LOW WATER CROSSING

Book 2 of the Sulfur Gap Series

DANA GLOSSBRENNER

Low Water Crossing

Dana Glossbrenner

Low Water Crossing: Book 2 of the Sulfur Gap Series
Copyright 2019 by Dana Glossbrenner

www.danagloss.com
dgloss@suddenlink.net

❀ Created with Vellum

Contents

For Jimmy Joe

Prologue: A Skeleton Arm--2013

J unior lurches in his cab and kills the engine. He pushes back his cap and stares at what dangles from the scoop of dirt—a skeletal arm dressed in tattered plaid, waving its bone fingers in the stiff West Texas breeze. My sweet sense of peace at the prospect of easy money evaporates.

"Oh, hell!" I jump from my truck, and Junior slams from his cab, both of us mouthing curses, our minds locked on the sight of that decaying piece of a human. He saws his arms to catch the attention of the dozer operators and truck drivers. He whistles to his father, Tuna, the foreman. When I signed the contract with their company to sell rock, I joked about their names—Junior and Tuna Berger. But now, they remind me of how ludicrous it was to hope for a hands-off source of income on the Cheadham ranch. No oil wells. No wind turbines. Is it too much to ask to have a gravel pit without a skeleton?

Tuna inspects the chugging gravel sorter. He straightens at Junior's whistle and fixes his eyes on the scoop, dangling the arm. Big trucks, other excavators and dozers—they all stop. Men climb from their cabs and jog to join me and Junior. In the sudden quiet, we stare at the limp arm. Tuna mutters as he reaches for his phone. He starts toward us as he makes a call.

"This is bad, Wayne." He barely looks at me as he meets us and puts his phone in its belt case. "Looks like we're gonna have ta suspend work awhile. We've found human remains."

"Have you ever seen the likes of this?" I remind myself it's not like we'll lose the ranch if the gravel pit doesn't pan out. After all, this is somebody's unofficial grave. We walk to the hole left by Junior's excavator scoop.

"Nope. I've dug up all kinds of stuff in my days, but I ain't never found no skeleton. Oh, man, look there." A skull grins up at us from a layer of rock.

"Damn. Could it be Indian remains?" I forget the shreds of plaid shirt and ponder for a moment. The Smithsonian might be interested, a desperate wish. Better an archaeological dig than a crime scene.

Tuna's quick to disabuse me of the idea. "Naw. It's not that old. We have to notify law enforcement, which is what I done. Sheriff Sparks is on his way."

"Oh, great." I try not to look too irritated.

We stand around and try to change the subject to weather, sports, anything but speculation about the skeleton. If we'd simply heard about it, we'd be all over the subject, but standing over a deal like this, we don't have much to say.

Within minutes, the cruiser bumps through the cattle guard and stops inside the fence. I turn away and shoot some bull with Junior. "This is an odd day of work, isn't it?"

"Oh yeah. Some find." He cuts his eyes at the skeleton arm. I wonder for a moment if he's about to cross himself.

"How'd you manage to stop so quick?" I ask.

Before he can answer, L.B. strides into our group, hitching his belt and resting his hands on his gear. His hat brim's as wide as his skinny shoulders.

"Howdy, Sheriff." Tuna offers his hand.

"It was hard to miss, Wayne," Junior says. "I looked up and saw a dried-up arm dangling. When you see something like that, you stop what you're doing purdy durn fast."

L.B. takes over. "So, there's been no other disturbance?"

"Naw," Junior says.

The sheriff looks down at the skull. "We'll have to get some investigators from Austin in here. And y'all have to stop digging."

"How long ya think it'll take, L.B.?" I ask.

"Looks like somebody intended to bury a body, so it'll be a homicide investigation. Might take a month or two."

"Aw, shit!" I slap my cap on my leg. The oil deposits are too deep in hard rock for drilling to make a profit, and a big wind farm butts up to my east property line. Damn and double damn. No oil, no wind turbines. And now this. A month-long shutdown will probably put me out of the gravel business. Tuna will have to relocate. He'll lose money, too.

"I'll have all this taped off, so don't tamper with anything,

Wayne." L.B. *steps toward me but rocks back like he intended to shift his weight. I walk to my truck and head off before I say something I'll regret, or maybe push L.B. in with the skeleton and kick in some dirt after him.*

EARLY THE NEXT MORNING, I'm at the back gate to meet the forensic team from Austin. L.B. shows up in his squad car as the investigators roll in from the opposite direction. Before long, search dogs stalk the area, sniffing.

"Why're you sending the dogs out?" I ask one of the forensics guys.

"Why's it important to you?" L.B. narrows his eyes at me. "Got any other bodies hidden here?" He's needling me, but it's not funny.

"Go to hell, L. B." I keep my voice low and steady. He slumps and looks away, realizing how lame his joke was. I feel a little sorry for him—he's a decent sheriff but he bugs the hell out of me.

The dog handler clears his throat. "It's a procedure to make sure we've found all the remains."

"Must be an interesting job," I say.

"Sure is."

I stick around and make small talk to shake off L.B.'s jibe. Today I'm bitter because I miss Luck. My son left the ranch for art school in Chicago several years ago. Some days I feel the empty spot. Take that and add it to the disappointment of the gravel pit, and I've got an ache that makes me want to throttle someone. Like L.B.

Each time Luck comes home, he's more removed from this West Texas ranch. But that's what I wanted most for him—to find his place. I go back to work, checking water lines and troughs and dropping feed for the cattle. The common rhythm cheers me. Nothing like the here and now to get rid of the "if-only's."

THE SECOND MORNING *after the skeleton appeared, I join my weekly group of coffee drinkers in town at the Navaho Café. News spread fast in Sulfur Gap. My buddies won't let me forget the body found in the gravel dig. The hats and caps at our table turn my direction when I come through the door. They must've come early to gossip before I got there. Can't blame them. It's a rare bit of excitement.*

"Wayne, do ya' think you'll be back in the rock business any time soon?" Don Runion pokes around for a story for the weekly newspaper, The Echo. He's got his glasses and notepad ready.

I hold up my coffee mug in a mock toast but say nothing.

"He don't want Don printing anything." My neighbor, Buster Standley, cocks his head toward me. His air of authority comes from the oil wells on his land. "And he don't want Charley talking it up at that hair salon of his."

"Hey, Buster, I have to listen to gossip, but I don't spread

it," Charley, the youngest, defends himself. He's used to it, though. Being a hair stylist and all. "Wayne, we're just curious. It's not every day you find a body buried in your pasture."

"I can report that human remains were found," Don says. "But it'd be nice to have a quote from the landowner."

"There's gotta be something else to talk about. How about them Cowboys?" I'd like for us all to share a frustration rather than focus on mine.

"I'm curious how a body would get there." Dick Raney, my most neighborly neighbor, stirs his coffee. "I'd be shocked to have something like that found on my place."

"Yeah, it was a shock," I admit. "Obviously, somebody put it there, in my field. It feels like someone broke into my house and painted graffiti on the walls. And don't quote me, Don."

"They'll probably never figure it out," Charley says.

"Don't be so sure. Don't you watch the CSI shows?" Don asks.

"Yeah, where they solve two or three murders in a night shift?" Dick Raney snorts.

"We don't know this is a murder," Buster says.

"What the hell else would it be?" Dick's a bit testy for a bystander. I chalk it up to shared outrage, glad I'm not the only one on edge.

The bell on the café door makes us look around to see L.B. entering. Damned if Buster doesn't move his chair over and pull up another one from an empty table. He probably hopes everyone will somehow learn more about the skeleton if the sheriff sits in.

"I'm meeting my deputy, so we'll find another table. Thanks, guys." L.B. turns away, but before he leaves, Buster has to smart off.

"Well, you should visit with us till he gets here. Wayne was telling us how he got rid of that nutty first wife of his. Turns out Lucy didn't head for Austin after all."

I feel the blood drain from my face. I can't believe the lengths Buster will go, trying to be funny. The other guys laugh, but not for long.

L.B. stares at me like he's considering a serious allegation. "Well, that'd be awful strange, since I see her around town when she comes back to visit her dad." He walks to his table and sits with his back to the group.

"Thanks a lot, Buster."

"Man, I'm sorry. I thought he'd just laugh and move on. Not act like it's an investigation."

"It's okay, you didn't know. Now can we talk about the Cowboys?"

My old gravel pit's quiet, except for the fluttering yellow tape and the occasional cow nosing around. Tuna, Junior, and crew have moved on to another project, like I figured. The rock is now being quarried from someone else's land to meet timely contracts.

I try not to look at those lonely mounds of sorted gravel when I have to use the south gate. Every day, more weeds sprout. Some are a foot tall already. Weeds are one thing that grows fast around here.

In the evenings, I sit on the edge of my bridge, dangling my feet, or I set a lawn chair in the middle. The rusty old steel bridge squats in the dry pasture across the front of the house. Rather than scrap it, I asked the county to move it to my place when a wider, modern bridge was built. Two cranes brought the old one, and it helps me in a way I can't quite explain. Some of the gossips said I'd finally lost it, gone haywire with collecting junk. World's largest yard ornament and all.

I wait each evening for a month. I watch the summer grass waving in the breeze or one of my cats stalking a field mouse. Finally, I decide it's time to call the forensics lab in Austin. A friend from high school works as a chemist there. I make an early morning call.

"Hey, Jim."

"Hey, Wayne, what's up?"

"I'm calling to see if you know what's been learned about the body they discovered on my place."

"Sure. I've been keeping up with crime news in my old turf. Didn't the sheriff call you? The report went to him a couple days ago, and he's supposed to be finalizing the investigation."

"No, haven't heard. Guess he's been too busy to let me know about a dead body that turned up in my field."

"Well, you've got a right to know. But don't quote me."

I dial the sheriff's office. L.B. answers with an official tone *when my call goes through to his desk. "What can I do for you, Wayne?"*

"Just wondering if you've been busy."

"Busy how?"

"Busy as in too busy to remove the crime scene tape from my pasture. The Austin crime lab tells me the investigation is complete. Maybe I should call Don and let him do an article in The Echo *that'll include how you're dragging your feet."*

"Hold on, Wayne." L.B. sounds tired. "I'll send a deputy out to put things back in place."

"You'd better come up with some conclusions from that report you're sitting on. The public has a right to know. As well as me."

"Wait. I still have to notify next of kin."

"What? You mean you've identified the body?"

"Yeah. But don't go telling anybody yet. I know it looks like I'm trying to stick it to you by leaving the crime scene tape up there at your place, but I really did forget about it the last couple of days."

Now I feel like a jerk for harassing old L.B. Oh, well, he knew what he was getting into when his daddy retired and he stepped into the job.

Later that afternoon, I'm sitting on the bridge when the cruiser appears, trailing dust up the road. The sheriff pulls to the fence. He's not wearing his gear belt. He takes off his hat and tosses it onto the front seat. Being a sheriff must be hard for such a narrow-bodied man. He looks small without his hat.

I walk him to the front porch and offer him a seat in one of the big chairs.

"Thanks," L.B. says. He rubs both hands down his face, looking older than a man in his forties.

"Well?" I'm anxious to know the results. "What's up?"

"You might want to close and block off your back gate. There's liable to be news crews crawling all over the place. They'll take pictures over your fence, but you don't want them tromping onto your property. They might even try their own digging."

"That'd be one way to get the scoop," I say.

"Ha-ha, yeah." Even L.B.'s laugh is tired. "The story of that body will make the news. Only reason it hasn't so far is that finding a body isn't that big a deal anymore."

"Why's this a big deal?"

"Turns out the body was a missing person from twenty-three years ago. Dental records turned up a guy named Tim Connelly. He would have been in his early thirties at the time of death."

"I don't remember him."

"He was ahead of us in school, and by the time he disappeared, he hadn't lived in Sulfur Gap for a long time."

"How the hell did he wind up buried on my property?"

"Cause of death was gunshot. Bullet in the skull was a 9-millimeter. No theories on the perp."

I freeze. My first wife, Lucy, owned a 9-millimeter. In fact, I bought it for her, taught her how to shoot. She was tempera-

mental and unpredictable, but could she have killed a man and buried him here on the ranch? It's possible. I stay composed. No need to mention Lucy.

"I've spoken with the victim's mother," L.B. says. "Tim was her only son, and she'd given him up for dead long ago. This finalizes it, so she's sad but relieved, too. Seems he'd always been trouble, and she feared something had happened to him and also worried he'd be back. Sad."

"Yeah," I agree. "Damn shame."

We sit and think about it. "So, when's the news gonna hit?"

"Tomorrow. TV stations, all the media. You need to block your back entrance."

"Thanks, L.B. I appreciate this," I say. The weight of the information he's shared makes our differences seem silly.

L.B. tips his hat as he drives away. I walk to my tractor, parked beside the shed, and drive it to the back entrance to add authority to the closed gate and "no trespassing" sign. I stop inside the gate and sit awhile on the tractor seat before I hike back to the house. I look over the abandoned piles of gravel. They don't take up much space, those little hills.

And they add some scenery. Maybe I'll think of the hills, sprouting life, as a tribute to Lucy. If she killed the Connelly guy, she had a damn good reason. I certainly don't plan to mention her as a suspect—for now, anyway. She was nuts, but she was full of life, the smartest person I've ever met. For a while, she made my life a living hell, when all I ever wanted was a good woman to be happy with. I wondered and guessed about what made her tick, but I never got anywhere. She could be such fun but turn on a dime and become a roaring terror.

But after all, she gave me Luck.

Lucy

Ho-Hum High School Reunion, Class of 1988

This Burger Buddy job sucks. From calculus to this. Only the fast food spots along the Interstate offer openings with enough work hours for a seventeen-year-old girl.

The lunch rush has passed, and Jimmy Lee's cleaning the grill, Sherry's mopping the floor, and I'm checking the condiments on the counter, ready to man the register (so to speak). I'm the one employee with a head for math. Something's wrong with the gene pool in Sulfur Gap.

The door jingles with the arrival of a couple of old high school friends (using the term lightly). I rejoice I'm not wearing the god-awful uniform. Hidden in back in case the manager stops by is the hat that makes us peons look like we'll break out a rap number any minute.

My "friends," Sheila and Camille, and I all say a

phony "Hi!" like we're singing soprano. I act like I'm in charge of the joint, a facade to prevent me from spitting in Sheila's face when I see her new Mustang parked in front.

"What can I get you?" I say, all business.

They order their shakes. In the awkward silence while I make change, Sheila, ever the condescending prom queen, asks, "Lucy, how do you like being free from the drag of school?"

"It's a big relief to get away from all the idiots," I say, handing them their receipt. "Your order'll be right out."

Sheila looks stunned for a fraction of a second, but Camille is oblivious. She laughs—forced and phony. At least they weren't directly in on the knock-down-drag-out fight in the locker room, the "incident" that got me expelled from the cheerleading squad. The principal blamed me.

That was when I decided to graduate early. I had honed my tumbling skills for years so I could be on the cheerleading squad. Some bitches are so jealous and self-righteous. Cheerleading ended, and so did the urge to stay in high school for the "social experience."

A couple of truckers come in and order Big Buddy Burgers, giant fries, and large Cokes. If either one of these pot-bellied, greasy guys offers me a ride right now, I'll throw my pinafore on the floor and climb aboard his eighteen-wheeler. One of them winks at me, like we share a secret. It reminds me of my babysitter's teenage son. Wonder what happened to that bastard.

My darling mother, Madge, charges me *rent*, so I need a job. "You're not in school now, Lucy," she said in her best "gotcha" voice, "so you need to work and pay your way." Her brief stint working as a secretary at the court house resulted in my going to a babysitter, a lady way nicer than my own mother. I would never have wanted to go home, except for the snaggle-tooth teenage son of hers, who took to poking things at me and in me. Both Madge and Daddy didn't believe me when I tried to tell them, but at least Madge quit her job—I have to give her that.

She encouraged me to graduate early so she could send me to work full-time at the ripe age of seventeen. Talk about sabotage. What more can I expect from someone who tells her second-grader when she gets home from school that she called the pound to come get Frito the cat, because said second-grader forgot to feed him that morning, and so Frito would die and be thrown into a lime pit?

I sobbed into my pillow until Daddy got home. "Your mother wants you to learn responsibility. What really happened was we gave Frito to Miz Melton, down the street."

To this day, I don't know for sure what happened to my cat. Daddy's a wimp, but a few kindnesses like that have been pinpricks of light at the end of the tunnel of despair.

Besides Madge's rent, I have to make payments and buy gas for the junker I'm driving. Madge doesn't know it, but Daddy goes to the insurance office and pays the premium for me in cash. It would be wonderful if just once he'd acknowledge what a piece of work she is. I've beaten my head on *that* brick wall so many times, I'm numb.

The door jangles as some more high school kids arrive. They're not in Sheila and Camille's crowd. A couple of skinny boys who run the school newspaper, such that it is. And their girlfriends—one who'd be pretty except for her huge nose and the other with no chances at all. I hand over their shakes and make small talk.

The Burger Buddy pinafore isn't the height of fashion, but with my tight jeans and T-shirt, I make it look good. Red's a good color for me—and with a white T-shirt and gold hoop earrings, I look nice. My eye sockets burn when I think about having to sneak around when I was twelve, just to have beginner make-up and something cute to wear to my first dance. Now that I'm grown and flourishing, I love it when Madge looks at me with angry envy in her eyes. I've got my hair piled on top of my head, a crown of gold swirls.

I check the paper cup dispensers, ignoring Sheila and

Camille and acting as if I have too many important chores to look their way.

Deputy Larry Bob Sparks pushes through the door. He's back from his stint at a community college somewhere, getting his Associates' in law enforcement. His father's the sheriff, so he had a job waiting for him. L.B. looks around to see who's there and perks up when he sees the high school kids. Poor dope. I hope he doesn't expect the likes of Sheila and Camille and their cronies to remember him—three years ahead of them and a huge nerd. He spies me behind the counter.

"Lucy! How's it going?" He drapes his forearm over the top of the register.

"Just amazing, L.B. What can I get you?"

"Your number!" He's feeling his oats with his new uniform and badge, more self-assured. Getting out of high school had to be good for him, but I don't want to date him. Someone's out there for L.B., and it's not me. Still, I recite my number. I don't want to give him the brush-off here in wide daylight.

He jerks a pad and pen from his shirt pocket and bends over the counter, scribbling furiously. He's such a dark, thin guy, he reminds me of a fly rubbing its front legs together.

"Great!" He pats the pad in his pocket.

He scans the menu posted above my head. "Guess I'll have a chocolate shake."

He hovers back a few feet and studies me while I

whip up his order. My neck prickles. He drives one of the old squad cars and walks toward it with a spring in his step. A shame I'll deflate him if he calls me.

To be realistic, high school was pretty miserable for me as well as Larry Bob. I was a mixed-up kid. Not that I've got the answers now. Still, I'm relieved the public education phase of my life is over.

I remember how mad I was at Madge for calling me "slut" when I went to my first dance. I was twelve, and that dance should have been a good memory. I decided that if I was going to be called a slut, I would be one. Under the bleachers where the whack-o, super-hormone-charged junior high bunch congregated during a football game. My first big make-out session was with Spencer Dixon. He got his hand inside my bra. Of course, he bragged to the other boys, so they were lining up for their turns.

The main thing boys in seventh grade wanted was to slide a hand inside my shirt and get as close as possible to touching a breast. If they managed to creep that far, they usually froze. But the next time, if there was a next time, they got faster and better, and I even enjoyed it. By the eighth grade, boys added lots of tongue to their kissing. By ninth grade, they were after my crotch. Spence had cycled back around, and he was the first boy who got to second base—or is that third?

When Spence got there, a spasm took my breath. He looked at me with triumph, like I was a dog he'd taught to sit. For a few days, I thought I was in love, but it occurred to me a boy who reads the right articles in *Playboy* should be good at doing what you like. Spence and I dated for a year. Eventually, he brought the condoms, and together we lost the last of our technical virginity.

His parents owned a lake house, and he sneaked the key and made his own copy in the next town. I can still smell the dusty staleness and the old towels we laid under us on the bare mattress in their parents' room. It felt like a honeymoon, especially when we'd sneak out and spend most of the night sleeping together and waking up to make out. Crawling back through my bedroom window as the sky began to lighten in the east never lost its thrill.

I'm glad it was Spence. He could be a real dick (no pun intended . . . well, maybe), but he was so afraid of his parents, he was the Condom King. He'd never knock up a girl. One night at the lake house, Spence said (when it was time to put our clothes back on, of course), "We ought to date other people. My parents are afraid we're going to get pregnant or run off or both. If I hear my dad say 'There's other fish in the sea' one more time, I'm gonna puke."

I wasn't too surprised. He, being a dick, frequently hinted that he could do better than me. But I was stung his parents had been campaigning against me. My social background wasn't equal to his, but I was silly enough to think good grades and other achievements would compensate. Not.

I spent a dateless weekend before the invitations began to roll in. I'm sure Spence had filled in the other boys on my enthusiasm for sex. I enjoyed the attention and the affection. But I still knew that I—per se—didn't mean a thing to any of them.

I strung each one along and wore their letter jackets until it was boring and I dismissed them with no fond memories. Or I let them have their tender moment and dumped them before they could dump me.

I'm pulled back to the present when two jocks from football practice swagger into the Burger Buddy. I'm about to dislocate a jaw, smiling like I'm enjoying the hell out of my life. Both of them dated me, but neither of them knew how to get things going. I don't give tutorials, after all.

I'm beyond glad Jackie and Denise haven't shown.

During our junior year this past spring, Jackie and Denise, biggest self-righteous bitches on the cheerleading squad, decided to have a come-to-Jesus meeting with me in the locker room. Jackie got too close to my face while she was telling me nicely what a slut I was, and how I should think of myself as a representative of the school and of Jesus, too. I doubled up my fist and punched her square on the mouth. I didn't give it my best—just wanted to shut her up.

She came at me looking like the crazy woman from

the attic in *Jane Eyre* and grabbed my hair with both hands. That gave me the boost I needed to slam her onto a bench and turn around on Denise. She tried to jump on my back while I was busy with Jackie. I shoved dear Denny into the lockers, knocking the breath out of her. As she slid to the floor, I kicked her in the stomach. I pulled back before the kick landed, which I realize doesn't make me a saint, but showed great restraint. I wished I'd worn steel-toed boots instead of tennis shoes.

On-campus suspension was my reward, even though I did my best to convince Principal Faulkner I didn't deserve it. Principal Faulkner informed me, right in the middle of "peace talks" with Jackie and Denise, that I would be removed from the cheerleading squad. I stopped my pleading in mid-air. My eyes froze on the principal, and he looked away. Smirks radiated from Jackie and Denise.

One of them said, "We'll pray for you, Lucy," and my fists doubled.

"Fuck you," I said, proud of my even tone. It took every ounce of self-discipline not to scream it—a primal scream that would have rung through the halls and classrooms of Sulfur Gap High School. I have to hand it to Mr. Faulkner that he overlooked the obscenity. As I left the principal's office, a reddish blur obscuring my vision, Jackie's and Denise's parents sat in the outer office. They all glared at me. Among them was a school board member, a city councilwoman, and a Baptist minister. I didn't stand a chance. No way would my parents stick their necks out to take up for me by coming to the school and raising Cain about those girls attacking *their* daughter.

I figured how many days I could legally be absent and played sick as much as possible. I took correspondence for the two courses I needed to graduate, and the high school mailed my diploma.

I've fallen a couple of notches, from varsity cheerleader to Burger Buddy cashier. At least I can say I'm glad I don't have the stupid hat on today—it looks like a damn crimson and gold Christmas tree ball on my head. With Sheila and Camille here, Jackie and Denise might show. At least I'll look good standing behind the register while I hate them for getting on with their lives after destroying mine.

Mr. Right-of-My-Way Outa Here

The door jangles with a new arrival to my burger haven, ending my trip down resentment lane. It's Wayne Cheadham. He was three years ahead of me in high school, too, a classmate but not a friend of L.B.'s. He used to watch me at pep rallies when he was a senior and I was a freshman. I did hand springs across the gym while the guys whistled. Wayne smiled down at me from the bleachers, showing his white teeth and dimples. But when I flirted in the hall between classes, he smiled and acted like I was his little sister. He was cute, though, tall and solid, with auburn hair and green eyes.

"Hey, Wayne. Remember me? Lucy Paxton?"

"Sure, Lucy." We shake hands across the register. "How's school? You're a senior by now."

"Oh, I graduated early." I give him a bullshit line

about being eager to start work and save for college. "What have you been doing since graduation? I haven't seen you lately."

"I went to Sweetwater for a course in welding." We talk about how a welding certification broadens his horizons, so he can move away from the ranch if he wants. Wayne is smart but not academically motivated. It doesn't matter, since he can work on his father's ranch— and take it over someday. He's set for life.

Truth is, I'll make it to college when hell freezes over. Madge won't let Daddy give out any tax information so I can apply for financial aid. I won't be eighteen till next August, which might change the game. Or maybe Madge gets squashed by an eighteen-wheeler and Daddy lets me use some of her life insurance for tuition. I laugh aloud at the idea. Wayne probably thinks I'm effervescing over the joyous prospects of my life.

"So, what'll it be, Mr. Cheadham?"

"The biggest iced tea you've got. Is it fresh?"

"It will be."

An older couple forms a line, and more jocks from football practice stop in, probably because they see Sheila's Mustang parked in front. The new Burger Buddy's already becoming a hangout for all the happy horseshit school crowd. I don't have time to play up to Wayne now, but maybe later. He's never been part of the gossip mill, and he might take me seriously.

Wayne takes his tea and sits in a booth. The old man

drops his money and stoops to pick it up. I scoot around the register, chirping at him to wait and let me help. I hope Wayne notices my tight jeans.

Again, it's hard to wait on the jocks. I know they looked at me as only a piece of tail—and not being around them is one of the great advantages of being out of school. They're a bunch of punks. They crowd around Sheila and Camille's booth. Wayne moseys past them and nods, but he keeps walking toward the counter. He seems eons older than the high school jerk-offs.

I roll my eyes toward the high school bunch, as if to say, "Aren't they lame?"

Wayne doesn't register my nonverbal communication. Maybe he doesn't translate cattiness.

"So, Wayne. Want some more tea? Free refills."

"No, thanks. But I was trying to think of a way to ask you out. I'd ask you to go for a coke, but it would be too much like work for you. At least we could go to the old Dairy Barn." Wayne lifts his hat and pushes back his thick hair. He's teasing about Dairy Barn.

"You can ask me to go lots of other places." I purse my lips so my dimples show. His eyes soften, changing colors from green to sort of amber, like they're glowing. He likes me.

"How about a movie in Big Spring?"

"Great!" I beam like he's invited me to the Bahamas on his Lear jet.

The next day, Larry Bob calls as I'm getting ready for

work. He gets right to the point. "So, Lucy. I thought you and I could go for a drive tomorrow, let me show you where we made a big drug bust last month."

He's looking for a cheap date, and the drug bust was probably in a good place to go parking. I don't feel too bad when I say, "Sorry, L.B. I have a date to go to the movies in Big Spring tomorrow."

"Oh! Mind if I ask who with?"

I do mind, but the conversation will be over faster if I come out with it. "Wayne Cheadham," I say. "You and he graduated in the same class."

"Yeah, yeah. Well, I guess he beat me to the punch."

"Yes, he did."

"Mind if we try for another time?"

He's persistent, I'll give him that. I'll have to let him down all the way and save him the planning and angst. "Right now, I'm going to focus on dating Wayne. I'm not a multiple-dater. But I appreciate the invitation." He can't question me further without being a true creep, so he gives up.

Getting ready, I celebrate that Madge can't say a damn thing about how I dress. I slip into my spaghetti-strap mini-sundress over a push-up strapless bra and walk right past her and Daddy watching *Family Ties* in the living room on the ancient RCA. Michael J. Fox's skin is green.

I meet Wayne at the door before he can knock.

Cocoon is showing. It's a re-run, but neither of us saw

it the first time around. We laugh like hyenas when the alien makes the nerd have a touchless orgasm in the swimming pool. Wayne seems nervous, though. Surely, he's not a Puritan? I'll fix that, if I get half a chance.

He holds my hand during the movie, and as we leave the dark theater, he holds onto my upper arm. His hand is rough, but he has a gentle touch. We drive so slow going back to Sulfur Gap, cars pass us like we're standing still. He'll get no objection from me if he wants to prolong the date.

The amber glow of our little town's lights appears on the far horizon, and he reaches into the glove box for an old Dr. Hook tape. The songs seem like an eerie match for the occasion— "Sharin' the Night Together," "I Don't Want to Be Alone Tonight," "When You're in Love with a Beautiful Woman," and "You Make My Pants Want to Get Up and Dance." I accept this as coincidence. Wayne is not that much of a schemer. I wiggle my shoulders in time to the music. My spaghetti strap slips down. He drapes his arm on the back of the seat, leaving his fingers dangling on my skin.

He clears his throat as he turns down the volume on Dr. Hook. "Remember how my mom invited the whole middle school to the ranch when my class graduated from eighth grade? She held it at the old windmill."

"Yeah, I was there, a little fifth-grader."

"I remember you. The windmill's hosted a lot of parties," he says. I don't tell him at least three boys took me parking there after I'd snuck out the window in the wee hours. "You know how it's on a little bit of ridge? The land drops off and you can see a long way."

"Sure—beautiful view," I say, lying of course. When I was there I either was too young or was looking at a car's headliner from the back seat.

"I recently got moved in to my brand-new house, west of the windmill."

"Lucky you. You don't have to keep living at your parents' house."

"Yeah, lucky me. I'm indentured to Ernie now for the rest of my life. He's holding the mortgage."

"Ernie?"

"My dad. I forget not everyone knows my dad's name. I've never called him 'Dad.' Doesn't fit."

"Funny. My so-called mother is 'Madge' to me. What do you call your mother?"

Wayne laughs. "I call my mother 'Mother.'"

I say, "I call my dad 'Daddy.'" And we lose it. We're lucky we don't get stopped, going so slow and weaving a little. We'd have a story to tell if Larry Bob pulled us over.

"Don't know when I've laughed this hard."

"Well, being a new homeowner with a mortgage from Ernie hanging over your head should make you more serious."

"It doesn't exactly thrill me. Ernie knows he'll get

every drop of blood, sweat, and tears he thinks he's owed."

"You'll have to show me your place sometime."

"How about tonight?"

"Drive faster," I say.

We speed to a turnoff onto a narrow county road and from there to a smaller dirt road. There's no moon, so it's too dark to see far. Beside us, the tall grass is silver in the truck's headlights. We turn again and rattle over a cattle guard onto a pot-holed road. A smaller road leads to the windmill, and past that, to the house, perched on the ridge. From there, I imagine he can spot a gnat a mile away if the moonlight's bright.

I'm disoriented, it's so damn dark. I'm a town girl, and I have no idea about the nocturnal habits of snakes —they come to mind anytime I'm around high grass. Wayne holds my arm as I get out of the truck, lighting the ground with his key chain light. "Hope you don't mind that I'm treating you like an old lady," he says. "But getting out of this big old truck in the dark is treacherous."

I put my arms around his neck as he helps me down. "I don't mind a bit." He keeps his arm around my waist. A covered porch stretches across the house front, with a bay window. The entry hall is paneled in dark wood, a shotgun leaning in the corner. Wayne says, "I don't usually keep a gun by the door, but I haven't put it up since I shot at a raccoon trying to get into the cats' food last night."

The kitchen is neat, basic, homey. Way nicer than the house I'm stuck in—for the time being. He's picked all the features and furniture, and I wonder if he's a closet interior designer.

"I'm rattling around in this thing," he says. "Ernie wanted a house big enough for a family, in case I have one someday or in the event I move off and he hires a ranch manager with a family." He gets Cokes from the fridge, and we settle on a soft, brown leather couch.

"Cheers," he says, and we clink our cans. We reminisce about high school. Turns out he hated it as much as I did. He was bored and didn't go for a lot of the mindless parties and dating protocol. Pretty girls felt entitled to put their feet on his dash, just because they were good-looking. I agree with everything he says.

I ask about his family. His one brother is a grief counselor. Sounds like a crummy job, listening to people whine. His dad probably has the first nickel he ever earned. Katy, his mother, sounds like a saint, too good to be true. We need to change the subject, but he stands up so fast, I bounce on the cushion. He holds out his hand for me and says, "I better get you home. We both have to work tomorrow."

This didn't pan out the way I'd planned. But I smile and take his hand. "You're so right, Wayne. I completely lost track of time." Sheesh. He's a virgin, and it's going to take lots of patience or an all-out ambush to get past his iron-clad pants zipper.

"Thanks for taking me to see your new house, Wayne," I say when he parks in front of my little shack. "I bet it's nice during the day, when you can see the view from your back windows."

He takes the bait. "Sure is. How does Saturday sound? I can get you about ten. Can you ride? We can ride, and go to my house and appreciate the view."

Uh-oh. I've never gotten along with horses. "No, but I'd love some lessons!" I'm putting my life in Wayne's hands, but I want to be a good sport. It's a job to fake sincerity.

"Great. I'll saddle a gentle horse for you, and we can ride to the creek."

I plan to wear bug spray and sunscreen. "I can't wait!" I say. He walks me to the door and gives me a goodnight kiss that makes me feel as young as I am. My next chance will come in a few more days. I'll get someone to cover my Burger Buddy shift.

Happy Act Riding Lesson

Madge is dense as granite, which makes me think of a tombstone with her name on it. She forgets this little tidbit—she can't make me do a damn thing. She's clued in to the fact I'm not working the Saturday morning breakfast shift, so she slithers into my room to announce she bought a new mop this week, and it's time I did something to help by using it on the kitchen floor.

I ignore her and work the curling iron around my hair. I wish I had a can of Mace. I could say I thought it was hairspray. At last, I hear Wayne's pickup. I'm in my best jeans, some boots I found at Goodwill, and a clingy silk shirt. Maybe we'll become entranced with the view, then with each other, and forget riding. But when I meet him in my raggedy little front yard, I'm disappointed by his frown.

"What?" I stop and look down at myself.

"You look . . . really good. But your shirt won't look good any more if we get into some brambles. You need a T-shirt."

Well, shit. He's planning to do some *serious* riding. He wears a long-sleeved John Deere T-shirt. But I won't invite him in to my personal hell hole while I change into a crummy T-shirt, not even to save my best silk.

"How about I borrow one of yours?"

He reddens a little—easy to see on him. "Okay." As we drive away, the curtain drops in the kitchen window. Spying Madge. I'd better work fast or she'll figure a way to sabotage me and Wayne. But maybe if I snag Wayne, she'll be glad I'm moving out.

Near the intersection, we meet Larry Bob in his cruiser. I wonder if he's doing a psycho drive-by or if he's just driving. Sulfur Gap is the right size for meetings like this. I give a cheery wave in his direction and can't tell if he's waving back with the glare on his windows. But I can see the silhouette of his big hat.

Wayne lifts a finger from his steering wheel, the understated salutation that says, "I see you, but I don't give a damn."

"You and Larry Bob good friends?" he asks.

"No. I'm being nice because I recently refused him for a date and dashed any hopes for our 'future'."

"I'm not surprised."

"At what?"

"That he asked."

"I hope you don't mind. I mentioned your name, said I had a date with you for the day he asked me. That was true, but I told him I just date one guy at a time, which implied we were dating regularly. Best way to let him down."

Wayne smiles. "Let's say we're dating."

"Okay," I say, with little enthusiasm because it's hard to tell if he wants to go out with me or to irritate Larry Bob.

At his house, Wayne leads me to his bedroom and opens a bureau drawer neatly stacked with tidy whities and T-shirts. He hands me a dark blue one and beats a hasty retreat, closing the door behind him. With his T-shirt flopping on me, we get back in the truck and wobble along the rutted road past Katy and Ernie Cheadham's house.

We pull to the empty corral. The odor of horse droppings and cow patties fills my head, but the cool, cloudy day lightens the effect. A breeze stirs the mesquite leaves and plays with the branches on big trees beside the Cheadham house. A modest home, considering they are among the longest-entrenched ranchers in Sandstone County. It's positioned with a view of pastures sloping to a creek lined with catclaw and mountain cedar clutched in a meandering line.

Under a deep awning and through another gate to the paddock, the horses graze on broken bales of hay.

Wayne slips a halter on a bay named Shivers and gives me the rope to hold while he gets his roan, H.A.

"What's 'H.A.' stand for?" I ask as we lead the horses under the awning to a gate, where Wayne loops each halter rope on a rail. He disappears into the tack room and emerges with a bucket of brushes in one arm and two saddle blankets in the other.

"H.A. stands for Horse's Ass. I was eight when we got him, and Ernie always talked about riding 'that horse's ass,' so I named him that. Mother made me use the initials. Turned out to be a good horse." Wayne reaches into the bucket and pulls out a curry comb. He moves it in big, light circles over H.A.'s hide and follows up with a big brush that pushes clouds of dust off the horse.

I stifle a sneeze and clear my throat. Wayne hands me the bucket of brushes. "You can do the same for Shivers."

I up-end the bucket and stand on it to reach his back. Shivers draws up his skin and shakes like a horse fly bit him. Explains his name. I inhale a bunch more horse dust, but I get him slicked down. Wayne throws on the blankets and cinches the saddles in no time. He goes to all eight legs with a hoof pick, faster than my dad can tighten lug nuts on a spare tire.

Wayne makes it look easy, so I relax while he bridles the horses and leads them into the corral. It's a relief to get away from the smothering feeling of the tack room overhang, where the flies buzz and the dirt daubers hover. It makes me itch, but I keep smiling and petting Shivers' neck like we're best buds.

Wayne drops H.A.'s reins. The gelding stands with his head lowered, snorting and stamping. He startles me when he swings his rump my way. I've always heard you should stay away from a horse's hind end. Wayne ignores him.

"I guess you know how to mount."

"Yeah." I put my foot in the stirrup. It's almost high enough that I need a stepstool, but I pull up and throw a leg over. Wayne uses the lead ropes to walk both horses through the outer gate. He mounts H.A. and pulls beside me.

"You don't have to do anything but sit on Shivers. He'll follow H.A. But I can give you some pointers if you need them."

"Sure. I can use pointers. I haven't been exposed to horses enough to know how to ride."

He shows me how to hold the reins and how to sit in the saddle, stuff I never thought mattered. My feet must be in the stirrups just so. And I should relax my legs instead of squeezing with my knees and use my heels to move the horse to the left and right. I already know about steering with the reins.

"To keep from bouncing," he says, "soak up the movement. Relax your knees and move with the horse. Either way, don't roll back or lean forward—keep your feet from poking forward. If you bounce, it makes the horse sway his back and it gets rougher."

With each suggestion, he adjusts my hands on the reins, taps my calf to remind me of my feet in the stirrups, and pushes my back into straight position.

"Don't worry if you can't do all this the first day," he says, reading my mind. Oh, crap, he's planning on doing more of this. "Keep your head up as much as possible."

We plod down the dirt road. Shivers follows H.A. It's going smoother than I expected. H.A. veers left onto a narrow path fringed with brown grass. With the hint of fall in the breeze, it's so quiet—no cars coming and going, no doors slamming or neighbors calling in the children. At the creek's edge, Wayne disappears down a path I can't see. I wonder how I'm going to steer a horse down an embankment. Then I remember his pointers. Shivers will follow. As long as Shivers enjoys the walk— and he is, judging by his ears pointing forward—I can go along for the ride. The slope is easy but lined with brambles to the creek bed. Wayne stops to wait for us.

We ride the dry creek, hooves clattering on shallow sandstone shelves protruding into the gravelly bottom. There's an occasional puddle with gnats swarming, and I'm glad I put on bug spray. We've ridden for thirty minutes, and my little butt bones are getting sore. If they're sore now, they'll be crippling tomorrow. Thank God, we come to where a road crosses the creek. We stop.

"You ready to get back? We can take the low water crossing and follow the road back to the barn," he says.

Boy howdy, am I ready, but I have to ask. "Why does everyone call these things low water crossings if there's never any low water?"

Wayne laughs and looks at the narrow, rutted road plunging down one side of the creek bed and up the other. "It's not about low water—it's a low *place*, a low crossing, might take you through swift-running water if there's a lot of rain. You have to be careful. The rushing water could push you off the road. That's why there's always warning signs."

"So, the 'low' applies to the crossing and not water? They should hyphenate 'water-crossing.'"

"Yep, but it durn sure would be a pain in the butt for the sign painters." He nudges H.A. forward. "Let's get back. I don't want you gettin' saddle sore and bein' mad at me."

He leads Shivers and me back to the barn. I prop on a rail while he unsaddles both horses, brushes them down, and gives them each a bucket of feed. The saddling and unsaddling are a lot of work for an hour's ride. A whole hour, and I have survived!

The minute the thought crosses my mind, a spider plunks onto the back of my neck. I clipped my hair off my neck so it wouldn't get tangled during the ride, and now this cheeky-ass spider is trying to get to know me better. About that time, a dirt dauber flits in my face.

They supposedly don't sting, but if that's true, why do they have a butt built like a wasp's? The dauber hovering and the spider legs crawling toward my collar are too much. I swat at my neck with one hand while fending off the dirt dauber with the other.

Wayne laughs so hard that he can't catch a breath. I squeeze my fingers over the spider and make a paste of it. The dirt dauber has flown off, so I can stop dancing. I wipe my fingers furiously in dry dirt to remove the spider mash. Wayne gasps for air.

"I'm sorry," he says. "I never saw anyone fight a spider and a dirt dauber at the same time."

At my hurt expression, he says, "Oh, come on, you're okay." He puts his arm around me, and I lean against him. He turns me to him and kisses me a long time. A simple little cool kiss, lips barely parted. He slides his hand along my rib cage, toward my breast, but he stops, like he's scared. He backs away, blushing. The horses finish their oats, and he shoos them into the paddock.

I stand with my hands in my back pockets, on the lookout for spiders and daubers. A trickle of sweat creeps down my lower back.

"So," he says, "are you ready to see the view from my place?" He's recovered already. Good. We'll have another chance at the house.

He's still in low gear when we pass his parents' place, and there, at the corner of the yard, stands his mother, waving a red-checkered dishtowel. I remember seeing her around town. And there was the party. She probably won't recognize me.

Katy Cheadham wears the wind in her hair and the sun on her face like she's as much a part of the ranch as the tall grass and graceful mesquites. With her salt-and-pepper hair pulled back in a loose little pony tail and her oversized blue cotton shirt and comfortable stretch pants and loafers, she looks younger than Madge, though she must be ten years older.

Wayne pulls beside the fence and lowers his window.

"What's up, Mother?" His voice carries a tinge of impatience.

"I wanted to invite y'all in for a glass of tea and a sandwich."

"No, Mom, sorry. We're headed to my house. I already made lunch. And by the way, this is Lucy Paxton. I'm sure y'all know each other but haven't been formally introduced."

Katy waves. "Hi, Lucy. I'm glad I caught y'all so I could at least say 'hello.'"

Wayne snorts and shakes his head at the steering wheel.

"Hi, Mrs. Cheadham! It's nice to meet you. Hope to see more of you."

"Call me Katy, all right?"

"Yes ma'am." I'm all giggles and grins, maybe over-doing it.

Wayne raises his window and takes off. I'm so glad

he didn't drag me to have lunch with his mother so I would have to make nice with her for an hour or so. We cover the short distance to Wayne's house. He pulls under a carport at the west end.

"Hope you don't mind goin' through the kitchen," he says.

"Not a bit. It's my third time here, so I'm not special company anymore."

"Oh, you're special." He brushes my cheek with his fingers and winks.

We climb steps to the side entrance, and he holds open the big screen door to a huge utility room with its own sink. There's a chest freezer that no doubt holds plenty of steaks. The washer and dryer are new. In the kitchen, the table is set. Nothing fancy—plain dishes like you get at J.C. Penney.

"Have a seat." Wayne pulls out a chair for me, so I plop down.

"This is a nice surprise," I say.

"I wouldn't make you work and not feed you," he says, washing his hands at the sink. I join him to clean off the dirt and spider mash. It's sweet to stand at the sink together. I feel like a kid playing house. He pulls two big salad bowls from the refrigerator.

"Hope you like steak salad."

After lunch, I excuse myself to use the bathroom off the hall. Wow. Double sinks. That's so two kids can share. Two extra bedrooms for two kids, at least. That's a downer. While the faucet runs, I open cabinets and have a peek. Nothing shocking.

I station myself in front of the big living room window. The sun begins to lean to the west, and the view extends for miles. Could all this be the Cheadham ranch? The afternoon shadows deepen the contrast between fenced pastures dotted with cattle and cedar brush, and planted acres, deep green from the beginnings of something—winter wheat? Beats me.

Wayne joins me in the living room. "Nice, huh?"

"Beautiful."

We stand at the window for several minutes. I'm itching to move along with the romance, but I wait for Wayne's Disney moment to pass. I count in my head. If I get to three hundred—five minutes—I'll pull him from his trance.

I'm to a-hundred-sixty-seven-Mississippi when Wayne comes to. He puts both arms around me. We kiss—another slow, tentative caress. He holds me to him.

"You feel so good," he says. "Let's go to the couch."

We kiss for a few more minutes, and his hands begin to roam. But he stops and looks me in the face. "You okay with this?"

"So far," I say. I'm breathless, more stirred up than I expected. While I've been thinking about closing the deal, I'm missing the fun of the negotiations. We kick off our boots and lie on the couch. As his hand finally creeps under my T-shirt, the phone rings. I say, "Don't answer it."

He shakes me off. "Ernie probably needs something. He'll know I'm here. If I don't answer, he'll come knocking."

He pads to the kitchen in his sock-feet. I can tell from the conversation it's Ernie. Wayne's answers are testy, more than with his mother.

"I did check the gate in the south pasture. . . . No, we don't need to go out there. I know it's secure. . . . Yes, I dropped feed early this morning and fixed the old trough so it won't leak. And the water's running in it. . . . No, I should have said 'dribbling.' I didn't leave it gushing. . . ."

Wayne defends himself on a few more "shoulda-done's."

He hangs up and pads back to the couch. I'm surprised he didn't slam the phone down. I figure Wayne will want to shuttle me back to town right away like he did on our first date. I could bawl at the idea of leaving here—the central air conditioning, the soft carpet—to go back to town and the house and my tiny room with only a fan to stir the air from a swamp cooler. But I have to suck it up.

We sit a few minutes, my head on his shoulder. I'm beginning to wonder if he's normal. We've been working on this project for an hour.

I touch him. "Looks like you're still happy to see me."

He presses my hand to him and pushes me back on the couch. Now his hands reach under my T-shirt. He unfastens my bra like a surgeon.

There's a knock at the front door, and the knob turns. This is surreal. Is there a sign on the roof saying, "Warning! Sexual activity taking place! Must be stopped!"? We sit up at opposite ends of the couch. He pulls a pillow over his lap, and I get my bra and T-shirt un-bunched.

"You in here, Wayne?"

"Yeah, J.J. Come on in. We're just sitting around." Wayne sounds casual.

Into the room steps the game warden, J.J. Rodriguez. He's a dark, towering figure. He and Sheriff Sparks keep watch on everything—pasture parties, places kids like to go parking, and parties going on when the parents aren't home. It's amazing they have time to do their real jobs, they're up in everybody's business so much. Fortunately, this is my first encounter with the game warden, but he's true to his rep—breaking up the party.

"You probably know Lucy Paxton," Wayne says.

J.J. glances at Wayne's pillow and at me. I hope my T-shirt isn't lumpy from my undone bra. I decide not to try to straighten my disheveled hair, since that would be a guilty gesture. I give a little wave. "Hi."

"Sit, visit a spell." Wayne waves at an overstuffed chair at the end of the heavy coffee table. J.J. sits and glances at our sock-feet and tossed boots. This guy doesn't miss a thing.

"You want some tea?" Wayne asks.

"Naw, I can't stay." The game warden shifts his eyes toward the bedroom door, revealing his thoughts—to me, at least. I don't miss much, either.

"I wanted to ask if you've noticed any signs of night hunters."

"Nope. Lucy and I rode the creek today, and I was out feeding earlier and checking the troughs. Didn't see anything before or since sunup. Why?"

"I've gotten several complaints from Buster Standley. He's seen some vehicle lights where they shouldn't be on a couple of occasions."

I want to tell him school started recently, and kids are back from vacay, hooking up and going on dates and looking for country roads outside town where they can park, drink beer, . . . whatever. But J.J. knows about kids.

"I'll let you know if I see anything."

As he gets up to leave, J.J. reminds me of a big totem pole rising from the chair—a scary figure for law-breakers.

"Nice to see you," I say.

J.J. nods. Wayne jumps up to walk him to the door, and I hear them in the foyer.

"Sorry, man. Didn't mean to interrupt."

"It's okay. We're just visiting."

"Right."

I hear a little shoulder slap as J.J. salutes Wayne's

naiveté in thinking he could pull off the "just visiting" story.

"We're barbecuing tonight. Y'all come if you can," J.J. says.

"Sure, if Lucy doesn't have other plans. I'll call Pam and let her know if we're coming."

The door closes behind J.J., and Wayne's back on the couch with his arms around me. He's like a lean bear— solid, and warm.

"I should know better than to try to make out during the early afternoon," he says. Anybody can see my truck. At least I should lock the door."

"J.J. kept us out of trouble," I say. "We might be rushing things a bit." I can afford to be noble, since we're going to J.J.'s.

"Just putting off the inevitable, I hope." Wayne says.

My, but he's getting cocky (so to speak). But he's obviously not a Puritan—or a virgin.

"I need a shower," I say, lifting my hair off my neck.

Wayne points to the master bedroom. "Right through there. Get yourself a towel from the cabinet. I'll go in after you're done."

I wrap my hair in a hand towel and step under the cool gush of the shower head. I rub a bar of soap all over and lather up. I increase the hot water as much as I can stand and watch the soap bubbles spin down the drain. I dry with a big, soft bath towel and use some of Wayne's stick deodorant. I step back into my aired-out, lacy black bikinis. And my clingy blouse is still fresh.

Before I finish dressing, I lean from the bedroom door and see if Wayne might want to come in when he sees me with nothing on but a towel. I peek into the living room and—damn! He's gone. Through the front kitchen window, there he is—on the porch holding a bag of—cat food? He's feeding the damn cats! All I can see of the critters is the tips of five tails milling around his legs.

I dress, and as I plop on the sofa, he bangs the side door and clomps into the house. I'm pulling my socks back on and trying to compose my face. Cats? Really? When you've got a cute girl naked in your shower, you're going to go feed the cats?

He stops. "What's the matter?"

Gotta come up with some excuse for the pout. "Are you sure you want me to go?"

"To J.J.'s? Sure. Why not?"

"Well, you might want to visit with your friends without me. I mean, J.J.'s what? Thirty? I'm not sure I'd fit in."

He laughs. "Sure you will. J.J. and I've been friends since I was sixteen. He doesn't put an age limit on friendship. But he might kid us some, so be ready for that."

Then he shuts the bedroom door.

I watch television for the next hour, flipping through the few channels he can pick up with his antenna. No cable here. No MTV. Nothing.

Chew, Brew, and Barbeque

J.J.'s house by the lake looks like it was airlifted from Santa Fe or Taos. Like maybe someone broke off a piece of a Native American pueblo and set it by the muddy little lake. It fits into the landscape better than all the bleak little cabins dotted on the weedy slopes overlooking Sandstone Lake.

J.J.'s wife, Pam, opens the carved wood door. She's a Former Beauty Queen type, and phony as hell. The last person I would expect to be married to J.J. Rodriguez, who looks like a member of Montezuma's Royal Guard. Her blond, Goldie Hawn hair is fluffed and as fresh as her creamy skin. She throws herself on Wayne for a big hug. I keep smiling like I can't wait my turn, while I'm conscious of my own squashed dishwater blond do, limp from the day's doings.

"Wayne!! It's good to see you. How're Ernie and Katy?"

"They're good."

Pam draws back, holding both Wayne's hands. "And how do you like your new house?" So far, she hasn't glanced my way.

"I like it."

"Do you have it all furnished? You know I'd be glad to come help you decorate, pick things out."

"It's pretty much done for now. I'm taking my time. No rush."

Wayne drops one of Pam's hands and turns her toward me. "Pam, this is Lucy Paxton. Y'all might know each other."

I hold out my hand and open my mouth to say hello, but Pam beats me to the opening salvo. She leans to shake my hand like she's talking to a little kid and says, "And Lucy!" Her voice swoops down along with her face as she bends to greet me, the afterthought, the extra baggage. "It's so nice of Wayne to bring you."

"Yes, but Wayne *is* a nice guy," I say, and she looks a little iffy, like maybe I'm mocking her. I'm sure the sarcasm crept in a smidge.

She sweeps us into the living room, where we sit while she clatters around and brings out a tray of iced tea in tall glasses. We sit and sip, as Pam focuses on Wayne. Finally, Wayne says, "Where's J.J.?"

The question of the hour.

"Oh, he's in the back, cooking steaks," Pam says.

"Well, hell, let's go keep him company!" Wayne jumps to his feet.

I get in a little word to Pam. "I love your house. Is the back yard as charming as the view from the front?"

She stares like she'd forgotten I was there. Finally, she says, "Oh, thank you, Lucy! Wayne, you trot out back and help J.J., and I'll show Lucy the house." As I suspected, the kitchen is mauve and almond, and the décor is so consistently southwestern I'd like to sneak over some night and paint the front of the house . . . Victorian pink?

I say all the nicest things about her attention to detail, and she relaxes. Maybe she felt awkward. I'm sure J.J. filled her in about walking in on us.

J.J. and Wayne bang through the back door, J.J. carrying a tray stacked with steaks. Aw, shucks. I won't get the backyard tour. Is steak all anyone can cook? But it's not like I come from a family of gourmet chefs. Madge always stocks up when frozen dinners go on sale, and we're set for the next two months.

While we eat, J.J. and Wayne discuss wildlife and ranching. I learn Pam's a nurse. I push food around to make it look as though I'm eating lots. Pam asks me about my plans, and I feed her the same line I gave Wayne about having college goals.

I smell brownies baking. Oof. I already feel like a

walrus. Brownies? Gag me. Pam retrieves the chocolate lumps of lard. I beg off, and finally get a reprieve after I threaten to be sick if I eat another bite. They nod and smile with the understanding that a short, top-heavy girl like me doesn't have as much room to pack it in as do an Amazon, a giant Comanche, and a bear.

I think we'll call it a night, but a deck of cards appears in the middle of the table. I hate cards. Wayne says, "Lucy, do you know how to play Spades?"

"No, I haven't played cards much." It's cards now instead of horses. They take turns explaining the rules. Pam's hover-y when we begin, thinking she has to explain every move, but it's simple. The pace speeds up when they're all satisfied Lucy-Goosey has figured it out.

Finally, Wayne says, "I can't play anymore," and tosses in his last deal. Thank you, Jesus. It's ten o'clock on a Saturday night, and I'm ready to go. But where? Please, please, not back to Madge's house.

"Wayne? I should get home. Daddy and Madge'll be worried." I pat myself on the back for the fine acting.

Wayne looks at his watch. "Sure, Lucy."

We drive away.

"Chew, brew, and bar-b-que," Wayne says, turning onto the highway back to town.

"What?"

"Oh, don't you know that's the Sulfur Gap motto? Chew tobacco, drink beer, and have a bar-b-que."

"I never heard that. Maybe they should add 'screw' in

there, in no particular order." Now we're laughing, and it's our first date all over again. The awkwardness of the evening slips away.

Calling the Cows

There's a sliver of a new moon, making the stars extra bright. They hang in the places they belong, while I'm being shuttled back to a place I've never belonged. But Wayne says, "Let's take a detour."

"Okay," I say, as neutral as I can pretend to be. Hot dog! I'm not going back to Madge's! Not right away, anyhow. Wayne drives another mile or so and turns onto a dirt road.

"Where we going?"

"A back door to the ranch."

"Back door?"

"Yep. The road past the windmill isn't the only way onto this place."

We cross a cattle guard. The truck rocks along a rutted road, past a plowed field, and into an abyss that must be the same low water crossing we rode up today. We climb away from the creek bed, onto level ground and turn into a pasture, stopping on a smooth surface. It's like a parking lot compared to the jostling way we've come.

"This is my favorite part of the creek," Wayne says. "There's a sandstone bluff here. Great place for a picnic."

"Looks spooky in the dark."

"Give your eyes time to adjust."

Wayne has his own private place to park where nobody can find us. For his next surprise, he hops out, unlocks his tool box, and retrieves a small cooler. He says, "These oughta be cold by now." He slides himself across the seat and unbuckles my seat belt. "You don't need that, unless you really are in a hurry to get home."

I could shout hallelujah, but I stay composed. I scrabble through the ice in the cooler and pull out a can of Coors. "You're a mind-reader." I pull the tab and savor the rush of carbonated air, spreading the fresh smell of beer. Better than a dozen roses. I hand it to him and grab another.

"You deserve a couple of these to relax after hanging with J.J. and Pam."

"I acted that bad?"

"No, you were fine. But they always want to play cards, and I hate cards. I got a bit of a hint you don't like cards, either."

"You are so right. But I go along to get along."

"I do, too. I like J.J. and Pam, so I play cards with them sometimes."

I wonder why we didn't go back to his place. Maybe he's not ready to break it in yet. I sip my beer.

"How'd you get beer? Fake I.D.?"

"I have my sources. I got it iced and put it in the tool box while you showered earlier."

Now I know he wasn't just feeding the cats. He was stocking his mobile bar.

Wayne turns on the radio. "At this location, I can pick up the Oklahoma City radio station—KOMA—with no static when the weather's right. Wolfman Jack's show broadcasts from there until midnight. We've got an hour to sit and listen."

And sure enough, Wolfman's gravelly voice says, "Here's a song for all you lovebirds in the outback. It's all about lovin' it up, so let's go!" "Baby I Love Your Ways" starts. We kiss for several minutes.

Wolfman howls as "Pour Some Sugar on Me" ends. We listen to more hits and banter from Wolfman and finish a second beer. Wayne pulls me onto his lap and starts unbuttoning my blouse. Before long, we're out of our shirts.

"Do you want to go back to my house?" he asks, pulling away slightly.

"Not now," I say. "We can go to your house another time."

We wriggle out of our pants. Here we are at last. And

he's no virgin. He has condoms in the glove box, but he's in no hurry. Wolfman Jack howls, and the disco overlay version of "Hazy Shade of Winter" plays. At some point, one of us pushes on the truck's horn with a foot or a knee, and the horn beeps several times. We snicker. Then we hear the thumping of hoof beats and mooing of cattle. We sit up to see twelve cows trotting toward the truck.

"Well, shit," Wayne says. "The horn honking made the cows think we're calling them to feed—at midnight."

But soon we're at it again, still laughing.

Happy Act Shooting Lesson, and the Prize
for the Happy Act

Wayne and I give Sulfur Gap a fresh topic for gossip. Working around my Burger Buddy shifts and his ranch duties, we spend our spare time together. On Friday nights at the home football games, we parade to our seats in the little grandstand under the floodlights. As the band toots the Sulfur Gap Gremlins' fight song, those cheerleaders with their pom-poms look silly to me, running ahead of the football players as they break through the paper banner beside the field house.

I bask in the envious glow of the girls' faces when I walk in front of the bleachers with Wayne, and I wink at some of the boys whose mouth-breathing expressions give away what they're thinking. The first football game we go to, Spence stands on the sidelines, holding his football helmet under his arm. He turns in time to see us taking our seats. His jaw drops a little and he whips his head back to focus on the field in front of him. L.B. stands around looking official on the track surrounding the football field. He enjoys standing there, inspecting the bleachers—looking for...guns? Someone waving a wine bottle? A fight?

We spend long, lazy afternoons in bed at Wayne's—doors locked and preemptive phone calls made—watching movies and making out. We drive around the ranch or ride the creek on horseback. I've improved. Wayne even trades off and lets me ride H.A.

Wayne invites J.J. and Pam to his house to pay them back for dinner. We decide to make lasagna to be different. We get them to watch a movie after dinner instead of playing cards. Pam acts like she's the hostess at Wayne's. Like I'm too young and Wayne's too helpless. She helicopters around him, barely missing his head with her boobs as she leans around on various lame pretexts. J.J. doesn't seem to care. I imagine myself ninja-jumping across the table at her.

Wayne and I discover a mutual fondness for horror movies. We go to Big Spring to see *Re-Animator* and laugh ourselves senseless. After renting and watching the first two installments of *Poltergeist*, we're ready for number three at the theater. A waste of money, but worth a few laughs.

Madge can't hide her curiosity. Every time I come home, if she's still awake, she takes a sneaky peek at my left hand, to see if there's an engagement ring. It'll be any day now. But sometimes I'm afraid this will go on only until Wayne finds someone better.

He takes me to dinner at the Navaho Inn. We sit on the same side of a booth, holding hands. We order their giant burger and fries. Wayne doesn't bitch at me about what I ordered when I leave more than half on my plate. In fact, he doesn't bitch at me about anything. How refreshing. I think he's reaching into his pocket to get some money to tip the waitress, but he puts a little black velvet box on the table in front of me.

It's a ring!

"Open it," he says.

I do, hands shaking. It's a small solitaire in a delicate silver setting. All I can do is look at it and let the tears slide down my cheeks. I've talked myself into thinking that even if he doesn't marry me and get me out of Madge's house, he's rescued me in a way. I have someone in my life who cares. And if it doesn't last but one more month, I'm better off. Since meeting Wayne, I'm different. Maybe happy? I sure haven't thought about being proposed to on a special occasion like this.

It fits perfectly. "How'd you know my size?"

"I'm a good guesser. But we can fix it if it's not right."

"So, this means we're engaged?"

"Yep. If that's okay with you."

I throw my arms around him and cry some more.

A COUPLE of weeks after the engagement, we're watching our usual afternoon movie, and he mentions setting a date. I had almost exploded, keeping the urgency to myself, waiting for him to bring it up. Pushing my hair back from my bare shoulder, he says, "So when do you want to get married?"

"Next month?"

Wayne's eyes widen. "Your parents won't be upset?"

"Why would they care?"

"You're only seventeen. I thought you'd want to wait till you're eighteen next August. Less than a year. And I'll be twenty-one in January."

"Daddy and Madge won't care. Besides, what difference does it make how old we are? We're at the age of consent." I know I shouldn't be startled that Wayne thinks about crap like this. Then I realize. It's the Cheadhams. The brother hasn't met me—he graduated from high school before I started school—and Ernie's said maybe two words the times we've been at their house. Katy's nice enough. But I bet the Cheadhams don't want us to get married. I'm too young, too low-class. I've trapped him, they think.

They think we don't know what we want. Well, I damn sure do. I want a life with Wayne. I want to sleep in his bed all night and get up in the morning and cook breakfast and clean house while he works. When I'm eighteen, I'll get a job at the courthouse and I'll help pay the bills. We can wait ten years to have kids and have a great life before then.

Wayne takes my alarmed look for curiosity, so he answers, "Age makes a difference. We're not geniuses, you know."

I'd forgotten I'd asked the question. "I suppose we've got lots to learn." I give in. He kisses me and we're off the subject for the time being. At least we discussed a date. I think about calling Katy, going by her house, and setting her straight. I'll tell her I love Wayne and want to be with him. But none of that will matter to her.

Wayne shoots from the bed. He stands there naked with his hands on his hips, the posture of a coach on the sidelines. "I have an idea," he says. He looks miffed when I laugh into my pillow.

"What? It's funny that I have an idea?"

"No! It's funny the way you jump up when you have an idea. And you look like a coach who forgot to dress for the game. Go ahead, call your play."

He looks down at himself for an instant, but he's not sidetracked. "You need to learn how to shoot."

I'm disappointed. I thought his idea involved plans for a quick wedding. But I recover. "I was pretty good at spit wads when I was in junior high. But I suck at darts."

"I mean a gun."

I've always been afraid of guns. I don't trust myself. I

might get depressed and blow my brains out. Or I might shoot Madge. Or someone else.

"Why do I need to know how to shoot a gun?"

"If you live on a ranch, you need to know how to shoot. Come on. Get dressed. You'll need to shoot snakes and varmints here."

"From horseback?" I'm being a smart-ass.

Before I know it, we're in the pasture behind the house. He's got a pistol in a holster slung over his shoulder. I carry a 16-gauge shotgun, pointed at the ground so he doesn't have a seizure at my inattention to a cardinal rule of gun safety. He's got a .22 rifle under his arm and a bag of ammo. Looks like I'm in for information overload.

My lesson begins. "This 9-millimeter is for self-defense. It's simple and light. Best used closer range because aiming a pistol accurately at long distances is nearly impossible." Next, I get the shotgun and rifle briefing.

"Why would I shoot a snake?" I hope my unwillingness to become a mighty huntress isn't a deal-killer.

"Every time you see a rattlesnake, you're duty-bound to shoot it, especially if it's close to people or livestock."

"Can't I just call you?"

"Raccoons, bobcats, and an occasional mountain lion come through this place. You might have to shoot a feral hog. You'd need a high-powered rifle. But never shoot a javelina."

I'm not sure what a javelina is and don't want to admit it.

An embankment rises behind a distant mesquite. "This is a good makeshift gun range." He shows me how to release the pistol clip and fill it with bullets and cock the gun to chamber a round. He shows me the safety lock and stresses how important it is to know at all times whether the safety is on or off. He stands behind me with his arms around me and shows me how to use both hands to hold it and aim. I wiggle my butt against him. "Now concentrate," he says. I'm supposed to keep my finger off the trigger until ready to shoot. He finds a big white rock and dumps it ten yards away and comes trotting back, not at all concerned with my trigger finger. Well, I wouldn't shoot *him*. He stands behind me, adjusts my stance, and tells me to squeeze the trigger. He backs off so I can squeeze off a round, like they say in the cop shows.

Ka-ching. A piece of white rock flies off. I can't believe it. I shoot several more times, and the bullet craters fill the rock. Wayne is shocked. "Wow! You're a natural. Are you sure you've never shot a gun?"

Wayne moves the rock further away, and we go through the same motions with the .22 and the shotgun. By the time we're through, I can tell my shoulder will be sore from the kick of the 16-gauge, but I'm proud of myself. I have natural talent. "Since I'm such a good shot, wouldn't it be appropriate for us to have a shotgun wedding?" Wayne doesn't find this at all funny. He's the poster boy for safe sex, but he doles out a chuckle to acknowledge my razor-edge wit. By the time we hike back to the house toting the guns, the sun is starting its dip behind the mesas. I'll have to get back to town soon so I can be bright-eyed and bushy-tailed for tomorrow's shift. But my days at Burger Buddy are numbered and I am glad.

Claiming the Prize

The January wedding will be small. No attendants, but we want to have it at the Episcopal Church with a few relatives and close friends. I don't have any relatives to invite other than Daddy and Madge. My friends from school—people I've grown up with—are still doing their high school thing. Whenever I run into the girls, they take a step back and look for an exit strategy. The boys angle sideways and look at the ground, like they're embarrassed. A few former classmates talk to me like they always did, but they're not the ones whose company I once sought. My best friends now are Burger Buddy cohorts.

Wayne argued with Ernie and Katy and got them to agree I'm a decent catch, smart and mature for my age, with plenty of potential. Especially once I get a chance to further my education. I didn't need to convince my parents. All I did was tell them.

I stood in front of the television and said, "Wayne and I are getting married."

Madge actually smiled—for her it was a smile. Anyone not familiar with Madge's facial twitches wouldn't have seen it. "Congratulations," she says.

"Thank you."

Daddy stood and hugged me. "When's the big day?"

"January 16, so I've got a couple of months to get ready."

"Where you gonna do this?" Madge sounded like we planned to rob a bank.

I shared our simple plans. Little does Madge know, she's not getting a penny of rent between now and then. I have to buy a decent dress and maybe a bridal bouquet.

As far as making a big show, I don't care about any of it. All I want is to move to the ranch and be with Wayne. To prepare, I've started trying to cook a few things at home. I never took home-ec or gave a good goddam about cooking. I check recipe books out of the Sandstone County Library and plan some meals. I learn where things are in the Shop-Tight Grocery Store. I should know a couple more things, besides lasagna, to make with hamburger, so I find recipes for hamburger beef stroganoff, meat spaghetti sauce, and meatloaf. I discover an old home economics book with instructions on how to fry, bake, and smother chicken and pork chops and make pot roast. Vegetables . . . eh. Anyone can make a salad. I'll get more creative after the wedding.

I'm an expert at cleaning, after all the odd jobs I've worked. I know a thing or two about yard work, and when spring comes, I'll fix up the yard. There'll be lots of spare time since I won't be working. The anticipated relief settles over me like a soft blanket.

The wedding dress worries me. The catalogs are all filled with Christmas stuff, so I'll have to venture from town to shop. Sherry's going with me. She and Jimmy Lee aren't as dumb as I thought. It takes a certain kind of know-how to get by with the least effort possible. Sherry props up with her romance novel during her breaks, a different book each day. Jimmy Lee can fix anything. The Coke dispenser began to leak, and he was back from the hardware store in ten minutes with hose and clamps. Speaking of hoses, he replaced some on my '75 Monte Carlo. And he wades in and unstops the toilets as needed.

"You could get rich as a plumber or mechanic," I say.

"Yeah. You wanna pay my tuition to tech school?"

"You could get a grant. I'll drive you to Abilene or Sweetwater."

"Okay."

And he walks off. Maybe someday he'll do something.

The day before Sherry and I head to Abilene, Jimmy Lee pronounces my engine belts roadworthy, along with the tires and transmission. Sherry's excited. You'd think we were doing a moon launch. I pick her up early on a Tuesday morning. The bridal shop in the Abilene mall has a big sale this time of year. Sherry doesn't open her novel the whole way. She's too excited. She's never been to Abilene.

I almost slam on the brakes, I'm so surprised to learn this tidbit. In fact, she says she's never been out of Sandstone County. I had no idea there were people in the world who had never taken a road trip. I slow down and look at the scenery—what there is. She gets fidgety when the traffic increases, and I feel like a metropolitan woman introducing my country mouse friend to the big city as I take the loop to the mall.

We browse the stores, spray perfume samples, and push through racks and racks like we plan to buy a stack of clothes. I find some good jeans on sale and make a mental note to come back if I have any money left after buying a wedding dress. At the bridal store, I'm overcome by the yards of gathered lace and netting and giant white bows. I do not want to look like chiffon topping on a pie.

"Do you have something without any gathers and fluff?" I ask Verna, the sales lady. "And no ruffles. Preferably something on sale. I'm on a limited budget." Madge would be embarrassed for me to announce this. Me, I don't give a shit what the sales lady thinks. I bet she'd be on a limited budget, too, if she were buying a wedding dress.

Verna leads me to the back and pulls three dresses off a rack. "These were just marked down fifty percent," she says, "and they're your size, if you can stand the long lace sleeves on this one." She holds up the dress I already have my eye on. The plain V neckline plunges just enough, and the whole dress is a form-fitting sheath. The one gathered part falls from the back of the knees into a small train that barely drags the floor. I look at the price tag. Perfect. I'll have money for a bouquet. I already have shoes that'll do. I'd bought them before I knew I wasn't going to junior prom. I hold my breath as I try it on. Perfect again.

Sherry takes a deep breath as I exit the dressing room. "Lucy, it's beautiful."

Verna agrees. I can't believe my luck. I've got my dress, I've got Wayne, and I've got a new friend in Sherry. When will the other shoe drop?

Madge is the wild card. I learned early in life not to let Madge know I cared about anything, because she would sabotage it. Letters to Santa? A set-up. I hid my excitement the first time I was invited to a dance in junior high. There would be a DJ and a spinning disco ball, all in the Sulfur Gap Community Center. It turned out to be the dance that fanned the animosity between Madge and me to a furious blaze.

But this has been a great day so far, and I'd like to

avoid thoughts of the junior high dance. Sherry and I roam the mall. I buy the jeans. Sherry is even gladder than I am to escape Sulfur Gap. I wish I had a mother to shop with me for my dress, and before I can stop myself, I'm back to replaying the junior high dance. That day, five years ago, concluded any hope of Madge participating in my life at the important times.

"A couple of the girls are hosting a dance," I remember saying, sounding casual as I tossed the invitation on the kitchen table. She would find a reason to ground me if I showed enthusiasm. All the girls planned to wear those one-piece slinky jumpsuits, cinched at the waist—the "in" look for 1983.

I've always been resourceful, I think, laying my wedding dress and jeans in the car trunk for the trip back to the Gap. I remember the urgency to get an outfit for the dance—an outfit that didn't make me feel like a kid in foster care. I hiked across town and spent a Saturday knocking on doors in the well-to-do neighborhood and asking if I could clean house or do yard work. I replaced one lady's kitchen shelf paper and bonsaied a juniper bush for another. I made twenty-five dollars—pretty good wages for a Saturday in '83.

When I got home in the late afternoon, Madge said, "Where've you been?"

"I made ten bucks today," I lied, downplaying my take. She might garnish my earnings to pay back some debt she's suddenly remembered. "I worked for some rich ladies. Thought I'd save to buy myself my first makeup, when I'm allowed to wear it."

A pleased look flickered across her face, but she shrugged and turned back to the television. Little did she know, my locker at school was stocked with make-up I'd bought on sale at the pharmacy. I wondered how I would find a dance outfit until opportunity surprised me.

When I came home from school on Monday, Daddy was sliding into his windbreaker and gathering his car keys to drive to Big Spring to deliver some paperwork for the accounting office where he worked. So, I piled my books on my bed and hollered to Madge that I was going along to keep him company. I'd seen an ad for a clothing store sale in the Big Spring *Chronicle*, with a slinky jumpsuit pictured. Sulfur Gap had some little boutiques, but they were too expensive, and a sales lady might tell Madge.

Once we got on the highway, I told Daddy I needed to get some underwear with my earned money but didn't want Mama to know. We pulled to the curb and I dashed inside, found a royal blue jumpsuit in a junior size 3, and was out in a flash.

I'm so deep in the memory, I forget I've got a passenger. Sherry's got her nose buried in her romance, leaving no one to chat with, so I'm left with my memories. I wish I could turn them off.

My teeth clench as I remember hiding the sack containing my carefully-folded outfit far back under the seat of the car. The Friday before the dance, I snuck it in the house and stayed in my room so Madge wouldn't go snooping. I pushed a chair under the door knob, pressed my jumpsuit, and tried it on, admiring myself in the mirror of my little dresser.

On Saturday, I dressed for the party in straight-legged pants, cheap slippers Madge let me order from the Sears catalog, and a big shirt. Nothing Madge could find fault with. Modest, unpretentious. Not very attractive but not downright ugly. After all, she didn't want to look like Cinderella's stepmother. I played it right, all the way to the dance—Daddy would take me and pick me up.

On Saturday afternoon, I slipped my outfit in its sack back under the seat of his car. Daddy didn't see me grab the bag as I hopped out at the community center. Inside, the lights were dimmed, the disco ball sparkled, and a clutch of girls—the "in" crowd—stood in the center of the floor. I was not assured of a position with the preferred clique, but they included me sometimes. I could tell a good dirty joke and fix everybody's hair, so I was invited to the larger slumber parties.

I waved and hollered, "I gotta change in the restroom. Just got back in town!" Flashing a bright smile and waving like it was no big deal to bring clothes to the dance and change there, I flounced into the prison-like bathroom. I had a small make-up bag hidden in my waist band, and I'd already made sure every curl on my head was in place.

My thoughts are wrenched back to the Abilene highway, because Sherry has decided to talk. She's telling me all about this boy she's been dating since she graduated and how he wants sex, but she's holding out for marriage. I wonder what century she thinks we're living in. I listen with one ear to Sherry's Romantic History for twenty minutes and say, "Good for you." She continues reading, and I'm back to the memory like a fly on a cupcake.

The first part of the dance was like another world. The music throbbed, and the blinking lights kept time. I joined in, outfitted as well as any girl there. Spencer Dixon raised his chin and winked at me. We danced toward each other. I fit in, more than ever before. I wanted to dance all night.

When the beat slowed, Spence pulled me to him. After a close dance, we held hands and made our way to the refreshment table for a cup of punch. We leaned against the wall, heads together, at the darkest edge of the big room. The casual chaperones chatted, letting the kids have the floor for their first adolescent fling.

"I wish I could kiss you, but the parents'll spaz," Spence said. We leaned toward each other and touched foreheads.

That's when my mother grabbed my arm. I hadn't smelled her coming. Not a whiff. She jerked me toward

the door and smiled her phoniest at the surprised chaperones. "I'm so sorry to bust in like this. We've got a
slight emergency and Lucy's got to come home," she
announced to their startled faces. They nodded,
pretending to understand.

Once outside, she grabbed my hair. A few roots gave
way as she got a grip and shoved me toward the car and
jerked open the door to push me in. She'd found my
other clothes on the table with the purses, inside the sack
bearing the name of the Big Spring boutique. She lobbed
the sack into the back seat and slid in behind the steering
wheel and turned on me, slapping at me with both
hands. I shrank and held my arms over my head. Her
voice alternated between gravelly and squeaky as she
cursed. "Slimy little slut, all ready to put out. Sneaky
bitch of a whore." And so on. She'd called me names
before, but now she came up with some new compound
curses, all involving me being a slut.

We drove home in silence. I figured I was busted for
getting the dance outfit, but she never said a word about
it. It had disappeared by the time I got out of the children's emergency shelter. She probably returned it to the
store and kept the money. I never knew how she found
out or if something else had stirred her up. No telling.

Sherry and I are almost back to Sulfur Gap, and I turn
down the narrow highway to the side of town where
Sherry lives with her mother. At her house, a little square
box that couldn't have more than three rooms, I think I

would have traded places with her before I met Wayne. She and her mother are tight, like two close sisters. We say good-bye, and she reminds me, "Don't forget! If you want that dress altered in any way, Mom and I would love to help." I almost cry.

I drive past the community center where the dance was held. After Madge dragged me away so unceremoniously, I wanted to have a cover story to tell my friends at school on Monday. A story to stop the questions.

But my brain had clicked to a novel idea. Why was I covering for her? Mark Twain said if you tell the truth, there's not so much to remember. A circle of wide-eyed girls crowded me at the lockers. "I'll tell you why I had to leave the dance in such a rush, but this stays among us." That last part guaranteed the news flash would be all over school in a minute. "My mother is mean and crazy. She loses her cool all the time. But only in front of me and my dad. He's scared of her. She jerked me out of the dance and dragged me to the car by my hair. She slapped me and called me all the names she could think of. I'm not sure what I did, except sneak around to buy my outfit. She probably saw it when she came to the dance to spy on me."

I touched my head, where the roots were still sore. A few tears crept into my eyes, but I shook it off. After the cat episode, I'd vowed Madge would never make me cry. Some of the girls touched my arm, teary-eyed. I trembled with the effort to hold back tears at the unfamiliar sympathy.

Sure enough, by afternoon, the school counselor called me in.

I told her the story of life with Madge. For all I cared, they could throw her in jail. What I didn't count on was the ride in the sheriff's car to the children's emergency shelter in Briargrove. I stayed there overnight while Child Protective Services assessed the situation. I felt safe, and the staff spoke in soft, reassuring voices. I again had trouble keeping back the tears. In the interview, I stuck to the truth. I told about the times Madge had turned her unhappiness on me. Sending my cat away, never allowing me to express myself, demanding I be invisible so she didn't have to be reminded I was there. The beatings came when I didn't stay invisible. Only my father's presence provided safety. I left out the part about the babysitter's son—the part where Madge claimed I made up what a pervert he was to get attention. A four-year-old, making that up. I was teetering on a cliff's edge saying as much as I did, and I didn't want to dive onto the rocks at the bottom.

My punishment for telling on Madge was the brief exile to a strange place, my school week disrupted. But it was worth it. When I got back home, she thought her icy silence hurt. It was welcome. Now she knew I was old enough and smart enough to tell.

I push my thoughts back to reality as I turn toward

home. My gas gauge shows I've got just enough to go to work and back tomorrow. I park carefully beside the driveway, leaving plenty of room for Daddy to pull up when he comes home.

After my "outcry" and the intervention of law enforcement, we were required to get family counseling, but Madge kept calling and putting off the appointment until CPS gave up or forgot about our case. CPS had bigger fish to fry. Madge simmered and kept her hands to herself, a big improvement. She was required to take a series of parenting classes. She couldn't get out of that— had to drive to Abilene every Saturday for ten weeks. What a farce. But I became a much more interesting person to all the kids at school—a noble survivor. Teachers went out of their way to be nice to me. My new popularity came with a heavy tinge of weirdness.

I let myself in the house and carry my wedding dress past the back of Madge's chair, where she sits, watching *Family Ties*.

Thanksgiving Mud and Madness

Katy invited my parents and me to Thanksgiving dinner. She said, "Since we'll be in-laws, we might as well celebrate the holidays together." Of course, the parents knew each other by sight but had never said more than routine greetings. I tell Katy I'll bring a zucchini casserole—from a recipe in *Redbook* at the library. Madge isn't about to get cozy with the Cheadhams, but she plans to go. I'm amazed.

On Thanksgiving morning, lumpy black clouds in a gray sky foretell nasty weather. I know Wayne and Ernie are standing in their front yards looking at the sky and praying for rain. It starts gently, but before long, it's a steady downpour.

Wayne calls to give some pointers. "Be sure Baker doesn't miss any of the turns," he says. "Tell your dad to watch for potholes on the last road. We don't want him to get stuck."

Jinx.

Madge bitches about what to wear. She finally comes up with a skirt and jacket I didn't know she had. Of course, we rarely see each other, especially the last couple of months. I keep my mouth shut and put together my casserole. Daddy makes a special trip to gas up the car. You'd think we're driving to Dallas for dinner.

I cover my dish with foil and wrap it in plenty of newspaper. Even though I've put it in a paper sack that'll rest in a cardboard box lid, Madge says, "Now don't you spill none o' that on Daddy's clean floorboard." I set the casserole on the floorboard and sit in the back seat.

The drive is smooth until we get to the last road leading to Katy and Ernie's house. Even in good weather, it's a bumpy ride for a sedan, and today, the ruts and potholes are filled with water. I remember one especially bad dip that's probably full of mud by now.

Madge peers over the dashboard, her head bobbing. I scoot to look out the windshield and watch for the bad spots. The most treacherous dip appears, so I say, "Daddy, keep going steady through this next puddle, and veer right as far as you can. This is where you're most likely to get stuck."

Daddy slows to a crawl and veers to the edge of the

road. A prickly algerita bush scrapes the side of the Plymouth.

"Baker, you stay in the road!" Madge yells.

He steers back to dead center.

"Daddy," I say, "you'll get stuck if you head straight into that big mud puddle."

"It's just a regular old loblolly," Madge yells. "Lucy, you shut up and quit back-seat driving."

"Really, Daddy, if you don't speed up and get over to the right, you'll get stuck in the middle."

Madge whips her head around like a striking snake. Her jowl lines and straight mouth make her look like *Chucky* and *The Exorcist* rolled into one. Then I see it. She's having a panic attack.

I keep my voice even. "I've been up this road at least twenty times, and that's a deep depression, right there."

Daddy, fearing Madge more than the prospect of getting the car mired, decides to plow through, and sure enough, our back wheels spin. We're stuck.

"You're digging us in deeper!" Madge continues to yell. "Damn it, Lucy, you shoulda told us it was this deep. So now what're we gonna do? We don't have no car phone. We gonna sit here until someone comes looking for us?"

"Shut up, Madge," Daddy says, like he's telling her what time it is.

My mother and I freeze. I've never heard him stand

up to her like this, even in a calm voice. "Lucy, how close are we to the house?"

"Less than a mile."

"Why don't you run get Wayne or Mr. Cheadham to come with the pickup and pull us out."

"And we're just supposed to sit here?" Madge's voice verges on a shriek.

"Yep. And I'd appreciate some peace and quiet while we wait."

I don't linger to see if Daddy gets his way on the peace and quiet. The mud is deep, so I stuff my jeans into my boot tops. It's good I brought my hooded windbreaker. It takes me less than ten minutes to jog to the house. Flipper and Fran, the mongrels who patrol the front yard, bark when I'm fifty yards away. Wayne steps onto the front porch. When he sees me, he jumps down without taking the steps and runs toward me. I'm so boiling mad at Madge, I don't know how I can be with her the rest of the day, but Wayne's concern melts a little of the ice in my chest. Wayne and I are in the pickup and back to the Plymouth in a few minutes.

"Happy Thanksgiving," I say in my most ironic tone. "I tried to tell Daddy about that spot, but Madge kept yelling at him not to scrape the car."

"It's okay. I've had to pull people out of that spot before." The Plymouth sits in the mud like a big green bug. Wayne stuffs his jeans into the tops of work boots and ties the car to his trailer hitch by a long rope. He and Daddy make a plan.

Madge's mouth chops away during it all. Wayne pulls the car free. He rolls his rope, takes off his work gloves, and stands on the running board to toss his muddy work boots into the pickup bed. He has a clean pair in the cab. We caravan to the house on time. If we hadn't gotten stuck, we would've been unstylishly early.

Madge's mouth is set in a straight line and her hands tremble. A coat of mud cakes the back half of the Plymouth. I kick off my boots in the mud room on the way in and carry my zucchini to the kitchen while Wayne formally introduces my parents to his and to his brother, Vince, and his wife, Elizabeth.

A heavenly aroma of turkey and dressing, potatoes, and pies fills the air. I haven't met Vince and Elizabeth, so I shake their hands. Vince seems nice, but Elizabeth gives me a quick, appraising up-and-down look, mostly down her nose. Wayne has his hand at my back, like he's presenting me at an ingénue ball. Daddy and Madge are backed up against a love seat, waiting for an opportunity to sit down and stare at the TV, which is what Ernie is doing from his recliner. Football is on every channel.

We finally find our perches, and Katy says, "Well, the next time we're all together will probably be for the wedding."

"Oh, I'm not at all expecting to come," says Elizabeth, like that's the most important thing for all of us to know.

She's a school administrator in Frisco, and she's too indispensable, don't you know, to get away for her brother-in-law's wedding.

Wayne and I sit at one end of the long couch, holding hands. Katy makes another conversational effort. "Vince, how's your practice doing?"

Vince isn't interested in the football game. "Great. I've got a contract with Child Protective Services that'll send a lot of business my way."

My ears perk up. "What do you do for them?"

"Oh, family counseling. Parenting. Grief counseling's my specialty, and it comes in handy."

"How's that?" I ask.

"A lot of family problems can be traced to a sense of loss a parent has never dealt with," he says.

My eyes automatically shift toward Madge. Her face is pinched shut. As we make eye contact, she jerks her head away.

"C'mon, Vince!" Elizabeth interrupts. "We're not here to talk shop."

I would have liked to "talk shop," but never mind me.

Dinner goes the same way—Madge tensing up over every topic, Daddy acting like he's not in the room, Ernie focusing solely on his food, and the rest of us making awkward conversation, worsened by Elizabeth's constant steering of subjects. She makes a slip.

"Katy, I love your zucchini casserole," she says. Katy

looks disappointed and has to admit I made it. Then Elizabeth tries to cajole Madge into the conversation.

"Madge, does Lucy have any brothers or sisters? Anyone off in college?" Like *everyone* sends their kids to college, my dear.

Madge looks like she's been handed a turd. "No, it's just Lucy." Daddy says, "And we were lucky to have her."

That's news to me. Elizabeth doesn't know where to go from there, so she hops up and runs into the kitchen for the tea pitcher to do refills. How can the world get by without someone like her to whoosh in and pour tea? During all this, Wayne squeezes my knee under the table every time Elizabeth stirs the air with a comment or question. It keeps me smiling, at least. Katy sits back and lets her serve pie. Smart move. Katy has a two-butt kitchen at best, and Elizabeth sucks up the air and space for three.

We're finally finished. Ernie pushes away from the table and looks at Wayne, Daddy, and Vince. "Football?" he asks. He doesn't wait for an answer, but heads for the den and his recliner.

Daddy says, "We better be heading back to town."

After some stiff farewells, Daddy and Madge take off. I'm spending the rest of the day with Wayne, and I'm grateful not to be riding with Madge when Daddy runs the Plymouth against an algerita bush.

D addy brings a package to the table. "Your mother and I wanted to get a wedding gift, and we thought Christmas would be a good time to give it to you."

Double-dipping on the gift occasion. Madge's idea, no doubt. I am as gracious as possible as I open the gift. It's a four-slot toaster. Well, halle-fucking-lujah. My dowry. I'll be bringing a toaster to this marriage, by God.

Christmas is quiet at the Paxton house, as usual. The Cheadhams have gone to Frisco to Vince and Elizabeth's new house for Christmas day. Wayne invited me. Not on your life am I going to Elizabeth's. I tell my parents I'll cook. We haven't done anything for Christmas since I was little, when Daddy wanted a tree so Santa Claus could come. I stuff Cornish game hens with instant stuffing and cook frozen asparagus topped with

Hollandaise sauce—from a package mix. For dessert, a Sara Lee cheesecake. It's not a bad holiday meal, but of course Madge won't say so.

A FEW WEDDING gifts dribble in. Waffle iron, skillet, dish towels. I work at Burger Buddy until the day before we tie the knot, saving money and buying clothes. Finally, it's time for the rehearsal, which takes ten minutes. Wayne's relatives and my parents gather at the Navaho for the rehearsal dinner. Bonnie and Janette—Wayne's cousins—and their husbands, Vince, and all the parents all sit with us at a long table. Madge shrugs out of her chair to hobble to the bathroom—she does the hillbilly hobble step for effect. There's nothing wrong with her.

"I can't wait to move out. She hates me," I say, to no one in particular. Nerves and exhaustion have taken their toll on being able to edit my comments before they tumble from my mouth.

Katy clears her throat. "Anyone for dessert?"

Bonnie laughs, "Oh, Lucy. I know you're kidding. Your mother doesn't hate you."

I shoot all the daggers I have in my head at her. She's one to talk, with *her* mother looking like she pees icicles.

After dinner, Bonnie's husband, Lloyd, backs Wayne into a corner across the room. They've got their heads lowered, chewing toothpicks and having a confidential talk. I can tell Wayne doesn't like it. He straightens up and raises his voice. "Lloyd, I tell you what. You mind your own marriage and I'll tend to mine."

Lloyd says, "Okay, sorry, man. Just had to get in my two cents. I'll forever hold my peace." He shakes Wayne's hand and pats him on the shoulder.

"What was that about?" I ask when we're outside in the parking lot.

"Oh, Lloyd thinks we're too young."

"Is that all?"

"What else would there be?"

"Well, if he's passing judgment, he doesn't know me."

"No, he wasn't. He thinks we're young to be getting married."

"Are you sure that's all?"

Wayne looks me square in the face. "Yes, that's all."

I can tell the discussion is over.

THAT NIGHT, I lie in my single bed. I pushed it under the window years ago for a better boost when I snuck out. I can't sleep, knowing this is the last night I will ever spend on a little-girl bed. The moonlight gives it all a glow that makes my old dresser and mirror look like a black and white photo, like something from the past, or a dream. I whisper a prayer to a God I don't believe exists.

I pray to keep the past not real to me, like an old newsreel in its box. I want to live the rest of my life in living color, with the moments bright and joyful. My best chance to be happy starts in the morning. Finally, I sleep.

I'm at the church by 9:00 a.m. Sherry meets me to help with my dress and last-minute details. She also has the job of waylaying Madge if she tries to come into the bridal room before the wedding. Madge won't bother, but Sherry's in the hallway in case Madge decides to try to suck the joy out of it. I admire myself in the long mirror. I wish I could get married every day, just to wear this dress and look this good.

It's finally time. The organist manages to play some introductory music and swing into the wedding march without missing too many notes. As I walk down the aisle with Daddy, Wayne waits for me at the end, the glorious end, the escape hatch from hell.

The ceremony is a blur. I don't notice my mother, except when Father Jones asks, "Who gives this woman?" and Daddy says, "Her mother and I do." I look away from Wayne for a moment as Daddy retreats to the pew to sit with Madge. I snap my attention back to Wayne. I concentrate on his face, his eyes, and I think, "I'll be Mrs. Cheadham any minute now." Sherry pats my arm for me to hand her my nosegay. It's ring time!

"Mr. and Mrs. Wayne Cheadham," Father Jones finally announces. It's taken ten minutes, if that long, with the off-key music thrown in, and we adjourn to the fellowship hall for punch and cookies. Katy arranged things for the little reception.

The church's punch bowl and cookie platters sit on a long table with a white cloth and white bows tied at the corners. Lloyd brought his camera. We all pose and make happy faces. Fortunately, there's only one picture with Madge in it.

She finds a folding chair against the wall and sits, gripping her purse on her lap. Daddy stands in a circle of men, listening and laughing. How did he wind up with someone like Madge?

Wayne shakes all the hands, and I kiss and hug everyone. My Burger Buddy co-workers clean up nicely, and I'm surprised by how happy they are for me. Before I know it, we've changed our clothes and grabbed our bags, and we head for San Antonio.

Married. Now What?

Four months feels like four years. Time has dragged since the honeymoon. We stayed at the Four Seasons Riverwalk Hotel in San Antonio for a week, mostly in the room, but also sightseeing, shopping, and enjoying the nightlife as much as we could without a fake I.D. to make me twenty-one.

Settling in to the routine has been an eye-opener (literally). Wayne gets up every blasted morning before the butt-crack of dawn. For the first three months, I rose with him and made breakfast.

One morning, he asked if I knew how to make pancakes.

"There's mixes for that. You can make your own damn pancakes," I say, only half joking.

"I appreciate you getting up with me, but you don't have to," he said.

That's all it took. Now I revel in the warmth of late mornings in bed with a book. He's invited me to go with him on his morning rounds, but I think not. I'll pitch in on the ranch work if worse comes to worst and I have to be a cowhand. Ranch work never stops, with all the animals needing to be fed or doctored or moved or found. An endless list.

On weekends we go to the movies or have Pam and J.J. over or some other buddies of Wayne's from around town. There's an occasional low-key party for a basketball game or some such. I invite my Burger Buddy friends. Our activities consist of card games, board (should be "bored") games, or, if the weather is right, yard games—washer pitching, volleyball, badminton, croquet. Yawn!

I can't get motivated to work on that front yard. I insisted Wayne buy some ash trees and plant them around the house for shade. He did it in a morning, using his mechanical post-hole digger. Those trees will grow fast enough and soon we won't be so exposed to the wind and sun. I nag about a fence, so at least I have an idea of how much territory we'll be looking at to get grass going.

Sherry and I make a couple more trips to Abilene to shop. I have my own checkbook for our joint account—and a credit card. Wealth beyond my wildest dreams. I walk to Katy's once in a while. She asks questions, and I can tell she's checking off the plus and minus columns on how Lucy's treating her baby boy. But I go see her, so she won't come see me—or us. I don't want her appraising my housework.

I ask Wayne if Katy is badmouthing me.

"Why would she do that?" Wayne can be so naïve.

"I'm sure she thinks you shouldn't have married me."

These ongoing conversations lead to reassurances. He loves me up so I stop worrying, but he's tired of it. The last time I mentioned my fears about his mother, he shut down the dialog. "I apparently can't convince you my mother doesn't have anything against you," he said. End of discussion.

Ernie is impossible. If he doesn't know Wayne's whereabouts every second, he calls the house. I tell Wayne he needs one of those new mobile phones in his pickup. He says they're too damn big. "They're like holding a boot to your ear," he says. After he comes home, Ernie always thinks of something to double-check, so there's at least one inevitable phone call each evening. We plan our lives around Ernie's heavy hand. I tell Wayne I can't believe he puts up with Ernie treating him like a five-year-old.

Wayne says, "He's antsier if there's no rain."

And doesn't it figure, there's been not a drop since the bluster that created the Thanksgiving mud puddles. I overhear him one evening talking to Ernie. Yes, he called the vet to come check the colicky horse, and no, he didn't forget to try such-and-such medicine, and yes, he'd ordered new tires for the tractor.

"Why do you take that shit?" I ask.

Wayne shrugs. "I think it's in the Sermon on the Mount. It says, 'Agree with thine adversary quickly. Lest he take you to court and take the shirt off your back.' That's the gist. If it's something that doesn't matter, I agree, or pretend to, and the discussion ends a lot quicker."

What a philosopher. I decide to pick a fight to see if "agreeing with the adversary" applies to me, too. I wait until the next evening:

ME: Where are those kitchen shears? (*I hid them in the top of the closet.*)

WAYNE: Haven't seen them.

ME: Yes, you have. You used them last. You used the gripper handles to pry open the jelly jar last night.

WAYNE, *walking to the drawer and looking in*: For some reason, they're not in the drawer. Maybe I left them in the utility room.

ME, *while Wayne rummages*: I don't think they're in there but be my guest.

WAYNE, *coming back into the kitchen*: You're right, they're not there.

ME: Well, where *are* they?

WAYNE: Let me see if I left them on the porch bench. (*He goes out the front door and is back soon.*)

ME: Well????

WAYNE: Not there. Are you sure you haven't used them?

ME: Oh! So, it's *my* fault! You lose a perfectly good set of kitchen shears, and I'm to blame.

WAYNE: It's not about whose fault it is.

ME: Yes, it is! You lost those shears and don't want to take responsibility!

WAYNE, *infuriatingly calm*: Okay, I misplaced the shears. I'll buy a new pair tomorrow.

Wayne sits on the couch and holds the TV remote. I slam the bedroom door. He's probably thinking I'm on the rag, the male chauvinist pig. Then I remember. Oh yeah, I am on the rag. And it'll take a lot more than a battle over who lost the scissors to goad him into losing his cool. Now I'm all upset, and he's enjoying the latest episode of *Cheers*.

Bastard.

Maybe I should cut him some slack. He works his ass off and doesn't mind me not working—in fact, he takes some pride in rescuing me from the Burger Buddy job and Madge. He slaves away for Ernie and never gets a bit of credit.

Ernie's the bastard, not Wayne.

I feel guilty for dishing out the crap. I stand on a stool and push those kitchen shears all the way to the back of the closet shelf. *I'm a crisis junkie.*

IT's no time before we're sucked into another card game. Why the hell can't Wayne tell people we just don't like to play cards? We're at Pam and J.J.'s, and Wayne's my partner. I've got it all figured. He should play the nine of diamonds, but instead he plays the six. I groan, so he looks again at his play and groans, too.

"Sorry, Lucy, thought it was the nine."

"Then maybe you should stand on your head to play cards," I snap.

The next time we see J.J. and Pam is when Wayne and I make our monthly-ish appearance at church. The Aztec warlord and the Norwegian princess stand out in the Episcopal Church with all the stooped blue-hairs and ordinary people. Pam and J.J. are something from a graphic novel—kind of surreal, all straight-backed and proper in their bright Sunday clothes.

We go to the Navaho for the Sunday buffet, and Wayne sits down with his plate full. He's not a big fan of fish, but he's got a big, battered fillet on his plate.

"Wayne," I say, "when did you start eating fish?"

He's confused for a moment. "Oh," he says, "I thought it was chicken."

"Was someone pushing you through the buffet line so you couldn't go slow enough to read the sign that said 'fried filet of sole'?" My tone is vicious. Wayne looks at me like I ought to be ashamed. Pam and J.J. look at each other and at Wayne. I can tell they're holding hands under the table, congratulating themselves on the solidity of their marriage. But I'm not fooled. Pam can't hide how her eyes cut over at Wayne to make sure he's aware of what he's missing. The Alpha Goddess of Love and Domesticity. *Yuck.*

I feel guilty again. It seems like the guiltier I am, the more I want to shred him.

AT LUNCH ONE DAY, Wayne, out of the blue, says, "You know, you could go ahead and start college this summer. I bet you're pretty bored hanging around here."

"What about the money?"

"You could probably get a scholarship, just on your test scores."

I wonder when he became a guidance counselor. I did brag to him that I had high SAT scores, and that was when I was a junior. "Yes, I suppose, for the upcoming fall term."

"Maybe we could scrape up the tuition for the summer term. I'm sure Mom and Ernie will help."

He's being all too agreeable. He thinks he can get rid of me if I get educated and have some career potential. But he can make all those plans he wants while I go to college. I'll be the one leaving him.

"Sounds like you and your parents have already discussed this. Why not include me in the conversation?"

"Well, we would have if you'd been there when it

came up."

"So, the subject of me just 'came up'? Sounds like someone, no doubt your mother, was taking advantage of my not being there."

"You weren't the subject."

"If I wasn't the subject, how did y'all start talking about me?"

"We were looking at the pictures of the senior class in *The Sulfur Gap Echo*. Your junior class picture was there and you were listed as an early graduate. We talked about how smart you are and how you should go to college."

"And Ernie and Katy are eager enough to either get rid of me or put me to work teaching or something equally lame, they'll pay for my college?"

"Just help with summer school. No big deal. To see if you like it."

This could work—cutting my time on the ranch in half and giving me a huge distraction. I never dreamed I'd go to college, and I decide not to look a gift horse in the mouth.

I enroll at Angelo State University. Wayne doesn't want me driving every day, so I'll stay in the dorm during the week. I test well enough to get credit for twelve hours of English and math. They're giving me a scholarship for the fall, too, a high-level award to pay all but a few of my expenses. I'll be a sophomore by December, and I figure I can get a degree in two more years.

Graduation on the Fast Track—December 1991

I don my cap and gown and take my place in line for the processional of December graduates. It's been a fast couple of years, I reflect, as I add the extra sash and cord to mark my status as a *summa cum laude* graduate. Katy, Ernie, Wayne, and Daddy are somewhere in the stands at the coliseum, waiting for me to cross the stage. Madge died of an aneurism last year. She gave it to herself because she was wound so tight.

It's been easier to stay married and live on the ranch on the weekends and during breaks. Weekend reunion sex is pretty damn good. But one recent development makes my chest hurt and heart pound and never leaves my thoughts. I'm swimmy-headed with the added pressure of commencement exercises. I tried to avoid going through the formality, but Wayne insisted. "It's your big day," he said. I feel undeserving after what I did, but there's no one I can confide in. Lonely guilt is the worst kind.

I shouldn't have made that stop at the Suds Shop after classes were over. My car was loaded, and I should have headed straight home. I got a fake I.D., and I've had the chance to kick up a little dust here and there. Nothing wild, just underage drinking. At the Suds Shop, you can do your laundry next-door to a bar with passable live music or a D.J. and a little dance floor. I can truthfully tell Wayne I've been to the laundromat.

I force my mind to the present. The graduates sit in their rows, listening to a bunch of humbug about our great achievement. To the contrary, bachelors' degrees like my political science diploma are so common, one advisor told me I should go on to graduate school if I want a decent job for the effort of going to college. More scholarship money will get me through a Masters' in Public Administration program. Lotta good an MPA will do me in Sulfur Gap, but I might get a good county job. The ideal outcome would be to move to Austin. Wayne, though, would consider that a fate worse than bubonic plague.

Right now, I'll do anything to stay away from the south field on the ranch. It's an awful reminder, and I'm not ready to examine what happened—what I did—only a few days ago. The guilt drags on me. I'll have to avoid the ranch as much as possible. No dust will settle before I start on the Masters' in the spring term.

They're calling our names now, almost to the C's, so I'm filing toward the stage and ready when they call "Lucy Cheadham." I shake the dean's hand, and it's over. I wish Madge could see this. I remember when Daddy called and described her condition—the intolerable headache, the loss of consciousness. Then the ventilator, Daddy's pacing, and unplugging the ventilator. The certainty was underlined. She wouldn't ever be the mother I wished for, because now she was dead. I gave up the last shred of an occasional fantasy that she would mellow. I even fantasized that getting a college degree or two would make her respect me. But she's not here today as I walk the line of graduates. I miss her, like a limp I've gotten used to.

Driving home on the long, straight highway, Wayne squeezes my hand.

"I'm proud of you, Lucy."

"Thanks, Wayne."

We pull into the drive toward the house, and the headlights illuminate an unfamiliar gleam under the carport. Omigod, it's a Mustang GT.

"A little graduation present," he says.

I jump out before he can stop completely. I wasn't unhappy with the used Toyota Cressida he'd gotten for me when I started driving back and forth to school. I never dreamed I'd own a muscle car. I run my hands over the cool blue metal of the roof and pull the door open. The interior is white leather. The dash and console glow in the light of the carport.

It's like the night he gave me the engagement ring. I'm undeserving, especially now. "It's not that big a deal, me graduating," I say.

"It is, too, Lucy. To graduate with top honors in under three years is a big deal."

Then I get this bug up my ass and I say, "You're not feeling guilty about something, are you?" I know from my psych class I'm projecting my own guilt onto him. I'm not serious, and I hear the accusing words as if someone else said them.

First, he looks puzzled, then stricken at how quickly I can suggest he's done something wrong. He knows I don't trust Pam. Maybe he thinks I'm accusing them of sleeping together.

"What?" All he can do is gawk at me.

"Oh, never mind! I'm just making a lame joke." I try to wave it off.

But he's cut to the quick. He gives me a Mustang and I give him the shaft. Boy, did I step in it.

THE NEXT FEW DAYS, I'm as appreciative as I can be. I call Sherry and Jimmy Lee—and make sure Wayne hears me —and tell them how proud I am of my college graduation gift. "It's the nicest thing anyone ever did for me—I never dreamed I'd marry someone as wonderful as Wayne—letting me traipse off to college, and then giving me such a gift." It's a public relations campaign, a sales blitz.

I talk to him. "Wayne, I don't know what made me say that. I'm paranoid. I think stuff, and when it spills out of my mouth it's a pile of crap that I can't believe. Maybe I need counseling."

He's kind. He says, "I know, Lucy. You don't wake up in the morning determined to cut me down. Sure, check out the counseling route if you want."

He's understanding, but there's a distance now. When we turn out the light at night, he turns his back to me instead of scooping me into his arms and spooning with me. If there's any sex, I have to start it, and he's automatic, like it's a chore to get through. His feelings for me have changed, the balance tipped by that one stupid remark.

WE GO through the motions of Christmas. Katy's having the festivities at her house, with Vince and Elizabeth and the rest of us, including Daddy. She's also invited Guillermo Sanchez and his little grandson Billy. Billy's mother doesn't want him, so Guillermo took the boy as his own, adores him. Guillermo's a regular ranch employee who rotates between the Cheadhams, the

Raneys, and the Standleys. He manages the seasonal laborers and translates as needed. This year in third grade, Billy has a new friend, a little blond boy with startling blue eyes—Charley Bristow. Guillermo asked if Charley could come—he hasn't had much of a Christmas lately because his stepfather died a couple of years ago and his mother isn't coping well.

The boys rush into the den, eyes wide at the sight of the decorations and lights. The mantel is festooned with cedar boughs, and on the stone wall above, a huge wreath of bows made from red bandanas takes the place of the usual barbed wire and burlap ribbon wreath. The tall tree reaches the arch of the cathedral ceiling and is decorated with bows of more bandana cloth and lacquered apples and pears. Sounds tacky, but it works.

The boys spy presents for them under the tree and look to Guillermo for the go-ahead. Katy says, "Santa Claus knew there were some good little fellers coming by here, so he left some of their presents."

Elizabeth claps her hands and shrills, "How exciting!"

We all watch the little hoodlums shred wrapping paper. They rip into model airplane kits, walkie-talkies, and a couple of hand-held games that make obnoxious beepy noises. Billy runs to show his *abuelo* one of his toys.

"You boys need to thank Miz Katy and Mr. Ernie for having Santa Claus," Guillermo says. Billy turns to the

Cheadhams and starts saying "thank you," the way kids do when someone makes them, but Charley's not sure which of us is Miz Katy or Mr. Ernie, so he runs to Wayne and grabs his legs and looks up at him with a face that could melt a glacier. "Thank you!" he says—and means it.

Wayne bends down and returns the hug. He ruffles Charley's hair. "Any time, pardner," he says.

Charley might turn into a project for Wayne—a distraction. Maybe it'll help until my latest foot-in-mouth episode blows over. Yeah, Wayne needs a nephew, and it doesn't look like Vince and Elizabeth will provide one. Elizabeth wouldn't let any of us touch her kid, anyway, so I hope Charley stays in the picture.

Games of 1993

I've finished my Masters' degree. Got my thesis in early, so the job search is on. I found out Sandstone County jobs pay peanuts. No surprise. Anyhow, I need to get away from the ranch and the south field after that terrible night just before getting my first degree. I still haven't framed it in my mind yet. Growing up the way I did, I learned to compartmentalize horrid events so I don't have to think about them. The disadvantage is that later, it's hard to make sentences about them, but the feeling of guilt lingers.

Wayne keeps a painful but civil distance. I wish he'd slap me. That would be a tangible thing. I could at least call him an S.O.B., point to the violence as proof, but this passivity drives me bonkers. All I can do is imagine what he's thinking. I stir things up to bring his new disgust with me into the open.

ME: L.B. pulled me over today.

WAYNE: Why?

ME: Speeding down Main.

WAYNE: Did he give you a ticket?

ME: Nope. Just a warning.

WAYNE: Good.

ME: Do you want to know *why* he didn't give me a ticket?

WAYNE: Okay. Why?

ME: Shit, Wayne, your wife was in a potentially compromising situation, and you don't care. You don't even care about my driving record.

WAYNE: How would you be compromised?

ME: Well, you know Larry Bob's *always* had a thing for me.

WAYNE: So?

ME: He might have suggested something.

WAYNE: Like avoiding a traffic ticket by giving sexual favors? *He laughs.* Larry Bob has more sense than to suggest that. And he knows you're married.

ME: Well, how nice to know you're on Larry Bob's side.

WAYNE: I'm on your side, of course. Did you say you got a ticket?

ME: Goddammit, Wayne! I already said he didn't give me a ticket, just a warning.

WAYNE: Oh, yeah. Well, good then. *He grabs a rifle from the gun cabinet.* See you later. J.J. called and wants me to help him corner a wild boar on Dick Raney's place. Adios!

And he's gone about his business. I try something less superficial the next day.

ME: If my education is going to mean anything, I should get a decent job.

HIM: You will.

ME: Not around here. We should be living in a larger town.

HIM: Get a job offer and we'll see.

ME: I don't want to go to all the trouble and then have you say you don't want to move.

HIM: I can't promise that won't happen, but you sure won't find a job if you don't apply.

ME: And if we move, what will you do?

HIM: Weld.

ME: You're toying with me—you don't want to admit you'll never leave this ranch.

HIM: Suit yourself.

ME: Goddammit! What the hell does that mean?

HIM: Go ahead and entertain your suspicions. I'm not going to keep defending myself.

I snatch his dress hat from the wall rack, throw if on the floor, and stomp the crown in.

He looks at me and the smashed hat and turns to the door. He drives away and I go to bed, leaving the hat on the floor. He comes back in an hour, but he sleeps in the guest room.

The next day, he's out before I get up. I drive to the horse paddock. Lately, I've been taking some solitary rides down the creek, but I need to ride along that south field and try to get used to the fact it's there, a patch of land with the effect of a mirage in a nightmare. Is it really there? Did everything happen the way I remember?

Shivers stands at the paddock gate. He's heard my car. In the tack room, I gather my currying tools, and I hear the clomp of boots outside. Ernie's form appears in the door.

"Hey, Ernie."

"Where's Wayne?"

"I don't know for sure. He left the house early."

"Humph." He turns away.

I decide to plunge in. "Ernie, can I ask you something?"

"Shoot."

"What if Wayne and I move off the ranch?" We're facing each other, me in the tack room, Ernie outside, and I'm glad to have the raised floor to put me closer to his eyes.

"Why?"

"Jobs."

Ernie clenches his jaw and swats his work gloves against a thigh.

"When?"

"When and *if* I find one."

"Well, I guess I'd find a ranch foreman." He straightens his shoulders.

"Would you let us come back if it doesn't work out?"

"I'd have to think about it."

He turns to walk away.

This is the longest conversation we've had in the four years I've been married to Wayne. I wait for the ricochet. At noon, Wayne comes blowing in the carport door.

"Why'd you talk to Ernie about us moving?" He's pissed. *Hallelujah.*

"Well, hello to you, too." I get to be the calm one for a change.

"Why?"

"Why not?"

"It opens up the subject, and I don't want to discuss it until it's certain we're moving."

Okay, so now I know he would go. It could breathe new life into this marriage.

"The subject isn't as iffy as you think. I've got a few positive leads on some jobs for me."

"You could've told me. Where?"

"Midland, for one."

"Doing what?"

"Assistant director of human resources for the county. It's a good entry-level job."

Wayne slips his fingers into his pockets and looks at me. I swear there's a hint of pride in his eyes. "I'll see if I can find a job. We'd have to live in an apartment until we can afford a house. Would you be okay with that?"

"Yes, yes!" I say, and I run to him and jump and wrap my legs around him. He catches me and returns my kiss. I gulp with relief. We'll be together a while longer.

"I'm sorry to be such a bitch," I say, and bury my face in his neck.

He doesn't dispute that I've been a bitch, but he gives me a squeeze as I breathe in his scent of wind and hay and sunshine. We'll be together, away from the ranch. The only regret I'll have is leaving Shivers. I'll go to the western wear store today and have his hat fixed.

Starting Over

We hitch a trailer to the truck and pile everything we'll need for our little place at the Conquistador Apartments on the outskirts of Midland. J.J. helped us load, and will ride with Wayne to help unload. The sofa, chairs, tables, bed, lamps, and boxes are piled and strapped securely on the trailer, even covered with a tarp. I argued about the tarp before we left.

"Don't you think this thing will work like an umbrella to create drag and guzzle more gas? It's not like it's going to freakin' rain anytime soon," I said, waving a hand at the steel blue sky.

J.J. took a step back as if to say to Wayne, "I'll let you deal with her."

Screw him.

Wayne said, "I guess you'd rather have bug juice

spattered on everything?"

"Oh, to hell with it." I flounced into my car.

I'm a true hussy these days, nervous about my first professional job—and whether Wayne and I can maintain this fresh start. I'm running away from the south field, too. Escaping the proximity of the most horrible experience of my life should allow me to focus on positive changes so my marriage can survive. Surely the guilt will fade the longer I'm away from the ranch.

I follow the trailer and listen to classical music on my new satellite radio. Contentment sets in, even peace, as I imagine Wayne and J.J. sharing observations about the land, the game, the buzzards circling, oil wells, and more on the list of manly topics.

Outside Midland, we pass Wayne's new job site—Quality Craft Mega-Pull Trailers. Tank Hammer owns the John Deere dealership in Sulfur Gap, and he's good buddies with Lester Bartlett, Wayne's future employer. With Tank's recommendation, Wayne was hired with only a phone call.

The next chore was telling Ernie.

"I'll go with you," I told Wayne.

"No, Ernie'll think we're ganging up."

The conversation, as Wayne reported it, had the ring of truth, with Ernie being Ernie all the way. I was sure he deleted the part where Ernie talked shit about me. Wayne walked the road to the parents' house. Ernie was in the barn, and Wayne hated that he couldn't tell both parents at once. Katy claimed she'd miss us living close by. She said she understood we needed to pursue new endeavors while we're young. Wayne found Ernie in the tack room, hanging his bridle on a peg. I know how the conversation went.

ERNIE, *seeing Wayne:* "What?"

WAYNE: Hey, Ernie, uh, Dad, I need to let you know about something that's come up all of a sudden.

ERNIE: Let me guess. Lucy wants to move. *Wayne steps aside as Ernie moves toward the door.*

WAYNE: It's not just Lucy. We're both ready. She's got a job in Midland. I put out some feelers and got a job right away.

ERNIE, *like Wayne's an idiot, not knowing he'd be hired immediately:* 'Course you did.

WAYNE: I'm supposed to start the beginning of the month.

ERNIE, *walking away:* Okay, I have time to find a new foreman.

Wayne's comment was, "Typical Ernie." My thought about Ernie was, "Emotional moron." But I didn't say it, because the comment would shed light on me, too.

So here we are in Midland, moved into the Conquistador Apartments. It's funny after growing up in a cracker box of a house, how quickly I got used to all the space in our ranch house. The apartment isn't a cracker box, it's a shoe box with the shoes still in it. That's how tight it is with our furniture.

The first day of the new job, my supervisor, Wanda, shows me a desk, where she's stacked folders containing instructions for projects she wants me to work on. I met her at the job interview. She's motherly and sweet, like Sherry's mom.

After informing me that my first no-brainer job is to create a new job application form, she gives me a greater challenge. Wanda says, "You'll need to gather a task force with key reps from all departments to re-work and update job descriptions—from grounds keepers and trash haulers to city attorneys." Okay, that sounds a bit more like what I went to graduate school for. There were some minor to-do's—following up on some complaints by dissatisfied citizens to determine if a county employee should be written up and choosing the best applicant for a road crew job. Wanda's orientation also includes the following advice: "You're young and pretty, so don't you let anyone disrespect you." She doesn't know what I'm capable of if someone *really* crosses me. Wanda makes herself available should I have a question, but the tasks are simple.

Wayne should like his job. He has definite hours, but he's not confined inside. The company's fabrication warehouse is bordered by cotton fields, so he can go outside and stare at the horizon during breaks. Most work goes on inside, climate-controlled. Best of all, there are no phone calls from Ernie.

We rock along for a couple of months. One Saturday,

my nerves frazzled, I'm looking forward to some quiet time at home with Wayne, but of all things, he's agreed to put in overtime to help meet a deadline. I decide the day's not miserable enough. I'll go to the laundromat, by golly. It takes me two trips up and down the stairs to load the laundry into the car and drive to the friendly neighborhood washeteria. I get all the clothes, linens, and towels sorted into five washers, churning away. I sit and read a best-seller. It'll take only two dryers to finish, but I'm out of quarters.

At the 7-11 next door, I plop a dollar on the counter. "I need some change," I say to a lady with her broad ass facing me, even though she knows I'm standing there. As she turns, I see her nametag: Frieda.

"Sorry, hon, but we don't make no change," she says in a hillbilly twang. My head resonates the chords of the banjo/guitar duel from *Deliverance*.

Well, shit. "You *have* to make change," I sputter. "How the hell can all your customers have the right change?"

"We don't change no dollar bills. You have to buy something."

I grab a pack of gum and slam it on the counter.

"Now, you don't have to throw no temper tantrum," she says, in hillbilly monotone.

"You ain't got no i-dee what no tantrum is," I say, mocking her.

"I seen lots o' brats in my time, and you ain't no different."

"Just give me the goddam change."

So, she drops a Kennedy half-dollar, some dimes, and some pennies on the counter, knowing I need quarters. I swoop up the coins and throw them in her face as hard as I can. The Kennedy sails past her head and thunks against the window, but a dime hits her in the eye. She holds her eye and whines, "Trailer trash," as I stomp out. A little voice inside me agrees.

I gather my wet laundry, lob the heavy baskets into the car, and drive to the supermarket. I buy a few items, write a check for more than the amount, and get *change*, by God. At another laundromat, I dry the damn laundry. That evening, Wayne comes home to the smell of a pot roast on the stove. I've got the laundry put away, and everything is as clean and airy as possible in our tiny apartment.

"How was your day?" I ask.

"Fine. But there was one guy who had to leave when his wife called him from the emergency room."

"What happened?"

"She injured her eye somehow."

"Oh, my." Now I've managed, in all of Midland, to maim the wife of one of Wayne's co-workers. I hope it isn't so, but I'm afraid it is. It's not *that* big of a city.

"How was your day?" Wayne asks. My turn now.

"Fine. I got the laundry done."

Temper-Mental Pitfall

I get home from work on Monday and find Wayne sitting in our tiny living room with a bald, flabby-chinned guy from work. Oh, dear God, don't let this mean I have to *entertain*. This new job makes me more tired than anything I've ever done. I say hello and whisk toward the bedroom door, which I plan to stay behind until Turkey-Wattle leaves. But before I can escape, Wayne stands and says, like the high school principal, "Lucy, we need to talk to you."

I walk back to the end of the couch where Baldy sits.

"This is Lefty Powers, from work."

"Hi, Mr. Powers. I offer my hand." Why is he here? Surely Wayne hasn't let him in to give us an Amway pitch.

"Miz Cheadham," Lefty growls, as if saying my name

leaves an awful taste in his ugly mouth. He ignores my proffered hand.

I sit. "What's up?"

"Lucy, Mr. Powers says you assaulted his wife at the 7-11 Saturday." Wayne sounds like he's offering condolences at a funeral.

"What?" I don't have to feign my surprise. How did they make the connection?

"Frieda says you done throwed a bunch of coins at her and hit her in the eye. It got to hurtin' and she had to go to the emergency room."

"Why would she say it was me?"

"Drivin' home from the emergency room, she saw your car, and then she saw you, hauling laundry into this very apartment. She knows the manager, and she got yer name."

Busted.

"I think she's mistaken," I say. Let's see, a partial, credible truth…"I do remember a lady named Frieda gave me change when I bought a pack of gum, and I knocked the coins out of my own hand. I, uh, don't remember that any of them went flying."

"She's got a scratch on her cornea, the doc said." Lefty stares at me, and Wayne is pink with embarrassment—or maybe anger.

"How much is the bill? I'll be happy to pay the bill if that will help," I say, acting noble.

"You damn right you'll pay the bill. And we might file charges."

This is enough. I bristle. "Listen, Lefty. There wasn't anyone else in the store Saturday. It's my word against hers. How do we know she didn't run into something and scratch her own cornea? I'm making a generous offer, but I'm not admitting I threw anything *at* her. If you don't want to take my money and let things be, then to hell with you."

I start to leave.

"Wait," Wayne says. "We need to put things to rest. Lefty, I'm sorry for any miscommunication my wife might have had with your wife." He pulls out his wallet and counts out three hundred-dollar bills. "This should cover medical expenses. I hope you and I won't have any problems with each other because of this."

Lefty scoops the money from the coffee table and pockets it in the bib of his overalls. "It'd be nice if your wife would apologize to my wife."

Before Wayne can say anything, I say, "No way. That would be admitting I did something to her, and I'm not about to set myself up for that."

I walk out and slam the bedroom door. I lean against it to catch my breath. I think I played it pretty smart— indignant, noble, and willing to help to a point. I'll wait till Lefty leaves, and then I'll apologize to Wayne for my part (however innocent) in creating an uncomfortable situation at work for him.

I hear the front door close, so I peek out of the bedroom. The living room is empty, so I venture into the kitchen. Empty, too. Lefty and Wayne are both gone.

From the window, I see the receding tail lights of Wayne's pickup leaving the parking lot.

I heat a can of soup for supper and watch television the rest of the evening. As I get ready for bed, I can't remember a single program. I set the alarm and try to fall asleep, but fear of losing Wayne has a grip on me. What if he doesn't come back?

I don't deserve him, especially after what happened beside the south field, but I didn't think I had a choice. The guilt rushes over me for the thousandth time. I wish there were someone to ask for forgiveness. Since I don't believe in God—not one that cares about *me*—I decide I need to forgive myself. I'm awake anyway, so I retrace every step. I examine my actions to see what I could have done differently.

THAT EVENING, more than two years ago, I made my last visit to Suds Shop before leaving for the end of the semester. It was a few days before commencement exercises. I'd parked in the lot outside, the Toyota Cressida loaded with the contents of my dorm room. Since all the students were supposedly studying for finals, of course Suds was doing a booming business. Everyone had to get all their "laundry" done before leaving for the semester. It was convenient to leave the wash going in the adjacent laundromat and step over to the bar for a beer and some dancing. I was exempt from all my finals and didn't have a care in the world. I was going home. There was no live band, since it was a week night. Just a D.J., so I joined a line dance to "Cotton-Eyed Joe."

After the line dance, some of us high-fived, and I returned to the table to join Charlotte, my roommate. I'd had three roommates who never knew me well. I didn't hang around the dorm or get involved in any campus organizations, of course, what with taking the maximum number of hours and going home for the weekend as early as my schedule would allow every week. My first roommate dropped out, the second got married, and Charlotte was transferring to Texas Tech next semester.

I sat down to finish my beer. A guy at the bar was staring at me, so I pointedly turned my back to him, but he moved two tables away and continued to stare. This guy was at least ten years beyond the average age of Suds Shop patrons. His weasel-like face and dark, curly hair reminded me of someone—I couldn't think who. I rifled back through memories of creepy teachers, through Burger Buddy co-workers, and then broadened my mental search to the whole town of Sulfur Gap. I knew I'd find him there.

Then it hit me. His name was Tim Connelly. He was the babysitter's son. The one who watched me some-

times when he got home from school and his mother
needed to run an errand. He was fun at first, swinging
me around and letting me ride pony on his back. I
loved it. But then he started taking me in his mother's
room, comparing my undies with hers, holding me in
front of the mirror, and telling me how pretty I was. He
laid me on the bed and tickled my feet and behind my
knees, and then one day, he caressed me between the
legs. I rolled off the bed and ran to the living room. He
came after me and said, "You wanted me to do that.
Don't tell anyone, or I'll deny it and say you're a dirty
girl."

The next time Mrs. Connelly left me with Tim, I
thought if I concentrated on the TV cartoons, he
wouldn't pay any attention to me. But he sat beside me
on the couch. Before I knew it, I was in his lap and his
finger was inside me. He put me back down and said
something like before, about not telling. I'm not sure
how often that happened. One day, he carried me into
his mother's room and opened her dresser drawer where
she kept her makeup. He pulled out tubes of mascara
and lipstick, anything cylindrical, and laid them beside
us on the bed. I cried as he held me down. I told him it
hurt, and he laughed in this weird, high laugh. When
Mrs. Connelly got home, Tim had returned me to my
spot in front of the television, but my face was red from
crying. She immediately looked at Tim. "What's wrong
with Lucy?"

Tim shrugged. "She was jumping on the couch and fell off."

She came to me. "Lucy, are you alright?"

I should have told her, but I could only nod and sniffle. When Madge picked me up at the end of her workday, she looked at me a bit longer than usual after we got into the car.

"What's wrong, Lucy?" Her voice sounded resigned, worried I might introduce some fresh new hell into her life. I told her as best I could what Tim had done and said I was afraid to go back to Mrs. Connelly's house. Madge's face was mashed and hard with anger, like wadded-up aluminum foil. She drove extra fast going home and screeched to a stop in the driveway. I feared she was extra mad at me and I would get a whipping if I went inside. I refused to leave the car.

"Fine," she said. And she turned to go inside.

I sat in the car for what seemed like hours to a four-year-old, but it was probably thirty minutes. Daddy drove a little motorcycle so Madge could have the car to drive to work at the courthouse. When I heard the high thrum of his bike turning into the driveway, I ran to him, sobbing. He picked me up and looked at the house. He already suspected Madge.

Inside, he took me to my room and said, "I'll figure something out, Lucy." Then he left. Their voices echoed down the short hallway to my room. I could hear things like Madge saying, "How do we know she's not lying?"

and Daddy saying, "I thought *you'd* done something. Honestly Madge, if you did, I'm not letting it go on." I didn't know what Daddy meant at the time, but I realize now he was relieved Madge wasn't the cause of my trauma. He was glad Madge toed the line so he wouldn't have to upset his apple cart. He came back to me and said, "Was it the babysitter's son?" When I nodded, he scooped me up and took me to the kitchen for supper.

I overheard more conversations during the next few days.

"Why would she make it up?" Daddy would say.

"Because she wants to be the center of attention," Madge would counter. And she kept saying, "I just can't deal with this, Baker, I can't."

Madge called in sick and stayed home with me. We didn't talk about going to the babysitter, so I didn't know if I was going to be delivered there or not. She finally phoned in her resignation at the court house and called Mrs. Connelly to tell her I wouldn't be coming anymore. In short, my parents decided there wasn't anything to be done but to pretend it didn't happen. I thought they didn't believe me, but maybe they did. I don't remember anyone telling me to keep my mouth shut about Tim, but that rule stuck in my brain. They must have thought I'd forget in time. And while I didn't forget, I learned to keep the memories locked in a little room I created in my imagination. A room where the bad things lived. I imagined myself baring my teeth at them and daring them to try to get out.

On that night, close to the day of my graduation from Angelo State University, Tim invaded my life again. He stared at me the same way he must have before he preyed on me as a child. My chest tightened and my hands went numb. "Charlotte," I said, "I remember something I've got to do. Here's money for the tab. See you at graduation Saturday." And I ran out into the parking lot on stiff legs.

It was one of those cool December nights—sweater weather. The waxing crescent of the moon hung—a sharp, bright blade in the sky, guiding me to my car. A shadow dashed by and ducked into the passenger side as I unlocked the car and opened my door.

It was Tim. I leaned in to look at him, and he grabbed me by the collar and jerked me toward him so I was half-lying across the console. Cold metal pressed against my throat.

"Scream, and I'll cut you," he said.

"Okay. Just let go. I've got all my stuff loaded to go home. You can have the car and everything in it. Just let me go."

"Shut up and close the door and drive. And don't do anything to make the cops stop us. You might get out alive, but you'll at least lose an eye."

I pulled my feet in, struggled with the key in my shaking hand, and cranked the engine.

"Back up!" he growled. The knife blade pressed against my ribs.

I drove to the edge of town. He ordered me to turn toward Sulfur Gap. He must be planning to take me to a place he knows of, I thought, off the deserted highway. He doesn't know who I am, or that I know the highway better than he does. I began to work out how to save my life. Maybe he doesn't want to kill me, I thought, but if he rapes me, I'll be as good as dead.

I was so glad I almost cried when I remembered how Wayne insisted I carry a gun. With his prompting, I'd taken it from its holster beside the driver's seat lots of times to clean it and practice shooting and loading. It was loaded, a round in the chamber, and the safety on.

Tim reached to play with my hair. I winced away. "I'm not going to be able to drive if you do that."

"Whatever you say, bitch. You won't be calling all the shots for long." He brushed his hand across my breast before he withdrew to his side of the console.

I shuddered and nausea peaked, so I slowed down.

"I'm going to throw up," I said and opened the door to retch on the pavement. I thought about diving out. But he held me by the belt and dropped the knife long enough to grab the steering wheel. The car idled along the deserted highway with me leaving a trail of puke.

I sat up and clutched the wheel. I wanted to jump from the car and run. I'm fast, but I wasn't sure I could outrun him.

"Turn here," he said. A dirt road met the highway, but I wavered and pretended not to see. We passed the turn-off.

"Idiot," he said. "You better follow instructions better or I won't be nearly as nice when I find a place." We'd driven thirty miles, and he spotted another place to turn. But headlights approached from behind, so we kept going, allowing a car to pass. It would be at least twenty miles before we came to another turn-off that wasn't a locked and gated ranch entrance. At the intersection, a pickup waited to pull out. It was J.J.! His game warden insignia stood out on the side of his white truck. He was patrolling the southernmost part of Sandstone County. I wondered how to get his attention, praying he'd come our way, but he turned the opposite direction. I wanted to cry, watching his tail lights in the rearview mirror.

My frantic thinking began to organize. We'd passed the main Cheadham ranch road. Tim saw the distant lights around the houses—my house and Katy and Ernie's. With the houses close and my gun beside me, I gained confidence, and I would mean business when I pointed my gun at the bastard. Once we got far enough out in the boonies, he would make me pull over. I'd need to be fast. I reached beside the seat to un-holster the gun, releasing the safety with my thumb. He was intent on the next turn, so he didn't notice. The turn led to the back road to the Cheadham ranch. I steered the car onto the familiar dirt road.

Calm swept over me.

"Pull over here," he growled, still thinking he controlled me.

I braked a few yards from the cattle guard leading into the south field, where Wayne had just plowed for winter wheat. Tim opened his door and grabbed my arm. With one foot out the door, he was ready to drag me across the console, but I jerked my arm from his grip and swung the gun up.

I yelled with an authority that surprised me. "Don't make a move toward me, or I'll shoot you in the face. Get out of my car. Slow. Or I'll shoot you in the ass."

Terror filled his little weasel eyes. He stood in the road.

"Throw the knife into the bar ditch."

As he pitched away his weapon, I spun out of the car and gripped the gun in both hands. "Walk toward the cattle guard." A culvert ran beneath a ramp to the crossing.

I followed him. "Turn around."

He shook and cried. "Look," he wheedled. "I didn't mean nothing. Just wanted us to have a good time."

"Oh, like the time you had with me when I was four?"

A bewildered veil dropped over his eyes as his memory pinged. "What?" he said, in the voice of the doomed, when they realize it's time to pay up.

"In case you don't remember which four-year-old I was, I'm Lucy. Lucy Paxton."

"I don't know no Lucy!" he whined. Tears dripped from his chin. "Please! I don't know you."

"*Sure* you do. *Tim.*" I intended to kill this bastard.

He fell to his knees. "Please, I didn't mean . . ."

He didn't finish his sentence. The bullet blasted a hole in his forehead, and he fell onto his back. His body fell close enough to the culvert to roll him into it with a couple of good kicks. I found the knife and kicked it toward him. I was shaky, weak, and smelled like fear—sour and sweaty. I needed to get to the house, but I took the time to stand with my back to the culvert and my face to the breeze, looking at the moon and stars and wondering how many women and little girls he'd preyed on. No more victims for Tim. I unbuttoned my shirt to air out, kicked off my boots, and peeled off my socks and jeans. The fine, dry dirt between my toes, the cool breeze carrying the smell of wood smoke from a distant fireplace slowed my heart.

After a few minutes, I dressed. Under the bright crescent of moon, I pulled my overnight bag from the trunk and gargled and spit mouthwash until the bottle was empty. I sprayed perfume and let the breeze blow it back at me gently, subtly. Ever so slowly, I drove home.

In the carport, I honked, and Wayne appeared in the door in his sock feet.

"Lucy! You're earlier than I expected."

"I made good time getting away." The gold light spilled around him. He hustled down the steps and hugged me, lifting me off the ground.

I patted his back. "Wait, my man. I've got to get inside and pee. And then I need a shower in the worst way. I'm totally pooped!"

"Okay, I'll unload the car. You tend to business."

I scrubbed myself and cried in the shower. After a few minutes' release, I tamped myself down and pulled on my nightgown. Soon, we lay next to each other. Home. In bed in the dark with Wayne. I began to ponder my next steps. Maybe I should tell Wayne what happened. I could explain it all to Sheriff Sparks—my history with Tim, the ride of terror from Suds Shop to our back gate. But what if no one believed me, like Madge and Daddy when Tim first preyed on me. At best, everyone would know I was a molested child whose outcry went unheeded. Or worse, they would think I was lying about that, too, a neurotic adult creating a wounded past.

I didn't want to put Daddy through that. After years of feeling betrayed by my parents and finally making a sort of peace with the fact Tim got away with it, I didn't want to have to use it to convince people I'd had only one choice.

I watched the glowing red numbers of the bedside clock until 4:00 a.m. Then, I got up and began to dress quietly. I knew Wayne would stir, so I was ready.

"Lucy, what's up? Where you goin'?"

I sat on the bed beside him. "I wanted to take Shivers on a ride before sun-up. I need some time to decompress, so I thought since I'm awake anyway, I'd go watch the sunrise with my favorite horse."

"Want me to go?"

"No, no. You need the sleep. And I'm starting a long vacation, so I can afford to squander the time."

"Take your gun."

"Oh, don't worry, I will." If he noticed the fired round from my gun, I could say I shot at a snake. I drove to the paddock.

Shivers nickered and stamped. Under the dim yellow light of a bare bulb, I gave him some oats and curried him. I rushed to get away before Ernie rose. I fastened a shovel to the saddle and threw a long coil of rope over the saddle horn. In record time, we hit the trail toward the south field. Guilt prickled my mind for making Shivers, my sweet old horse, an accomplice.

At the cattle guard, I pulled on my work gloves and dismounted, dropping Shivers' reins onto the ground. I laid the shovel beside the freshly plowed furrows. Wayne had commented that the topsoil in this area was several feet deep. Digging a grave should take a solid couple of hours. I crossed the cattle guard gingerly, so as not to sprain an ankle. I scanned the horizon all around for signs of car lights. J.J. had to sleep sometime, and so did Sheriff Sparks and Deputy Larry Bob.

In the culvert, I wrestled the stiffening body, aiming the feet toward the cattle guard. I tied the rope around his ankles, stuffed his hands under his belt, and secured the knife back in its sheath. I tied the rope around Shivers' saddle horn and backed him so the body slid up the culvert incline and onto the road. As Shivers stepped back, the body followed, the head bouncing on the rails. Finally, it rested between the plowed furrows. I shoveled dirt as fast as I could, until I hit rock. I took Tim's wallet from his back pocket and laid it aside, rolled the body into the narrow grave, and covered it, piling the dirt to conform to the shape of the furrow. I crossed the road and, twenty feet into the next field, buried the wallet deep.

The sky lightened in the east, close to seven o'clock. The barn was still dark as we trotted back to the paddock. The Cheadhams' kitchen window, though, cast a yellow glow. Katy and Ernie were having coffee. I reined Shivers in when Ernie's figure moved past the window and toward the back door. I was ready to dismount and find a place to hide the rope and shovel for now, but I heard Ernie's pickup ignition. The headlights swung across the low-hanging mesquite beside the path. Some early errand in town.

I returned the rope and shovel to their spots in the tack room, unsaddled, and gave Shivers more oats. I laid my forehead on his nose and thanked him. By the time I drove back to the house, Wayne was up, ready for work.

I'd left my boots in the utility room, but he eyed my jeans, where dirt clung. "I had to jump off and re-cinch the saddle. Landed in some loose dirt," I said.

We made a date for lunch in town, and I showered again and went back to bed. Later in the afternoon, I took the Toyota to be cleaned and detailed, inside and out. It was like new when Wayne traded it a few days later for my new Mustang.

I dreaded the thought of the south field. I became desperate to move when I finished grad school. Awful images flickered through my mind all the time, like snatches of a horror movie as I peeked through my fingers—the visions made me ill, set me on edge. I became an even bigger bitch from the nerves. I couldn't blame PMS, although it doesn't help. I was in a mental fog from the shock of murder, all during my graduation ceremony and riding home with Wayne. My intruding thoughts about my mother not being there for my graduation, to see that I had value, didn't help. Wayne was so proud of me. He didn't know how worthless I really felt. Out of the fog, I sputtered a lame, hurtful comment when he gave me the Mustang for graduation. He never knew what a true gift that new car was.

I don't know how to remedy the situation. I hope that, as the years pass, the bad memory will fade. If I can stay away from the ranch, I stand a chance.

A Perfectly Unsatisfying Trap

I f Wayne thinks I'm the Hussy of the Universe for throwing a dime in Frieda's eye, I can imagine what a freak he'll think I am if he learns what's in the south field.

Wayne stays gone for two more days. I trudge to work. I've put one foot in front of the other under worse circumstances, but I'm as sad as I've ever been. On top of that, my period's late. I'm on the pill, but I wasn't able to get my last refill before I ran out because of the move and changing pharmacies.

I come home from work and see his truck. My heart leaps. Inside, he sits on the couch. He's got a two-day stubble going, and his eyes are red. I see this hasn't been easy on him, either. I sit beside him. I touch his shoulder, but he leans away.

Finally, he says, "Lucy, I can't do this anymore."

"What?"

"I keep thinking if I do certain things, you'll get better."

"Better at what?"

"Getting along. Not starting fights. Not humiliating me."

"So, this is about *Frieda*?"

"No, but the deal with Frieda has ruined it for me at work. Lefty loves to have someone to pick on, and now he's got an excuse to make my life a living hell."

"Tell the boss."

"That won't work. Lefty's got seniority—lots of it—and knows he can be a bully. But this isn't about Lefty . . . or Frieda. They're the end of a string of crushed hats and feeling bewildered by your latest blast of meanness. We've made it this long because you've spent more than half our married life away at school."

"You never told me."

"I never felt like I could win an argument with you, and it would be an argument if I tried to tell you."

"You want a *divorce*?" I panic.

"I do love you, Lucy, but I can't live like this. You've got so much to offer, and I'm proud of you, but I'm living in a mine field. I haven't slept the last two nights, trying to think of another solution, but we've tried everything." He tells me he called in sick at work the last two days and spent the sleepless nights in the Motel 6.

"What about marriage counseling?"

"You'd have to be willing to change."

"I can change." I'll promise anything. I don't want to be thrown away.

"We could try it, but I want to separate."

"So that you can find your next wife?" The viciousness erupts before I can curb it.

"Ouch," he says, staring into my eyes.

"Well," I huff. "You think you've got the solution, but there's a new wrinkle."

"What?" His voice is tired.

"I'm pregnant."

He didn't see *that* coming. His eyes glow a moment, but flatten. He'd love to be a father, but not with me. Talk about a dilemma. Finally deciding to divorce the bitch and she's pregnant.

I explain about the pills so he won't think I trapped him on purpose.

Wayne says, "If you're pregnant, a divorce is out of the question. We have to make this work."

His unhappy resignation has a withering effect on everything we do. He's polite and answers questions or responds to my comments, but most of the time he stares at the television when he's at home or buries his head in a magazine. I'm sad and infuriated, but there's nothing I can say. I've lost my leverage. He tolerates my presence because I'm incubating his child. It'll always be this way. I'll play mommy, and he'll play daddy, and we'll both be miserable. How can he, in his wildest fantasy, think this will work?

Gotta Go

Wayne finds another welding job, so he won't have to work under the cloud of Lefty's hatred. I continue my job because of the medical benefits. That's what I tell Wayne, anyway. It's also because I'm developing other career plans.

Plan B. I've always been good at having a Plan B. A skill I learned in the University of Madge.

Wayne is attentive—to my pregnancy—asking me how I'm doing, if I need help with this or that, as he regards my growing stomach with reverence. Meanwhile, he sinks into a furrow of resignation to a life with me. His happiest times are the weekends we go back to the ranch. Ernie hasn't given the house to a foreman's family. He's hired extra help, but they stay in one of the hunters' cabins. That threat was B.S. Wayne spends time with young Charley Bristow, whose mother suffers the exhaustion of the working poor and the depression of a woman who sees few options.

The marriage counselor gives us an assessment test. Wayne takes forever, as he chews his pencil and holds his finger on each question. I finally leave the office and go for a walk, having turned in *my* assignment to the receptionist. At the follow-up appointment, Dr. Burke talks to me alone, then Wayne. He tells me I am clearly a high-functioning person suffering from mild (ha-ha) bi-polar and complex post-traumatic stress disorders. As he explains both of these diagnoses, I recognize that being bi-polar saved my life by allowing me to switch into murdering mode so I could take care of Tim. But it also explains throwing coins at Frieda, stomping Wayne's hat, and a whole list of unseemly conduct. I ask him how I've managed to keep a lid on it most of the time, and he says it has a lot to do with other factors, such as body chemistry, stress levels, and other circumstances, blah, blah, blah. The C-PTSD is what you'd expect, growing up with Madge, being molested (which I haven't mentioned to the doc) and neglected—and the shrink doesn't know it's compounded by the fact I killed someone, buried him, and got away with it—legally, anyway. He says I'll need lots of counseling, meds, and an outlet for my talents.

But there is hope, he says. And the rest is blah, blah, blah, because I know there isn't any hope for Wayne and me. And no hope for this baby with me for a mother.

On with Plan B. I find a job opening in Austin and

drive there for the interview with the excuse to Wayne that I am looking into a treatment facility so I can get some intense psychological help before the baby comes in two months. I tell him when I return I've decided I don't need treatment. He's disappointed, I can tell.

I interview for a job as assistant to a powerful state senator. I intercept the mail days later and rejoice and cry over the letter of acceptance. And Austin will have a smorgasbord of choices for counselors. This job experience will set me up to become a lobbyist or congressional aide. Duties won't start until after the delivery. My employers don't mind that I will be a new mother, starting a new job. It's the nineties, after all. I even find an apartment and pay a deposit. Wayne won't know—I handle all of our finances. I know he will miss my efficiency, my business head, and my body—but not my mood swings.

"I have an idea for a name," I say as the due date draws near. "What?" he says with an 'oh-no' face, a look I've learned to tolerate and that expresses all his fear of what I'm going to do next, thanks to my "disorders." He doesn't have any disorders except passive-aggressive tendencies, natural offshoots from dealing with Ernie—and me. We're a regular alphabet stew of craziness, with me providing most of the letters.

"Luck," I say. It sounded good when I came up with it.

"*LUCK?*" He's incredulous. He's being less passive, like the doc told him, so he straightens up to argue.

"What's wrong with it? Think about it, Wayne. So much of our lives depends on luck—from birth, with all the coincidences from brain chemistry to talent. That name is a gift. And it's just one letter off from my name."

Wayne, of course, doesn't know this name is the only thing I'll be giving this child, except life, which any breeder can do. Look at Madge. I won't be giving him my sulks, tantrums, and unpredictability. But neither will he know my passion, tenacity, and sense of humor (albeit dark at times). I want Wayne to agree on this name.

"How about Luck for a middle name?" he says. "If you'll come up with something else that sounds good with 'Luck,' I'll consider it, preferably as a middle name."

"Why don't you think of something?"

"Carson," he says, so quickly, I know he's thought about a name, too.

"That's Mother's maiden name. Carson Luck Cheadham. We can call him Luck, if you insist, but not 'Lucky'. That's a dog's name. When he gets older, he can go by Carson so he'll be taken seriously if he enters a profession not involving being a male stripper."

"Deal."

So, Luck gets his name.

My stomach and chest take turns aching at the thought of leaving. I know it'll be harder if I see the baby and hold him, so I wonder how I'll avoid it. I've built up an account in an Austin bank and bought the bare basics of furniture and had it delivered via an arrangement with the apartment manager. I've gradually added clothes to the big suitcase in my car's trunk.

I worry about my physical ability to get up and leave the hospital on my own. I'm still spry, wiry, and wily as the due date draws closer. I wonder if I'll be able to avoid seeing the baby. I've felt him moving—sometimes romping, the little turd (affectionately said! Sort of).

The beginning of labor pains wakes me at 4 a.m. I want to drive my own car to the hospital, so I breathe slowly, timing the intervals. They're still twenty minutes apart and don't hurt. They feel weird. I go through our morning routine of breakfast and getting dressed, still timing those contractions. They're getting stronger.

"Bye, Wayne! I'll call you if there's any labor pains!" He's been watching me closely the last several days.

I make it down the stairs and into my car. I drive straight to the emergency entrance of the hospital. I check in and get whisked off in a wheelchair to the obstetrics wing. Only then do I ask a nurse to call Wayne, my husband for these few more hours.

The delivery is fast and easy, but I cry uncontrollably and babble nonsense when I know the baby is out and I hear his cry. It's not a total act, but I do add embellishments to give the delivery staff pause. Wayne is ready in his surgical mask and gown to take the baby to the nursery while they tend to me. They think I'm having a psychotic reaction to childbirth. I know Wayne, Katy, Ernie, and Daddy (all have made it to the hospital by the time Luck comes) will be cooing through the nursery glass at the baby. I'm alone in my room, wondering how soon I should try to get up, when Wayne opens the door.

"Lucy?"

I pray he hasn't brought the baby, maybe checked him out of the nursery. I don't know how all that works. But he's alone.

"Hi, Wayne." Good. I thought I'd seen the last of him, but he's so decent and good, he'd want to check on me, the woman he thinks he's shackled to for life, because I am a human being after all, and the mother of his son.

"How are you?"

The tears are real. "I still can't quit crying."

He strokes my hair. "We have a perfect baby boy."

"Thank you, Wayne."

"No. Thank *you*."

At this moment, he thinks we'll be happy, our little family. But he'll see I'm still crazy and a lousy mother, and he'll resent me again, with greater fire. Katy and Ernie and Daddy all come to give their congratulations and all I do is cry. They think that it's post-partum blues, but it's departure blues. I won't be seeing any of them for a while. A nurse gives me a tranquilizer. I spit it out and flush it on my first trip to the john, but they think I'm knocked out for the night. I sleep from the exhaustion of childbirth and grief.

I wake up as the early morning sun streams through my window. It's time to go. I dress and gather my things. I know I'll need some pain reliever, but I can stop at a pharmacy on the way out of town. There are plenty of hotels between here and Austin if I don't make it to my new apartment.

I leave a note for Wayne on the bed. It says,

Dear Wayne, I love you and the time we've had together. I love our baby, too. But I love you both enough to know I need to leave. I'll be all right. I have a job in Austin and will be in touch, but I won't interfere with your raising Luck or getting on with your life. Go ahead with the divorce. You'll be a wonderful father, and Katy will be a great mother. Maybe someday soon I'll be able to meet Luck. I hope you all will understand.

Love, Lucy

I drive into the sunrise in my Mustang. In the rearview mirror, I see Wayne's truck in the golden light as he pulls into the hospital parking lot.

Interlude: Low Crossing

In the moonlight, I stare at Luck's face. Tomorrow he'll be a little bit different, and I want to catch the moment. Even asleep, he bunches his blanket in tight fists. Poor kid can't relax. He's got my hair—thick reddish brown. I'm sure Ernie never did this with me—drive around until sleep comes and the colic lets go. Maybe I didn't have colic. Here at the creek crossing I remember Lucy and me riding the horses that first time. Further down there's the sandstone cliff where I took her parking. I can't regret getting physical so soon—that's what it was about with me and Lucy. If we hadn't, I wouldn't have Luck.

Lucy and I fit together so well, and I was so young... I thought good sex guaranteed a good marriage. I knew how to stay out of arguments—they couldn't be won with her, and anyhow, victory didn't prove anything but who can argue best. I'd married a woman with Ernie's personality, only more *unpredictable and with lots more words to spew. No way to figure her out. Seemed like no way out when she got pregnant, so I looked forward to having my own little family but feared the kind of mother she would be. In the end, Lucy was more realistic. She cleared out without making a scene, leaving only a note. I've read it a hundred times. She's helped me along without meaning to. She got me out of a rut by talking to Ernie about us moving. That's when I learned I'm not chained to the ranch. I stay because I love this place—work, weather, animals. I can watch the sky and feel the wind, see how long a red-tail hawk will sit on a telephone pole. None of that fits Lucy's flinty personality.*

The morning after Luck was born, I drove into the hospital parking lot by sunrise. I'd wanted to stay the night, sitting with Lucy, but she ran me off. Said she had to sleep and couldn't do it with me hovering. I got back as soon as I could. Couldn't wait to hold Luck again, wanted to be with her when she met him.

I walked onto the maternity wing, and a clutch of nurses stood around Lucy's door. Something was wrong. I sprinted down the hall. Hushing hands reached out, and the soft voices scared me. Don't touch me with those hands. Don't pity me. "Mr. Cheadham, she's not here. We just finished shift change, and we found her room empty. It looks like she left a note."

I panicked. "Where's the baby?" My voice cracked. I had to block off the fear.

"The baby's fine. He's in the nursery, sound asleep." So professional, these voices.

I didn't believe them. I ran to the window to look at the rows of bassinettes, and there he was. I sank to my knees. Luck wasn't gone. But Lucy abandoned us. Luck would have no mother. Why didn't I see this coming? I sobbed as the hand of a hospital social worker patted me. He waved off people who watched the spectacle. I didn't give a rip about them. Ernie's not here, with his face of stone to shame me. Mother's not here to fly into protective mode and distract me. I have this moment to fall down from shock. But I need to pull myself together. In a few days, I can take H.A. to my favorite water tank. In a week, I'll be on the tractor with only the sky to listen in.

I pulled myself together in a tiny chapel where they left me alone. Mother, Ernie, and Baker were enjoying their breakfast at the hotel when I called Mother's phone. Mother said, "No! and How could she?" I heard Baker in the background. "What? What happened?" I'm sure Ernie hardly looked up from his omelet. I left it to mother to fill them in. At the hospital, Mother and Baker hung together and cried, and Ernie sat with his head down. Eventually, we began to make a plan. Mother said, "We'll set up the nursery at our house." She gave Ernie a look that told him to stay quiet. "I will be a mother to this boy as long as I'm alive," she said.

"I'll help any way I can," Baker said.

I decided I'd stay at Mother's and be a parent. If I didn't start then, it would be too easy to gradually distance myself.

"Looks like this kid's got it made," Ernie chimed in. For once, his sarcasm rang true.

We changed plans without a blink. We were all adaptable,

even Ernie—at least he had no comment. I felt at home in my old room. I've slept on a small bed close to Luck's crib. It was good to be back home, Mother caring for the baby, Lucy gone. She would have been put out to have to devote attention to Luck. No kid needs to grow up feeling like an intruder. I'm sorry for Lucy, such a broken, smart woman. She copes, but she'll never know how it feels to hold Luck and watch his fingers curl around hers.

I'll stay to myself for now. Maybe I'll make friends with a woman. Friends first, and for long enough to know if she's got a bad disposition. If she comes at me with easy sex, I won't get roped in. I'm in no hurry, but if it's in the cards, I want a family woman—a sweet, intelligent person. Good looks won't hurt, either. If it's in the cards.

I drop the truck into low and drive up the slope.

Cynthia

Mﾠay 27, 1993
Columbus, Mississippi *Dispatch*
Yesterday evening, a motorcycle accident claimed the life of U.S. Air Force Lieutenant Casey Rust, age 27. The accident occurred on Jolly Road east of Highway 45 at dusk.

Rust was driving his motorcycle at high speed, heading west when, according to a witness, an eastbound car rounded a curve and veered into his lane. He collided with an embankment. The car, a dark blue sedan, possibly a Chevrolet Impala, did not stop. Anyone with knowledge leading to the identity of the driver is asked to contact local police. Investigation of other factors, including Rust's blood-alcohol content, is pending.

Casey Rust was the only son of Carl and Daisy

Combest Rust of Reno, Nevada, where he graduated from Robert McQueen High School. After completing a degree in mechanical engineering at Texas A&M University, where he joined the Air Force ROTC, he received his commission. He advanced to Pilot Instructor, stationed at Columbus AFB as of January of this year.

In 1991, he married Rachel Sidenor of San Angelo, Texas. He was the father of a three-month-old son.

During his Air Force career, Casey served in Operation Desert Storm. He was scheduled to receive his Captain's bars in June.

Base Commander Connie Mathison said, "Our prayers are with Casey's family. We all feel his loss. He was a vibrant presence, not only in the Air Force community, but in the city of Columbus as well. He was a rising star."

I SCAN the newspaper while I rest from packing. The movers come tomorrow. The headline catches my eye— front page, bottom right. "Local Traffic Fatality." My heart thuds. The blue Chevrolet that failed to stop—I was the driver.

Yesterday while driving home, I was distracted by the rush of errands and afraid of the girls staying alone with Leo. A gust of wind pushed the car. A blur whipped past, barely missing my front left fender. I was looking down, turning on my headlights. The thought of stopping to see if I had caused an accident brushed across my mind, but I had to hurry home. Leo looked up from his book when I burst through the door. "My God, Cynthia. Are you running from a cheetah?" I ignored him and went to check on the girls.

The paper slips from my hands onto the kitchen table, and I stumble past half-filled moving boxes to the bathroom. I retch as tears run down my cheeks. My carelessness has caused the death of a young father. I could go to prison, be sued, or have to serve probation. I wouldn't be allowed to leave the state or even the county. If I go to prison, what kind of parenting would the girls have with Leo? Leo would try to be a dad—he isn't a monster—but he would populate the girls' lives with a string of live-in girlfriends who would set horrid examples. He would drink himself to an early grave.

We're moving because Leo signed a contract with Angelo State University in San Angelo, Texas—a tenured position in the chemistry department. In fact, he's teaching a summer school course, so we'll begin the two-day drive tomorrow to gain a few days to settle in before classes start.

I blot my face with toilet paper. I must remain nameless… unless a witness caught my license plate number. Not likely, in the shadows of dusk. I'll pray fervently, every spare moment, for the wife and son—and for the soul of Casey Rust. I must think of the greater good.

Eliza and Abby need me. I don't know that Casey Rust wasn't drinking or going too fast—contributory factors in the accident. It might not be all my fault. If I come forward, the focus will be on my mistake of driving on, and not on whether the accident was completely my fault. Who can know? I'm sure of this—I have to think of my girls. What kind of justice would be gained by separating me from my family? Still, I should have stopped.

"Mommy?"

Three-year-old Abby stands in the bathroom doorway.

"Hi, there, sweetheart. I was just cleaning the toilet."

I get up and carry Abby to the kitchen. Eliza will be awake soon.

Necessary Loss—1998

Leo wants a divorce. For the last month, he's stayed with his girlfriend. I've crumbled into a million pieces. I take one step at a time and cry after the lights are out, quiet as possible. The future is a yawning, black tunnel I have to pass through, while my brain is a muddle of conflicting thoughts. Maybe I *am* being punished.

Moving from Columbus, Mississippi, to San Angelo, Texas, required adjustments, but the role of college professor's wife didn't call for new skills. We went to the usual stiff parties where Leo drank too much and I smiled until my cheeks hurt. Leo remained indifferent to my opinion of his drinking. Our few friends helped create the illusion that we had a social life. My church life saved me. I have friends at church, good works to do, and singing. I do love to sing. Eliza's more reluctant these days to go to all the church activities, but she'll come around. Leo, of course, has never shown any interest in church.

My cardboard cut-out of a marriage served as a backdrop to the nagging doubt I wake up with every day. Every day, I pray until I can move on. I can't change the past, I tell myself. It's spiritual pride to refuse God's forgiveness and try to punish myself. Sometimes I do feel forgiven, but the weight of hypocrisy pushes me down. I live a surface life, being the best mother, wife, and church member I can be while carrying my dark secret. Every time I think I'll tell my pastor, my heart pounds. He might want me to confess it at church. I even thought for a while Leo would be the most rational person to confide in, but now he's divorcing me.

My girls are in third and fifth grades—good girls— but sometimes I get calls from teachers telling me they're disruptive—talking, fidgeting. I sit them down and tell them about the discipline of the tongue as it's described in the Bible. They wait with placid faces for me to finish my spiel.

Meanwhile, my insides are being worked over with a bottle brush. Just as I thought I'd be able to tolerate the dull hum of guilt in my mind and carry on, here comes Leo, wanting a divorce. Life is supposed to offer us opportunities to grow, but how much more can I stand? Maybe I'll remarry. Only if I meet the right person—

someone who loves me and won't decide I'm not enough and leave me for someone else.

I'll carry on. I'm not the type who snaps mentally, although sometimes I wish I could run screaming down the street. The settlement money will run out eventually, and I'll need a job. What can I do with a degree in Voice? I could teach private lessons, be the music director of a big downtown church, or work with the symphony or the Cultural Affairs Council. I don't have a teaching certificate. I could substitute teach or work in a private school, but no job around here would support us. I could combine several jobs and never see the girls. The thought hurts my chest.

We've sold the big house on Douglas Drive. I'll need some furniture for my new little house. I gave Leo the bedroom furniture, since I found out he'd slept with his girlfriend in our bed every time I went back to Columbus to visit my mother in the nursing home. As he left, what I thought was our final fight reached a crescendo when he said, "Enjoy that king-size bed, Cynthia. Brandy and I have." And he drove away with his U-Haul full of books and diplomas.

Leo exploited my absences to have his flings. What sort of woman would go to a man's home when the wife was away and sleep in their bed? I hope Leo finds out real soon. I hope she leaves him high and dry and flopping around, feeling like I do.

Maybe I deserve all this because I'm a coward and a hypocrite.

Anyway, I'll go to the furniture auction to find bedroom furniture. My neighbor says they have good deals there.

A New Bed to Lie In

The warehouse is jammed to the roof with dining sets, bedroom suites, couches, and coffee tables. I admire a decently priced, solid mahogany canopy bed with all the matching pieces. The moldy smell of old stuff reminds me of all the great antique places in Mississippi and Alabama—large emporiums and little shops along the back roads.

As I stare at the bedroom set, I move a few steps and bump into a big cowboy.

"I'm sorry, ma'am," he says. He picks up my purse.

"That's all right. I wasn't watching where I was going."

His green eyes might blend out to blue or amber, the type that change depending on what color he's wearing. He holds his hat to his chest and hands me my purse. His auburn hair, which he really should wear a little

longer above his ears, has a natural spring to it. Nice
smile. Nice-cut jaw—handsome, in a crisp, snap-button
western shirt.

"Are you bidding on this bedroom set?" he asks.

"Yes, but I've never been to an auction and don't
know what to do."

"I know the auction owner, Eddie Dennis. You can
pre-bid and don't have to wait for your item to
come up."

"Can you help me?" I smile more than I've smiled at
a man since I met Leo.

"I'd be happy to, uh . . ."

"Cynthia." I offer my hand.

"I'm Wayne." He enfolds my hand with his dry,
warm paw. "I'm a regular at the auctions. I've got too
much stuff, but it's a hobby I've developed the last
several years."

This Wayne fellow dips into the little cluttered office
in the corner of the auction barn. He's back in no time.
The bedroom set is mine, for far less than I was prepared
to spend. He offers to help deliver it to my new house.
I'm wobbly over the attention, but I focus enough to
write a check to Eddie, who takes it in a dusty hand.

I finished cleaning my house yesterday, so it's ready
for furniture. The rest will come this weekend, in a
moving van paid for by Leo. I feel a rush of accomplish-
ment as I drive to my new home.

I'll get the girls from school at 3:00. They're sad to

have to change schools next week, so soon after the school year began, but I explained to them that at least they won't have to answer questions about the divorce. And they will be blessed with a whole new set of friends.

I'm relieved they're changing schools. I met the assistant principal of their old school at open house. Her name is Rachel Rust. Surely, she's not the widow of the airman who died on his motorcycle that night in Columbus over five years ago. If she's Casey Rust's widow, she might notice in the school records that we're from Columbus. But then, so what? It won't occur to her I had anything to do with her husband's death. I almost dismiss the idea that she's the widow, given the low probability she would be here in San Angelo. But I remember the news article mentioned Casey's wife was from here. And there's an Air Force base here as well as Columbus. The possibility nags at me, like I don't have enough of a load, with my fury at Leo and near-panic about the future.

I sit on the steps of my new-to-me frame house in the Santa Rita subdivision. It's so neat and well-tended, all I have to do is place the furniture inside and decorate. Wayne pulls up with my furniture loaded in the back of a large pickup that's seen better days. He pulls a dolly off the back and muscles the heavy dresser and armoire into the house. He carries the other pieces easily.

After he's maneuvered everything in, he looks

around the otherwise-empty house. "Did you say you're moving here from Mississippi?"

"Oh, no. I've been in San Angelo for five years, but I'm moving from another part of town. I'm getting a divorce." Shame tinges my voice.

"Sorry to hear that. Divorce hurts, no matter how much it needs to happen."

His blunt assessment rings true. I hadn't thought about this simple truth. "It sounds like you've had the experience."

"Yep. She left me. I probably would've hung tight until one of us died. She put us out of our misery."

"Well, I was left, too. And I was planning to hang in there, too." A tightness loosens in me with this frank admission.

"Any children?" he asks.

"Two girls. You?"

"One boy. He's five."

"Do you get to see him often?"

"Every day. He lives with me. His mama left us from the hospital when he was born. She comes back to visit him a couple times a year, but she's like a distant aunt as far as he's concerned."

"How can a mother just leave like that?"

"That's a long story. It was for the best."

A picture of this woman begins to wriggle into my mind. Maybe she's even more guilty than I am. Maybe she left without a backward glance. Time to change the subject. "I haven't been very polite. My name is Hastings. Cynthia Hastings."

"I'm Wayne Cheadham."

He ranches outside a little town called Sulfur Gap. I remember blowing past Sulfur Gap as we headed to Colorado on vacation a couple of summers ago.

Wayne says, "I might be completely out of line here, but I'd like to call you sometime. I come to town a lot, and maybe we could have lunch or dinner."

"My divorce isn't final for a few weeks."

"Give me a call when you're ready for a not-very-serious lunch date. Here's my card."

Wayne waves as he pulls away in his pickup. I've never ridden in a pickup that large.

Tug of War

I've kept Wayne's card in a corner of my purse for the past weeks. Leo picks up Eliza and Abby every other weekend and on Wednesday nights, when they go to dinner. It's worked well, so far.

One night when they come home, Abby says, "Mommy, have you met Brandy? She's nice."

My heart seizes, but I take some slow breaths. "Who?" I say in my calmest voice.

"Daddy's new *friend*," Eliza says, with air quotes around "friend."

"I think your Daddy has known Brandy for a while. You're just now meeting her." For the hundredth time, I think how the name sounds like a bartender.

Eliza says, "I bet Brandy is the reason for the divorce."

"You're right." No need lying in the face of my smart

girl. I have to ask. "I haven't met this *Brandy*. Tell me about her."

"She's okay," Eliza says, giving Abby a warning look to shut her mouth.

But Abby says, "She's not nearly as pretty as you are, Mommy."

I give her a pat.

THE DIVORCE DECREE arrives with the morning mail. That's why Leo had the audacity to take his girlfriend to supper with the girls yesterday. I left the court appearance to him. Everything was settled—visitation, child support, property division. I seethed with helplessness, knowing I couldn't make any stipulations about keeping his girlfriends away from my children. I wanted a stipulation to drive a stake through his heart, but with that possibility also out of the question, I let the court date come and go, and now Leo knew there was nothing I could do to him. His hypocrisy is staggering, not to mention that he could leave *me* for someone named *Brandy*. Helpless rage ripples through me. I think for the millionth time—maybe I deserve this.

Anger energizes me to call Wayne. I tremble as the call goes through. When he answers, loud rumbling almost drowns out his voice.

"Hi, Wayne. This is Cynthia Hastings."

"I'm sorry, I can't hear you. If you can wait, I'll call you back in five minutes." Then it's silent on his end.

Well, that didn't go as planned. But in five minutes, my phone rings.

"This is Wayne, calling back."

"Hi, Wayne, it's Cynthia Hastings."

"I'm sorry, Cynthia, I didn't know it was you. I was unloading cows at the auction barn. How are you?"

"Good," I lie. Then, to change the focus, "I didn't notice any cattle at the auction back in late August."

Wayne laughs. "This is a different auction."

Now I feel stupid. "Oh. Anyway, I thought I'd take you up on that offer of lunch." We make plans. An hour from now, I'll be on my first date since college.

Wayne takes me to a little place that's been written up in *Southern Living*. The menu lists selections you won't find anywhere else in San Angelo, some of them with French names. He wears a pressed shirt and starched jeans. Both times we've met, I've caught him unprepared, and he looked good anyway. I tell him so.

He laughs. "You should see me digging up the plumbing around the house."

"You must welcome the days when you don't have to get dirty."

"I sure do. Today I'm only dusty."

During lunch, we talk about our kids. His son's name is Luck, of all things. No doubt, there's a story to that. I wonder why his wife would leave him and the baby? I'll be cautious until I know more. What was she running from? We walk to the water lily collection in the nearby park. No blooms in the big concrete ponds—it's too late in the fall—but we walk around pools of massive floating fronds—some resembling giant green crepe pans.

Wayne takes my hand and I stiffen. "You there?" He leans toward my downcast face.

"I'm sorry." I look up. "I feel awkward. This is my first date since college."

"Then I'll go easy on you." He pats my shoulder.

He's so warm, in body and spirit. Still, it's only a first impression. At my house, he walks me to the door.

"I'll call you next time I'm heading for Angelo." He waves goodbye.

I look at myself in the hallway mirror. I'd forgotten I'm pretty. I could still win Miss Watermelon Queen in Columbus, and I don't look like I've had two babies. But then, I don't look like someone on the lam for manslaughter, either.

WHEN LEO COMES for Eliza and Abby for the weekend, he has the gall to bring *her* to the door. And they *both* follow me into the house, gawking at every detail. But subtleties elude him. And Brandy *really* should stay out of my house. For an intellectual, Leo sure is dumb. I stand in the middle of the living room and cross my arms. Then I realize. *He's drinking.* I know his slack-jawed expression as well as I know my own shoe size. And I can smell him.

Leo grins. "Cynthia, I want to introduce you to Brandy."

Brandy holds her hand out, but I stare at her.

"Hello, Brandy." My voice drips icicles. I want to ask her how she likes my mattress, ask Leo if he's trying extra hard to hurt me, leaving me for this skinny over-bleached blond and then marching her into my house. How can he suppose we can act like they didn't sneak around for months? That he didn't spear me with the news he was leaving me? But Leo would be blind to this. He's a complete narcissist.

"I guess we should have called," Brandy says.

"That might have helped," I say, with sharp under-statement. "And Leo, I know you've been drinking. The girls can't go with you if you're drinking."

"Oh, come on, Cynthia. I had one drink when I got home from work."

"Do what you want at your house, but you're not driving under the influence with my girls."

Brandy takes Leo's arm. "Come on, Leo, let's go."

Her whispery Marilyn Monroe voice matches her wispy, over-processed hair. She's headed toward anorexia, she's so skinny, but she's still managed to find a pair of jeans that fit like a second skin. And she's spent too many sessions on the tanning bed. On top of that, her bosoms *cannot* be real, so firmly pushed up to arch above the low neckline of her tight sweater, a fashion contradiction indeed. Why wear a sweater if you plan to freeze your boobs?

Leo says, "At least let me talk to the girls."

I call them, and they run in and hug their father. Brandy wisely stands aside. I'd knock her down if she touched my kids now.

On one knee, he holds both their hands and says, "Look, chickadees. I'm sorry, but something's come up this evening. Would it be all right if I get you in the morning?"

The girls are disappointed, but they have a video to watch. No big heartbreak. They'll see a sober father in the morning. They bump off to the den.

"Brandy, may I have a private word with Leo?"

"Okay. I'll see you in the car, Lee. And it was nice meeting you, Cynthia." Her saccharine voice sickens me. She heads out the door.

I say, "Listen, Leo. You're not my husband anymore, so I'm going to tell you some hard truths. If you drink and drive with Abby and Eliza, I'll make sure you never see them again, not without supervision. And if you drink and drive and wind up hurting the girls, I'll kill you."

Leo's never heard me threaten violence, but he's not

so stunned he can't bite back. "Still a self-righteous drama queen, I see."

"And you're still an alcoholic."

He turns away and waves me off, dismissing me as usual. As he leaves, I relax. I join the girls in the den to watch *The Sound of Music*. We sing along and rewind the tape to sing our favorites over and over. We yodel on the lonely goatherd song until we collapse in a pile, laughing. It's a wonderful evening spent with the kids after taking a bite out of Leo.

Chaperones

B ringing Brandy to the front door was so like a drunk Leo—insensitive and stupid. Surely, he won't bring her back this morning. Yesterday evening, his judgment was impaired by liquor, but even sober, he's capable of such self-absorption, there's no telling. Just because I feel guilty about causing a death and not owning up, I'm not going to be a doormat. He's not God and not entitled to punish me.

While I look out the front window for Leo, Wayne calls. He wants to stop for a cup of coffee. He has a couple of young friends with him.

"Is your son coming?"

"No, Luck has plans with his grandmother. It's Charley and Billy—friends of the family."

Wayne and the boys arrive in five minutes. I'm fully dressed, with my hair swept up in combs on each side and falling down my back. It makes me look a little intimidating, styled for Brandy's benefit in case she shows up.

"This is Billy Sanchez, a friend of the family." Wayne pats Billy on the head. "And this is Charley Bristow, another friend of the family." He puts an arm across Charley's shoulders. Charley's eyes are the bluest I've seen, looking out from under a haystack of hair.

"What brings you guys to town?"

"Wayne's gonna buy us new boots," Billy says. He answers before Charley, because Charley is looking at something behind me.

"How nice, Wayne," I say. I turn to see what's drawn Charley's attention. It's Eliza. She stares back at Charley. Abby is close on her heels as they roll their overnight cases from their room. Abby does a double-take when she sees the boys and forgets what she's about to say. I can't believe their sudden interest in boys. Much older boys. Maybe Abby's shy, but it's clear Eliza's having an experience. Help me, God.

Fortunately—I'm reluctant to use that word in association with him—Leo pulls up. Red-eyed but sober, he eyes Wayne's pickup as he walks to the porch. After stiff introductions, I send the girls off. Eliza casts disappointed looks over her shoulder, but Abby skips to the car. It's nice that Eliza's more fascinated with what's at home than with whatever they do at Leo's. My heart does a little victory dance to see Leo—a seedy, slightly-stooped chemistry professor—next to Wayne—a tall, virile cowboy. Leo's going downhill fast, and in a few years, Brandy, if she's still in the picture, won't have much of a prize. At the moment, though, women think Leo's a real catch, with his professor-like demeanor, academic status, and sharp, witty observations.

I make coffee while the guys sit around my kitchen table. I offer Charley and Billy milk or juice, but Charley says, "No, thanks. I like my coffee black." I bring out a plate of Danish tea cookies. The boys scarf them like potato chips.

Wayne laughs. "They're eating machines."

The boys look at each other like they're proud to be garbage disposals, so I bring a whole tin of cookies from the pantry. "Have at it. I don't need these here. I've got to watch my figure."

They give my figure the once-over, then inhale the cookies. Wayne invites me to go boot shopping. I've never been to a Western store, but Wayne claims I might find something for myself. Billy and Charley rivet their eyes on me from the backseat of the crew cab as I climb into the front. I'm a specimen under a microscope. Testosterone forms a cloud.

At the store, they scan the large boot selection. They tug off their old, tight boots, revealing worn, mismatched socks. I wander away to look at women's wear. I'm not the leather fringe and silver medallion type, but the store does carry some pretty skirts. But I'm watching my budget. At checkout, Wayne tosses a few pairs of socks beside each of the boxes of new boots. It's lunch time, and I can't believe those boys are hungry, but they jump at the suggestion of a steak.

The uneven restaurant floor and booths of duct-taped plastic from the seventies are lit by light fixtures coated in dust, also from the seventies. Billy and Charley wolf down their steaks. Wayne and I brush elbows a few times. Such good steak, so little ambience.

"Who wants cobbler?" Wayne says cheerily. Charley and Billy come to full alert. I pass, but I enjoy the aroma while the boys dive in.

Back at my house, Charley's and Billy's eyes track us from the pickup as Wayne walks me to the door. So far, I detect only decency in Wayne. No signs as to why his wife fled the hospital.

MY SUNDAY MORNING routine of singing in the church choir lifts my soul. I haven't sung with such heart since before Leo dumped me. I feel hope, but I'm not sure why. It's as if there is a yet-to-be-revealed fork in the road ahead, a path to carry me beyond guilt and sadness and anger. As the sun goes down, Leo's car lights flash through the living room window. I hug the girls, but Leo stands around, like something's on his mind, so I send them to unpack. I'm not about to offer him a seat, especially with the smirk on his face.

"When did you develop a taste for rednecks?" he says.

"What do you mean?"

"You know what I mean. That cowboy and those little hicks with him."

"My goodness, Leo. I thought *I* was the judgmental one. At least that's what you always say. I'll have you know those 'little hicks' are some kids my friend Wayne has taken under his wing. And I'll remind you of what you always said, if I complained about rednecks in Mississippi. You said being a redneck is a state of mind, not a matter of dress or appearance or social status. And that rednecks live anywhere in the world, just as ignorance and intolerance can be anywhere."

"Wow. So *now* you agree with something I said."

"What's your point, Leo?"

"I simply can't picture you with a cowboy, riding in a giant pickup. It's a culture clash. You're not the 'yippee-kai-yay' type."

"People change. And you're drawing conclusions mighty fast, considering how you always harp on how one shouldn't deduce something from one observation. Science Guy."

"Oh, the irony is sweet."

"It's none of your business who my friends are. At least I'm not *living* with someone already."

Leo looks past me, so I turn to see the girls at the door, hurt looks on both their faces. I want to punch Leo for drawing me in to this fight.

"Nice job, *Cynthia*." He spits my name. He goes to Eliza and Abby. "Girls, I'm sorry, but we're having some trouble getting adjusted to the divorce. We're acting childish, but we both love you, and we'll work to get along and be there for you. I'm sorry, Cynthia." He waits for me to say my line.

"I'm sorry, too, Leo."

A fine speech by Leo, nicely orchestrated to make him look noble.

The letch.

First Date Disaster

Wayne and I finally have a real date. The girls are at Leo's and I'm free from church obligations. I've unpacked from the move and decorated the house, so I feel more relaxed.

We're going to a dance at the VFW, a private party. I haven't danced in forever, and never at a VFW. I asked Wayne about the dress code, and he said "casual Western." I assume it means nice jeans are okay. I told the girls I had a date and made it sound like a teenagers' night out. They liked the idea.

Abby asked, "Are Charley and Billy coming to town?"

"No, Sweetie. They don't go *everywhere* with Wayne. He has a son who is five, and you'll meet him if Wayne and I keep dating."

"YEWWWW!" Eliza looked like she'd eaten a caterpillar. "A five-year-old *boy*? I bet he's a pain in the butt."

"Eliza! Watch your language. And don't judge!"

"I'm not judging. I see the dopey five-year-olds at school."

"That's judging."

"Well, you judge Daddy."

This was a turn in the conversation I didn't bargain for.

"And what makes you say so?"

"You talk to him like he's a moron. And he's not, he's a college professor!" Eliza must have looked for an opportunity to blast me for talking down to her brilliant father.

"I don't mean to. We disagree, but I don't think he's a moron."

"You judge him and hate him for who he is because he's not perfect, like *you!*" Eliza's eyes blazed, her voice dripped with sarcasm. The divorce has pushed her into early teenage defiance. Abby soaked up every word of this conversational U-turn.

"Listen, Eliza. I am NOT perfect and don't pretend to be. I believe Paul when he says, 'All have sinned and fallen short of the glory of God.'"

"Does Daddy have Jesus?" Abby asked.

"It's not my place to comment on Daddy's relationship with Jesus. And I don't hate him. After all, the

Lord's Prayer says, 'Forgive us our debts, *as* we forgive our debtors.'"

"Does Daddy owe you money?" At this question, Eliza swatted Abby on the back of the head. Abby howled, and I banished Eliza to their room, the logistics of which were lacking. Abby couldn't get into *her* part of the room until Eliza's punishment was over. I tried to explain to Abby about debts and debtors.

NOW IT'S DATE NIGHT, and I wear my best-looking jeans, red heels, and a red turtleneck sweater. I pull my hair back with a red satin ribbon clip. Faux ruby earrings and gold chains complete the outfit. I'm adding blush when the doorbell rings. My stomach does a flip. I hate these nerves, this dating ritual, and I ponder what it would be like if we didn't have to date, if our parents arranged things. Well, mine *did* sort of arrange things with Leo and me. Daddy was friends with Leo's father, so they arranged for us to meet. Leo had finished his Ph.D., held a tenure-track position at Mississippi State, and looked like the kind of college professor that girls signed up for to make goo-goo eyes in class. My parents harped on what a catch he was, and Leo persisted, until I decided I could love him.

I answer the door, my heart pounding. Wayne could be a Western-wear model, he's so handsome.

"Hope you don't mind, but we're meeting my friends, J.J. and Pam."

"No, that's great." I'm glad it won't be just the two of us, possibly relegated to a table by ourselves. But I doubt if Wayne ever sits alone anywhere for long.

At the dance, friends of Wayne's greet him with hand-shakes and back-slaps. Pam reminds me of Michelle Pfeiffer, and J.J. looks like Antonio Banderas. This world is light years away from the stodgy faculty gatherings, bridge games, and lecture circuit attendance by the San Angelo intelligentsia.

Before the band starts, I ask J.J. what he does for a living. "I'm the game warden for Sandstone County. Pam is the head E.R. nurse. What do you do, Cynthia?" J.J. asks.

Darn, I've let the conversation lag. "I've been a stay-at-home mom up to this point."

"Are you looking for a job?" Pam asks.

"I will be eventually."

"Being a mother is an honorable profession," Wayne says. Pam and J.J. nod.

Pam says, "We couldn't have children." She and J.J. look at each other for a split second of shared sadness. Then she says, "I'm so sorry, Cynthia. That's TMI from a brand-new acquaintance."

"That's okay. And I *am* sorry," I say, and my hand reaches out automatically. She takes it and squeezes it.

Even if Wayne and I weren't dating, I would want to be friends with this nice woman.

The band begins to play, and we move onto the dance floor. Wayne leads well and keeps time to the music. Once he finds out I can follow him, he tries a few fun maneuvers. I feel so safe and natural here, even with all the drinking going on. Wayne sings off-key to "Margaritaville" as we slip into a rhumba. He's not at all self-conscious that I'm a trained vocal musician. He's the most straight-forward man I've known, and a good dancer and friend. But a bad singer. Really bad.

On the third round of drink orders, Wayne replaces his beer with water, which is what I'm drinking. What a relief. Pam asks if I mind if Wayne dances with her, and I tell her to help herself. J.J. asks me to dance.

"Wayne tells me y'all met at the furniture auction," J.J. says, once we've gotten in sync.

"Yes, that's right. He helped me bid, and then he delivered my purchase. We've had a couple of lunch dates."

"Charley told me about going out to eat with y'all."

"Oh, yes, those boys didn't take their eyes off us during the whole time we were together.'"

"They're curious. Sulfur Gap girls don't hold a candle to you."

"Pam is beautiful," I say.

"Of course, but she's not from Sulfur Gap." We laugh.

Back at the table, a couple J.J. and Wayne know stops

by. I meet the bright-eyed Dorothy. She says, "If you're ever in Sulfur Gap, come by my salon—the Wild Hare. I'm the manicurist." The couple meanders off and finds a place among the dancers circling the floor to "If I Ever Need a Lady, I'll Call You."

Someone else hovers beside us. Good God, it's Leo. "You guys seem to have a Barbie doll competition going on. Which one of you has the best-looking blond?" Leo winks at Pam. He's completely trashed. I never dreamed I'd see Leo Hastings at the VFW. Brandy, no doubt the instigator of Leo's social comedown, hovers behind him. She wears a sequined cowboy hat and displays her whippet body and surgically-enhanced chest in the tightest possible jeans and clingy shirt. I remember what Dolly Parton said— "It takes a lot of money to look this cheap."

Brandy pats Leo's shoulder and says in her childlike voice, "I'm gonna make a run to the toy-toy." She gives me a little wave. I don't wave back.

Leo zooms in on my right hand. We've fought about the wedding ring. I'm careful not to wear it when he's around. It belonged to Leo's grandmother, and he wanted it back.

"It's a family heirloom," he said. "My mother wants it back in my family so she can pass it on to a niece who's getting married."

"And Eliza and Abby aren't family? Did you divorce

them, too? You should have thought about the ring before you ditched me."

"Come on, Cynthia. It's only a ring."

"It stood for lots more to me. One of the girls should have the ring someday."

"You just want to wear it."

I hung up.

Now he's caught me wearing his family heirloom. He says, "Oh, so you *do* want to wear the ring!"

Wayne leans back in his chair. Pam and J.J. shift uncomfortably.

I ignore the comment. I introduce Pam and J.J. "This is my ex-husband, Leo Hastings."

Leo doesn't look at them. His bloodshot eyes focus on me as he weaves over us. I'm shocked numb when he grabs my hand. Wayne moves so fast, he's a blur as he reaches to grip Leo's wrist. He squeezes until Leo lets go.

"You're getting awful close to an assault charge, Bubba," Wayne says as he stares up at Leo. Calling Leo "Bubba" is the best dig he could have used.

"Mind your own business, Shitkicker."

Wayne stands up so fast, Leo's slack-jawed. J.J. gets up more slowly. He pulls a badge out of his shirt pocket and holds it up. "You don't need to create a disturbance here."

Leo looks from one big man to the other. He aims at me instead of the big guys.

"Cynthia, if you don't give me back the ring, I'm taking you to court."

"The divorce is done, Leo. Leave us alone. And who's watching the girls while you and Brandy party?"

"Brandy's teenaged sister, if you must know. The girls like her." Leo's practically hissing now.

"You need to leave," J.J. says. His badge, now hooked to a clip on his shirt pocket, is eye-level to Leo.

"I don't have much choice, being outnumbered as I am." He grudgingly turns away. Brandy's finished powdering her nose and advances toward our group. Leo steers her toward the exit. Maybe there's a party they can crash somewhere else tonight. But I imagine Leo's evening is finished, he's so drunk. The band starts playing the next song, and the crowd goes back to yammering and laughing.

Wayne and J.J. sit. Leo's pall weighs on me. Pam doesn't mean it, but her look of pity increases my embarrassment.

"I wonder who in the hell invited them?" Pam finally says.

"I'm so sorry," I say. "Leo sure put a damper on things."

"We'll recover," Wayne says, chipper as can be. I'm not convinced. I detect the slightest trembling coming from him, the kind you get after a big adrenaline rush.

The fun drained out of me, we sit. I wish for a trap door under my chair so I can disappear. Finally, Wayne pulls me onto the dance floor. We dance every dance as if to prove that Leo couldn't ruin our evening. Pam, J.J., and Wayne pretend nothing happened. I feel their sympathy and their effort to cheer me up, but my shame deepens.

Before I know it, the night is over. The band closes with a gospel song, their signature, "May the Circle Be Unbroken." Everyone holds hands and stands in a circle and sings at the top of their lungs, me included. Singing always helps me ease tension. I'm doing high harmony to let out steam, and people look my way, so I tone it down.

On the way home, Wayne says, "Lady, you've got some pipes."

"Sometimes I forget myself and belt it out."

"You have amazing talent. Never hide your light under a bushel."

Wayne's profile is silhouetted by street lights as he drives along Beauregard Avenue. I still feel the shame of Leo. I decide to be honest. "I am so embarrassed by my ex-husband."

"You should've seen what my ex-wife was capable of. I tried hard to understand it, but never did."

"Leo can think of so many ways to be a complete ass. And now he's made a disaster out of our first real date."

"I had fun in spite of Leo. I thought you did, too."

"Well, yes. I wish we could 'ex' out the part where my ex comes in."

"It'll make the dance more memorable. Leo coming after your wedding ring while both of you are with other people." He chuckles. "I thought he was going to fall backward when J.J. trotted out the badge."

I fail to see any humor. I've spent the evening feeling like a low-life for having such a bastard for a former husband. I look at my hands.

"Oh, come on, Cynthia. It's not your fault. You'll laugh eventually."

We'll see. But the shame blinds me to any kind of funny spin to put on the night's events.

Hyperventilating 101

I overhear Eliza telling Abby something along these lines: "Daddy says Momma is stooping low, dating a shitkicker."

"What's a shitkicker?"

Eliza sighs. "It's someone who kicks shit, doofus."

"A plumber?"

"No! Not people poop. Animal poop."

"A dog catcher? A zoo keeper?"

"No, idiot. A cowboy! They work with cows?"

"Ohhhh."

I burst into the room. "Eliza! Such language! And calling your little sister names." I hug Abby. "Honey, you are not a doofus or an idiot."

Eliza zips her empty overnight bag and tosses it into the closet. She turns to me. "Maybe Abby's not a doofus, but your boyfriend's a shitkicker."

"That does it, Miss. You're grounded next weekend. You're not watching television or movies or talking on the phone. All you'll be allowed to do is play board games with Abby and me." Abby barely stops herself from clapping her hands. She loves board games.

Eliza shoots me a chilling look and slams the bathroom door. I toy with the idea of inviting Wayne here while she's grounded, so she can experience first-hand what it's like to hang out with a shitkicker. I wonder why Leo drags the girls into his insecurity. It occurs to me that I didn't dispute—even with myself—that Wayne is my boyfriend. And we've had one bona fide date. I can't let this relationship get too far without telling Wayne what happened in Columbus. And I need to find someone I can trust, to tell them and try to find a way to answer for my part in Casey Rust's death.

It turns out Eliza is a bully. And Mrs. Rust delivers the news. When she calls me, I argue that Eliza no longer attends the school where Mrs. Rust works as assistant principal. I learn she covers two campuses, so I haven't escaped. As we talk on the phone, pressure builds in my chest and sweat seeps along my temples, but at least my voice is steady.

Eliza tripped a girl in the school cafeteria. The girl fell on a fork which barely missed her eye. I argue the girl must have done something to Eliza, while the pounding in my ears makes me wonder if I'm having a stroke.

"This is a serious problem," Mrs. Rust says.

"Are you sure it was Eliza? After all, kids bear false witness against each other all the time!"

"Her teacher, Mrs. Sims, says the other girl came to her last week. She talked with them and thought they had reached an understanding. After today, we need you involved. Whitney's parents have taken her home, and I'd like to see you at your earliest convenience."

"I'll be right there," I gasp, and hang up. I'm wheezing, hyperventilating. I crawl to the cabinet under the sink, grab an empty bread bag from the trash, and breathe into it until I can breathe normally. I'll carry the bread bag in my purse, in case this happens again. It could serve in a pinch as a sick-sac.

I have to focus on Eliza and put a lid on my own fear and guilt. I don't *know* the assistant principal is the Widow Rust from Mississippi. It's upsetting enough Eliza is in so much trouble. I tremble all the way to the school and manage to park beside the curb.

A tired secretary points to a door sign, "Assistant Principal." Mrs. Rust invites me in, and I take a seat in front of her big desk. She's a lovely woman my age. Her dark hair is pulled back with a large clip, her deep brown eyes are kind. A little boy resembling her gazes from his picture, which hangs behind her, along with diplomas and plaques.

I clutch my purse.

"Thanks for coming in," she says.

"You're welcome." My voice pitches high, like Brandy's. Do all women sound this way in the presence of someone whose marriage they've ended? At least Brandy didn't *kill* my husband. I remind myself I'm here for Eliza.

As my tears spill, Mrs. Rust pushes a box of tissue toward me. She takes charge, outlines her concerns, and says kids become bullies for a reason. I assure her no one is picking on Eliza, but I tell her about the divorce.

"Maybe Eliza feels her life is out of control. Changing schools, moving, meeting Dad's girlfriend. That's a lot to take in. It would have a huge effect on a girl her age."

"I can see what you mean. But to turn her into a bully… I've always taught them the Golden Rule."

"Well, the idea of the Golden Rule is good, but some kids don't *know* how they want others to treat them. They feel bad about themselves, and they find ways to express their anger. The Golden Rule breaks down. But let's not get side-tracked. Let's say Eliza feels bad and is taking it out on Whitney."

"How did this get started?"

"Whitney borrowed Eliza's pen from her desk without asking. After she wrote her name on her paper, she returned the pen and told her thanks. Eliza was outraged, as if she'd stolen from her. At recess, Eliza started an argument. She called Whitney names and made threats until Mrs. Sims intervened." Rachel Rust tells me about several more incidents, ending with today's fork to the forehead when Eliza tripped her victim.

"I have some recommendations," Mrs. Rust says. "First, get Eliza to a private counselor. The other thing is that I would like Whitney's parents and you, Whitney, and Eliza to confer at a later date. We need to communicate our care for both girls but that bullying is unacceptable."

Eliza will spend the rest of the week in In-School Suspension—required to occupy a desk beside the tired secretary, with a sack lunch and no recess.

Mrs. Sims brings Eliza to the office. She turns her shoulder toward me when I try to hug her. The teacher tells me how smart she is, like I don't know. "It's often a surprise when a smart child misbehaves," she says. "We tell them they should know better, but they're still young and often don't know how to take care of themselves emotionally."

I promise to take Eliza to a counselor and thank the ladies. As the last bell rings, I maneuver into the pickup line to collect Abby. She climbs in the car and knows something's wrong. "We'll talk when we get home," I say. "For now, let's focus on getting there in one piece."

At home, I shut myself in the bedroom with Eliza, feeling like I've entered a lion's den. She's lying on her bed, facing the wall. "Leave me alone," she says. "Go ahead and deal the grounding, but leave me alone."

"Not until you talk to me about why you bullied Whitney. We have to meet with Whitney and her parents eventually. You'll need to apologize."

"No."

"Why not?"

"She's a slut."

"*What?*" My sheltered Eliza, calling another ten-year-old a slut? "You don't know what a slut is. What makes Whitney a slut?"

"She flirts. Boys follow her. She's already got boobs, and she wears clothes to show them off."

"She's developing early. Some girls are flirtier than others. Does she *do* anything with the boys?"

"I wouldn't be surprised. I bet she's the first girl in middle school to screw a boy."

I'm stunned. I finally stutter, "She's not... it's not... Eliza, if she acts that way, we should be sad for her. We shouldn't condemn her. Jesus said, 'Let he who has not sinned cast the first st---.'"

"Oh, stop it, Mom!" Eliza rolls away from the wall and glares with bloodshot eyes. She sobs. "I hate her."

"Okay, Eliza. You hate Whitney and there's nothing anyone can do about it."

"Good, because it's all bullshit."

"What is?"

"All the Bible verses you always spout." My tears start to roll. Eliza's eyes are hard.

"Why do you say so?"

"Look what it's done for you. Daddy left, because you're so superstitious—and self-righteous."

"Did he tell you that?"

"No, but he says you're superstitious." Eliza's smart, but she doesn't know how to apply the term "self-righteous." She continues, "And now *we're* crammed into this tiny dump, and Daddy and *Brandy* are looking at new houses. You never got mad! All you do is forgive everybody, and act like you're perfect. You never *even* got mad!!" Now she's screaming. "I hate Whitney! And I hate you and Daddy and *Brandy*! And I *really* hate Whitney!"

"I love you, no matter what you say." No further words occur to me, so I leave the room quietly. Later, I take her a sandwich for supper, but we don't speak the rest of the evening. Abby and I do homework. I have to stop to dry my tears and blow my nose. Poor, sweet Abby's being extra careful, watching everything I do, trying to do her homework perfectly and helping straighten up before we go to bed.

I lie awake, my thoughts alternating between prayers and cursing Leo. And I wonder if Wayne will be interested in me, with such a troubled child. But then, I haven't met Luck. And I don't understand why his ex-wife—I've learned her name is Lucy—would desert her husband and child. In the morning, I take the girls to school. As we're pulling to the curb, Eliza sucks in her breath. "There she is. *Whitney.*"

A thin, light-haired girl steps from a car ahead of us. She turns our way, and I get it. Whitney looks like a ten-year-old, early-developing version of Brandy. From the perspective of another ten-year-old girl who's had her home wrecked, I can see why the sight of her would be despicable.

Thanksgiving with Norman Rockwell

I hope Brandy humiliates Leo. But, to be humiliated, one must care what others think, and Leo is impervious. They're taking the girls to Mississippi to see family, as Leo and I have done the past years since we moved to Texas. I'm outraged, too, that Leo flaunts *his* wrongdoing, while I hide in shame.

At least I haven't had much time to think about Thanksgiving because I've been finding a counselor for Eliza—the "plus" side of having a child diagnosed as a school bully. Still, I wallow in feelings of abandonment, until Wayne calls asking me and the girls to come with him and Luck to Frisco to his brother's house. At least I'm not forgotten. I tell him the girls' plans and add that I would be bad company.

"How about Luck and I come see you the Saturday

after Thanksgiving, maybe go to lunch and spend a little time?"

What a relief. No long, lonely weekend with no one but church friends and my simmering disgust at Leo. I can't discuss Leo with church people. They would tell me not to feel how I feel, and then I'd feel worse, because I would want to push them all off a cliff.

Later, I call Leo during his office hours to tell him Eliza's trouble. I tell him she's transferred her anger at Brandy onto Whitney. He says, "Good gosh, Cynthia. You're over-analyzing. Brandy and the girls get along great. And of course, you're reaching a conclusion favorable to your point of view."

"I don't see how this favors me in any way."

"You're proving to yourself and your imaginary world that Brandy and I are the bad guys."

"Let me remind you—you're the ones who screwed around."

"Wow, you're getting less priggish about language. Is the cowboy bringing you along?"

"I see you're better than ever at avoiding the subject of your infidelity. You make light of what you and Brandy did." My voice rises. "You remain nonchalant, even when the repercussions of your actions appear in Eliza." I've become shrill, so I drop my voice an octave. "Anyway, Eliza will be going to a counselor, and you'll be getting the bill, whether you want to accept *personal* responsibility or not."

"You're a complete drama queen."

"I'm not the one who's creating the drama. First, it was you. And now it's Eliza. Draw your own conclusions."

I hang up, my heart racing. But I'm proud of the pounding I gave Leo. I return to the counselor search. A chat with an objective person could give Eliza something to hold to on this crazy trip where Leo plays "same old dad" after he's torn us apart. Maybe I'll have a chat, too, if I like the counselor. Perhaps I can unravel my tangled emotions.

"I'M NOT SPEAKING TO A COUNSELOR," Eliza announces for the fifth time since I told her she was going. I was lucky Dr. Harris had a cancellation.

"Why?"

"I don't need any help."

"Oh, yes, you're fine. You've spent a week in ISS for bullying."

"Seeing a counselor is part of my punishment, then."

"No! It's to *help* you."

"I said I don't need help!"

"Okay, you don't need help. But you're going to a counselor as part of the deal with the school. You don't want to be sent to the school where the gang-bangers go, and everyone must pass through metal detectors at the door."

"They're bluffing."

"I doubt it. The school has to document everything—so if anyone else gets hurt, they can't be sued for negligence."

"Like I'm going to plant a bomb? Shoot someone?"

"No, not you. But sometimes bullied kids go to extremes—they show up with weapons at school. The school people can't know you're not making a career of this, like I know it."

Eliza snorts. "You don't know. Maybe I'll become an axe murderer."

I pull the car over and stop. I turn to face Eliza. "I know you. You're my daughter, not a budding psycho. You're a good Christian at heart."

She sneers. "Forget Jesus."

I want to touch her face, stroke her hair, but I also want to slap her. I say, "Being a Christian doesn't save any of us from hardship, but it does help us through it."

"Bullshit," she singsongs.

I wonder what kind of language she'll come up with as a teenager, what kind of defiance she'll show, since she's so adept at being a rebel at ten.

In Dr. Harris's waiting room, I tell her, "Look, you've got a chance to have a new friend here. Why don't you look at it that way?"

"Yeah, a friend for hire, paid to listen." Eliza sits with

her arms crossed. The door opens, and Dr. Harris, the shortest, roundest woman I've ever seen, shakes my hand and nods to Eliza. She looks like an elf—short haircut, impish little ears, and slanted eyes.

I start to sit, but Dr. Harris beckons me into her office. Eliza smirks and plops back on her chair. I hadn't thought about talking to the counselor myself. After a quick discussion of why I've brought Eliza, she says, "Can you tell me more about the tensions in her home life?"

I relate the divorce and all the other changes we've made.

"And how are *you* with all this?"

I raise my chin. "I couldn't survive this without my faith."

"Does Eliza share your faith?"

I cry for the hundredth time in the last week. I admit Eliza shows contempt for my beliefs.

"I'm sure that's hard for you."

"Yes, it's unbearably sad." Dr. Harris hands me a box of tissue. "She's blaming religion for our family failure, when it's her father's adultery."

"I see. And do you point this out?"

"No. She knows Leo initiated the divorce so he could be with his girlfriend. She figured all that out by herself. She has blamed me some—she says I'm too Miss Perfect, so Leo turned to someone else."

"Advanced thinking for a ten-year-old."

"Yes. She says God hasn't done us any good, that my beliefs are bullshit."

"How do you respond?"

"I let her lash out. It would make her more rebellious if I tried to force my beliefs on her."

"It's good you realize that. It's hard for someone with your strong convictions to get along with children who think another way." She stands and says, "Let me talk to Eliza. If we need to, we'll call you in. And, if you have concerns, give me a call. Just know that once I've become Eliza's therapist, I cannot tell you about what goes on in our sessions except in the narrowest of parameters." She hands me a pamphlet on parents' rights.

Back in the waiting area, Eliza's eyes widen when she sees my red face. She walks into the psychologist's office and the door closes, leaving me to chew my cuticles and pretend to read a magazine while I ponder the irony. My religion tells me I'm forgiven, but guilt drags me down. And my religion is Eliza's excuse to channel her anger at me. Again, I wish I could have a psychotic break to get a break.

ON THANKSGIVING MORNING, the house feels hollow. The kitchen echoes as I clatter around. I decide to clean. I dust, scrub, and mop every surface. Before I know it, it's late afternoon. As I put the hall runner in place, exhaustion overtakes me. I lie on the rug. It's an interesting perspective from the floor. The attic door fits into the ceiling above me. I haven't been up there at all. There could be a skeleton in my attic, for all I know.

The ladder creaks with a pull on the dangling cord. Once I'm up, my flashlight beam reveals draped cobwebs and seasoned rafters. I walk along the center joist, sweeping the attic with my light. Next to the chimney sits a stack of old issues of the *Saturday Evening Post*, tied with thick twine. The top issue is from 1943. Back at the attic opening, I drop the bundle to the hall floor and hurry down the ladder. For the next hours, I pore through these old magazines.

Images of American battleships, patriotic pleas to buy bonds, and ads for seamed nylons show my parents' world. I come across a Norman Rockwell painting inside one magazine. His pictures were always on the covers, I thought. It's called "Freedom from Want"—one I've seen on calendars—a woman serving a gigantic turkey with the man of the house standing proudly behind her. Happy, young faces beam from the dining table. I've always loved this picture, but now it makes me sick.

I leave the magazines strewn on the floor and settle onto the couch with a ham sandwich to watch the rerun of Macy's parade.

To hell with Norman Rockwell and his fat turkey.

Luck Runs Amuck

How do I entertain a five-year-old boy? The good weather should hold, so we'll have lunch on the patio, maybe a picnic in the back yard. I'll dig the croquet set from the garage storage.

I fry buttermilk battered chicken and stir up potato salad. We'll have chilled pickles and olives to go with it. And of course, biscuits and butter and honey and a peach cobbler will round it all out, all to show off my Southern roots.

A DIESEL PICKUP ENGINE CLATTERS. By the time I get to the front window, Wayne stands beside his truck door and holds out his arms in time to catch a little boy who launches himself from the cab. The little rascal bangs on the front door as hard as his knuckles will allow. I open the door, and he streaks to the middle of the living room and stops on a dime to look around. Wayne sweeps in and grabs me in a bear hug. My neck almost snaps while I crane to keep an eye on the dart-monster.

It's good to see Wayne. I've been so busy addressing Eliza's troubles, I haven't realized how I miss him.

"Luck," he says. "Come meet Cynthia."

I bend to shake Luck's hand, but he holds it above his head, palm out. "Gimme a high-five!"

I give him a high-five. He's a child version of Jim Carrey.

"Luck! What do you say?" Wayne has coached for this encounter.

"Nice ta meet ya. Can I play your piano?"

"Okay." I fear he will try to bang harder than I would like, but he sits gingerly on the bench and makes a show of cracking his knuckles like Bugs Bunny. He plays random notes, leaning over the keys to examine the tone. When the new wears off of playing piano, we migrate to the den. I ask Luck about kindergarten.

"I know how to count to a hundred, too. Want to hear me?"

"Maybe later, Luck," Wayne says quickly.

"I can do science, too. Have you got any baking powder and vagina?"

"Luck! It's *vinegar*." Wayne reddens.

Luck is unperturbed. "Oh yeah. Vinegar. We'd have to go outside to make a volcano. Do you have any play dough? You can make your own, you know. You can make it different colors. I like to finger paint, too. Do you have any finger paints? You have some girls around here, don't you? I want to see those little girls."

"Luck, remember we talked about it. We might not get to see them," Wayne says.

"I'm going to be a senator when I grow up. Or maybe a chef. I'll go to France. Do you have a dog? I have two—Rufus and Redneck. They're not allowed in the house. They have ticks. They swim in the water troughs. I'm not supposed to get in the water troughs."

"Luck, why don't we go in the back yard?" I say when he pauses for a breath.

We troop through the kitchen. Luck runs laps around the yard and somersaults in the dead November grass.

Wayne and I watch from the patio chairs.

"I've never seen a child with such energy," I say.

"Yeah, he's like one of those Jack Russell terriers. Definitely hyper."

There's no point trying to play a real game of yard croquet, but I bring out the balls and mallets. Luck hits the ball a few times but he can't make it go far, so he swings the mallet and sings, "I've been working on the railroad, all the livelong day!" He drives an imaginary stake into the ground.

Wayne says, "Stop it, Luck. If you can't hit the balls with the mallet, you'll have to put it down."

Luck drops it. "When do we eat?" he says, rubbing his stomach.

I haul lunch out in a big picnic basket. We spread a blanket on the yellow grass. Food slows Luck down. He gobbles chicken and potato salad and even a dill pickle and biscuit, all while swilling a whole bottle of lemonade. He lies back flat with his little belly sticking up. And he burps with a grand flourish.

Wayne says, "Luck! Remember what I told you!"

"Sorry, Dad." Looking at me, he asks, "Are you my dad's *girlfriend*? He said you were a friend, but I think you're a *girlfriend*."

"Yes, I'm a *girlfriend*."

"Good, 'cause you sure are pretty." Wayne and I laugh, and he takes my hand.

"Does he need a nap?" I ask hopefully.

"Are you kidding? He hasn't napped since he was six months old."

My cell phone plays the short, foreboding Wagner passage I've selected for Leo's ringtone.

"We've landed in San Angelo," Leo says. "The girls are ready to come home. Is that all right with you?"

"Absolutely. Tell them a little boy named Luck wants to meet them."

My weary travelers arrive soon, toting their bags.

Luck stands beside Wayne, scoping them out. They all say "hi" and the girls head to their room. Abby eventually comes to the den, where I'm going through a stack of videos with Luck to see what he'd like to watch.

"Do you have any Transformer movies?" he asks.

Abby says, "Oh, Luck! Let's watch *Mary Poppins*. You'll like it."

Luck smiles and bounces onto the couch, patting for Abby to sit beside him, which she does. Luck widens his eyes at me in mock seriousness. "Where's the popcorn, *Ma*?"

Wayne groans.

"Where's Eliza?" I ask.

"Oh, she's writing in her journal. Her counselor told her to keep a journal," Abby says.

"Oh." That sounds interesting. A journal. And Eliza cooperating.

While the kids watch *Mary Poppins*, Wayne and I sit at the game table in the corner. I talk about Eliza's woes, but I steer the conversation elsewhere as soon as possible. Wayne collects stray or unwanted animals. He buys old horses and keeps them as pets until they die. And he takes in llamas (he has two, Dolly and Ding-dong—after the Dalai Lama and the old song, "Shama Llama Ding-dong"). Three emus wandered to the barn at least ten years ago, abandoned by their owners after the bottom dropped out of the emu market. He still has them.

Eliza finally flops on a floor pillow. She doesn't say much, and Luck instinctively keeps his distance. Maybe he's had experiences with girls her age, those pre-teen mysteries who can be so precious, yet at the drop of a hat, terrorize teachers, parents, boys, and each other.

Bethlehem with Emus

"It's not always this sparse here," Wayne says, as we cross the cattle guard. "We haven't had enough rain. I hoped it would snow and cover up the dead stuff, but the cold front didn't make it past Lubbock."

Five years I've been in Texas, and I haven't been on a ranch yet, not that I consider it a huge void in my life. At the end of December, the countryside is bleak with dead wood, brambles, and dry-yellow clumps of grass. Coming from Mississippi to this feels like leaving a palace to move to an orphanage. What a place to celebrate Christ's birth. But this is probably more like Bethlehem, minus the barbed wire.

"There's my house, past the windmill." From the direction Wayne points, two wolf-like creatures bound toward us.

Oh, my God. "What are those *beasts*?" My voice
quivers.

Wayne laughs. "Rufus and Redneck. They're showing
off." Eliza's sigh says more clearly than any words,
"Mom, you're an idiot."

We wallow along a dirt road to the main house, the
dogs leading the way. It's limestone-brick and adobe,
with a silver metal roof blending with the December sky.
While I gawk, there's a tap on the window. A small
floating head with huge brown eyes looks at me.

"What on earth?" I gasp. Eliza and Abby shriek.

"That's Seymour." Wayne nods with pride toward
his pet.

"An emu?"

"Yep. I've got three of them now—Seymour, Sidney,
and Psycho."

"Do they know their names?" Abby asks.

"No, but they recognize my truck. I'm the bird feed
dispenser. But don't worry. Seymour won't bother you. If
it were Psycho, I'd warn you to stay in the truck while I
shoo him away. He pecks."

"Thanks, Wayne," Eliza says, sounding saucy.

"Welcome, Eliza." Wayne either doesn't care or
doesn't notice Eliza's smart mouth.

When we step out of the truck, Seymour runs away
with smooth, easy strides. On the wide porch, Katy
Cheadham waits for us. The house smells of spiced apple
cider.

Wayne introduces me and asks, "Where's Ernie?"

"Guess."

"Watching football." Wayne tosses his hat on a hall table.

"Cynthia, please excuse my husband. He's not sociable, but Vince and Elizabeth are here. Come on in the den." Katy is down-to-earth, with a face full of laugh lines.

Ernie looks up from the television to shake my hand. We greet Vince and Elizabeth. She steers the conversation while Vince leans into a corner of the sectional couch. She's a school administrator. I've had more than my share of administrators lately.

"And what do *you* do?" she asks.

"Stay-at-home mom, but I hope to find a way to put my degree in Voice to work."

"Sounds like teaching is the only option. Unless you're planning to break into show business." I wonder if this woman has any friends.

A ruckus erupts in the dining room, and Luck zips in. "Hey, Gramma! The guys are here!" He spots me and runs to hug my knees.

"I like these soft pants." He rubs his little hands in my lap to appreciate my black velvet stretch pants. I lean forward to hug him, but he spins away to high-five the girls.

"Everyone, listen! I'm going to recite "Twas the Night

Before Christmas,'" Luck poses in front of the stone fireplace.

"Wait, Luck," Elizabeth says, "Let Cynthia get acquainted with our new arrivals."

"She's met Charley and Billy," Wayne informs her. The boys stand inside the door with their hands in their jean pockets. Abby and Eliza perk up. "And this is Guillermo," Wayne says. "He's our partner on the ranch —and Billy's granddad."

"Let's open presents!" Billy rubs his palms together.

Before long, a rubber-dart gun war shapes up in the den. Charley's and Billy's Gameboy games and Luck's Teletubbies and giant Rugrat Chuckie lie in a pile.

"Stop that now! Go outside! Not in the house, fellahs!" All the adults yell at the same time. Except Ernie, who never looks away from the football game. They scoop up their darts and head to the yard. Eliza and Abby follow close behind.

Ernie says few words at dinner, but no one need worry about the conversation dragging with Elizabeth around. The kids eat and excuse themselves to go back outside. I'd like to help, but Elizabeth bustles around, making it hard for Katy to work in her own kitchen.

Charley strides back in, Eliza close on his heels, and says, "Would y'all mind if we walk the girls to the creek." I'm glad Elizabeth isn't in the room to answer for me.

"What about snakes?" I ask.

"They should be denned up for winter," Wayne says.

"But it's sixty degrees!"

"There's some cold weather due, so they'll stay in, and sixty is pretty cold for snakes."

"What about the water? How deep is it? How fast is the current?"

Ernie, surprisingly tuned in to the conversation, turns away from the football game. "It's a mostly dry creek bed," he says, "with pools here and there, and swirl holes."

"Charley, will you and Billy be careful?" I stop short of batting my eyelashes. He's got a face that makes your eyelids flutter, no matter how old you are.

"Yes, ma'am." Charley takes me seriously.

"Okay, but don't be gone more than an hour. If you are, we'll send the bloodhounds after you," I say, although the ancestry of Rufus and Redneck is a mystery. We watch from the porch as the kids follow a trail across the rocky pasture to a line of cedar brush growing along the creek.

Back in the den, we make small talk. Vince, as much out of the conversation as Ernie, has given up. Elizabeth won't let him talk. I'm nervous about the kids hiking into the boondocks, but I don't want the girls to miss out. If Wayne feels it's safe to let his five-year-old roam the creek, the girls should be fine. Still, I look at my watch every five minutes. Wayne puts his arm around me and pats me on the shoulder.

After an hour, I'm antsy. "I'm sure they're on the way back," Wayne says.

When they're ten minutes late, my heart begins to pound.

"Maybe Wayne should go after them," Elizabeth says, and for the first time today, I feel she's not squared against me in a contest to be alpha female.

Vince is concerned. "Yeah, Wayne. I'll go with you if you want."

Guillermo speaks up. "Let me go. I'll have some words with Billy for making Cynthia worry like this."

I'm ready to burst into tears, until I hear the dining room door. But it's only Charley, panting and red-faced.

"Abby fell in a dry swirl hole," he says.

"Oh, my God!" I say, close to shrieking.

"She's okay! I climbed in with her to give her a lift, so Billy could pull her out, but I couldn't lift her high enough. I could get footholds and climb out, but Abby's too short. I figured I'd come get Wayne. He can pull her out."

"Where's Eliza?" I ask, still breathless.

"Everybody stayed to keep Abby company."

"How'd she fall in?" I clutch my crossed arms.

"She leaned to look in, and—I don't know, she sort of slid off the edge. There's soft dirt in the bottom, so she's not hurt. Might've turned an ankle."

"I should go. She'll be terrified." I head for the parlor, where my jacket lies on a chair.

Wayne touches my shoulder. "Cynthia, Guillermo and I can jog all the way. And you don't have the shoes for it," he says, pointing to my pumps.

Charley says, "Abby's not all that scared. She cried at first, but then she laughed, especially when I got in there with her."

"Lead the way," Wayne says to Charley. "I'll take rope in case we need it." He squeezes my shoulder. "Give us thirty minutes. We should be back before then."

"It'll be all right," Katy says.

"I've never heard of a swirl hole," I say. "It sounds awful."

"It's where the water eddies and eats through the sandstone. Shows when the creek runs dry. Come back soon, and we'll have our own hike to see the creek."

"That'd be nice," I say, not too sincerely.

Twenty minutes later, I see spots, my breathing is so shallow. Elizabeth tries to distract me by asking questions, but I finally say, "Elizabeth, I'm sorry, but I'm not feeling too chatty right now." She leans back next to Vince and pats his hand, the first time she's acknowledged his presence except to interrupt and correct him. When she looks the other way, Vince catches my eye and gives me an approving wink.

Finally, the kids clatter through the door. Eliza looks happier than I've seen her in months. Charley follows, looking pleased, too. They're all filthy, carrying the acrid smell of sweat and dirt. Abby runs to me the way she did on Christmas morning when she believed in Santa Claus, showing me what he'd brought.

"Look, Mommy!" She opens her sweaty hand to show me an arrowhead. "I found it while I was in the swirl hole. Wayne says it looks like one of the old ones—over a thousand years old!"

Ernie's out of his chair, looking closely at Eliza's discovery. "I thought all the old arrowheads had been taken. Good find, Abby." He pats her on the head and shuffles off to the bathroom.

Abby runs to Wayne and hugs his legs.

"This was an adventure," Eliza says.

Truth

Wayne has invited us to the ranch for the weekend and assured me that the girls and I will have our own room at his house.

When I tell them, Eliza, with her quick eye for the negative, says, "Luck's a squirrel on steroids!"

"You're right, he'll dart and chatter most of the time," I say.

Abby says, "Luck is funny."

"Yeah," Eliza admits. "But Charley and Billy might be there, and even if they're not, Wayne said we might get to ride horses if we come back!"

I realize the kids are all getting attached, and the girls are bonding with Wayne. I need to have a serious conversation with him before this courtship goes any further. The thought tears me apart, but it's also the opportunity I've waited for to have enough trust and a good enough reason to stop the charade with at least one human being. And while I'm at it, I might reveal my misgivings about Lucy.

I invite Wayne for mid-morning coffee while all the kids are in school. I say I have something important to discuss with him. He agrees to make the drive to San Angelo. When I open the door, he looks a few inches shorter—stricken. Poor guy expects me to break up with him. I'm sure I look frightened, too. I'm afraid he'll tell me I'm not the person he thought I was, and he'll be right. We'll part ways, and the girls will suffer another loss. But not as huge as it would be if we fall into a rhythm with Wayne and his family and he learns later that I could have gone to prison for manslaughter. Or if I learn that Lucy had a good reason to leave.

We go through the coffee-pouring routine with little to say. I finally sit down to face him. He says, "I can't stand the suspense any longer. Tell me what's up."

My confession begins. A box of tissues sits handy. "Back in Mississippi, my erratic driving caused a motorcyclist's death." As I tell my story, something melts away inside so I can speak evenly. It's right to tell Wayne. If he decides he can't stand me, it's still right. I tell him my reasons for not coming forward—my concern for my daughters, how their lives might be destroyed—the possibility of Casey's speed and possible alcohol use as mitigating factors. There was no good excuse for driving on except my fear of Leo—perhaps drunk—keeping the girls.

I say, "I care about you, Wayne, but you deserve the truth. It'll be your decision whether we continue to see each other."

Wayne listens, so still I want to nudge him to see if he's turned to stone. When I'm through, he sits, quiet. I'm proud of myself for the first time in six years—I have the courage to risk losing Wayne, because the truth is more important than a phony relationship like my marriage to Leo.

"Thank you for being honest with me," he finally says. He looks at his hands, folded on the table. "It'll take a while to soak it in."

"I'm sure you'll need some time." I have the urge to fill in the long silences, put words in his mouth, ask how he feels.

Finally, he says, "I'm disappointed. I guess I had you on a pedestal."

Oh, what an uncomfortable place to be. What a role to fill. "I'm the last person who belongs on a pedestal."

"Are you going to turn yourself in to the authorities?"

"The person who most needs to know is Rachel Rust. I tried to tell myself she isn't Casey's widow, but I know she is. I have to speak with her. It'll be up to her."

"That's a good plan, Cynthia. But why haven't you talked to a pastor or a counselor?"

"I haven't trusted anyone enough to be able to tell them until now." He's too deflated to be flattered. He stares at the back yard. "Whatever you decide, please know I'm glad I met you. You're so honest, so real, I can't keep up the act of a wounded divorcee. I'm a hypocrite, a mess. You've drawn me out of hiding, and I'll always be grateful." I can't bring myself to ask questions about Lucy—clear everything up at once. Not a good time.

"Thanks for the kind words." He stands, picks up his hat, and looks at my kitchen as if for the last time. He walks to the door and gives me a cool peck on the forehead, maybe the last kiss. I've lost so much in a few short months, and maybe that's what it's taken for me to realize that even though I'm forgiven, I'm not much of a Christian until I take responsibility for my actions. I watch him drive away.

My next hurdle is to tell Rachel Rust. Before I lose resolve, I call her office and make an appointment for the next morning. I'm distracted that evening as the girls and I go about our routine.

Eliza's helping me load the dishwasher. "So, Mom, are we going to the ranch this weekend?" Her excitement saddens me.

"I don't know yet, honey. Wayne had some conflicts in his schedule. He'll let us know if he gets things worked out."

Abby's little shoulders sag, but that's the last of the questions, thank heavens.

I manage to doze for maybe an hour the whole night. I drop the girls off and park my car in visitors' parking. The buzz of a new school day greets me as I walk toward the office. The principal's voice resonates over the intercom as she gives the morning announcements. I pass the care-worn secretary and tap on Mrs. Rust's office door. Once inside, I sit in a chair in front of her desk. It's become an all-to-familiar hot seat. Eliza's folder lies on the desk. Mrs. Rust clearly expects a parent conference.

"This isn't about Eliza. It concerns your husband, Casey." I say.

She looks up sharply. Yes, she is the widow indeed. "How did you know Casey?"

I've rehearsed this sentence in my mind. Now's my chance, no backing away. "I was involved in the accident that resulted in his death."

She closes Eliza's folder. "You? How?"

I tell her my story. She listens in stony silence.

"I'm not asking for forgiveness," I say. "I'm not begging you to keep quiet about it. I will face the consequences. I've lived too long with this secret. I might go to prison, I might lose custody of my daughters, and my ex will certainly use the information against me."

She holds up her hand to stop the flood of words. She stands and walks behind her chair. She looks at the picture of her son. "I don't know what to say, what to do.

Leave me with this. Let me think about it. I'm completely blindsided." She doesn't turn as I leave.

Back at home, I sit through the silent afternoon, waiting for the phone to ring. It might be the Mississippi police or whoever sets the extradition process in motion in Texas. It might be Wayne saying he still wants me, or calling off the courtship. It might be Rachel Rust, with a fuller sense of loathing for what I've done. But the phone never rings. As usual, I pick up the girls. I'm relieved that it's Leo's night to take them to dinner. Before their father comes, Abby's the one to ask. "Are we going to see Wayne and Luck this weekend?"

"No, honey, I don't think so. When I know more, I'll be sure to tell you." I twirl her pigtail and kiss her on the head. Eliza watches from the doorway. She knows something's wrong.

I FINALLY SLEEP, and I wake up at peace with it all, knowing I'm on the right track. Maybe I'll speak to an attorney who can communicate with Mississippi law enforcement. But first I'll see how things unravel here.

My phone rings mid-morning. It's Rachel Rust. She's much less brusque than yesterday, even with her business-like tone, and she wants me to come to her house this afternoon. Her address is in the Twin Oaks subdivision, where some very nice, new houses have been built in the last five years.

Leo agrees to let me drop the girls off at his office after school so that I can take care of "errands." He's working late, getting ready for the beginning of spring semester. It's the first time I've asked him for extra help since we separated.

At Rachel's house, I linger in my car. I suppose administrative pay is decent, but I wonder if she's inherited a lot of money. Her house's brick façade spreads across a landscaped yard. Every shrub is perfectly sculpted, with rows of winter pansies growing at neat borders. A tall portico accents the front, with an outdoor chandelier dangling above the front door.

I say a prayer and check my makeup in the visor mirror. I don't think Rachel will throw a vase at me or come after me with a fireplace tool. Facing her contempt is the scary part. She opens the door before I can ring the bell. "Mrs. Hastings. Come in." She's still dressed in her professional suit—jacket, dress pants, low heels.

She ushers me into a marble-tiled hallway. An ornate dining room lies to our left.

"Come in and have a seat." She leads me down the entry hall into a high-ceilinged den. I sit on an expensive leather couch and look around at all the artwork. She obviously travels and brings pieces back from her destinations. It's carefully hung and displayed—a variety of genres. A large window reveals a deep, cool back porch.

She sits in an armchair, the dark, marble-topped coffee table forming a barrier between us. "I wanted to finish this business away from work. My husband and son have gone to prowl the mall while we meet."

"Thank you." So, there's a husband. I didn't know she had remarried. Now the beautiful home makes more sense.

"I can't say I admire you, but I think I understand," she says in a low voice. The seconds tick by. "This has been a lot to take in." She looks at the wall behind me. "I guess you thought you—all by yourself—ruined my and my son's life."

"I'm so, so sorry!"

"Stop thinking that."

I straighten.

"The first newspaper article didn't tell the whole story."

All I can do is stare at Rachel. She settles in her chair, as if deciding how much she wants to tell me. With a sigh, she begins. "The story in the newspaper, the one you read the day after the accident?"

I nod.

"As I recall, according to that first account, Casey's speed as he entered the curve was in question—and also his blood-alcohol level. The story left the impression, though, that the driver of the blue car caused his death."

"Impression? I think I contributed. I'm guilty of manslaughter."

"All of it was resolved in the following weeks. He was going so fast and had drunk so much, he slammed into the embankment at high speed and caused his own death. Of course, had you stayed in Columbus to see it through, you would know all this. The examination of the accident scene concluded that he lost control going around the curve. The police stopped being concerned about the driver of the blue car. Someone driving behind you had reported they thought you caused him to veer off the road, but he would have crashed whether you'd been there or not."

All I can do is blink. I understand the words she says, but how can they fit with what I've believed for the last six years? It begins to soak in. I wasn't at fault. But my cowardice has cost me. All these years, I've been tormented with guilt for my culpability in a death and for hiding it. I'm off the hook, but will I always feel tainted?

Rachel says, "You also need to know that Casey's death gave me a chance to be happy. I'm sorry he had to die, but I don't know how else I'd have gotten away."

She gives me a brief history. She met the handsome officer from Goodfellow Air Force Base in San Angelo. She was finishing her master's degree, and he was taking an instructors' course at the base. She sometimes hung out at the Suds Shop near campus with friends, and one day, he and some other airmen stopped by in their flight suits, no doubt knowing they were the best outfit to wear to pick up college girls.

"I got swept up in his hyper-drive. A jet pilot, an engineering graduate from A&M—of course he let me know all this in the first thirty minutes after I met him. I didn't know that trotting out the impressive resumé right away should have been a red flag. I was taking a break from my college boyfriend—Jackson. He's my husband now.

"Casey kept calling me and drove with me onto the base, where the guys at the guard house saluted him. And we went to the military ball with all the pomp. I was thrilled to be with such an important guy. Jackson was sidetracked by a determined girl at the time, so— long story short—when Casey proposed, I accepted." She shakes her head. "Bad decision. He was abusive."

She looks out the big window. "I debated telling you all this, but you should know the rest of the story. Even with a baby, I was planning to leave. My parents were helping me find a way to get back to San Angelo without having to confront Casey. It wasn't safe. We braced ourselves for a nasty ordeal with restraining orders, custody battles.

"I'm not glad he died. It's too bad he never had a chance to grow up. But I'm glad my son didn't have to know him. Jonathan wants to change his name to Cald-well, my husband's name. He'll have to wait until he's eighteen, since Casey's parents back in Reno would make trouble. I'll change my name then, too. Casey's dad is a control freak, so I keep our contact to a minimum. I've kept the Rust name to give my son solidarity."

My brain won't click into focus, but a tiny peephole of relief etches itself on the horizon. By hiding, I've lived with unnecessary remorse. I feel a wash of gratitude for Rachel's openness in telling me all this. She could have said, "I don't care. Go away," and never talked to me again. A mourning dove swoops in under the porch awning and thuds against the window glass. He drops from sight, but in a few seconds, flutters back up and flaps away to a nearby tree. He's left a bird-shaped smudge on the glass. I thank her for hearing me out. "I'm sorry for both of us it's taken me all these years to talk to you."

"I'm sorry, too, Cynthia. I haven't obsessed over it, but for a while, I wondered who was driving the blue sedan."

"Do what you wish with the knowledge."

"The story of how Casey died is finished. There's nothing to add."

"I guess you'll need to tell Casey's parents."

"No. I want to be involved with them as little as possible. And please know—this won't affect how I deal with the girls at school."

I PICK UP MY GIRLS. They've been punching holes and putting papers in notebooks for Leo. Very important work! I feel lighter. From survival mode, I feel my strength return after the years of sapping guilt. Even if Wayne wants to cool it with me, I'll be fine. I'll be open to whatever kind of work comes along so I can support us.

Later that evening, I look through the newspaper's classified ads, and I see an ad in the real estate section. A music store for sale. I've never run a business, but I can learn. I'll have to put together the finances, but with my music background, I'm the right person. It's a huge risk, but it doesn't amount to anything after what I've done the last few days.

I wonder if I should call Wayne, and the phone rings.

"Cynthia, I wanted to see how you're doing," he says.

I tell him what I learned from talking to Rachel Rust.

"It took a lot of courage for you to be honest, Cynthia. A lot of people wouldn't have done that."

"Well, my confession is done, and I'm in the clear, but I feel stupid."

"You were looking after your family. Anyone would be confused about what to do, given the information you were working with."

"Yes, but I rationalized away my negligence in leaving the scene, too."

"You were protecting Eliza and Abby, as far as you knew. They were smaller then, and you moved to San

Angelo. It adds up. You've got a conscience, so it was rough on you."

I sigh. "Thank you for understanding, Wayne. I'm relieved in so many ways." I still don't know if Wayne wants to see me again.

But then he asks, "So, are we still on for Saturday?"

Questions Answered

I thought Luck would wear thin, but he minds Wayne, and living in the country is ideal for him. We spend most weekends at the ranch, when the girls aren't with Leo. All I know about Lucy is she fenced a wide front yard, inspired Wayne to plant ash trees, left her baby and husband, and created scenes.

Abby, Eliza, and I sleep in Wayne's guest room, the three of us sharing a queen-sized bed with a huge, wooden headboard that looks like something from a Dracula movie. On Sunday, we sometimes go to church with Wayne, but I find the Episcopalians tepid. I prefer the nondenominational church, Faith Gospel, and they've already asked me to sing solos, often without notice.

One Saturday afternoon in the cool of February, Wayne and I sit on the porch drinking coffee. The subject of Lucy still bothers me, and the girls are exploring the creek again with Charley, Billy, and Luck, so I launch into it. "Wayne, I can't help wondering why Lucy would leave like she did. Do you have any theories?"

Wayne takes a moment. "Lucy was fun and clever when I met her. Pretty wild in high school, but I didn't let that bother me. Her dad's a real nice guy, but her mother was barking mad. When she died, not many tears were shed. Lucy was an only child, so there's no telling what she went through growing up."

"I guess when we're young, we don't think about those things."

"I sure didn't. I was twenty. She was seventeen. But she was so smart, I figured she'd be miserable if she didn't get educated. Finished high school by correspondence. Got her bachelors' and masters' degrees in about four years."

He's proud, not bitter. "Was she more cut out for a career than for marriage and family?"

"Without a doubt. The pregnancy was accidental. I'd decided to leave her. She'd become moodier and more unpredictable since, oh, I guess since about the time of her first graduation ceremony. But when she told me she was pregnant, I figured we'd have to stay together. No way would I let her be single with my child. Then after Luck was born, she left me a note on the hospital bed. I cried for days. She'd started a big job in Austin. She didn't come back to see Luck till he was one."

"Do you know what happened to make her worse? Looks like she'd be happier, more fulfilled, getting all that education."

"I've pondered it more than I'd like to admit. *Something* happened. I blamed myself for a while, but it wasn't me. Something made her go sour on everything. She would've never wanted kids, and I did. So, like I always say, she did Luck and me a favor. Only reason we stayed married for five years or so was she stayed away at school more than half the time, and after that, she was pregnant. Then it was over. I'll never know the whole story."

AT HOME, when Leo picks up Abby and Eliza, I don't see Brandy lurking in the car, so maybe there's a new girl-friend. I'll wait for the girls to tell me.

At last, we're ready for a school conference Mrs. Rust proposed before Thanksgiving. Eliza has behaved with Whitney, according to Mrs. Sims. Dr. Harris still sees Eliza, and she's so much less prickly, it's worth Leo's money and my initial battle to get her to go. I was standing at the kitchen sink when she announced she was ready to make a formal apology to Whitney. I almost dropped a plate. With new confidence, I called Mrs. Rust, and we set a date for the long-delayed meeting. Rachel Rust acted as though nothing had happened between us. In fact, she was friendlier than before.

This is big stuff at the elementary school. Sitting around the conference table in the head principal's office, we face each other—Whitney and her folks and Eliza, Leo, and I, and as many school personnel as can squeeze in to sign off on a behavior plan for Eliza so they'll have something to put in the file to show the next inspecting state bureaucrat that they were proactive about school violence.

I'm proud of Eliza. Not for being a bully, but for apologizing. The head principal, Mrs. Davis, makes a little speech on why we're gathered, while the school counselor takes notes in triplicate. Mrs. Rust introduces Eliza, giving her the prompt to say, "Whitney, I'm sorry I picked on you. I was feeling sad about things, and it felt better to be mad, and I arbitrarily selected you to be mad at." Everyone beamed and congratulated Eliza for her nobility and Whitney for not retaliating. I'm proud of Eliza for saying "arbitrarily." Poised, repentant, and reformed, that girl is bound for law school. Eliza still tells me to cut the Bible talk, but she's stopped calling it bullshit.

Meeting over. All of the conference participants shuffle away. Later that afternoon I look at my bank statement and figure I'll have to get a job soon to supplement child support. The owner of the music store already had a contract pending when I called, but

I told him I'd still be interested if the deal falls through.

I'll have to get a job or start a business. I flip through magazines searching for inspiration. I could start a Deep South bakery, sell my chocolate chip caramel poke cake, sweet potato pie, Mississippi mud pie, and other special desserts passed down in my family. It would be labor intensive and high overhead. I could start a boutique, but that's a huge risk. Looks like I've got some praying to do.

One Saturday night after we've been to a play at the Civic Theater, Wayne sits in my kitchen and says, "Cynthia, you know I love you. And . . . well, I was wondering if you would ever consider marrying me."

I'm surprised. I didn't think we had reached this point. "I love you, too, Wayne, but I hate to uproot Eliza and Abby too soon after the divorce."

Wayne sets his coffee cup down and frowns a little, but he says, "I understand. I wouldn't want to uproot Luck, take him away from his support system."

"Luck's support system is more closely tied to the ranch than Abby and Eliza are tied to San Angelo," I say. I could talk to them instead of speaking for them—then I can decide for myself.

Wayne watches my wheels turn. "You're considering it?"

"I'm considering it, yes!"

He jumps up, pulls me up, and plants one of those expert kisses I've learned to appreciate so much during the past few months. Other than some great kissing, I've kept him at arm's length. I feel so close to him at times, though, it's as if I already know his body.

When Eliza and Abby come home from Leo's, I usher them to the den right away. They're crestfallen, expecting horrible news or a lecture they didn't see coming.

"I have something important to ask you girls," I say, once we're all sitting. They both lose the stricken look. They're being consulted for a change.

Eliza pre-empts me. "You want to marry Wayne and move us to the ranch!" she blurts, her eyes dancing. As usual, Eliza's several steps ahead of me.

Abby catches up and squeals. "You mean Wayne will be our stepdad?" She claps. "And Katy will be our grandma?" She claps again. "What will Charley and Billy be?"

"Technically, no kin, but you could think of them as cousins."

"But if we marry Wayne, we'll be living with Luck *all* the time." Eliza drops this point in mid-celebration, cooling Abby's exuberance.

"That's right," I say, smiling at Eliza's "if *we* marry Wayne." "We'll always have to remember Luck was there first. We'll be welcome, it'll be our home, too, but we can't come between Luck and his daddy."

"Hmph." Eliza crosses her arms and flops back into her chair.

"Luck's all right," Abby says. "He'll be at his Gran's

most of the time anyway." I'm glad Abby figured this out, so I don't have to say it aloud.

Eliza says, "What if I don't want to move to the ranch?"

"Then I won't marry Wayne."

"I don't want to make the decision, Mom! *You* decide!" Her voice becomes a shout, and she races to her room and slams the door.

Abby and I look at each other. Abby grins at me and I can't help smiling. We hold our hands over our mouths to muffle the giggles. We both know Eliza will be on board after a few theatrics.

After the girls are in bed, I call Wayne.

I say, "I believe we'll have full cooperation on your proposal."

Wayne exhales. "When?"

And we begin to plan.

"I CAN'T BELIEVE you're moving to the sticks," Leo says.

"Some people think *San Angelo* is the sticks, Leo. Let's not be snobbish about the size of city we live in." Wayne once said some people think they're more important because they live in a big city. And then they retire and buy a place in the country where there aren't any theaters, museums, or libraries.

"There's lots more opportunities for the girls in San Angelo," Leo argues.

"You just don't want to make a long round trip to get them. It could be worse, you know. I could be moving back to Mississippi."

I picture Leo sitting in his office, his steady decline showing in the spreading grayness of his hair, skin, and whites of his eyes. Add tobacco-stained fingernails and teeth, and you have a dissipated old fart.

"You're a hard woman, Cynthia," he says, trying to shame me.

"You're a self-centered narcissist," I retort. I realize I've committed a redundancy which Leo surely noted. "You get to play musical girlfriends, and I'm not supposed to pursue any love interests."

"You are especially pursuing *this* 'love interest' because it'll take you up the road away from me."

"Sure, Leo. It's all about you."

"I've got a class I have to go teach. We'll talk later. We might have to change the custody and visitation arrangements."

The line clicks to silence.

Sifting Junk, Lucy, and Ernie

With a June wedding slated, our work is cut out. To combine households, we're building a family room, with a section of special nooks for the kids.

The front living area will show off the rosewood piano and serve as a formal living room. Lucy wasn't a decorator—she was a ladder-climber. Wayne's ranch décor—I'd call it Early Prairie—is a mix of cow hide rugs, leather, rusty things, and burlap.

I stand in the front yard and try to distract myself. Lucy will be here soon. Rather than think about it, I envision how new porch columns will complement the new roof and the trim color. I've ordered a door painted deep red and set with beveled glass.

Lucy's on her way. Raggedy nerves keep me moving

little orange landscaping flags around. I think about how much nicer this house will look after I get through with it. She's due any minute. Sure enough, I see a dust cloud rising from the county road.

Luck calls her "Lucy." I still can't believe she didn't try to see him until his first birthday. Since then, she's come by for a few hours every three or four months. Wayne's parents hated her for that, but they decided to buck up and count their blessings. She's got a big job involving flying back and forth between Austin and "D.C." as Katy calls it, swiping her hand stylishly in imitation of Lucy. Katy often adds a comment about Lucy making *piles* of money, with more than a tinge of snark. Wayne says at least she knows her strengths and weaknesses—she can make money but can't parent. I sometimes wish he weren't so damn nice. He always puts the softest spin on the asinine things she did. Katy never speaks ill of others, so her snide tone tells me Lucy was trouble.

The dust cloud draws nearer, so it's not just a dust devil. Well, "dust devil" might be the best way to describe Lucy's coming. *Something wicked this way comes.* And Wayne's away repairing a leaky pipe. I'm on my own.

"You two can meet without me in the mix," Wayne said. "It'll only last a few minutes. She'll take Luck to Mom and Ernie's."

"Is she required to have supervised visits?" I asked.

"No, but she's not confident about being alone with Luck. He's a handful for her. She doesn't trust herself." Indeed, I thought. I'm good with kids, and he's a handful for me.

She's here. Her bright blue two-door Audi rolls to a stop. The first part of her I see is a small, red shoe with a gold buckle covering the instep, like something Louis the Sixteenth would wear. The tiny leg is encased in close-fitting ankle jeans of the same red as the shoes. She raises herself from the car, revealing a bright blond, spiky hair-do. The thin, flesh-colored spaghetti straps on her swingy, light-weight tank top make her look practically naked. I can tell what she's all about, and it isn't Sunday School.

I wave. I'm glad I'm not wearing a dirty, paint-spattered T-shirt and old jeans, my usual attire these days. My hair is slicked back in a ponytail, but it flatters me. My T-shirt is stylish, my jeans are clean, but my sandals are far out of league with those designer shoes.

Wayne never gave details, but he said she picked a lot of fights. I remember the verse in Proverbs: "*It is better to live in a corner of the housetop than in a house shared with a quarrelsome wife.*" I didn't understand why he married her in the first place, but seeing her now, ten years later, I imagine she was quite becoming. She still is, but hard-looking.

Lucy smiles and waves, walking up the gate path. She reminds me of a very short runway model—or maybe she feels like it's a gangplank. Her smile—I detect some expensive dental work—says she might as well be at a White House reception.

"Halloo! You must be Cynthia!" She advances with her arm out straight, offering her hand. We shake. I can do the stiff-arm salute, too, and serve up the marmalade.

"You are so right! I'm the one and only Cynthia— around here at least. It's nice to meet you, Lucy."

"Oh, I hope so, after what I imagine you've heard about me."

I'm taken aback by her frankness, but, like I said, I can dish it, so I say, "Oh, it wasn't *all* bad!" We laugh, but her eyes narrow with hard caution.

"So, you guys are getting married in a couple of months?" she asks. She doesn't beat around the bush. Might as well talk about it, since Wayne is all we have in common.

"Yes, in June." I gesture toward the house. "We're making some changes so it'll fit a family of five."

"When I lived here, I rattled around in it." She appraises the new shape of the roof and my landscaping flags. "It's a good thing you're fixing up. It was getting seedy."

Before I can take exception on Wayne's behalf and remind her that running a ranch *and raising a son* takes time away from home maintenance, Luck pops out the

front door. "Lucy!" he yells. He races down the steps to
grab her legs. Lucy takes a step back to brace herself for
impact, so Luck gets a hold on one leg, which he
squeezes like it's his favorite baseball bat.

He swings from Lucy's hand, and she smiles at him,
but she's stiff and hesitant. Luck babbles to her about his
latest toys and the bobcat skulking around the house last
night, news that widens my eyes and makes me look in
the direction he points. Lucy smirks at me like I'm a big
wimp.

Fortunately, Abby and Eliza bang out the door. They
screech to a halt. For a moment I see her through their
eyes. Tinkerbell with a wicked twist. Luck says, "Hey,
Abby-Eliza! Lucy's takin' me outa here!"

She waves to the girls with her free hand. "I guess
you know all about me! It's nice to meet you." She looks
down at Luck. "Ready to make a getaway?"

Lucy buckles Luck into the back seat of her Audi for
the short ride to Katy's and they roll away. I take a breath
of Luck-free air. I love the little monster, but I'll be so
glad when he's older.

"Lucy's pretty!" Abby yells, not so much from
surprise, but from tension release. The Mystery Woman,
finally revealed.

"Yes, she is. Now let's go in." My hands are doubled
into fists to stop them shaking. Lucy unnerves me. She's
so carefully cultivated—the accent has no trace of Texas.
Her arms look sculpted by a personal trainer. Every

spike of hair is arranged. Such staging hides a great sense of personal inadequacy.

THE GIRLS TAKE the four-wheeler for a spin, and I decide to inventory the empty closet space. The large walk-in was Lucy's. And now I have a true picture of the creature who inhabited this space. I'll repaint, re-carpet, and hang a mirror on the door, and with my clothes, Lucy's imprint will be eradicated. I'll need to move a few hats of Wayne's. Standing on a step ladder, I inspect the mostly-empty top shelf of the smaller closet Wayne uses. As I dust the shelf, my rag catches on a pair of scissors with hot pink handles shoved all the way to the back. Back in the kitchen, I drop them on the countertop. Wayne's in the utility room taking off his muddy boots and changing into clean jeans.

He charges in for a bear hug but spies the scissors. "What's that?" He's descends on them and turns them over in his hands, examining them. "Where were they?"

"I found them shoved to the back of the top shelf of your closet."

His puzzled expression clears. "I think Lucy hid those from me years ago." Then he falls in a chair and laughs.

"What's so funny?"

"Way back when, Lucy picked a fight with me about

misplaced scissors. Looks like she hid them. She was always trying to get me riled. I was a challenge."

"Well, that was cruel of her."

"I guess it was, but it's funny, too." His laugh tapers off. "It's a little pathetic when you think about it. She tried to play with my head."

Leave it to Wayne to have compassion. I never.

"Speaking of scissors, how did your meeting with Lucy go?"

Before I can answer him, the phone rings. From Wayne's side of the conversation, I can tell it's Ernie. Wayne says "uh-oh" a few times but it's mostly Ernie, wound up about something.

"A cow grazed your fender? Yeah, we can do without stampedes caused by four-wheelers." Wayne hangs up.

"What happened? Are the girls all right? Did you say *stampede*?"

Before he can answer, I hear the hum of the four-wheeler. At the side door, the girls take their time wiping their feet. Abby's face scrunches as if she's about to cry, but Eliza frowns.

"Ernie's *mean*," Eliza says.

"Yep," Wayne says. "Ernie can be real mean when he's mad. He doesn't realize he hurts people's feelings. I guess you heard some choice words?"

Eliza looks up. "Yeah, he said 'goddam son-a-bitchin' four-wheeler.'" She glances at me. "We drove at the cows, but I thought they'd walk away. They take their time moving away from cars. But there was this one cow that raised up on its hind legs and ran off, and the others ran, too. One bumped against Ernie's truck, and . . . gosh, I didn't know a cow could do that."

Wayne says, "Yep. Cows weigh a ton. Add a little speed, and they can sure bend a fender."

Abby adds, "It was like Eliza said. We laughed about the cows running. And that made Ernie madder. He said some things and told us to 'git on to the house.'" Abby's imitation is perfect.

Eliza seizes the opportunity to use her total recall of conversations, a talent she has often deployed against me. "He said, 'Don't you kids have the sense God gave a flea? You've gone and spooked the goddam cows and now my goddam truck's dented.' Then he told us to 'git on back to the house,' like Abby said."

Wayne says, "I'm sorry he scared you, but this is Ernie. If something happens that's sudden and not to his liking, he'll fly off shouting in all directions. And yes, Eliza, he can be *mean*."

"So, do we lose the four-wheeler?"

"It's your mom's decision. But there might not be a problem with y'all keeping it as long as you stay away from cows and Ernie. The cows aren't used to the four-wheeler. And they can be dangerous. They could charge at you if they have a calf."

I speak up. "I'll agree, Wayne. But you should tell

Ernie I don't appreciate him cursing at the girls. Or I can tell him. How do you want to handle that?"

"I'll tell him, Cynthia. But you're welcome to talk to him about it any time you want to."

I hate to admit it, but there's no point. Ernie won't change.

A Well-Staged Blend

My nerves are crawling out of my skin. Cheri Venable, my matron of honor, fusses with my hair as we wait in the aqua and pink bride's room at the Episcopal church. Eliza and Abby run in and out, blurs of pink and lavender.

Luck sticks his head in the door and his eyes almost pop out on stems. Vince, Wayne's best man and designated Luck Patrol, reaches a hand in to grab his shoulder and pull my soon-to-be stepson out of the room. He manages to yell loud enough for everyone in the next county to hear, "Good God-a-mighty, you look purdy!"

Luck's the ring bearer—fake rings stitched to a pillow. If Luck were entrusted with real rings, he might decide to use them in a washer-pitching match on the church lawn.

We're expecting a hundred people—my friends and Wayne's best friends and family. I wanted my pastor at Faith Gospel to conduct the ceremony. Wayne explained his family's long relationship with Father Jones and the Episcopal Church.

I said, "But it's so tiny."

He said, "How many people will come, do you think? It'll hold 150."

I had to admit the acoustics would be better in the Episcopal church. Still, I wasn't happy to be married on the spot where Wayne and Lucy said vows. My next objection was that there would be too much ritual, but Father Jones said we could do it my way. I gave in to the dignified Episcopal sanctuary, with its deep wood tones and stained glass.

Worries about Luck and all the strategizing are the least of my concerns. What's really haunting me is *tonight*. I'm squeamish, leery of sex. But here I am, in a nice ivory sheath dress and matching heels with my hair piled on my head.

The girls are in favor of the marriage. They've had the time of their lives on the ranch—exploring, riding horses, four-wheeling. They like Wayne, and even Luck—I know they'll love both of them someday.

Everything's good, except the prospect of sex. Leo and I once enjoyed sex, but I thought he wasn't interested as much anymore because his drinking made him impotent. Apparently, Brandy was up to the challenge. I know Wayne won't have that problem. It'll be real. I'm afraid, and I'm insecure. I feel a little responsible for Leo's straying—maybe I did something wrong and I'm not good enough to keep Wayne.

For our honeymoon, we'll fly to Asheville, North Carolina, to stay in the bridal suite of a bed and breakfast. I've got enough makeup on right now to make a bloodied boxer look good, but my ears and neck and collar bones will blush as I stand in front of the altar. I begin to feel panicky. Cheri sees the signs and makes a quick trip to the drugstore for smelling salts. She's a sorority sister, and she knows I sometimes get the vapors before singing performances.

"Look at you! You're all flustered about this wedding, and you've sung in front of thousands! National anthem at football games, gospel at big revivals. It's just a little old wedding, and you can put it all behind you in twenty minutes. And you don't have to sing."

"I know, Cheri. But it's such a big step."

"Many a girl would give her right arm to be in your place, marrying a hunky cowboy, living on a real ranch with him. Focus on how lucky you are."

The words "hunky cowboy" make my stomach flip. I smile my phoniest, but she sees through me and says, "Oh, sweetie! It'll be all right. It's like riding a bicycle." That does not reassure me. For a moment, I hate Leo. Then, I realize if I'm angry with Leo, I'm not so afraid. I decide to run with the anger—a familiar feeling—long enough to get me through this. I think, "Yes! I'm marrying a shitkicker! Yes! We're going to screw tonight... or maybe tomorrow or the next day! So, screw you, Leo!" Now I am energized, defiant. I have survived this divorce, by golly, and I am marrying a great man. I have a second chance at life, so take that, Leo.

The organ plays Pachelbel's "Canon in D." Thank goodness, I was able to get my friend Annamarie from San Angelo. The regular organist here doesn't use the right stops and all the music would sound the same, in addition to wrong notes. But Annamarie can play the Canon and switch into the Wedding March with her eyes shut.

As the prelude winds down, meaning Wayne's family has gone in as a group, Cheri peeks out the door. "Okay, processional music starting. Don't worry, I'll be on Luck's heels. And anything that goes wrong will just make the wedding more memorable—in a good way." I hear the strains of "Trumpet Voluntary." That means Abby and Eliza are strewing rose petals, while Luck follows. Cheri will glide in, stately in her light blue sheath dress and matching shoes, her dark eyes and hair shining.

I hear the rustling of people standing at a signal from Father Jones before Wagner's "Bridal Chorus" starts. Wayne stands at the end of the aisle, relaxed and smiling.

As I walk toward Wayne, I'm startled. I had grieved

about the empty front pew on the bride's side, where my parents would sit if they were alive, or where my siblings would join them if I had any. But the pew's not empty. Katy, her sister, and the cousins and their husbands stand on the bride's side. On the groom's side, Ernie, Charley, Billy, Guillermo, and Baker—Luck's other grandfather, Lucy's father—balance the family group. I'm so touched, I slow down and almost stop. Katy nods to me, and the other women smile. They all told me last night at our little rehearsal dinner at the Navaho how glad they are Wayne's marrying me.

The processional is over, and Father Jones begins.

We've included the children in the ceremony. Eliza rolled her eyes, Luck clapped and jumped up and down on the sofa, and Abby said "thank you" when I told them they would be part of the wedding vows. The children join us. Wayne and I pledge to support the children in their dreams and build a family together. Luck starts into a little dance, hopping from foot to foot. He hears a few titters from the crowd, and I feel his energy ramp up. He's been standing next to Cheri, so I reach back and grab him by the elbow for the next part. I hand off my bouquet to Cheri and take both of Luck's hands.

Luck is fixed on me, like we told him in the rehearsal. I squat down to tell him my promises to love, guide, and support him along life's paths. After I say each phrase, Luck pumps my hands and says, "Yes!" He just now decided to add this feature, but it's working. Instead of bringing down the house, Luck's enthusiasm has our wedding guests and family members actively listening. Sniffles ripple around the church. They all know the story of Lucy's desertion. Wayne holds hands with Eliza and Abby and repeats the same words.

When we're through, Luck whips around and runs past Katy, but she catches him with one hand. She's worked with baby goats, so she's quick at catching strays. She hands him off to Ernie, who gets a grip on Luck's shoulder that says "stay put."

The priest prays for a long time, and Wayne and I finally say our vows, exchange rings, and turn to the wedding guests while the father asks if they will support our union. The on-the-ball Episcopalians know to shout, "We will!" The rest miss the cue, unless they were following along with the printed program.

We kneel at the altar while Father Jones intones. The Episcopalians also know to say "Amen" at just the right time.

I like those pew-jumpers at my church—they're spontaneous, to say the least.

Finally, we face the wedding guests while Father Jones pronounces us husband and wife. We kiss. Everyone claps, and the organ kicks in with "Ode to Joy." Before I know it, we're hustling down the aisle. In the vestibule, Wayne pulls me into the bridal room. "This is for Luck," he says, as he locks the door, and I know he means Luck with a capital "L." He pulls me to him, to his natural smell of hay and sunshine and a little fresh sweat. He holds me so tightly it doesn't matter that I'm wobbly-kneed. And he kisses me like I've never been kissed before. His kiss says he's my husband now, and tonight's the night.

Hyperventilating on the
Honeymoon

I've washed off the grime of the day, and I'm talcum-powdered, scraped, and brushed. I sit on the edge of the big whirlpool tub in our B&B bridal suite in Asheville. My nightgown is no more revealing than a sundress—white cotton, with lace and little satin bows on the straps and edges. I'm sure Wayne isn't expecting me to enter in stiletto heels and a baby-doll see-through.

My main problem is I'll have to come out of the bathroom sooner or later.

Eliza and Abby will stay at Katy's until Leo picks them up tomorrow. I gave him careful directions for getting to Katy's house and warned him about the road in case it rains. "You don't think I can negotiate a muddy road after living in Mississippi most of my life?" Leo said when I warned him about a place where people get stuck. I'd heard the story about Lucy's dad getting stuck and Lucy having to run to fetch Wayne to come pull them out.

"Of course, you know how to drive," I say. "But this part of the road I'm talking about is treacherous, unless you have four-wheel drive," I said. Leo's so ungracious. Why can't he just say, "Thanks for the heads-up"?

"So, I'll get to see the place you're taking my kids to live, out in the backwoods of Bumfuck, Egypt."

I hope it rains tonight and Leo gets stuck. It'll serve him right.

I hear Wayne shuffling around, his feet padding across the carpet, a drawer opening and closing. The television mumbled for a while, but now it's quiet. He clears his throat, coughs. The pages of a magazine rustle as my heartbeat escalates and my breathing becomes labored. I'm feeling so light-headed, I'm afraid I'll pass out on the bathroom floor. The thought propels me to my feet, and I stumble out.

Wayne throws the magazine on the floor and jumps to catch me as I'm falling and carry me to the bed. "You're hyperventilating, Cynthia. You'll be okay." He's matter-of-fact, even in his stretch boxers. He glides to the closet, where he yanks the plastic laundry bag from its coat-hanger clips and makes a circle with his thumb and fingers, cinching the bag to hold it on my mouth. "Breathe into this," he says, and I do. He sits beside me on the edge of the bed.

As I begin to breathe regularly, I say, "I'm sorry, Wayne. I'm so scared."

"It's okay. You know, you're not required to do anything."

I burst into tears. Wayne shoots into the bathroom and brings back a big wad of tissues. I pull myself together. I've made my grand exit from the bathroom, and here we are, him in his underwear and me in my nightgown.

"Thank you, Wayne," I finally manage, pushing myself up to lean against the padded headboard. Leo would have scoffed at me a million times over by now and told me I have a terminal case of Southern Belle. Or I've got religion up the wazoo.

"Listen, Cynthia. I don't want sex to be some kind of duty you have to perform. We've had a big day, so why don't you relax on your side of the bed and I'll do the same? We can talk or sleep, or whatever you feel like."

"Okay," I say, and slip down under the sheet. He gets into his side. There's a good three feet of distance between us, and I relax. He turns off the lights and I relax some more. Before I know it, I sleep the sleep of the exhausted.

At some point during the night, I wake up just enough to see his silhouette and hear his light snoring. I'd like to stroke his cheek, but I don't want to lead him on. I'm not ready. I fall asleep again, comfortable beside him.

Over the next several days, we scout downtown Asheville to the strings and horns of buskers, and we visit workshops where glassblowers and potters line their shelves with bowls and figurines. We gawk in our rent car along the Blue Ridge Parkway, hold hands at scenic overlooks, and hike past waterfalls, breathing in the misty air. We rubberneck through the Biltmore mansion. This is what honeymoons were for, once upon a time. To get comfortable with one another.

Finally, the night before we catch our plane to go back home, we reach toward one another at the same time, and we slowly come together. I think, *This is why they call it "making" love.*

Luck's Quandary

"Okay, Mother, we'll give him a few more days." Wayne sets his phone on the kitchen counter and rubs his hand over his forehead.

"What does Katy say?"

"Luck wants to live with her. He doesn't want to come home."

"Why? Has something happened?" I'm stunned.

Eliza, Abby, and Luck have practiced a mix of détente, fighting, and crazy fun the last several years. Some initial drama involved screeching when Luck walked in on the girls in the bathroom, piercing his ears so he learned to knock. Shrill accusations were hurled when Abby blamed Luck for losing her Nintendo, which appeared under her bed. And when Eliza accused Luck of stealing her allowance money, which appeared where she had hidden it in the back of a drawer.

Luck's revenge took the form of pranks—rubber snakes in the bathtub and a tarantula in a Mason jar left on their dresser. He never left the girls alone with Billy and Charley—because he wanted to be included and because he knew he was frustrating their plans to escape him. But I was glad he stuck with them when they were together, especially Charley and Eliza.

Eliza's fifteen, and Charley's so darn good-looking, I'm afraid he'll get her involved in a physical attraction. Charley doesn't have any religious upbringing to keep him out of trouble—he must have experience with girls. He's so relaxed and seems to know they're drawn to him. And he gets no supervision or guidance from his mother. Wayne says she struggles and copes the best she knows how.

The problem now is that Luck spent the weekend at Katy's and wants to stay there. He and Katy made a trip to Abilene, while Abby, Eliza, and I went to San Angelo to see old friends.

Wayne says, "Nothing's happened in particular. Luck says he likes how quiet it is at Mother and Ernie's. That's all he's told Mother so far."

"It won't be quiet for long with Luck there," I laugh.

The idea that Luck wants to stay for now with Katy and Ernie galls Wayne. He hangs his head as he leans against the kitchen counter. "I'm sorry," I say. I put my arms around him. "Have we failed him somehow?"

"No, not you. He couldn't have a better stepmother."

After we married, I convinced Wayne that Luck needed some kind of therapy for kids with Attention Deficit Disorder. Katy and I took him to Fort Worth every week for months. It was the closest place we could find with a child therapist to fit Luck's needs. He can do somersaults across the classroom during his first lesson in long division and catch on anyway. But he won't finish a test. He knows the answers but doesn't care if the teachers know he knows. He thinks solving the first and last problems in an assignment and maybe one or two in between is enough to prove he's got it.

Wayne appreciates all the efforts I've made. He knows I care. I do love a project, and Luck's the project of a lifetime. But if he weren't so cute, I might have to wrap him in a sheet and beat him with a coat-hanger.

Wayne's voice is thick. "I think it's because Lucy hasn't contacted us in nearly a year. He's become aware that his mother *chose* not to raise him. Maybe he wants more time with his grandmother." Wayne stands at the sink, staring out the window. "What really bothers me is that I've been a much better father than Ernie. But it's not good enough."

The situation burns him. Lucy is so focused on her own life, she's forgotten she has a son. I resent her leaving Luck for someone else to raise and I envy her freedom to flit around the world with various boyfriends. She's a Congressional lobbyist now. I often recite the Bible verse to myself about the tongue being capable of setting a forest on fire, to keep from saying what I think of Lucy. I pray not to be angry. I'll get mad at her later, when I'm chopping weeds in the front yard.

Wayne sits at the table with his head in his hands. Finally, he says, "I love that kid more than my own life, but I don't know how to deal with him most of the time."

"That's not true, Wayne. You're a great father. You're better than my father was, and better than Leo, and I'll remind you how impressed I was the first time you brought Luck to my house."

Wayne needs to meet Guillermo to work on a fence, so he shakes off his mood and pushes away from the table. "Thanks, Cynthia," he says with zero enthusiasm as he leaves. "I appreciate your encouragement."

I've made some version of the speech many times in the last four years. I tell him he's a good dad, and it seems to quell his feelings of guilt when Luck is on a spree. When Luck was eight, he snuck out one night and drove off in the pickup. He got all the way to the county road before he thought better of going any further. We all knew he didn't want to face his daddy if he took that truck off the ranch.

The current disappointment swept in unexpected. I had planned to get Luck after school today, but Katy asked if she could pick him up and let him stay with her a few days. When I took all three kids to school this morning—I circled to Katy's to gather Luck—he was unusually quiet on the drive to town, but he didn't get a

chance to talk much. Both girls play in the school band—
Eliza on flute, and Abby on clarinet. They've been
rehearsing a duet for State solo and ensemble contest,
and they started arguing about how a phrase in the
music should go, humming back and forth, until it
became a duel.

Eliza said, "Don't spaz if you make a mistake. Just
keep playing." Eliza is still the bossy one, and sweet little
Abby lets her take the lead.

I dropped Luck at the elementary school, and he
waved a limp goodbye. Eliza and Abby continued their
discussion as we drove to the secondary school. They
bounced out of the Suburban to grab their instruments
and backpacks from the deck.

I watched my girls walk up the front steps, greeting
their friends. I'm grateful for the Sulfur Gap school
system. There were gifted classes for Eliza and honors
classes for Abby. They even got involved in 4-H, which
meant cooking projects like making jelly. Livestock
projects got us into the sheep and goat business.

I had to veto Luck's proposal to set up a bee colony
and make honey. But extracurricular involvements help,
since Luck doesn't have many friends—he wears them
out—and he's got such a different quality about him,
besides being hyper. Academically, his reading level is
far above his classmates', his math skills fall in the upper
percentile range, and his memory is amazing. He doesn't
remember dates from history, because he doesn't care.

He's a good writer, but he doesn't care about punctuation. When he went into third grade, I argued to his teachers that he was gifted, and they looked at him more closely and said, "Yes, that explains a lot."

Leo has mellowed the last few years. Eliza's high school schedule now requires that she sometimes stay in Sulfur Gap for parties or club meetings rather than traipse off to San Angelo with her dad. He looked bad for a while—fish-belly gray, in fact, with droopy pouches around his eyes. He still had all his hair, basically handsome, but he looked like he suffered from chronic flu. One day I noticed his color was better. I said, "You're looking healthier. New diet?"

"Thanks. I've stopped drinking. The doctor convinced me it'd be best, last time I got a check-up. I went to Alcoholics Anonymous rather than going it on my own, and I'm surprised. I like AA. And I've cut way back on smoking, aiming for a clean break."

He introduced his latest girlfriend to me last time we made the child exchange. She's an English professor at the university, more mature and stable than the others. Not a live-in, I gathered from the conversation.

After Wayne leaves to meet Guillermo, I change the bed linens. I stop to smell the crisp sheets that dried on the clothesline. Wayne and I love those sheets. Just smoothing them over the bed gives me a tingly feeling, which goes away when I think about Luck. I still can't figure out why he's distancing himself.

Clash of Belief

I feel hollow, so I can only imagine how Wayne feels. Luck has cloistered himself at Katy's for three weeks. He helps Wayne with chores in the afternoon. Finally, one afternoon, Luck told Wayne, "I would like to come home, but Cynthia wouldn't understand me. I don't want her to send me to some *Christian* counselor." Other than these mutterings, he clammed up. I'm hurt to the core that Luck feels this way about me.

Leo is due any minute. Rufus and Redneck bark in tandem and charge up the road, doing their best to get run over by an approaching car. Sure enough, it's Leo. Good. He doesn't have his girlfriend with him.

When he opens his car door, the dogs swing their tails and look sheepish. They haven't banished the invader, so they ingratiate themselves. I whistle to them. It's so much easier and better for my voice than yelling. Wayne loves that I can whistle like that. He's had me do it for Pam and J.J., Charley and Billy, his cousins, and everyone we're around. Who knew whistling like a cow hand would become a major life skill? The rascal dogs trot to the porch and stay.

"My God, Cynthia, you amaze me," Leo says, truly complimentary about my whistling ability. We're actually becoming *friends*.

I invite him in for tea.

"Where's Luck?" Luck always blows through to chat with Leo when he's here.

"He's at Katy's. He wanted to stay there for a while." My voice carries a tinge of sadness. "I don't know what's the matter. All he's said is I might send him to a therapist over something going on with him." At one time, I would never admit any of this to Leo, but he's stopped trying to ambush me over some foible. He's smart, and I need to tell someone who won't repeat anything that would spread around the Gap.

Leo cocks his head. "Having trouble fitting in, is he?"

"I suppose."

"Well… you know he's a pretty unique kid. I think he'll do great things, on his own terms. But he might be shaping up to have a different sexual orientation than folks around here are ready to accept."

The idea staggers me. I'd never thought of that. I struggle to remain calm, and I'm irritated at Leo for dropping this suggestion, out of the blue. *And* he's making it sound like the "folks around here" are all duds. He doesn't get it that those "folks" are everywhere. Then I remember the admonition— "Don't shoot the messenger."

"Luck is not the least bit effeminate," I say. "And he's certainly too young to have had sexual thoughts."

"Straight boys start paying attention to girls in the preteen years—and Luck's that age. He probably wonders why he feels different. Kids these days are savvy. He's beginning to wonder why he's different."

"Besides being hyper?" I laugh. "But he's always admired pretty girls."

"That's not the same as being attracted to them."

"Well, maybe he *feels* different toward girls because of his mother issues."

"Oh, science has blown that theory out of the water. Sexual orientation is inborn."

I'd read about it being inborn, but the Bible says homosexuality is a sin. Yet there's other things in the Bible that don't make sense from a modern perspective. "That's something to think about." I change the subject. "So, do y'all have some exciting plans for the weekend?"

"I thought I'd take the girls to the art museum. Have dinner at the Mexican food restaurant, take in a movie." He gazes out the window onto the porch, where Rufus and Redneck peer back at us, tails thumping furiously on the concrete. "I think I'll get a dog," he says. "There's an adoption fair at the mall, and we might find the right rescue dog. The girls will enjoy helping me pick one out."

Abby and Eliza are happier than usual to be going with Leo. Maybe it's because Leo is healthier and doesn't have an anorexic girlfriend on his arm. He seems more real, like a regular person and not a vapor of bourbon and cigarettes. For a moment, I'm jealous, but I've enjoyed the rank of the "better parent" all this time, with Leo a distant second. I decide to be happy for everyone.

"Dad, will you let me borrow the car? I need to practice driving in traffic, and there's no traffic in the Gap." Eliza begins angling for the favors on her agenda.

"Sure. But don't I have to ride along?"

"No. I have a hardship license. Kids living in the country can get those."

Abby jumps in. "Dad, can I go to the movies with Stacy and Leslie tomorrow?"

"We can work that in, as long as Stacy and Leslie are girls."

I've gotten used to Leo taking my daughters, but I always feel uneasy when they're gone. As they load up, Wayne pulls in and stops to say goodbye and shake Leo's hand before driving under the carport.

He kicks his boots off and comes into the kitchen. This weekend, we'll have some rare moments to be alone, and we smile at each other, looking forward to it. I'm booked to sing in San Angelo tomorrow—a wedding in the morning and a program at the museum in the afternoon. But I'll be home before bedtime. I decide to mention the theory Leo expressed.

"Did Luck give you any more indications about what's bothering him?"

"No. I'm not pressing him. All I know for sure is something's eating at him. Maybe it's religion. Maybe he's toying with the idea of declaring himself an atheist."

I never thought Luck had any particular religious leanings. He goes along to church, refuses to go to church camp, and remains lukewarm about youth activities. In fact, he and Eliza are right there together. I'm thankful I've learned it's not their own faith if they don't find it for themselves.

I say, "Do you think that's all he's questioning? Religion?"

Wayne looks startled. He's picked up on what I mean much faster than I thought he would. "What do you mean?" he asks. He wants me to say it.

"While Leo waited on the girls, we talked, and he told me Luck is at an age where boys start feeling confused if they're wired differently—sexually."

"Hmmm. To tell the truth, I've thought the same thing, wondered if this is what Luck says you wouldn't understand. But I want him to say it himself. Mother feels the same way."

I've been left out of the loop. Once again, my religious beliefs are creating a schism. I feel defensive. "Well, I'm sorry everyone's tiptoeing around *me*."

"Mother and I felt like we shouldn't make a big deal
—for Luck's sake."

"Well, aren't *you* considerate? You're so careful of our
feelings, not even bringing me into the discussion."

"We love you both."

That knocks me off my high horse. My tears sneak
up. "I'm sorry I've alienated Luck. I don't know any
other way to be. When I was a kid, I was so lonely, and
the church was my refuge. Whenever I question some of
the beliefs I grew up with, I feel like that lonely child
again, so I go back to my faith. Leo, then Eliza and now
Luck—people get sick of me and my religion. You'll
grow tired of me, too."

Wayne takes my hand. "I admit, it's hard sometimes,
Cynthia. I wish you'd chill. I really do. But I can deal
with it. I love you. Marriage is about accepting one
another's quirks. Mostly, your faith is a bonus. But if
Luck feels different from the other boys, it would be
scary for him to be around someone who believes being
gay is a mortal sin. When he went to your church once,
he heard a sermon on it. It made enough of an impression that he came home and talked to me."

I vaguely remember a sermon. I did think there were
more important issues we could hear about than
condemning gay people, but I never took a stand. It's
time I did. I say, "I can't believe God would condemn
Luck for who he is. If he's gay, I don't think he chose it,
any more than he chose to have A.D.D. or be gifted. How

do you feel about it—if that *is* what he's struggling with?"

"I'm okay. There's nothing he could do or be to make me stop loving him."

"It'll mean some of the things you'd hoped for his life won't happen."

"You're right. He'll probably leave home and move to a city where there's more of a community for him. I probably won't be a grandparent. But it's not for me to like or not like. It's who he is, and he doesn't need me shaming or pressuring him. Anyway, we still don't know for sure."

We decide to wait until Luck's ready to talk openly. I promise Wayne that in the meantime, I'll do my best to let Luck know I love and accept him. Maybe all the efforts I've made to keep him on the right track school-wise have given him the impression I don't accept him. I'll set that straight.

BEING A SINGER HAS PAID OFF. After I became a Sulfur Gap citizen, calls came for me to sing solos for weddings and funerals. An honorary payment for the singer is custom-ary, and I began to receive more than the recommended amount. Word of mouth is my best advertisement, and now I sing for all kinds of occasions in our area. I also give voice lessons, often in San Angelo at Annamarie's home or at the schools after classes, to coach students for contests or simply help them reach their full potential. Singing and teaching is a great part-time job. When the girls go on to college, I'll take more business—unless Luck needs me. Katy covers that territory quite well, though.

The morning wedding goes well, and as soon as I can discreetly leave the museum after the program, I slip out a side door. Wayne and Luck planned to spend some extra time together today, with me and the girls gone. I hope they made progress.

I call Wayne on my cell as I'm leaving town. He answers before I hear a ring.

"I'm on my way home! I can't wait to see you," I say. Life looks good. I'm so in love with my husband, and I love him more every day. Whatever happens, we'll deal with it.

"I can't wait to see you, either, Cynthia. I love you."

"Love you, too. Bye for now."

THE SUN SETS FASTER than usual, it seems. Traffic picks up —people on their way to Saturday night events. I join the flow of cars, and before I know it, I arrive at the exit toward Sulfur Gap.

I turn on the radio and set the cruise control to sixty. No need to hurry. The road narrows to a two-lane as I drive past fields of wheat planted in the winter months, ready to harvest, and more fields plowed and prepared for cotton in the coming summer.

The sun slips below a mesa. The road curves past undeveloped acres of mesquite and mountain cedar and straightens toward a gentle hill—one in a series where the girls and I always have contests guessing how far away we are from the next crest. I think, "Two and a half miles." As I get to the top of the hill, I look down at my odometer to see if I've guessed right, but something invades my peripheral vision. It's a large pickup, and it's coming toward me, entering the reach of my headlights.

I slam my brakes, wrench the steering wheel away from the pickup, and slide into a sideways skid. The front of the pickup smashes my side of the Suburban, and I become a rag doll enveloped in air bags as my car rolls over the top of the truck, and I wonder why I can't feel anything—why there's no pain as the roof crushes in —and I think, "My girls!"

Interlude—Higher Ground

L ate Saturday evening, L.B. shows up instead of
Cynthia. My stomach tightens. My scalp crawls at
the sight of the sheriff. I stand at the door.

"Wayne, I'm sorry to tell you this. Very sorry. There's been
a bad wreck on 237. Miz Cheadham didn't make it."

I slump against the door jamb.

"It was a head-on. Coming over the rise. Pickup in her lane
with his lights off, trying to keep from getting caught hauling
dope. No way she could avoid it. Unlucky timing."

I shove my hands into my pockets and stand as straight as
I can. My mind won't formulate words.

L.B. says, "Are you here alone? Is there somebody to be
with you?"

"No, I'm alone."

"J.J. was at the scene. He called Pam. They're both on their
way. I should stay till they get here."

I turn aside and gesture L.B. to the kitchen. He sets his hat on the table and takes a chair. L.B. has to keep an eye on me, part of doing his job.

"Want me to call your folks?"

I shake my head. Minutes pass, maybe hours, as we sit, still and quiet. A tightness creeps up my rib cage and into my throat, about to stop my breath. I'm glad L.B. is smart enough not to try to talk. A car, followed by a pickup, stops in front. Pam and J.J.

Pam says, "Wayne, I'm so sorry," and she throws her arms around my neck. She slips through the house, inspecting the bathrooms. I guess she expects people will come by. That's what Cynthia would do—inspect the bathrooms. She empties and reloads the dishwasher and makes a pot of coffee, then hurries away, sniffing and dabbing her eyes, in time for her shift at the hospital.

J.J. stays until close to dawn. He was close to the scene, waiting to intercept the drug runner if he eluded L.B, his deputy, and the highway patrol. L.B. sure summed it up when he said something about bad luck. Sure was. Cynthia got between the S.O.B. and his escape path. Can't say I'm sad to hear he died, too.

I have to call Leo, so he can tell the girls. I can't do it, so I hand the phone to J.J. when the call rings through. He grabs it and tells Leo what's happened. I'm thankful for my good friend who knows how to deliver the worst news in the world. I wonder if Leo will remember when he met J.J. at the VFW. Probably not. What's happened now puts all the other stuff in miniature perspective. Leo's gotten sober and matured since then. We're friends. J.J. answers a few questions—short, to the point. Finally, he says, "Let me ask him. Wayne, can you talk?"

I gesture for the phone and say hello. Leo says, "Oh, my God, Wayne, I'm blown away. This is horrible. How will I tell Eliza and Abby?"

"I'd hate to be in your shoes, Leo."

"Well, I'd hate more to be in yours."

"Thanks. Tell the girls to call me, or you can bring them to the ranch if you want. It's up to you now." My voice cracks. I've lost those two stinkers, too, unless Leo. . . . Hysterical money siphons at times but they warm me whenever they come in a room. I'll be alone in the house, unless Luck comes home. This sudden, new lifestyle—I can't picture it. Maybe I'm meant to be alone.

Next, J.J. calls my folks. He talks to Mother. "Will you tell Luck?" he asks. Good, I think. She'll know how.

It's not long before Mother and Luck come. They both hug me at the same time. I back away and nearly fall onto the couch. Alone. Mother holds my hand, and she and J.J. talk in low voices about what a tragedy this is. Luck leans against my arm, but at some point, he drifts down the hallway to go sleep in his room. Watching his little back, I begin to sob. J.J. rests a hand on my shoulder. Mother sets a box of tissues in my lap. Alone.

J.J. leaves and Mother is asleep on the couch. I leave a note.

"Gone for a drive." I carry my boots to the carport. The sun is just beginning to rise.

I pass my parents' home. Ernie, a bucket of feed in his grip, stops as he crosses the corral to raise a hand in my direction. I lift mine in return. Ordinarily, we would ignore one another. I drive along the fence line and turn at a crossroad. At the low water crossing, I plan to stop and let go of the dam in my chest. I park in the swale and cut the engine. Shallow water stretches on each side of the crossing, remnants of a recent rain, a rain that fell when Cynthia was still alive.

My chest is tight, crushes my heart. I might get relief if I cry without an audience. I remember Luck in the car seat next to me after Lucy left ten years ago. So many times, we drove through this spot, waiting for the colic to pass. I can't form a coherent thought yet about Cynthia being gone. Every day, she loved me. Abby and Eliza—what will it be like for them? At least they have a decent father now, and I hope I can still play a part.

The trees that overhung the bank when Lucy left are bigger now. More boulders lie at the base of the cliff beside the creek bed. That's where I fell for Lucy. There was a layer to Lucy I could never see. Cynthia, even with her old secret, was an open book compared to Lucy. I bang a fist on the steering wheel at this ludicrous, capricious fate for Cynthia.

No tears come. It'll take more than a few good cries, too. The dam will have to crumble a little at a time. No choice but to give it time. In low gear, I climb to higher ground and drive home.

People show up Sunday afternoon. Pam answers the door and lists the visitors and the dishes they bring. J.J. shows them in to see the family. Guillermo, Charley, and Billy come. Billy cowboys on his own these days, and Charley's a successful hair stylist, of all things. Charley grips me in a tight bear-hug. He lets go just as I think I can't stand any more and says, "I'll come stay with you for a few days after the funeral, Wayne. You and Luck'll need some company."

"Thanks, Charley. That'd be nice."

Pam serves coffee and cake to people who come bringing more cake. It fills the empty hours of shock. Friends from both our churches, the coffee group, business buddies, ranch neighbors, high school pals—all traipse through Cynthia's parlor. Mother stays on. I pitch in to tidy the house on Monday morning, the beginning of my second day without Cynthia. Mother and Luck drive into town—people don't bring toilet paper to a sitting after a death. An excuse to get away. I drop a T-shirt into the hamper. The one I wore at the door when L.B. came on Saturday night. I'll take it to Goodwill. Never want to see it again.

Cynthia's blue nightshirt lies on top of the clothes in the hamper. Her shampoo scent lingers on her pillow, and on mine. Should I change the sheets or try to keep breathing her in a little longer? In her closet her perfume hovers. She's everywhere. A coffee mug in the dishwasher with her lipstick on the edge, a crescent moon of wine. A stack of stamped envelopes on the counter addressed in her writing. A wad of long, blond hair in her brush. Bottles of lotion and makeup on the bathroom vanity. Her rosewood piano. I sit on the piano bench and pick at the keys and cry. A bit of the dam crumbles.

I'm on the porch with Luck, Mother, and Ernie in the afternoon. We stare at the grass. Cynthia convinced it to grow. The accident made the front-page headline of The Echo. *It lies on the table next to me, under the junk mail. It tells the same story I got from L.B. and J.J. The other guy was traveling in the wrong lane with his lights off. He'd blasted through town and drew L.B.'s attention. The pickup was the subject of a BOLO. A deputy and highway patrol unit joined the chase. J.J. waited to intercept the fugitive at an intersection where Cynthia had recently passed. Then there was the hill and no way to avoid a collision.*

The newspaper included a tidbit I didn't know. The guy was carrying five kilograms of cocaine concealed in his wheel wells. The paper quoted L.B., and I have to say, he summed it up pretty well: "This is the most senseless tragedy I've seen. An unnecessary loss, all because a drug dealer was running from the law."

"So what have you heard from the insurance folks?" Ernie asks. He holds a fly swatter and takes a swing at the empty air. Leave it to Ernie to think of money.

"No, I haven't. I'm not worried. Jim Garvey called me and told me not to fret. He's setting a claim in motion."

"What about life insurance?" Ernie won't let it go.

"Cynthia's life insurance was with Jim, and so was the car

insurance. And he'll look into the other guy's coverage, too, or the company will." My voice shakes with extreme peeve.

"Ya know, it might cover what we've borrowed from the bank to do all the upgrades she wanted before she'd consent to move in here."

"Ernie!" Mother finally shuts him down. "Wayne's just lost his wife. Not a good time."

"No kidding," I say. "Anyway, I wanted the upgrades as much as she did." I don't tell him her ideas were fancier than mine.

Ernie's silence doesn't mean he concedes, only that he's being his usual self.

Luck says, "What about Abby and Eliza? Will they come back home?"

"I don't know, Luck. I'll ask them if they want to. But Leo's in charge. I'm not their legal guardian."

"Do I have to go to school tomorrow?"

"No, you won't have to go until after the funeral at the earliest."

"What about Abby and Eliza?"

"Leo's bringing them up Thursday. Would it be all right if Leo stays in your room? You can bunk with me or stay at your Gran's."

"I don't care." Luck shrugs.

"It's still your room," I say.

"I know."

Mother touches Luck's shoulder. "I imagine Leo will want his daughters to live with him, Luck."

For the first time, Luck cries.

"I feel bad," he says. "I'd started to hate Cynthia, and I wished she'd go away."

"That's okay, pard," I said. "I got impatient with her, too."

"You did?" Luck's eyebrows shoot up.

Mother and Ernie both lean in and wait for me to say more.

"When I met Cynthia, I thought she was the most beautiful woman I'd ever seen. She knocked me over. She was so . . . graceful and elegant."

"She didn't know how beautiful she was," Mother says.

"I agree. She was a good person, but she needed to be doing more and doing better, so she was always . . . ." I reached for words. "She always worried, like she might come up short," I say. "She tried so hard, she could be a pain in the ass sometimes."

Mother smiles, Luck's eyes widen, and Ernie cackles.

"I thought you loved her. You married her." Luck says.

"I do love her. Just because she was a pain in the ass doesn't mean I don't love her. Everyone can be a trial to their loved ones on occasion."

Mother nods, glancing at Ernie.

"She never liked me," Luck says.

"Yes, she did. You exhausted her with all your energy, but she loved you. I wouldn't've married her if she didn't like you."

"She was always making me do stuff. She made me go see a special doctor in Fort Worth so I'd be different."

"That was to help you," Mother says. "We told you."

"I know." Luck looks at Rufus and Redneck, whose tails thump against the porch. "The dogs miss Cynthia."

"Dawgs know when something bad has happened," Ernie says.

"I didn't want to live here anymore because she was always watching me and finding something wrong," Luck says.

"Too religious," Ernie says. "Too much Bible-poundin'."

Mother says, "She was nice about it, just more fervent and different beliefs about some things. But we loved her. She made a beautiful home, and she would do anything for any of us if there was ever a need. She was completely dedicated to her family."

"She loved me," I say.

Luck asks, "If Cynthia was so religious, how come God didn't protect her?"

I redden at the simple "you-do-this-you-get-that" notion. "I don't know, Luck, and neither does anyone else. And if you hear anyone say this was God's will for Cynthia to suddenly die like this, remind yourself they're full of crap."

Father Jones is due any minute. He married us, and now he'll preside over Cynthia's funeral. I'll make one musical request—the old hymn "Higher Ground." I'll ask Cheri to sing it and Annamarie to accompany. It would be a closed-coffin funeral, but I like the idea of a classy urn, her ashes on a pedestal at the front of the church, beside her beautiful portrait. If she's looking down on it all, she'll like it, too, even though she did once tell me she didn't belong on a pedestal.

NEARLY TWO YEARS *since Cynthia died. I feel like expanding my life beyond the safe trails I've stayed on. I have an idea, an urge to make a big gesture. It'll be better than a scrapbook left to mold in a storage room and be thrown into a rubbish pile by people who don't know me. It involves a familiar, old bridge. I want it placed in the pasture in front of my house, on the dry land. It's an old, rusty,1940s bridge from the county road that runs past the ranch. A memento of sorts.*

When the county commissioners approved the plan to put in a new bridge, the old one was slated for the scrap pile. I called Shirley Sylvester, our precinct commissioner and old family friend.

"Shirley, can I get y'all to save the bridge on my county road?"

"No, Wayne, no way. It hasn't been safe for years. It must be removed. It's way too late to campaign to save the old bridge."

"Whoa, Shirley! I guess I'm not being clear. I want *the old bridge. On my place."*

"Hell, no, Wayne. What are you going to do with it? Is it for the cows to cross the creek? They'd fall through and break a leg, and anyone driving over it would take a risk, especially after it's moved."

"I don't want to put it across the creek." Shirley drew a sharp breath, so I rushed to finish. "Hear me out, now. I don't

want it for practical use. I want to put it outside my front yard, across the front of my house. It might wind up being cheaper for the county to bring it to my place than to scrap it."

Shirley was so quiet, I finally said, "Hello? Did I lose you?"

"Not the connection, Wayne, but, yeah, you lost me. Let's see. You want the old bridge in front of your house. World's largest yard ornament."

"Yep." Lots of other features in places around the world could outstrip that bridge as the world's largest yard orna- ment. Versailles, Taj Mahal, just to name a couple.

"I'll have to see. . . If I do the research on this, you've gotta give me your word of honor you won't change your mind. You know, the wheels of bureaucracy grind slowly, but once they're started, it's hard to change directions."

Shirley agreed to arrange an impromptu meeting if needed. I was relieved she didn't write me off. My coffee group would have never let me finish. They'd have laughed me under the table. Maybe not Charley.

The bridge is my statement. Charley might get it, when he slows down enough to think about it. Vince would understand. Lucy would catch on, if she came around. But she's stayed away a few years—alive and well—that's all Luck and I know. Cynthia wouldn't get it, but the idea for the bridge would never have occurred to me if Cynthia were alive. If she were alive, I wouldn't be allowed to place it where it messed up the view of the house. Curb appeal in the country—not important now.

TWO LARGE CRANE *trucks trundled the forty tons of steel bridge along the road. After all the chugging and swearing, I get to enjoy the new view from my porch, my 2005 Christmas present to myself. I build up dirt ramps on each end, for light traffic. Charley humors me and drives over the bridge in his VW and stays a while.*

"Wayne, you're loony tunes. This is a whole new angle on hoarding."

"I'm not a hoarder," I say. I hand Charley a beer.

"It's such a great big thing, this bridge. I'm just saying it's kind of weird."

"I know. But come look at the view."

"There's no view in front with the bridge in the way."

"You'll see."

We climb the bridge's west ramp and sit, feet dangling into the tall weeds. My longneck serves as a pointer, sweeping along the horizon.

"Hmm." Charley gazes at the countryside. "Yeah, this is a better perspective than from the porch."

"Glad you see it. I drove back and forth on this bridge from the time I was big enough to see over the steering wheel."

"Yeah. You've made lots of trips on that road."

"I drove over this bridge bringing Luck home from the hospital in Midland. I got to thinking about stuff like that when I heard there was a new bridge going in."

"Lots of history."

"Yep. Lucy and Cynthia both drove over this bridge."

"Those were some good and bad old days, huh?"

The tall grass stirs, and Claude—he's as big as a bobcat—bounds toward us. "Vince will give me a hard time about this bridge."

"How's Vince?"

"Single—so he's good. We even get to talk to him when he comes. Elizabeth always did the talking."

"I remember. She could sure suck the air out of a room."

"I was settled in for life with Cynthia. I miss her every minute. Even Ernie had started to appreciate her."

"Yeah, she was a good lady." After a moment, Charley adds, "Ernie's not a bad guy."

"No, I guess not. Lots of folks hold him up. The quintessential cowboy. His admirers don't live with him, though. Mother set us an example of how to stay married, so both Vince and I stayed married until they left us in one way or another."

As the dark spreads from the eastern sky, Charley heads back to town. I'm not quite ready to make my way past the dry weeds in the front yard, so I linger.

I remember the aftermath of Cynthia's wreck. The sudden, eerie silence made the whir of the crickets and sounds like a calf bawling louder. Everything sounded sad, desolate. Vince wanted me to see a therapist.

I considered it—I thought I should be better, into the second year. I heard about the bridge. I like my bridge. From my porch, it blocks part of the horizon. I have to make a point of getting on the bridge to see it. Reminds me I don't know what lies ahead, but I'll get there. For now, I'll appreciate the view.

Lou

My father's sudden death changed everything. He planned to go fishing that day, but his buddy arrived at 6:00 AM to pick him up and instead found him crumpled on the driveway of our suburban Tulsa home. Doctors said it was a heart attack—a "widow-maker." He left a letter to the family with his will. It wasn't just goodbye—it was an info bomb—telling us about his other daughter named April. Never heard of her. And I'm thirty-six.

Pop wanted the family to find April if we could. He specifically asked me, good old Lou, the oldest, to get some money and a message to her. Mom, my brothers, and I might have let it go—no need to disturb someone who's gotten on with her life. But the investigator found hints that she needs our help. She lives in Sulfur Gap, Texas.

I sing an improvised song to cheer me up as I drive the highway to meet April for the first time. Every step toward meeting her has brought misgivings. As I approach Sulfur Gap and April, I turn to music for comfort. It's my natural drug of choice. My father was a drummer. He toured with some big names, especially country music stars, stayed on the road or lived part-time in Nashville, Vegas, or some other music hot spot. I'm a drummer, too, but I like to stay home, except for summer gigs. I'm a middle-school music teacher, following my mother's lead. Mom's an elementary music teacher, and together we waited for the times when Pop was home.

I drum a beat on the dash board and sing. These last forty miles into Sulfur Gap feel like the road to Hell—the one paved with good intentions. Longest forty miles in the universe.

When I learned April's address, I googled it and found a trailer park on the edge of a town I'd never heard of. Pop requested that I deliver $20,000 he'd left for her. April was suspicious—actually, she was paranoid, hearing from a total stranger claiming to have information she'd want to know.

A deer standing on the shoulder reminds me to slow down. I grip the wheel and stop drumming. I'm getting close to The Gap, as I've dubbed it. I sing another two verses of my song and drift into the closing.

Ba-dump-dump. Sulfur Gap city limits, population 2,365, according to the sign. No city in sight. The speed-limit changes to thirty-five. I brake as soon as I can react, but not soon enough. A light flickers on top of the Sandstone County sheriff's car sitting on the curve—a speed trap. A wide cowboy hat is silhouetted in the front windshield as he homes in on my bumper.

I pull over and watch in the side mirror as the Law ambles my way. He's a funny little man, willowy, with his thumbs in his belt and a comical swagger. This will be the first person I meet from Sulfur Gap, besides my telephone time with April.

"Good evenin', ma'am." He touches his hat brim. "You headed through town?" I can tell he's sucking in his skinny stomach. Maybe he doesn't meet many decent-looking women on this job, and I'll catch a break.

"Actually, I'm booked at the Navaho Inn for the night. I have some family business here."

"License, please."

I hand it over. He glances at my driver's license and makes a note on the back of his ticket book. Making sure I'm not a drug dealer coming to town, I guess, or smuggling Canadians into Texas. It would be Canadians since I'm coming from the north with Oklahoma plates.

He hands my stuff back. "No ticket today, Miss Trainer. Not a proper welcome to Sulfur Gap." He reaches into his shirt pocket. "Here's my card. If you need any help, just give me a call." He's an all-right guy. His card is black with gold lettering that says, "L.B. Sparks, Sandstone County Sheriff." He tips his hat again and turns back to his squad car.

"Thank you!" I say. As he walks away, he waves without turning.

In downtown Sulfur Gap, Main Street consists of several blocks of patchwork store fronts. Many of the buildings, made of big, limestone bricks, take me back a hundred years. A two-story court house dominates the town square.

This sweet little town, with Sheriff Sparks standing sentinel at the entrance, feels like a trip back in time, despite the late-model cars and pickups on the street. Time has slowed here, like Shangri-La. Beside the railroad tracks, a dark green railing guides my eye toward an old train depot. A big sign across the eave reads, "SANTA FE RR, Gap Branch. WELCOME TO SULFUR GAP." Another sign says the old depot is now a museum.

Across the tracks, the Navaho Inn and Restaurant looks respectable enough, with its fresh terra cotta and brown paint. I check in and haul my overnight bag up the breezeway stairs to my room. Not exactly four-star accommodations, more like a solid two. I toss my bag on a chair and flop on a surprisingly comfortable bed.

April expects me tomorrow morning at 10:00 a.m. I hope she'll let me in.

The first time I phoned her, I hardly introduced myself before she hung up. Okay, so she thinks I'm a telemarketer. I wrote a registered letter introducing myself and asking her to call me regarding some information about her family that she would be interested to hear. I waited ten days. No call, even though I got the delivery receipt. I called again.

When she finally answered, I dove right in. "Hi, April. Please don't hang up. I need to talk to you. I'm Lou Trainer, and I've been trying to get in touch. I don't blame you for being suspicious, but please, hear me out."

April breathed a whisper of cigarette smoke into the receiver. "Okay, then. Speak away, Lou Trainer. But don't be surprised if I hang up. I don't have anything worth conning me for, so if you've targeted me, I'm not a very good mark."

"No, April. It's nothing like that. My father was Darrell Trainer. You met him in Las Vegas when you were fourteen. Your parents had taken you with them to do some kind of mission work. Do you remember Mr. Trainer?"

"Maybe."

"He left a letter in his will. He and your mother were close in college. He left you some money. I know this sounds like bait, but please don't hang up. I'm no con. I'm a middle school music teacher in Tulsa, Oklahoma. I live with my mother. And I'm trying to carry out my father's last wishes." On this sentence, my voice broke.

"I don't like company."

"I'll stay in a motel and be out of your hair in no time. I was thinking I'd drive to Sulfur Gap, meet with you, and drive back home. It would be a two-day trip for me, but it'll take less than an hour of your day."

April agreed to see me, like she was bestowing a favor. Now, I call her again to let her know I'm in town at the Navaho. "I'll see you tomorrow at ten!"

"Okay," she says, resigned, and hangs up without a "goodbye" or a "thanks for coming." Not big on social skills. I don't begrudge the money she'll get, but I'm not keen to meet someone who likely won't give a damn that I'm her sister. I repeat to myself, to crowd out the misgivings, "I'm doing this for Pop."

I look in the bathroom mirror. Frazzled. I brush my hair and re-fasten the clip. I'll at least change into a fresh T-shirt for dinner, I decide, sure there's no dress code at the restaurant.

I GIVE my order to a skinny waitress with spikey pink hair. While I wait, Sheriff L.B. Sparks enters. In small towns, you bump into people you've recently seen somewhere else —like in the last hour. I'm not used to that, so my "yikes" alarm goes off. The sheriff lifts his head to see if it's me, sitting in a far booth. I nod, and he nods back and looks away. With a sigh of relief, I plow into my sandwich and give in to the tiredness of a long day's drive. As I leave, I look into my purse so I don't have to speak, and I skitter past the sheriff's table. In my room, the tension drains away, and I sleep.

A Sister... and a Nephew

I wake with a yen for a breakfast burrito and strong coffee. The thought of food blunts the fear of meeting April. More of a crowd in the restaurant this morning, with a sea of hats and caps of good-ol'-boy coffee groups. A group close to me is loud enough, I can hear the banter.

One guy says, "I hope you'll let me run a story in my column about buyin' that bridge, Wayne. It's a perfect story for 'Echoes from Stinky Holler.'"

I smile at the title of his column and the idea of someone buying a bridge. The "Stinky Holler" columnist says, "The story of a bridge for pasture decoration will entertain the readers." A few laughs ripple around the table.

A younger voice says, "He's just sentimental. It's been a tough couple of years for Wayne."

The newspaper guy says, "Oh, I'm not gonna give him too hard a time. I'll write that he'll need to move his house if that bridge attracts a creek." More laughs.

"Give it a rest, Don," another voice chimes in. "Charley's right. It's sentimental, and y'all don't deserve an explanation." That must be the Wayne guy talking. He's at the end corner of the table, blocked from my view.

A gravelly voice says, "Good thing Wayne's such an amiable guy, Don, or he'd be takin' exception to you makin' light of his collectible." Another heckler says something about Wayne being mighty young to have a dental problem. The men haw-haw at all the quips, but the subject wears thin.

As I stand to leave, I get a better look at the coffee drinkers. The Wayne guy, the one with the bridge, looks my way, and our eyes meet. He's handsome, in a wind- and sun-burned way, with bushy, auburn hair. We both look away.

To kill time before my ten o'clock meeting, I walk to the railroad museum in the next block. It's a tribute to local history. Pictures behind plexiglass tell the story of how a small settlement grew from a buffalo camp to a railroad stop. A large antique emporium sits at the corner past the railroad museum. The glass cases are full to bursting with old glass dishware, their sparkle dimmed by neighboring egg beaters and cast-iron gadgets of bygone days. The historical marker at the court house tells its story.

Nerves nibble at me as I load my bag in the pickup at the Navaho. The mobile home village, practically around the corner, is a mix of property owners settled on smaller streets branching off a central lane. Some homes are well-kept, with gardens and neat fences. Seedier homes sit further back. One of the last lots is April's place. It looks like an older unit with mismatched siding repairs. A face peeks out the window. At least I won't have to beat on the door. The door opens, and there stands my sister in a muumuu, an expanse of pleated tropical color. I take her hand and look into her drained, blue eyes. Pleasantries are not welcome. She stands aside and waves me in.

The reek of stale cigarettes and tar-drenched surroundings hits me. At the end of a short hallway, an open door reveals a bed piled with laundry. I know the odor of stale alcohol, since I've played drums in many a dive that stunk of spilled beer and old dishrag.

April lowers herself into a recliner and gestures toward a wobbly captain's chair beside the TV table separating us. "I'm sorry I was rude on the phone. I should have heard you out."

"That's okay. I understand." April looks haunted. Her apology took an effort. I feel less reluctant to be here.

"I don't have much to do with people these days," she says, as if she's ancient—waiting to die. She's only thirty-nine.

"I'm sorry, April. I wish we could have met under better circumstances. You'll see what I mean. I'll leave a copy of my father's letter for you to read."

"Well, give me the short version," April says, business-like, as if she's got a little spunk left. I wonder how life has beaten her down so.

"The short version is this. I'm your sister." I planned to be blunt, and it works.

Her puffy eyes widen. "My parents didn't have other children."

"Frank and Ann Bristow didn't, but Frank Bristow wasn't your real father." Not the time to mince words. "Your mother apparently married Frank Bristow around the time you were born, but my father is your father."

She considers my revelation. Her lips form the beginning of a smile. "Frank Bristow isn't my father?" She shakes her head. "All I can say is *hallelujah*. If this is true, it's . . . maybe the best news of my life." Tears form in her eyes. I grab a box of tissues on the breakfast bar, camouflaged amid sacks of snack food.

She presses several tissues to her face. I kneel on the floor beside her and put my hand on her arm. "Please don't string me along," she sniffles. "You don't seem like a cruel person."

"April, I'm not lying. Look at me. Don't I look like someone who could be your sister?"

"If I turned back the clock fifteen years or so, yes."

"You're still in there, April."

Another wave of tears comes, and I begin to worry about her blood pressure. She looks unhealthy enough that such startling news could be dangerous.

"Daddy—Frank—was a mean, self-centered S.O.B. Every year, he got meaner."

I tell her the name of our father—Darrell Trainer—and how he tried to find her after meeting her in Vegas and learning she was his daughter. But Frank and her mother disappeared, taking her. People were harder to find in the 80's than they are now.

She rubs her hands over her face. "So, he was my father. And they didn't tell me."

"Maybe Frank was afraid of losing you."

April looks beyond the dingy window. "All the moving we did while I was growing up was Frank disappearing. In fact, for the last twenty or so years, I haven't heard from him or my mother. They disappeared on *me*. Something happened to Mother, or she would have contacted me."

"Your mother must have been a good lady. I can't see Pop with someone who wasn't."

April nods. "I think Frank killed her. My biggest fear is that Frank will show up here. I even thought you might be in cahoots with him to work some sort of con on me. But meeting you now—you wouldn't be dealing with the likes of him. My mother was the last good woman he could work his way with."

I explain that Dad's letter tells how he'd lost touch

with his college girlfriend in Lubbock—she was pregnant and he never knew. A communication snafu thwarted any chances of finding her. He married my mother a couple of years later. He had learned about April when they met in Vegas, but he put off telling us. Who knows why? But I can't judge those who procrastinate. At thirty-six, I still live in my girlhood home.

April blots a few remaining tears. "One more reason to hope Frank rots in hell. He kept me from my real father. I'm sure my mother was miserable about it, but she would have had to stay quiet, for our safety." She shifts in her chair, lights a cigarette, and drags on it until the tip is bright coral. She looks like an unkempt sixty-year-old, with swollen fingers and gray-streaked hair.

"Do you have any children?"

She smiles. "Yes. I have a son in his early twenties. Charley. He's the only thing that keeps me going. He's got his barber's license, and he works at the Wild Hare Salon. He's so good, people come from all over to get him to cut their hair."

"Great! I'd love to meet him!"

"Oh, but please don't tell him who you are yet! I'm still taking this in."

"Okay." I'm not surprised. "Well, I could stop by the salon as I'm leaving town. I'd like to see your son, even if he doesn't know who I am."

"I can't stop you," she says, not happy. I'll have to

tread lightly. I hand her a cashier's check for $20,000. She sets it carefully next to her ashtray.

"Thank you, Lou," she says. "I'll put this money away for Charley. He'll be real surprised one day when he gets more from me than this broken-down trailer."

I tell her about my brothers, Ronnie and Dwight. She sighs. "I suppose they'll be wantin' to meet me, too?"

"Sure. They'll call. They have busy lives, but they'll be in touch." That's hard for April to accept. She thought she'd buried herself on the back lot of a trailer park. I'll tell my brothers what to expect. "If I write or call, you'll open the mail and won't hang up?"

"I'll try not to be twitchy. I'll call you, too, if I have any questions about this letter." She taps a finger on the back of her copy.

"You're welcome to come see me, but I'm probably moving to Alaska for a while."

"Well, seeing as how I haven't been out of the county in a couple of decades, I probably won't be making a road trip any time soon." She gestures toward a decrepit van sitting on the dirt drive.

I made plans for Alaska in knee-jerk mode after it dawned on me that I needed to live my own life. I automatically assumed having a life would entail moving far, far away from Tulsa. I hadn't counted on feeling drawn to Sulfur Gap, thought I'd put it behind me once I'd given April the money. My mission to find April and deliver the check is accomplished, but I sense there is so much more to April. We say good-bye, but I have an urge to meet Charley. The way April described him and the change in her face when the subject of her son came up pulls me toward the Wild Hare Salon. Maybe he'll take a walk-in client. I find the salon in the middle of a horseshoe-shaped row of shops I'd driven past on the way into town.

Inside, I ask a manicurist who seems to control the traffic if Charley is in, and if I can get a quick trim. "Sure," she says, "Let me catch his attention." She cups her hands to her mouth and yells toward the shampoo bowls. "Charley!!! You've got a walk-in!" She looks up at me and says, "Sorry. I'm the only PA system we've got. By the way, I'm Dorothy, the owner."

We shake hands. A tall, blond man with April's blue eyes walks toward us. In his early twenties, she said. No wonder April is proud. He's the one who keeps her trailer home from crumbling around her. He wears Wranglers and a white T-shirt with an open, short-sleeved snap-button shirt. His smile is disarming. I want to run at him and holler, "Hi, Charley! I'm your Aunt Lou!" But April put a muzzle on me. Dang.

"Hi, Charley, I heard you're a good stylist. I could use a trim."

"You're just in time. My next client isn't due for a half hour." He beams. He has to know the effect this has on women. Before I know it, I'm caped and he's running deft fingers through my hair.

"How about I spray on a little water and give you a damp cut?"

"Sure. You're the expert," I say.

We make small talk, and in no time, he's sweeping up a pile of my hair, now on the floor. My new layers are the most manageable style I've ever had. He blow-dries the dampness, blows the hair off my cape, and shakes it off before wadding it and throwing it into a hamper.

"That'll be thirty dollars," he says.

I can't get a haircut like this for less than eighty in Tulsa. "Quite a bargain," I say, adding a hefty tip.

I wave good-bye to Dorothy, and before the door falls shut, I hear a smart-ass toward the back. "Whoa, Charley! She's an out-of-towner!" Every decent-looking woman of any age probably gets vetted as a potential girlfriend by Charley's fellow hair stylists. Well, it's good to be considered in the running, even if I am his long-lost Auntie Lou.

On the sidewalk, a big man walks toward me. I scoot aside for him to pass, but he stops in front of me. He's wearing a western hat, not nearly as big as the sheriff's. I recognize his face from the diner.

"Hello there," he says, holding out a big hand. "I'm Wayne Cheadham. Are you new here or just passing through?"

Unaccustomed to the nosiness of strangers in small towns, I back up a step and clutch my purse. "I'm passing through." I don't take his hand.

"I saw you at the Navaho this morning." He nods toward the Wild Hare. "I'm stopping in to see my good buddy, Charley."

"Oh. I just met him."

"Good. Nice to see you again, even for a second. Hope you'll come back."

I feel guilty for my rudeness. "Sure, I'll be back. And I'm Lou Trainer, visiting from Tulsa." He's a good guy. Outgoing and down-to-earth. We shake. As I walk away, the rough, warm feel of his hand lingers in mine.

Escape from Alaska

I t took me three years to get back to Sulfur Gap. Echoes from my short visit there kept calling me. The evening I got back to Tulsa, Pop's old friend Wylie Spence called. I was pushing through the clothes in my closet, getting presentable to meet my boyfriend, Pete.

"You probably don't remember me, Lou," Wylie said. "We played together for a couple of weeks at a Juarez nightclub ten or so summers ago."

"I remember you, Wylie. How are you?"

"You're not going to believe this, but I live in Sulfur Gap now."

"You're kidding."

"Nope. I heard you'd come to town, wished I'd seen you. If you're ever this way again, let me know, and we'll round up some more players and give them what-for at

Sulfur Gap's hottest night spot."

"You heard I was in town?"

The small-town gossip mill brought news to Wylie that a lady named Lou stayed at the Navaho. Both Wylie and the Navaho owner and night manager, Dink Walford, were astounded to figure out that the lady was the Lou Trainer Wylie knew from the sawdust trail of nightclubs around Texas and Oklahoma. Wylie expressed his condolences about Pop. I told him I'd be back in town, that I was very interested in Sulfur Gap.

AND THEN I wound up in Alaska. My boyfriend, Pete, talked me into going. The good thing about it was it taught me I didn't have to stay in Tulsa. And I learned how to operate a construction crane. As Mom waved Pete and me toward security in the Tulsa airport, she wasn't forlorn, like I thought she'd be.

Pete secured a petroleum engineering job and I landed a secretarial job with an energy company's HR office. The fun of the bustling office began to pale after a couple of months of sitting on my butt at a desk. But it was a perfect way to see job openings.

Evenings, Pete's conversation centered on his work and how the higher-ups had their eyes on him. How had this jerk replaced the happy, sexy Pete I used to know? I kept my thoughts about Sulfur Gap to myself. I knew he would spew contempt at the idea. Not a place for the "up-and-coming."

As I perused job openings, I found an opportunity. My heart took wing with such energy, I realized I had been depressed.

"I'm going to work on the North Slope," I told Pete.

Pete spun and leaned against the kitchen counter, where he had been setting up his new prize—a pretentious Moccamaster coffeemaker worth over three hundred dollars. "Doing what?"

"Crane operator."

"But Lou, that's so *blue collar*."

"But Pete, it'll be fun. I've gotta get out of that office!"

Through a stiff smile, he said, "You'll come home a lot, I suppose."

He expected me to fold and come back soon—he couldn't see me doing something so *un-classy*. Before long, I was trained to move pipeline segments and unload heavy equipment from trucks. I flew back to Anchorage every month. Then every two months. Pete's priorities and mine were so different, the only reason we didn't fight constantly was that I was gone. At parties, he peered around the room to see who was looking at us. He had started to grouse about what I wore, even down to the toe ring.

One weekend, I watched him dress for some social-climbing function. I knew he didn't approve of the simple dress and shoes I'd donned—not chic enough.

Too big a feat to transition from the oil camp to a cocktail party thrown by moguls. Pete posed in front of the mirror and checked his cufflink, turning it just a hair to align it with the edge of his sleeve. Right then, I knew I'd leave.

Later, when I told him, he said, "You'll regret this for the rest of your life."

I said, "No, you will." And I rolled my luggage out the door. No point belaboring the obvious with someone who's oblivious.

"DON'T you come back here to keep me company, Lou." My mother was adamant when I told her I was leaving Pete. "I'm fine. Come only if you feel like Tulsa is calling."

What called me was Sulfur Gap.

April and I had kept in touch, superficially, as people do when they're beginning to become friends. We talked on the phone and shared a few old-fashioned letters. April didn't have a computer. She gave general information—it's hot in Sulfur Gap, everyone has allergies from the ragweed—nothing personal. On the phone, we discussed Pop's letter. She became less guarded and sullen as she learned she could trust me. Twenty thousand dollars helped, too.

Wylie and I planned to form a band and warm the

night life in The Gap. He told me about a great night club
—Hopper's. I'd make friends with Charley without
violating April's confidence. She hadn't told him—and I
didn't pressure her. It'd be easy to meet people if most
are as friendly as the Wayne guy.

I didn't expect the Hopper's gig to support me, so I
spent several weeks in Tulsa exploring my options. I was
looking for a small business when the Scissors 'n Such
Barber and Beauty Supply popped up on the radar. I
called the Sulfur Gap Chamber of Commerce to investigate. Brenda, a chatty woman with a small-town twang,
gave me the low-down. The current owner, Mo Jackson,
bless his heart, was struggling because he lacked the get-
up-and-go to keep the business afloat. "This could be a
goin' business if somebody'd pick it up before Mo
destroys it completely, poor feller," Brenda said.

I called Mo, and he gave me the sunny side of the
story but didn't shellac it too much. I asked for pictures
of his warehouse—a large storage building but with an
air conditioner, office, and bathroom. Records showed
inventory was down, as were orders.

My next quest was to find a place to live. Again,
Brenda was a godsend. "I know the place for you," she
said. "It's a few miles outside town—a farmhouse on
twenty acres, furnished. Hang on, and I'll give you the
landlord's number. Dick Raney. You'll like him."

Dick answered right away. "Yes, ma'am, the place is
available. The last tenants just moved out."

"Great, I'm pretty certain I'll be moving to Sulfur Gap."

"What brings you to these parts?"

"I'm buying the barber and beauty supply from Mo Jackson." I added, "Do you know Wylie Spence?"

"Sure, I do! He's a musician, hasn't lived here long. Don't know him well, but we got to talkin' one day over a bucket of bolts at the hardware store. Nice fella."

"That's Wylie. He was friends with my dad." I told Mr. Raney about my father and described my careers as a teacher and performing musician. I said I was single, childless, and not attached at the moment.

"Well, it sounds like you'll be fine. Hope you're not squeamish about mice. They sometimes try to move up in the world by moving in from the hayfield."

I assured him I'm not rodent phobic. I don't understand people who are. Now alligators and cockroaches—that's a different matter.

I'd move the last of March. My girlfriends wanted to party. They were winding up to have a shindig at Baxter's, with presents and a roasting. "No going-away gifts," I insisted. "I'm traveling light."

Once I had a plan, I called April.

"Hi, Lou," she said. She'd acquired a phone with caller ID, putting a toe into the new millennium.

"April, I'm moving to Sulfur Gap!" I'd told her I might. Still, her lack of enthusiasm was disappointing.

But she hadn't been enthusiastic about anything except Charley for the last two decades.

"When will you be here?" she asked in her steady monotone.

"End of the month." I filled her in on the details, and we were off the phone in our usual five minutes.

Keeping my expectations of April in check will be a challenge. Mainly, I don't expect her to turn over a new leaf because she has a sister in town. She's still keeping my existence a secret. My brothers—Ronnie and Dwight —and I have tutted about poor April, but we agree there's nothing we can do.

The Middleton Place--2008

The dirt road to the house runs for a quarter mile beside a pasture of hay stubble. Dick Raney's green pickup sits in front of the porch. A steep silver metal roof with attic dormers tops the white frame farmhouse, and tall windows on each side of the front door overlook the long porch and stubbly hay field. A massive live oak shades the south and west siding from the sun.

The front door opens as I step onto the wooden porch, my huaraches tapping a hollow beat. Behind the raised window sashes, gauzy curtains billow. A weather-beaten cowboy about Pop's age greets me with a grin and a huge, outstretched hand. He's got a broad Howdy Doody smile and hairline, but, unlike Howdy, his hair is gray.

"Hello-and-how-are-you!" he says, as one word.

"Great! So glad to meet you." I'm concerned mainly to see the house, to make sure it's not a dump. Brenda, my chatty Chamber of Commerce friend, would have told me if she knew any ill reports on the place, but Brenda can't know everything.

Mr. Raney and I make small-talk as he shows me around. There's a big parlor to the right of the front door, and behind that, a dining room and kitchen. A brass plaque high above the stove intrigues me.

"Dates it, huh?" Dick says, looking up. "That's where the stove flue used to be."

"Must be a hundred years old," I say.

"I left the flue cover in place there. Some of the older features needed to stay." He shows me across the hallway to a bathroom equipped with a claw-footed bathtub. There's probably a ghost or two here. I ask, "Who were the Middletons?"

"A family who lived here for several generations. The last old couple was alone—their kids all took off for Austin or Santa Fe. Both fell sick with pneumonia. When the doc phoned to check on them, there was no answer, so a sheriff's deputy checked. He found them both lying in bed—dead. Real sad for such decent people."

"The heirs sold you the land?"

"I only bought the house and twenty acres around it. Wish now I'd bought all the acreage. They're getting ready to drill for oil out there."

"Hindsight, huh?"

"Yep." He turns back to the kitchen, where lease papers lie on an oak table. He offers to make us a cup of coffee. The kitchen is stocked with what he calls "essentials," including an ordinary coffee-maker. Praise be.

He takes my deposit and hesitates. I'm ready to tell him to spit it out, whether it's a confession that the termites are close to bringing down the rafters or that a racoon family lives under the house. Finally, he says, "I'm no matchmaker, but could I introduce you to a friend?"

"Oh, Dick, I just got out of a long relationship. I'm not ready." Besides, how old is his "friend"?

"Let me know if you change your mind. He's a neighbor. Wayne Cheadham, a real good guy, about your age. Anyway, you'll cross paths with no help from me."

I remember the name because I've listed it in my mind the last couple of years as one of the five people I know in Sulfur Gap, along with Sheriff Sparks, Charley, Wiley, and April. I don't tell him Wayne and I have already met. Come to think of it, Dick was probably one of the hecklers teasing Wayne in the restaurant during my first visit to Sulfur Gap.

Dick waves goodbye and drives off into the sunset. I pile my meager belongings in the front room, dig out my cosmetic bag, fill the tub, and soak.

I'm spongy and relaxed when I hear scraping on the screen door, and hoarse howling. A dog might have a

person in tow, so I dry off, jump into my jeans, and pull
my nightshirt over my head.

I flip on the porch light to look out the window. The
tail-thumping and whimpering tell me it's a lone dog. A
skinny bird-dog mix backs away as I open the door. She
sits back on her haunches and raises her upper lip in the
best approximation of a smile a dog can muster. She
snuffles at my hand, saws her way past the screen door,
and circles to lie on the rug, as if it belongs to her.

If the previous tenants left her here, they deserve bad
karma, at least a lifetime of flat tires. A collar tag tells me
her name is Flo. Another tag is stamped with the phone
number for Harper's Veterinary.

She looks up at me with cinnamon eyes as I scratch
her ears.

"You must be thirsty, Flo."

Her toenails click as she follows me to the kitchen,
where I rummage to find a water bowl. While she
guzzles, I worry about her protruding ribs. She must
have been out for days, waiting for someone to come
back. A nearby creek holds spring rainwater, so she's not
completely dehydrated. But what to feed her?

She scratches at the cabinet door under the sink. I
open it to show her there's nothing there, but she noses
at the trash can. There's something behind it, and, lo and
behold, it's a bag of dog chow. Dick Raney might know
something about the dog.

An irritated female voice answers my call. It's only 8:30, hasn't been dark long, so surely, I didn't wake them.

"This is Lou Trainer."

"*And?*" she says.

"I'm your tenant. I have a question for Mr. Raney."

"What'd you say your name is?" She sounds suspicious, like she's protecting her husband from a stalking female.

"Lou Trainer. I drove in from Tulsa today, moved into your rent house, and now have a strange dog wanting to move in, too. It's a landlord issue, but I can ask you. Whose dog might it be? Is it permissible to keep the dog on the premises until we find the owner or a temporary home?"

I hear Dick Raney in the background. "Gimme the damn phone, Ida." He says, "Sorry, Lou. Ida thinks everyone is a telemarketer."

"Well, I don't blame her." I repeat my questions.

"Oh, it's Flo! My last tenants called and told me she ran off when they stopped at the gas station last week. They were leaving town."

Dick promises to call the owners so they'll know their retriever is retrieved. I'll call the vet and take her for a checkup tomorrow. But right now, I'm done in. I don't know what kind of sleeping arrangement Flo is used to, and, as if she reads my mind, she flops down on the mat against the back door.

Once I throw the sheets on the bed and turn in, I'm dead asleep.

A COLD NOSE in the palm of my hand wakes me. My eyes open to a high, plastered ceiling and light fixture from the 1920s. Flo shifts her eyes from my face to the front door, eyebrows in the worry position. I hit the floor to let her out. The last I see of her is the pads on her back feet as she disappears off the porch and around the side of the house.

Time to get moving. I'm supposed to meet Mo, and I have to unpack, rearrange, and make a list of what else I'll need. When they arrive via UPS, I'll set up my drums in the spare bedroom. Flo scratches at the front door. Inside, she leads me to the kitchen and stares at the dog food cabinet. It's eight o'clock sharp. This dog will serve as an alarm clock. I won't mind if she stays.

My phone rings. "I got ahold of Rhonda Farley," Dick says. "She's so relieved Flo's been found. Says it'll be a couple weeks before they can come from Odessa and get her. Do you want me to keep her at my house?"

"No, she'll probably make a beeline right back here. I found some food for her under the sink."

"Oh, I left that. Yeah, when she got loose, I took some dog chow to your house in case she showed up. I've done a drive-by every day to look for her."

I like the sound of *your house*. It's time I had *my house*. "She showed me where the food is."

"Great dog, that Flo. I'd keep her for myself, but Ida don't want no indoor dogs."

I ask Dick to give Rhonda Farley my number. I'm in a hurry, lots to do—take Flo to the vet, meet with Mo Jackson, and stock up at the supermarket. Flo's finished eating and now sits and stares at the wall above the stove. I follow her line of sight. She looks at the flue, tilting her head to one side. "Flo's lookin' at the flue, with Lou"—a little ditty of a tune starts to form in my head. "Well, all righty then. If that's what she wants to do." Another line. I wonder what's so fascinating about the flue. A chill runs over me. It might be a critter lurking behind the stamped brass. A bat. A giant cockroach.

I'm dressed and ready to go, and Flo still stares at the flue, her nostrils working like she smells something.

"Sorry to interrupt your reverie, girlfriend." I tug her collar toward the front door. I call the vet's office and talk to a friendly new voice--Shenika, the vet's assistant. I tell her I'm coming to town with a dog that has been out a while.

"Oh, is it Flo?"

Gosh, news travels fast in this town. "How'd you know?"

"Mr. Raney called a while back and said let him know if someone brought her in."

"I don't have a leash," I say.

"No problem. I'll meet you in front."

When I arrive, Shenika is waiting on the porch. Flo dances and whaps my arm with her tail as Shenika comes to the truck and opens the door.

"It's okay," she says. "She knows me. I kept her when the Farleys went out of town."

Small town. Everybody knows everybody's dog. Another song lurks in there.

A short-haired, thin woman in scrubs steps into the waiting room, protective glasses on top of her head. She peels off her plastic gloves and throws them into a trash can as she takes in the dog. "She's missed a few meals, looks like." She scratches Flo's ears. "I'm Andrea Harper," she says, holding my hand in a firm grip. In the exam room, she checks every orifice on the patient dog.

"Looks like those broken ribs are all healed nicely," she says.

"Broken ribs? Do you know what happened?"

"Her owner—Randy—said she got kicked by a donkey, but I think a person kicked her. I'm sure it wasn't Randy or Rhonda. But for some reason, Randy didn't want to name the real jackass."

After the exam, Flo rests on the table between us while we talk. I tell Andrea my usual spiel that I'm here to buy the barber and beauty supply from Mo and to play in a band with Wylie.

"I don't go to Hopper's as a rule—not big on dancing —but I'd love to hear your band. And you know, if you'd carry a line of pet products in your beauty supply, I'd open an account and start a dog grooming business. Shenika has the experience, and I've got the space."

With a clean bill of health, Flo and I drive away. The little warehouse where I meet Mo is on the edge of town, across from Wal-Mart and behind the VFW. Mo clings to his better days. Nothing gives that greenish cast quite like an anti-graying hair treatment. In his tiny office, he says, "Here, hon, you sit behind the desk. You'll be the boss from here on." I see why Brenda kept saying "bless his heart." He says, "Hon, you were a godsend, an absolute godsend. I haven't been keeping up, so you'll have to re-build the clientele. Brenda tells me she gave you the scoop."

Mo's shabby office boasts an early nineties computer capable of only dial-up internet. He says, "Computer comes with it, but it's awful slow. It has Lotus on it for bookkeeping."

"That's okay, Mo. I'll bring my laptop." I add a printer and wi-fi to my mental shopping list.

Mo and I make a date to meet at the law office in the afternoon. Flo waits like a good girl, so I decide I can make it to the United for more groceries, including dog food, and have her guard the pickup, windows cracked to let in the spring air.

Flo and the Flue

I could call Dick, but I don't want to be taken for a wimp. I've got my West Texas macho woman image to cultivate. While I put away groceries, Flo sat in the middle of the kitchen, staring at the flue. I walked around her, pantry to fridge, fridge to pantry, until she barked. A package of pasta flew out of my hand.

Maybe I should take a look.

The small barn smells of rotting tires and old dirt caked with tractor oil. A bare bulb hanging from the center beam lights the empty space. A step ladder leans against the far wall. Just right for checking the flue.

Back in the kitchen, I climb the ladder and step onto the stove-top. Flo watches. "Dial 9-1-1 if I fall and break my neck," I tell her. I'm ready to slide the cover over when it dawns on me that I'm unprotected. What if something jumps out? I climb down to grab a long barbecue fork from a hook beside the door. Holding the fork in stabbing position, I plant my feet on the stove top and listen for movement as again I push the brass disc aside. A one-inch opening appears, and two long, brown antennae flop out. I smack the wall with the back of the fork, hoping the giant roach belonging to the antennae will back off. No luck. The creature, at least four inches long, scuttles onto the wall. I swipe at it with the fork and knock it to the floor, where it lands with a thunk in front of Flo.

"Don't eat that!" I yell and jump down.

I skewer the mouse-sized insect. Flo and I run through the back door toward the burn pit, with flailing legs and antennae waving at the end of the fork. I stab it to pieces, rake dirt over it, and tamp it down with my foot.

"Aren't we a team?" I say as she trots beside me back to the house. "Lou and Flo's Organic Roach Disposal. No nasty chemicals."

I assume we've solved the mystery of what lies behind the flue cover, but no. Flo takes her position again and stares, her ears turned wrong-side out. I pray no passel of roach relatives wait to welcome me. Maybe I'll call an exterminator after all. Chemicals can be your friend, and the attic needs a good fogging.

No other life form ventures toward the opening, so I decide to take a closer look with a flashlight. My Mag light reveals a white object. It's a baggie full of . . . flour? Oh, shit.

"I guess you're a drug-sniffing dog, too," I tell Flo. This is a job for the local authorities, which will feature— be still my heart! —Sheriff Sparks! I call the sheriff's office. As a courtesy to my landlord, I notify Dick.

Ida answers in the same ill-tempered voice. She hands the phone to Dick, muttering something about "single lady tenants," communicating that I am a nuisance and not to be trusted with money, men, or maintenance of a rent house. Dick, on the other hand, perks up at the news.

Within fifteen minutes, here comes the sheriff, lights flashing on his cruiser, followed by another sheriff's car with two hats—Deputies Bill and Otis. In the kitchen, Bill steps up the ladder and plants his boots on the stove top to reach into the flue with a rubber-gloved hand. He draws the baggie out. I'm no longer a fan of charming old stove flues. I decide if I buy this place, the flue hole is getting plastered over. Old crap isn't necessarily special crap.

While the evidence is bagged, Sheriff Sparks and I catch up.

"Did I pull you over a few years ago?" He remembers both me and my little truck with the Oklahoma plates. He must have a lonely job.

"Yeah, thanks for not giving me a ticket."

"What brings you back to Sulfur Gap?" His poker

face gives no clues. Is this a social or an investigative question?

"I liked the town. I found a business to buy here."

He nods, says, "Uh-huh," ruling me out as a new drug distributor in town.

I explain about Flo's appearance on the porch the night before when I was settling in and her barking at the flue today. "She was the previous tenant's dog. Do you suppose someone trained her to sniff drugs?"

"Could be. I doubt the Farleys will be back to fetch her. This baggie-full is probably part of a stash Randy left. Flo must have watched him put it there. As much as we followed him and waited for an excuse to search this place, we never could bust Randy. He's probably in trouble with his bosses if he left this here."

Dick Raney steps into the kitchen. "I let myself in, Lou." We update Dick on the situation. He already knew Randy was a suspected drug trafficker, small-time. Dick was relieved when the Farleys gave notice they were moving to Odessa. "Sorry I didn't tell you, Lou, but I didn't want to scare you off. Didn't think it'd matter."

My line is supposed to be, "That's okay, Dick," but it's not okay. I'm pretty steamed.

Sheriff Sparks decides to check the rest of the house and the barn. Although I tell him the kitchen is the only place Flo's gone on alert, he takes her into every room to see if she finds something. I'm not thrilled about Sheriff Sparks lifting my mattress and checking the dresser and wardrobe. My undies and sundries are in disarray. Finally, we slide the barn door open to the scuttle of mice. Bill climbs the rudimentary wooden ladder to search the loft.

All that's left is the attic. On the screened-in porch, Sheriff Sparks removes his hat and gear belt, balances on the step ladder now straddling the washer and dryer lids, and crawls through the panel access. Dick and the deputies steady the ladder. The sheriff does the honors because he weighs at least a hundred pounds less than either deputy. There's got to be a good Aggie-type joke somewhere in this scene. What does it take to get Sheriff L.B. up a ladder? Two fat deputies and a jolly rancher. Ha-ha.

While the sheriff tromps around the attic, there's a knock on the porch door. A big cowboy peers through the screen.

"Everything all right in here?"

"Hey, Wayne!" Dick opens the door like it's his house and invites Wayne in. Dick doesn't miss a beat. "Wayne, I'd like you to meet my new tenant, Lou. Lou, this is Wayne, the one I was telling you about."

Wayne shakes my hand. "Oh, we've met before," he says.

I remember the warm, dry grip. "Yeah, I came through town a few years ago. How can we help you?" My tone is pointed. While I'm flattered both Wayne and L.B. remember me, I'm put out because my house has become Grand Central, with four big men crowded on my back porch. And I'm pissed that Dick is so tickled to play matchmaker. A baggie of cocaine in the flue makes me a mite testy.

Wayne says, "I stopped by when I saw the cruisers and Dick's truck. Thought I'd see if there's any way I can help."

I decide to be nice. "Oh, well thanks. I guess you're a neighbor?"

"Yep. A few miles that way." He jerks his thumb in a northerly direction.

Boots drop back through the attic opening. The support staff goes back to supporting, and the sheriff's down. I give him a wad of paper towels for the sweat pouring down his forehead. He glances at Deputy Otis's belly, and I read his thoughts regarding Otis's uselessness for accessing tight spaces.

"Nothing I can see up there, unless it's under the insulation. It's undisturbed, though, so I'm satisfied." Sparks buckles his war-on-crime equipment back on and grabs his hat. He eyes Wayne. "What's up, Wayne?"

"Just thought I'd see if you need any help here, L.B." Wayne's mouth twitches. I know a subtle heckler when I see one.

"We're just doing our regular jobs."

Wayne smiles disarmingly. "Good to know the county's safe."

L.B. forgets about Wayne for the moment. "Otis, go

get the preliminaries done on the evidence and call the DPS and the DEA. We have something big here." He looks at Wayne pointedly, inviting him to leave.

I throw in an olive branch. "Wayne, it was nice to see you. And thanks for stopping."

"You bet, Lou. Give me a shout any time, and welcome to Sandstone County." He hands me a card with a windmill logo. Then he's gone. I slip the card into my back pocket.

L.B. turns to Dick and me. "We think Randy can help us bust a good-sized ring of distributors."

I glance at the wall clock. "Oops! I've got a three-thirty appointment to close a business deal. I'd better skedaddle." Dick promises to lock up for me.

I'd hoped to dress more professionally, but the jeans and T-shirt I've been wearing all day to run errands, round up roaches, and search for hidden drugs will have to do. I'd rather be on time, even if it means failing to impress Mo and the lawyer, Wallace Derby, with my wardrobe.

Yesterday, I met Wallace Derby—a cute man, with a boyish face and thick salt-and-pepper hair, nicely cut. Although his law degree requires that he be subtler than a wolf-whistling construction worker, his once-over prompted me to reach for my hand sanitizer. Charley must cut Wallace's hair, it's so pretty. The office manager would be beautiful if Charley got hold of her hairdo. She did the stiletto heel walk into the office to shuffle papers at Wallace's little conference table, where we signed documents and exchanged checks, and I left as the owner of a beauty supply business.

Today I'm armed with a client list from Mo, an inventory of stock, and a strong but fluttering heart as I enter Entrepreneur World. I pat my doggie good-bye and set out for my first official day of work. In town, I park my red pickup next to the little warehouse. Mo gave me his magnetized business sign to snap on my truck door. I need to think of another name. "Scissors 'n Such" is a bit Betty Boop for me.

I'll install a do-it-yourself alarm and monitor it from my cell phone. If Sulfur Gap is a stopping point on the drug pipeline, I shouldn't assume it won't touch me. And, since one dealer recently lived at my house, I'll put an alarm there, too.

At Mo's old gothic desk, I call April. "I'm glad you're moved in," she says, actually sounding chipper. "Come by to see me any time but Wednesday night. That's when Charley comes."

"April, you know I can't dodge Charley indefinitely. One of us will have to tell him sooner or later. I want him to know I'm his aunt."

"I know. I'm trying to find the right time."

The "right time" should have arrived in the last three years, so I myself will have to find the right time. I say, "April, I'll see Charley often. I might beat you to the punch on telling him."

"Okay." She's resigned. Knowing my resolve, she can gird herself for whatever can of worms she thinks will fly open when he learns about the rest of the family. We make a lunch date at her house tomorrow. I'll take the sandwiches.

Now that I've resolved to tell Charley who I am at the first opportunity, the immediate task is to call clients. I'll start filling orders and stop by to introduce myself. The Wild Hare, where Charley works, is the biggest salon in Sulfur Gap. When Dorothy answers, I don't mention our previous meeting since I don't want to answer questions.

"Oh! I'm so relieved!" she says, thrilled to learn I've taken on Mo's business. "Let me ask all my stylists and see who needs what. I'll call you right back."

I have as much luck with the other shops in the area. I'm doing so well, I google the salons in Big Spring, narrowing the targets to privately-owned ones in the busiest locations. I make several new connections. Not having any sales experience, unless you count selling music appreciation to seventh and eighth graders, I'm doing all right. Andrea Harper's idea for a line of pet products sends me on another avenue of research, and I call some veterinarians.

Dorothy calls back with orders from her stylists. I have everything in stock. One item, though, I'll definitely have to order. Charley Bristow, my unsuspecting nephew, needs a new pair of precision scissors, a specific brand. I gather all the deliveries I can make today and begin rounds. I'll enjoy setting my own schedule, rather than being ruled by the tyranny of the school bell, with a new group of students filing in every fifty-five minutes. But I'll miss those funny kids, always testing the boundaries and telling silly jokes to see my reaction. As in the following exchange with a funny seventh-grader:

"Ms. Trainer?"

"Yes?"

"What did Beethoven leave on his piano stool?"

"I don't know. What?" I play along, even though I know the punch line.

"His fifth movement!" The kids break out in giggles and groans, while I keep a poker face that makes them laugh harder. Seventh-graders are so easily entertained.

My cell rings as I drive to the Wild Hare. It's Wylie, making sure we're still on for band practice at his house. "If I can bring my dog. She's home alone all day."

At the Wild Hare, Dorothy occupies her usual perch inside the salon door. She knows who I am by the box I'm wagging. "Hi, Lou! You can drop the box in the break room, and I'll collect your money if you want to run some other errands and stop back by."

I haul the box to the back. On my way, I see Charley intently working on a client. He looks up and nods absently. Vicky and Bethany both lean over a shampoo bowl, studying someone's botched color treatment. "We'll have to use ketchup and have her sit a while with her hair wrapped in plastic," Vicky says.

Loretta's voice carries from behind her partition, where she's giving a massage. "Honey, you've got as many knots as a Boy Scout jamboree." I wave good-bye to Dorothy, who looks like she's trying to remember when we've met before, and I head for Stripes to get gas. I remember the story about Flo running away when the Farleys stopped in town for gas, and again I wonder what spooked her into leaving her owners behind.

Flo stands on the porch and wags her whole body when she sees me driving up the lane. As I settle in with a plate of spaghetti and marinara, my phone lights up. Sheriff Sparks.

"Lou? This is Sheriff Sparks, uh, L.B. You can call me L.B. It's short for Larry Bob. Some folks that went to grade school with me still call me that, heh, heh."

"All righty, then," I say. "You're L.B. to me. How can I help you, L.B.?"

"My deputy tells me that when the Odessa sheriff's department paid the Farleys a visit at their most recent address, they'd already cleared out."

"Oh?" I glance at Flo. If the Farleys are in the wind, it could mean she's really my dog. Hooray! But L.B. has more news.

"Randy Farley probably got cross-ways with some pretty bad people. He thought he'd move out of their reach, and now he's moved again. Or that's the theory of the moment."

"Was he about to be arrested?"

"Yes, his fingerprints are all over that bag of cocaine, and there's no way he got wind that we have his stash— we've kept it out of the news—so we think it's his drug dealer friends he's running from. I'm telling you this because you should keep your doors and windows locked. Do you have a gun?"

"God, no. I don't like guns. I do have an aluminum baseball bat that I keep under the bed."

"So, you don't like guns, but you could bludgeon a person with a bat?" He chuckles.

"Well, I'm also a master-level black belt in Taekwondo. That counts as a weapon."

He quits laughing. "No kidding? How'd you get into it?"

I'm peeved that he drew me into bragging about my status in martial arts. "There are lots of martial arts gyms in Tulsa. I've been practicing since my teens. We had a Taekwondo club in high school."

"So, if an intruder comes in your house, you can *really* kick them out?"

Okay, he's making light again. "You bet your ass I can. Unless they know Taekwondo better than I do. But I would have the element of surprise, followed by the ambulance—and you sheriff guys." The banana peel of pride lies on my path, so I shut up.

"Well, I'd still feel better if you had a gun. You need one, living out in the country. It'd be hard to deal with a rattlesnake using Taekwondo."

"Ah, but for the snake, I have Taekwon-*hoe*."

L.B. sings falsetto when he laughs. "Okay, then. Keep your guard up. Those dealers Randy Farley is avoiding might circle back to check out his old premises. They're a nasty bunch. You might consider moving into town."

Well, shit. It's been a few days, and I'm getting settled in. We had drug dealers next door to us in Tulsa, even in a nice neighborhood. They got themselves wrapped up in the penal system and were gone before long, just as Mom and I predicted, but we still installed an alarm system. "I'll give it some thought, and thanks for the heads-up. Keep me posted!" And I end the conversation. "Gotta run. I've got a date." I'm referring to my jam session with Wylie and friends.

As Flo and I begin to drive away to Wylie's, the sunset spreads pink across the sky. I'm grateful for the security light that spills a yellow glow on the front of the house. What a painting it would make. Tonight, I'll leave the porch light on, too. I don't want to wonder what's lurking in the dark when I come home. With that thought, I dash back in and turn on a light in every room.

WYLIE'S simple brick and frame house is what you'd expect of a veteran bachelor—crooked Venetian blinds and the most basic of landscaping—a few skinny little bushes against the house and a poor excuse for a yard. Wylie has a so-so set of drums assembled in his living room for practice. He's the lead guitar and vocalist. He introduces me to Forrest, bass guitarist ("Forrest the guitarist" makes me think of a song, or at least a limerick — "There once was a fellow named Forrest"). Chad is the fiddler. We make a list of oldies from 1940 to 2000 that we can play and sing with our eyes shut, and we cross out a few because they're too slow to dance to, unless you're playing an assisted living gig. Lance, who'll play rhythm, steel, and acoustic guitar, arrives and adds a couple songs. We'll add more current hits later.

Driving home, I feel invigorated. As soon as I turn onto the hayfield road, I can tell something's amiss. I ease closer, the house looks dimmer—some of the inside lights have been turned off. I turn off my headlights and coast further. Flo begins a low growl. I hold up a finger to shush her, and she whimpers. I park the truck in the hay field. No sign of a vehicle in front of the house. I tell Flo to stay in the truck and run past the big oak to circle beyond the edge of the light and to the back. Through the screened-in porch and kitchen windows, I see a man walk through my kitchen. I pull my phone from my pocket and call the 911 dispatcher, and I wait.

The man crawls onto the stove-top and shoves his arm as far into the flue as he can. Satisfied the stove flue won't yield his sought-after baggie-full, he carries a kitchen chair out to the screened-in porch and tries to get into the attic, but he can't make it without a ladder. He leaves the chair perched on the washer and wanders back into the kitchen. Headlight beams swing across the big oak's high branches, and rocks ping as squad cars speed down the lane. Now, along with the sound of the County Mounties arriving, Flo howls and yelps her muted protest at being trapped in the pickup. When officers barge through the front door, the man slithering around my kitchen bolts out the back. He crosses the porch, smashes through the screen door, jumps over the steps, and runs straight toward me. He can't see me until he's practically on me. He lowers a shoulder as if he's going to tackle me, but I give him a side-kick to the jaw that connects perfectly. He's down, flat on his face. L.B. bounds out the back door, his gun drawn. I yell, "Don't shoot, L.B.! It's Lou!" He runs toward my voice, gun ready, and spots us—me waving my arms and the burglar in a heap on the ground.

The sheriff turns the groaning intruder while holding the gun on him. "Randy! What the hell?"

Randy Farley.

Otis and L.B. decide Farley is in good enough condition to be cuffed and escorted to a waiting patrol car. Farley protests, "I'm looking for a gold bracelet Rhonda thinks she left here. I was running toward that tall gal, and something hit me from the side."

I jog down the road to retrieve my pickup and dog, who has almost lost her mind. She licks my cheek frantically as we drive to the house. "Sorry, Flo, I didn't want you to get hurt, girl." I put an arm around her.

Inside, L.B. once again searches the premises. Farley

had turned off the bathroom light, probably from habit. He'd left the commode seat up after taking a whiz, also from habit. Some men never learn. He'd parked his car on a narrow road through the field behind me, and he closed the gate behind him like a good citizen while he proceeded to burgle my house.

"L.B., thanks for getting here so soon," I say. "Farley tripped and fell."

"And he *landed* on his jaw?"

"I dunno." Farley doesn't know what hit him, so he can't contradict me. L.B. doesn't believe me, but what's he going to do? I don't want tales getting around about me taking Farley down. He might have nasty friends.

"Do you think Farley's business associates will want to follow up?" I ask.

"They might. If they've got a shred of sense, they'll lay low. Anyhow, I'm going to keep you out of the report. I'll say a suspicious person was seen entering your house and Randy Farley was arrested, motive unknown. No one has to know you're involved."

"Thanks. I don't want to make the front page of the local news."

"Oh, and here's your key. Farley made a spare, thinking he might need to get back in. It's a good thing. Your front door stayed intact through it all."

Thank you, Saint Francis. I don't have to get the door fixed.

L.B. has paperwork to finish, so he says goodnight. I

lock the doors, pull down the shades, and pat the bed for Flo to join me. I need company.

Wayne's card seems to glow on my dresser. I'm tempted to call him, just to have a friend to tell about what happened tonight.

M y neck of the prairie has calmed down. Farley sits in the county jail, unable to make bail. I have no clue if he's giving information to bust up a wider ring of drug traffickers. But when one bunch of losers goes away, others take their place—a never-ending line of applicants for a career in drug distribution and sales. Farley's arrest was big news in *The Echo*, but, as L.B. promised, I wasn't mentioned. Looks like I won't have to go into the witness protection program after all.

My security system is installed and working. When I tested the alarm, Flo howled. If it goes off at night, I'll shoot out of bed with enough adrenalin to punch out a platoon.

April takes more pride in her mobile home these days. When I brought lunch one day, an old vacuum cleaner stood in the corner. She said, "I'm trying to be a better housekeeper now that I'm having company." The next time I visited, the ratty area rug was gone. The house smelled better.

I tell her about my run-in with the druggie side of Sulfur Gap. I know she's not telling anyone, and it's an entertaining story, so I don't leave anything out. I tell her about the baggie in the flue and Farley being in my house when I came home one night. She says, "There's always been lots of drugs coming through town because it's a good stop-off coming from Mexico, with the Interstate close by." April learned the seedy details from patrons in the know when she worked as a waitress at Hopper's and the VFW.

I tell her about Wayne peering through the screen door when the cops were there. She lights up when I mention his name. "Wayne is such a nice guy. He took Charley under his wing when he was eight." She tells me how he's been a faithful friend and mentor to Charley ever since. "The saddest thing that happened to Wayne involved the damn drug traffickers," she says. "He had this nice, pretty wife. I didn't know her, but he showed me her picture. I didn't go to the wedding." Of course not, I think. April was honing her hermit skills then. "I hated what happened," she says, and reaches for her cigarettes. She tells me it's been almost five years since Wayne's wife was killed in a head-on collision with a drug trafficker who was being chased by a deputy, a highway patrolman, and a game warden. She was coming home from a trip to San Angelo.

"How sad," I say. "Well, as the Bible says, the world is full of tribulation." I sigh, thinking there's really nothing to say about something so awful.

April laughs. "That's so funny you would quote the Bible. Cynthia was a big-time Bible-thumper. She was a nice enough person, but Charley told me she always said 'praise Jesus' and knew Bible quotes for all occasions. By the time Charley went off to barber school, he'd started avoiding her. She seemed to think he was trying to seduce her older daughter."

"Oh, she had children?" If I had a daughter, I'd keep an eye on Charley, too. Just as a precaution. His intentions might be good, but the daughter's might not.

"Yes, two, from a previous marriage. They went back to live with their dad in Angelo. When his wife died, Wayne lost three family members—her and the two girls."

Tragic. A nice, friendly guy with enough mischief to poke at L.B. A friend to Charley. He's single, and Dick wants us to get to know each other. Something to think about.

BUSINESS IS BOOMING. It's been fun meeting the salon people as I make my rounds. The band has played twice at Hopper's, and Brady Hopper, the owner, has convinced us to play every night but Sunday. We agree, but we make it clear we're busy people and won't be able to sustain the schedule indefinitely.

I'm setting up my drums tonight. They arrived unscathed, and I'll keep them at the club as long as we're the only band playing. I'm adjusting my stool when I see Charley and another guy walk through the door. Holy moly, it's Wayne. He makes a beeline for Dick Raney at the bar. They're in a heated but friendly discussion while Charley moseys around the pool tables. Finally, Charley and Wayne sit near the dance floor while we're testing the mics. Charley's grinning and talking, and Wayne's about to fall out of his chair, laughing. Wayne looks more closely at the bandstand, sits up straighter when he recognizes me, and holds up a hand. I wave back.

We play our first set. There's a nice crowd tonight. It's Ladies' Night, and the word is out about the live band. Brady Hopper took out a quarter page ad in the *Echo* about a live band with "seasoned" players. Most of the town regard Hopper's as a low-key place to dance and connect with friends. There's a relaxed, friendly vibe, and it's big enough for Brady to triple the clientele. That's why he paid our fee. Wylie, Forrest, Chad, Lance, and I don't play for peanuts.

The dance floor stays full through the first set. Dick Raney dances past the bandstand with Dorothy and nods at me. I'm not surprised Ida isn't here. I've known married men who relax at nightclubs with no evil intentions, purely for the amiable company.

During the break, I decide now is a good time to reacquaint myself with Charley and Wayne. On the way back from the restroom, I stop and introduce myself. Charley has a fuzzy look, trying to figure out how he knows me. He's slow on the draw, but Wayne jumps up and offers his hand.

"Remember me? Wayne Cheadham? And this here is Charley Bristow."

He pulls out a chair, and I sit down. A cute brunette passes the table with an eye on Charley. Looks like I'm spoiling his chances for now. Too bad, Charley. You'll have to settle for me at the moment. April told me Charley has already been in two ridiculous marriages that ended badly. Everyone thinks Charley is interesting, charming—downright adorable. Besides personal charm, he's got crazy good skills, and not just at cutting hair. He could play pool professionally but doesn't want the pressure, and he's known for swirling the women around the floor when they need a dance partner.

Wayne and I begin a getting-to-know you chat that Charley can't resist joining, even though he's sulking about missing his shot with the brunette. I mention I've been working in Alaska the past three years, most of it as a crane operator for pipeline projects. Charley tilts his head, taking it all in.

"Aren't you the new beauty supply lady? I saw you at the shop a while back."

"Yep. That's me—and you cut my hair when I came through town three years ago."

"Okay," he says, dim recognition lighting his eyes.

"I was here on business back then."

"I remember," Wayne says. "Wish you'd stayed long enough for everyone to get to know you."

I'm not sure how to respond, but Wayne knows a good exit line when he's said one.

"Well, I've got an early day tomorrow, so I'll have to say good night. Nice to see you, Lou. Are you coming, Charles?"

Charley doesn't want to go home yet. He's lonely. "I'll give you a ride, Charley," I say. He's reluctant to accept. Surely, he doesn't think I'm hitting on him.

As the band plays on, Charley and the cute little brunette dance. Good for them. After a dance or two, he leaves her on a bar stool so he can join his pals at the pool table. After the last song, I set my hat on my stool.

Charley follows me to my little red pickup. "Nice," he says, admiring my leather seats.

We pull onto the highway beside Hopper's, and a George Strait song plays over the pickup's sound system. It's "The Chair." The lyrics tell about a guy who picks up a girl at a bar and takes her home. Charley looks wide-eyed, and I assure him I didn't rig that song to play now. I'm about to assure him I'm not hitting on him, but he starts this mock helpless routine about not knowing if he should feel safe. I pull a serious face. "You shouldn't," I say. He's alarmed, so I laugh. He really doesn't know what to do with me, poor baby.

I've got to find a time—and soon—to tell him we're relatives. He's a bit surprised when I drop him off at the stairs of his apartment. Ay, yi, yi. He thought I might come upstairs. As he's about to close the car door, I lean across the seat and say, "Hey, if you come back to Hopper's to hear us play, I'm not gonna think you're in love." He laughs—fake, to cover his awkwardness. Charley, Charley. I shake my head and drive away.

I drive back across town and get home as quickly as possible. Flo stays in the house these days when I'm gone. She might try to be a guard dog and take on a drug salesman who's come to investigate that damn stove flue.

Dick Raney Plays Cupid

My phone rings during breakfast.

It's Dick Raney. "Hi, Lou. Good to see you at Hopper's last night. Your band is great!"

"It's not my band, Dick."

"People think it is. You're the one they watch."

Oh, please. "Well, thanks, Dick. What's up with you?"

"Just checking to see how Flo's settling in."

"She's good. It's like she's always been my dog." I know this is just a preliminary. Dick called for some other reason. So, I wait.

"Good! That dog deserves someone steady. I read where Farley was arrested. The story was vague on the details. Sounded like he tried to break into the Middleton place."

"Something like that. I wasn't home, though."

"Good. I never heard who called the sheriff's office."

"Me either." He must have something else on his mind. Again, I wait him out.

Finally, he says, "Looks like you and Wayne were hitting it off during your break."

Just as I thought. More matchmaking. "He's a nice guy. Charley, too. He's a beauty supply customer."

"Great guys. That Wayne, he's a real good person. Salt o' the earth." He advertises for his friend. "But he plays it too safe. He's dated a time or two lately, but those women backed him into a corner. Wayne's last wife died in a bad car wreck five years ago."

"His *last* wife? How many times has he been married?" Dick is not helping at all.

"Only twice. First wife left him and their new baby at the hospital."

I draw a sharp breath at the thought. What an awful way to become a parent. "That's a terrible thing to have happen. Why did she leave?"

"Word is, she didn't want to be a mother, and she took off to Austin to further her career. No telling about Lucy—that's her name. After Wayne helped put her through school all the way to a Masters' degree."

Boy, he really knows how to pick 'em. Deserters and Bible-pounders. "Bad luck with women, huh?" But no one can know what a person might become. I think of Pete.

"You bet. Charley's had some bad experiences, too. It's time both of em's luck changed. That's why I'd like to encourage you and Wayne to at least have coffee. Can I give him your number?"

"He seems nice enough. If you'd told me his history before I met him, I wouldn't want to touch him with a ten-foot pole." Snake-bit, poor guy. And we do keep running into one another. Kismet, maybe. He's a gentleman, and he looks . . . warm. Like cinnamon toast. Coffee won't hurt a thing. "Okay, give him my number. And I have his card. Maybe one of us will get around to calling the other."

Now I have to get going. Deliveries. Calls. More research on the pet product line. Andrea and Shenika want to become Sulfur Gap's first bona fide dog grooming business.

Time for local deliveries—Billy's—the barber—and Gladys's, Maude's, and Kitty's—run by ladies who work from converted garages. And I'll drop off Charley's new precision scissors at the Wild Hare. I leave the motor running in the truck to make a quick stop, and I see the outline of Charley's head, looking out the plate glass window at me. I make a beeline for his station. He's got this silly grin, like he's got a wise remark ready, but I plunk his scissors on the counter in front of him. He's confused, poor thing. Thought I was stalking him.

"Here's the scissors you ordered. Cash or credit?"

"Can I get it to you later?" he asks, after a bit of brain-searching.

"Hmmm." I don't want to get taken advantage of in my young business career. But it's Charley. "Okay," I say. "I know where you live." This last remark raises a collective eyebrow over the entire salon. The Selective Hearing God tuned in just in time for me to broadcast my statement. I skedaddle and leave Charley to deal with it. Dorothy, her nail polish brush poised in mid-air, is waiting for the door to close behind me as I leave so she can question Charley.

I've got to tell him soon, so we can let the town know we're *related*.

THE ROAD to Sprocket doesn't have shoulders or a center stripe. Mile after mile of plowed fields push up next to the narrow pavement. Out here, the land is so flat, only the curve of the earth keeps me from seeing the next town. The road sign says "Sprocket, pop. 867." Where are they all?

An intersection with a caution light and four-way stop forms the hub for a post office, a small-scale truck stop, and a cotton gin. A stucco building housing a shop with an open yard full of lawn decorations tempts me to forget everything and shop. Ironwork trellises and benches built to withstand all kinds of wind and weather are so unique in their craftsmanship, they're probably from a local metalworker. Across the street a tire store features tractor and truck tires. Beside that is the Hairport.

I park in front, with its red-lettered sign and red-striped wind sock. I'm surprised at the hum inside the small salon. All four stylists are busy, trying not to bump butts and elbows.

"You must be Lou!" a woman with white, huge hair yells. The stylists crowd around me.

Soon I'm on to Matilda. The state prison, with its guard towers, razor wire, and searchlights, dominates a cotton field about five miles from town. At the town stoplight—a stoplight gives Matilda a leg up on Sprocket (another song?)—the prospects are cheerier. The Main Street vibe buzzes more than in Sprocket. There are a couple of blocks' worth of small businesses and agencies serving the prison employees, oil field workers, farmers, and ranchers. The Wind and Waves hums with hair dryers, clippers, and chatter. Here, I'm shown the same hospitality I found at the Hairport.

On to Briargrove. It's larger than Sulfur Gap, even though The Gap is the county seat. Blocks and blocks of Victorian rooftops of old homes rise over the flat roofs of businesses. Cute Cuts is quiet, maybe experiencing a lull, so I assume there'll be time for a friendly visit. Three stylists gather at the front counter while I distribute supplies and shake limp hands. A fourth woman advances from a back room. She's gorgeous but sullen, stylishly dressed, about my age. My efforts at conversation fall flat, while her cohorts hover behind her, listening for what's coming, the way people do when a fight is brewing.

I would walk out in a heartbeat, but I'm trying to establish a business connection in a tightly-knit community, and I have to tolerate whatever bullshit comes my way—for now, at least. Bridgette, the dour one, finally throws a punch. "I heard you're also working Hopper's." She says it like I'm a prostitute, "working" Times Square.

"I play in a band there," I say. "It's for fun, more than anything. You all should all come over some night. Bring dates, husbands."

"I've *been* to Hopper's. We all have."

"Hmmm. Sounds as though it's not your kind of place." I keep my eyes on Bridgette but sense rising discomfort among the other women. Feet shuffle, someone clears her throat.

"It depends on who's playing," she snaps.

Good exit line for me, but I want to discover why the automatic hatred.

"Have you worked here long?" I ask. "I just arrived in Sulfur Gap a couple of weeks ago." My pleasant demeanor is insincere, and they know it. I've subconsciously widened my stance, and my invoice book and purse sit on the counter, leaving my hands free. That's

what half a lifetime of studying self-defense will get you
—readiness. Only twice in my life have I needed it, once
to defend my purse from a snatcher on the midway of
the State Fair, and once to convince my date that I was
NOT signaling I wanted sex.

"I've lived in Sandstone County all my life. And I
own this salon." She reminds me of a yapping dog.

I look at the other women. "Have y'all been here as
long as Bridgette?" They take turns muttering about
their tenure.

"I heard you were with Wayne Cheadham." Bridgette
lobs this little hand grenade, a full load of resentment
attached. My change of subject has not worked. We're
back to Hopper's.

"What do you mean by 'with'?"

She's thrown off. Her mouth draws down. "You
know what I mean."

"Actually, Bridgette, I don't. I visited during the
break with Charley, my old friend. He was *with* Wayne,
and I visited *with* both of them."

"Consider Wayne off-limits."

"If I happen to run into Wayne, I'll ask *him* about it," I
say with a wide smile.

Bridgette reddens. "Yeah. We'll see."

As I turn to leave, the others let out a collective sigh. I
can't imagine Wayne hooked up with this banshee. I
haven't made any friends at Cute Cuts, but I don't care.
On to Shear Heaven, where I find the atmosphere happy

and the walk-ins steady. Bridgette can drive to Lubbock for her supplies, for all I care.

Down the road, I spend a couple of hours visiting shops and distributing brochures in Big Spring. Heading back to the Gap, I decide to take Flo for an outing to the warehouse.

Flo waits inside the front door. She gets an ear-scratching and runs outside to take care of business. We load up and head to Stripes. While I gas up, Flo begins to bark in an odd, vicious tone. She's looking at a large, red-bearded man with a canvas sailor cap, sitting inside at a booth next to the window, eating a burrito. When I open the passenger door to calm her down, she bolts past me and bounds past the pumps and around the corner of the building, out of sight, looking at the man and barking the whole way. I wave at him and shrug hopelessly about my dog, but he levels a blank stare at me. Okay, so we won't make friends over a wacky pup. I sprint after Flo, but she's already across the highway and leaving the far side of Hopper's empty parking lot. She drops out of sight into the bar ditch, headed back home.

I forget about cleaning my bug-spattered windshield. Following Flo's route, I catch up and slow to thirty. That's how fast she's running. I tap the horn and slow to reach the passenger door for her. She jumps in.

"What is up with you?" When I start to make a U-turn, she yelps a protest, so I turn back instead, toward home. She stands on point in the seat, and when we arrive at each turnoff, she might as well be a compass, pointing the way. Back at the house, she jumps out and circles the place, sniffing the ground and finally sitting on the front porch. She plants her butt with a finality that says, "I'm staying here."

Maybe I can wait until tomorrow to go to the warehouse. I'm pretty tired, after all. And I can sleep in peace with the newly-installed alarm system.

Getting a Few Things Straight

C harley hasn't appeared at Hopper's since last week, so at lunch, I ask April about it.
"Has Charley given up pool?"
"I dunno. Why?"
"He hasn't been into the nightclub in a week."
"He's not a fount of information with me," April says, between bites of her chicken salad sandwich. After some thought, she says, "Charley has car trouble. He and Wayne brought my groceries Saturday and said they're going to Briargrove this week to find Charley a used car he can afford."

Later, I'm at the hardware store getting some new cabinet pulls for the bathroom, and I almost bump into Wayne on the plumbing aisle. We exchange pleasantries and I tell him about my busy schedule.

"Do you ever get a day off?" he asks.

"I can give myself a day off anytime. But right now, I take off Saturday and Sunday but play Saturday night."

"Maybe we can grab some coffee when you have down time."

My hesitation shows, so I decide to come out with it. "I would like that, but I ran into someone who hates the idea."

Wayne tilts his head for a half second. "That 'someone' wouldn't be named Bridgette, would she?"

"Yeah."

"Well, I stopped seeing Bridgette after a few dates. And that was almost a year ago. But she thinks I'll come to my senses."

"She wants to help you along with that by threatening the new girls in town."

"I'm sorry. But there's not much I can do about Bridgette until some guy comes along and sweeps her off her feet. It's only a matter of time."

I change the subject. "How's Charley? I haven't seen him lately except in passing at the Wild Hare."

Wayne looks a bit stricken but recovers quickly. Oh, hell, he thinks I'm *romantically* interested in Charley. Well, shit.

Wayne says, "Charley's great. He's slowing down and using his head more these days. He and I are going car shopping tomorrow so he can quit bumming rides and jogging everywhere."

"What's he looking for?"

"A Jaguar, but he can only afford a very used Chevy. He's never realistic about his finances. Keeps him in hock."

"At least you haven't given up on him."

"Never. The feller has potential. And he'll owe me one." Wayne's smile is evil. "He knows nothing about buying cars, so he can pay me back for my expert advice by helping clean my tack room on Monday."

"You drive a hard bargain, Wayne."

We carry the last part of the conversation to the register, where a woman who should be retired and enjoying grandkids checks us out. Scanning our items, she listens to our conversation and stares at me when she gets a chance.

"Thanks, Melba," Wayne says. "Melba, this is Lou. She's new in town."

I shake hands with Melba, whose curiosity makes her stand on tiptoe behind the counter.

In the parking lot, Wayne says, "Well, we're busted. Melba is Bridgette's cousin." We laugh and wave as we drive away in different directions, me to my self-appointed office hours, and Wayne back to his ranch to fix a toilet.

I MISS work at Hopper's Friday. Wylie and Forrest got food poisoning. We blame it on fundraiser tamales from

Briargrove. Without the lead singer and guitarist, and the bass player, the rest of us don't want to take our chances with unfamiliar fill-ins. Wylie finds a band to sub, and we get a break. I put up a porch swing last weekend. Always wanted one of those, but I never lived anywhere with a good porch. Flo and I sit and listen to the crickets. Very few times in my life have I seen as many stars as on nights at the Middleton place. I'm glad to be here, even with the brush with Randy Farley.

When Wylie and Forrest feel better, we meet to practice Toby Keith and Sara Evans songs on Saturday afternoon. Wylie wants me to sing as much as possible Saturday night. The new songs are a hit. The crowd goes nuts when we play "Get Drunk and Be Somebody." During the first set, I see Charley across the nightclub several times, and he's either playing pool or dancing with that cute brunette. Wylie tells me during the break that her name's Darla Buchanan, that he knows her stepfather, and that he's given her a ride to the club tonight. Toward closing time, Charley and Darla practically dance their way out the exit. I wonder if Charley is losing his head rather than using it tonight. Not my business.

I hatch a plan. I need to go to Lubbock on Monday to pick up supplies, so I'll get Charley to go with me and take the used Buick I heard he got last week. Road time is a good time to talk.

On Monday morning, I jolt him awake with a phone call. "Get off your butt, Charley. I need you to drive me to Lubbock in your new, used car."

"What?" His voice is full of sleep, as his hamster wheel brain gears up. Maybe too many wheels run at the same time.

"I'll be there in thirty minutes. You're in 207, right? Tell Wayne you're not available to clean the tack room today."

"Okay." Poor guy didn't have a chance.

On the road to Lubbock, I explore his car. I can't believe what good shape it's in. Not a dot of wear and tear on the velour seats. With Charley's permission, I nose into the glove compartment, where I find a small manila envelope containing a cassette tape labeled "'Skylark,' by Hoagy Carmichael."

"I love this song," I say as I slip the cassette into the player. "I'm impressed the previous owner had a theme song for the car."

We listen to the song for miles as it repeats. I love old jazz ballads, and I get lost in listening, until I realize Charley is barely breathing. I'm about to ask if he wants to pull over, but he slows beside the caprock's scenic overlook. The song must've gotten to him. My ears are still popping from the quick climb up to the high shelf of land that will carry us on to

Lubbock. In the parking area, he stops the car and stares ahead.

I say, "Let's get out and enjoy the view."

Charley moves to the lookout point like a robot. That song certainly flung him into a stupor. It was about longing for love. Not within his usual listening genre, it probably took him by surprise with its wistful loneliness. For me, it would be like the first time I saw the ballad "Memory" performed on Broadway. I had to stifle a sob. I was with Pete, and he would have ridiculed me for becoming maudlin over a song by a soprano in a cat suit.

It's hard on Charley, showing his buttered side like this. I wait a few minutes, enjoying the strong breeze and the view of a horizon fifty miles away. He's loosening up. It's wild how I can pick up his physical cues that resemble those of my father. Now might be a good time to tell him I'm his aunt.

As an introduction, I say, "Charley, I need to tell you something. When I was here three years ago, I came in for a haircut. Remember, I told you?"

"Yeah."

"Well, I came to Sulfur Gap to see your mother."

He comes to full attention. Mention his mother, and Charley goes on alert. While he recovers from the shock of the "Skylark" song, I ramble about how impressed I was with the way he turned out and how I've thought about him the last three years. I say I want us to be the best of friends, but I have to stop. His silly look puts me

off course—a raised eyebrow and the wrong kind of
twinkle in those blue eyes, followed by some smart aleck
remarks that don't bear repeating. So, I tell him his
mother and I are close, which slows his pulse a bit.

Then, the presumptuous twit says, "You know, Darla
and I have sort of started something."

I want to sock him right there. But I give him a good
lecture. "Listen, Mister. All women who are interested in
you aren't trying to get you in the sack." I cite Dorothy as
an example. Charley's concerned I've heard the bad
scoop on him, but I reassure him. "Everyone loves you,
Charley. Some folks think the right woman is all you
need. But I think it's looking for Miss Right that's gotten
you into hot water. Don't rush, and don't look at everyone, including me, as a potential partner."

He doesn't grasp my words, because he baits me
about maybe we could have a little fling. Scalawag. He
doesn't mean it, but, boy, does he need a lesson in
etiquette. I have to shut him up.

"Charley, I'm your aunt," I say. And that knocks the
wind right out of him.

I might have to drive. But he pulls his shock together
by the time we walk back to the car. Once on the road, he
glances at me with his trademark grin and says, "You've
got some 'splainin' to do, Lou-sie."

Charley's smartass attitude fades and we have a
genuine conversation. I'm glad he's able to be real and
not always "good-time Charley." He tells me about how

he grew up—about losing his stepdad when he was five, his mother waitressing at bars, and her retreat into oblivion. Other than having the trailer house roof over his head and food and clothing mostly available, he raised himself after his stepfather died, with the encouragement and support of Wayne and his family.

One Christmas day when he was eight, he went to the Cheadhams' with a little friend whose grandfather worked on the ranch. He felt a kinship with Wayne. April's boyfriends kept Charley on nervous alert, but by the time he left for barber college she'd settled in for a stretch of isolation and depression—the state she was in when I first visited three years ago.

After the Lubbock errands, we settle into a booth at Denny's where we spend the next couple of hours. I read him the letter my dad wrote, explaining he was April's father. I tell him how I picked up the trail of April in Sulfur Gap and came to see her and give her the $20,000 check my dad left. Meeting Charley is my bonus.

Charley's dumbfounded. "Darrell Trainer, a pro drummer, a Vietnam vet, and a family man. He was my grandfather?"

"Yes, and your mother would have had a much better life if she hadn't gotten separated from him."

"And Mom has known this for three years?"

I've dreaded Charley's realization that he was excluded from this news. He is rightfully pissed.

We drive back to the Gap, drained by revelations,

with scattered conversation filling in more of the past. When we reach Charley's apartment, he drops me off at my truck, unloads my beauty supplies, and zooms off to April's for the Big Confrontation.

I've done my part, and now it's time for April to do hers.

As I get back into my truck, a car creeps by. Pressed to the window of a late-model Toyota Camry is the hateful face of Bridgette. And she is steadily shooting the finger. I smile and wave at her and climb into my pickup, where I double over with laughter. Here I am, relieved to have Charley embarking on his journey toward self-knowledge, and here comes Bridgette, so outrageous, such a slice of cat-hissing life. Maybe she heard from Melba. And with my car at Charley's apartment all day, what other gossip might I have started?

Well, I'm not pussy-footing around Bridgette. I whip out my cell phone and call Wayne, glad I slipped his card into my purse. We'll get this message out: Lou Trainer talks to whomever she pleases.

"How about coffee?" I ask when Wayne answers.

"When?"

"Now."

"Sure. Meet you at the Navaho in fifteen?"

"You are on, Mister."

I'M disappointed Bridgette isn't at the Navaho, but the number of cars indicates someone who knows Bridgette surely lurks inside. Since I'm swimming in Denny's coffee from the afternoon spent with Charley, I decide one more cup won't hurt. Wayne and I are by God gonna have coffee.

True to his word, Wayne arrives in fifteen minutes. We make small talk about the warming spring weather, our jobs, and the rising prices on the Navaho's menu. Wayne is the first to confront the question that hangs between us.

"You want to tell me what's up? Your voice was calm, but your call seemed sort of last-minute and urgent. Something I need to know about Charley?"

Boy howdy, is there ever, but I want to let that ride for now, even if Wayne is confused by a possible romantic connection between me and Charley.

"No, it's not Charley. He's fine. I was spurred to call you when Bridgette rolled by me in her car, middle finger extended my way. She must have heard from Melba."

Wayne throws back his head and laughs. "Oh, so you're making a point! It's a good thing I parked next to your truck. Maybe she'll get the message."

"Yep, Briargrove Bridgette doesn't dictate who I have coffee with. How'd you wind up dating her, anyway? You seem like too nice a guy."

"That's my problem, Lou. I'm too nice. And I get lonely."

"I understand that."

"I've been married twice."

"Dick told me."

"Figures. Knowing Dick, he was probably unnecessarily hard on both of them."

"That's what friends are for."

"My first wife left me. She signed off of motherhood and me at the same time."

"How old's the child?" I'll stick to statistics for now, even though I'm intrigued.

"Fifteen in November. Name's Luck."

"Interesting name."

"Have you been married?"

"No. I was too busy minding someone else's business."

"How's that?"

"I kept thinking Pop would retire, Mom wouldn't be alone so much, and *then* I'd find a serious relationship. I didn't realize the rut I was building. Then Pop did retire, but he died. Boom. Plan foiled."

"Sorry about your dad. So, you were trying to take care of your mom?"

"I used it as an excuse not to date anyone serious. My motives were muddled. Like now."

"What about now?"

"I like you. Asking you for coffee wasn't just to make a point with your evil ex-girlfriend."

At this, Wayne's eyes warm and his cheeks redden. "Well, thank you. I like you, too."

"We'll have to do this again when we get a chance."

"Agreed."

We walk to our cars together and give each other a sideways hug.

"Ladies'" Night . . . Supposedly

Fighting Bridgette was not on my to-do list. Work had settled into a rhythm, with time for April, playing at Hopper's, and planning a garden. All the good dirt in front of my house called for at least a corner devoted to a garden. I rented a small tractor and hauled it on a trailer Dick loaned me. "Put up an electric fence, or the racoons will eat you out of a crop," Brenda advised, so I went to the lumber yard and bought the materials. I tilled up a good space, and I'll get Charley to help with the fence.

Tonight, the crowd is thick at Hopper's. Spring fills the air, and folks feel feisty, ready to dance, drink, and enjoy the fellowship of others who want to stop taking life seriously for a while. We're playing through our repertoire, and I'm singing "I Was Country When Country Wasn't Cool." The row of sillies at the bar sing along—Sandy from the bank, Brenda from the Chamber, and Dorothy, Vicky, and Loretta from the Wild Hare. They're not bad singers, really. Some night I'll invite them up for backup.

Then who should dance right in front of the bandstand but Bridgette, shooting eye-daggers at me? At least she's keeping her middle finger out of it while she gives me the stink-eye. I've sung through worse distractions than this, like the time a lady slipped on the dance floor and her skirt slid up to reveal, from the view provided by sheer panty hose, that "she" was a "he." That was in Minnesota. I don't think anyone would try to pull that off around here without giving advance notice.

Bridgette's with a decent-looking guy—tall, with neatly-cropped gray hair. He's holding her too tight to be a relative. I can't begin to guess the logic of her jealousy over Wayne while she's out dancing in full frontal contact with her date.

At the break, the band guys and I stand outside in the parking lot to shoot bull until it's time for round two. Here she comes. The guys back away when they see her, thinking we have some female bonding to do and proving what poor judges of body language they are. Bridgette stomps toward me, fists doubled at her sides. We should outgrow these things by the end of junior high. But here she is, trying to scare me.

She yells, "I told you Wayne was off-limits." Her raggedy, enraged voice gets the guys' attention.

Wylie is the first one to my side. "Hey, lady, let's calm down," he says.

"Don't worry, Wylie, she just needs to get something out of her system," I say.

"I'm gonna beat something outa *your* system!" she screams.

I wave back Wylie and the other guys.

"I can handle this." I have no intention of laying a finger on Bridgette, or allowing her to touch me.

"Oh, so that's what you think? You think you can handle *me*?"

"Yes. I think you should back off." I use the facial expression and tone of voice that caused many a middle-schooler to quake. But she's at the stage of drunkenness when, to her mind, she's bullet-proof. And *where* is her dance partner?

"And why would I back off?"

"It would be better if you did."

"Well, fuck you!"

She pulls way back before launching her fist at my face. I step aside, and her momentum propels her past me. She catches herself, stays in a crouch, and prepares to lunge. The word's out: Girl fight in the parking lot. Here come Dick, Dorothy, Loretta, Vicky, Sandy, Brenda, and a few other regulars, cell phones out. I don't look long enough to determine if they're taking pictures or calling L.B. I have to keep my eye on this crazed woman. I spin away from her next lunge and trip her as she staggers by. She splays out on the gravel but rises to her hands and knees, cursing and waving off her handsome date who has appeared to help her. Once up, she throws several more punches. I dodge them. I hear some people saying, "Come on, Bridgette, stop this." She's out of her mind, though. If she remembers this tomorrow, she might decide to check into rehab.

An unmistakable wash of red light from a patrol car lights the scene, silhouetting the onlookers. That was fast, but the sheriff's office *is* around the corner.

It's Otis. He hauls Bridgette up and cuffs and stuffs her in the back of the squad car. Her gentleman friend heads for his jeep without looking back.

"Otis, I don't want to press charges. Do you have to do this? It was all bluster, she didn't hurt me," I say. Bridgette sags against her seatbelt, shoulders heaving as she sobs.

"I'm arresting her for public intoxication," Otis says.

Brenda reaches me first. "Lou, this is a disgrace! I hope you don't think this is a regular thing in Sulfur Gap. Remember, she's from *Briargrove*."

Sandy, Dorothy, Vicky, and Loretta say, "Oh, Lou, this is awful. Just awful." "I don't know what's gotten into her. She hasn't always acted this way." "There's no excuse." They're all trying to soothe my ruffled feathers. And then I realize. I've got a group of girlfriends. They love me.

The guys are focused on the logistics. Dick says, "Boy

howdy, she would've broken your nose if you hadn't dodged."

Wylie marvels at the way I tripped her. "How'd you do that?" they ask, in one voice.

"I know some self-defense techniques," I say.

Break's over, time to get the dancing revived, a welcome change of pace to get my band guys to quit gawking at me. A beginner could have managed that fight. For the rest of the night, my chorus at the bar sings along extra loud. Despite Bridgette, I'm happy. These days, a spark flickers in April's eyes. My charming nephew Charley's maturing. And Wayne. The possibility calls to me.

Coffee, Anyone?

The middle of the Navaho's dining room is our meeting place. Six or seven of us squeeze around a table for four. April will join us someday.

Brenda and Dorothy know everything happening in town. They chatter about plans for the upcoming celebration of the hundredth anniversary of the railroad in Sulfur Gap. Idle for decades, it was refurbished a few years ago to answer the wind energy demand. A couple of slow-moving trains pass through each week, transporting wind turbine blades that look like wings for experimental aircraft. The railroad festival will bring carnival rides, civic and church group booths, food vendors, and street sales by the Main Street and Court Street merchants.

Later, I'm busy with warehouse work when Wayne calls.

"Lou, Dick told me about Bridgette's attack last night. Are you alright?"

"I wouldn't call it an attack. It was more like her losing her mind and everyone else watching."

"Dick said you're pretty good with the evasive maneuvers."

"Yeah, I am. Don't like to get punched." To change the subject, I say, "Let's have coffee."

"You're on."

By mid-afternoon, I'm back at the Navaho having coffee with Wayne. I might have to use the Dairy Barn sometimes, or people will think I've got a problem. We don't even talk about Bridgette. My phone rings. It's Charley, wanting to talk to me when I come by the salon. Wayne has cows to feed, and I have some deliveries, so we give each other a hug and a pat and promise to be in touch.

CHARLEY and I walk down Main Street toward the courthouse. He wants my advice. Darla's father doesn't like him, he thinks, and he doesn't know what to do.

I give him a pep talk and remind him, "Such an independent young woman as Darla isn't apt to let her father's opinion of you—whatever it is—get in the way."

Charley feels better. I love being Auntie Lou.

"Let's go get some coffee," he says.

"That'd be great, Nephew, but my kidneys need a break. How about tomorrow?"

"Okay," he says. "I've got more to tell you. You'll like it."

AT 8:00 a.m. the next morning, I'm at my "office" in the Navaho, waiting for Charley, when L.B. walks in. He stops at my table.

"I hear you did okay with Bridgette trying to break your face."

"Yes, I have a black belt in dodging."

"She's lucky she didn't fall on something mysterious and get knocked out." He moves on as Charley joins me.

"What's up, Charley?"

"You know how I raced to Mom's when we got back from Lubbock?"

"Yeah. You were spinning your tires."

"Well, I told her I would have liked to know about this family. I always wanted to know who my real dad was. She said I might as well know. He was this kid she went out with in high school when she was at the Girls' Home in Briargrove. He went off to college, and she stayed in the area, had me, and married my stepdad."

"What's his name?"

"I'll find out later." He brushes the question aside. "Anyway, what stopped me in my tracks was Mom saying my real dad came back to Briargrove a couple years ago, so I'll be able to meet him."

I'm excited. "Don't put it off! I'm the poster kid for wasting time." I tell him how I've put a chunk of my own life on hold, sitting on a fence with a good view and nothing to do. Another song. "How's Darla?" I ask, before the notes form in my head.

He updates me, and I pat his hand. "Good to see you holding off on the marriage proposal."

"She's a career woman. We both have goals to reach."

"In the meantime, have fun."

As we're leaving, I remember. "Oh, Charley. I need some help."

"What with?"

"What do you know about fences?"

We make a date to work on the garden.

Fence Project
Rescue

C harley shows up Sunday morning. He surveys my proposed garden project and shakes his head.

"Uh-uh, won't work."

"What? Why?" I can't believe he's torpedoing my plans.

"You can't keep animals out with just an electrified wire strung on some stakes."

"Then what do you suggest?"

"A six-foot chain link fence, fortified with the electrified wire."

"My God, this garden will put out some mighty expensive produce."

"Yep. But you could make your money back if you set up a vegetable stand by the highway." He stops to see if I catch the joke.

"Like I need another job." I punch his arm.

Charley and I hop in my truck, swing by Dick's to borrow his trailer again, and proceed to the John Deere outlet to rent a power auger to attach to the tractor. On to the lumber yard, I buy posts, concrete mix, chain link, a gate, and other hardware to construct a respectable fence.

Back at my place, Charley takes off his shirt and stuffs his jeans into his work boots. I'm wearing work boots, too, with cut-offs and a tank top. After we slather on sun screen, we go to work, me drilling the holes for the fence posts, and Charlie shoveling and pushing dirt.

We break for lunch. While we relax before the next round—the serious business of hand-mixing concrete to pour into the post holes—my phone chimes. It's Wayne.

"Hey, Lou," he says. "Do you want to go to Big Spring or Abilene for a movie tonight?"

"I'd love to, but you need to give a girl more advance notice. I'm working on a project."

"Okay. How about next Sunday?"

"Sure," I say. "Charley's here, waving hello to you. He's giving me advice on a fence for my garden."

"Charley's a good hand."

"It's turned into a bigger project than I thought. You're welcome to come help. Charley would love it, too. We're out of our depth."

"I'll bring Luck."

"Yes, we need all the luck we can get."

"Well, that, and also, my son, Luck. He'll come."

"Good, I'd like to meet him."

Charley and I drive stakes to mark the plot. I'm less and less thrilled about the idea of a raccoon-proof fence, if such a thing exists. Wayne's truck turns up the lane. He stops under the oak tree, and he and Luck walk toward us. The sight of these two fills me with confidence and relief. Charley's no slouch, but Wayne—fences are a big part of his daily life. I am awed by Luck's height and dramatic features. He's only fifteen, and as tall as Wayne. He's so slim, he'd have to hold out his arms to feel the wind. Despite the slender build, he looks like he can do a bit of work. His hands are huge and strong, like Wayne's. Both wear work clothes—light-weight cotton shirts, faded jeans, and steel-toed boots. Cavalry to the rescue.

"Hi, Lou. I'm Luck," he says, pumping my hand. "Dad tells me you need a fence. And I need some Brownie points, according to him." He throws an eye-roll at Wayne.

"I'm calling in some favors." Wayne rests an arm on Luck's shoulders.

"When I get a chance, I'll owe you a few home-cooked dinners." I can't think of a better way to show my appreciation.

Wayne decides we should pile into his truck and drive to the creek for rock. He says we need a small-rock mix in the post holes first, and he knows a good spot to find it. The pickup sways over the ruts. We reach a low water crossing, and he backs the truck down to the creek bed, where piles of small rocks have collected against the bank. Wayne pulls two shovels out of his big tool box behind the cab and hands one to Charley. I stand aside with Luck, and we supervise—or heckle.

Back at the garden plot and a few sweaty hours later, twelve aligned poles stand, ready to support a fence. The guys attach rails, and we plan to add the chain link tomorrow.

Time for a soak in the claw-footed tub.

Good-God-It's-Morning Ambush

Even Flo oversleeps on Monday morning. We both crawl out of bed, stretching and scratching. Flo bounds out the front, and I turn off the alarm. I jump into my jeans and T-shirt, put out fresh food and water my doggie, and start the coffee. In no time, she's in back, barking furiously.

I slip into my huaraches. Flo's practically screeching as she throws herself at the screen door. Footsteps thump behind me as I cross the back porch to see why Flo is so upset. Big arms snake around me. Son-of-a-bitch. I lower my chin to prevent a choke.

Flo snarls and jumps against the screen.

A rough, bearded cheek presses next to mine, and the stench of rotten teeth comes with a deep voice that says, "I'll break your neck if you give me any shit." I am caught prey, but not for long. With my right forearm, I push his elbow, pulling it toward me to force his grip loose. With a quick maneuver, I'm facing him, holding his arm so he leans back to keep me from dislocating his shoulder. I take the opportunity to knee him in the ribs. He's falling back but catches himself with his free hand and rights himself from a squatting position. I deliver a snap kick to his stomach, and he stumbles against the closed kitchen door, where his head cracks the glass. I have a chance to get a good look at him.

Holy crap. It's the guy from Stripes who sat beside the window—the one who inspired Flo's fury.

I know he'll come at me as soon as he recovers, so I give him a round kick to the side of the head. He staggers. He's solid, won't go down easy. His face is purple with rage, and he wobbles, but he reaches behind him and produces a gun. Before he can point it at me, I kick it from his hand.

He backs away, holding up his hands. "Wait. Wait!" So now he wants to talk? Choke hold first, gun second, talk last—I don't like his order of business.

A side kick to his groin doubles him over, and I smash at the base of his skull with a hand chop. On his way to the floor, he gets another kick in the ribs.

I grab the gun, grateful it didn't discharge, and run to the kitchen for my phone. I open the back door for Flo, who races past me to sink her teeth into my attacker's arm and shake it. I keep an eye on them both while I dial 9-1-1. I've set a record for the number of calls to the sheriff's office, as though my presence has set off an epidemic of crime around Sulfur Gap. I tell the dispatcher I have another intruder, this one trying to kill me.

Coffin Breath is starting to stir, and Flo backs off, barking again.

"Quiet, Flo!" To my surprise, she stops. "I would stay down if I were you," I say.

He is not too smart. He rises to his hands and knees, so I shove the ball of my foot into his sore ribs. He groans and falls over on his side.

"Who the hell are you?" he gasps. "Some plant from the DEA?"

"Yeah," I lie. "So how about telling me why you're attacking me this bright morning."

"You're law enforcement. You can't question me without an attorney. I want a lawyer."

This is too much. He's lying on his side holding sore ribs, so I stomp his knee.

"Goddam you, bitch, I'll kill you." He curls into a fetal position.

"I don't have to protect your rights." I stomp his other knee.

There's banging on my front door. "Around back!" I yell. I open the door for Flo, and in seconds, she's flying back to me, leading a motley crew—skinny L.B. ahead of Brad and Otis, each running as fast as he can.

Mr. Ambusher screams when Otis rolls him on his

stomach and pulls his hands behind him. "I'll sue every one of you!" Otis ignores him and rolls him onto his back and cuffs his hands in front. Otis and Brad raise him to his feet, but he can't stand. "She stomped both my knees!" I push a kitchen chair under his butt as he's about to fall.

L.B. holds his gun on the intruder. "Call an ambulance," he orders Bill.

"You'll never make a charge stick after what she did," my attacker says.

"She was defending herself," L.B. says.

"Excessive force," he says.

"That would apply to a law officer," L.B. says.

"She told me she's DEA."

L.B. turns to me and raises an eyebrow.

"He never asked me what DEA stands for. In my case, it means Death to Evil Assholes."

While the sheriff and his deputies laugh, I run to the bathroom to tape up my hand and give myself time to throw up. The urge passes, and I rejoin the Sulfur Gap Sheriff's Department, who might as well move their offices to the Middleton place. The Man from Stripes is hauled away, handcuffed to a gurney and accompanied by Otis. I hand over the gun he'd planned to use on me, and Brad takes a hundred pictures before he leaves. L.B. records my statement as we sit in the kitchen, drinking the pot of coffee that finished perking during the fight. After I tell him what happened, he says, "And why did you mangle his knees after he was down?"

"So he wouldn't get up. And he said he'd kill me."

When he turns the recorder off, I say, "This was about that dope in the stove flue."

"Yep. That was high-grade cocaine, street value in six figures. Farley realized he'd gotten in too deep. He thought he'd sell some marijuana and make money when he got laid off from his good oil field job. He wanted to keep Rhonda happy at all costs. He found the right contacts and got a small job. It was working fine until shipments got dangerous because of the grade of heroin and coke that came in—and the quantity.

"He found another oilfield job in Odessa and cleared out. He left the last big stash of cocaine in the stove flue so it could be retrieved. And he thought that would be all. But you moved in sooner than expected. A representative of the cartel caught up to Randy and told him it was his responsibility—or else—to return the cocaine. Randy finally confessed everything to Rhonda, and it scared her so bad, she left Randy and went back to Wyoming. He came here to get the coke, but got caught. Your visitor this morning was probably Randy's contact. When Randy got arrested, it looks like the buck stopped at Bruno."

"Bruno?"

L.B. looks at his notes. "Yeah. Bruno Metzger. That's what his license says, but it could be phony."

"I've seen Bruno before. At Stripes. Flo raised her hackles and sailed out of the car and headed for home."

"I've seen him before, too. He comes through town sometimes to deliver tooled leather products to the western store. Bruno's a middle man. Boxes of boots can hide lots of drugs."

Flo puts her head on my lap, and I tear up. I grab a paper napkin and dab my eyes.

"You alright?" L.B. asks.

"Yeah. I'm tired. Lots of adrenaline. Flo needs to sleep off the excitement, too."

Then I remember I've got a work team coming. "I've got some guys coming over to help me build a fence. I better call them off."

When L.B. leaves, I call Charley, who is not disappointed to have a day of rest. I tell him about the ruckus at my place.

"Gosh, Lou, you're lucky the bastard didn't kill you. Can I do anything? Bring you a burger? Take you for X-rays?"

"No, I'll be fine. Eventually."

I call Wayne next. As with Charley, I have to explain about the drugs in the stove flue and tell him to keep quiet—the information that the sheriff's office has confiscated the drugs hasn't been released yet, and I don't want to be recognized as the Combat Queen of Sandstone County. I tell him about Bruno bushwhacking me on the screened porch. He'd apparently slipped up the back just as I was letting Flo out the front.

"Are you hurt? Do I need to come over? Have you seen a doctor?"

"Only my hand is swelling. I'm all right, but I'm not in the mood to build a fence today. Maybe we can make the movies next week. In fact, screw the movies. Come over for dinner. Bring Luck if you want."

"It's a date, but aren't you afraid Bruno sent for backup?"

"I doubt it. He probably thought he'd get the drugs, maybe kill me, and leave."

"That gives me the shivers, Lou. Do you have a gun?"

Here we go again with the gun discussion. "No, and I didn't need one."

"You know what they say, 'Don't bring a knife to a gunfight'? Well, don't bring your bare hands, either."

"How many times in a person's life should they expect to have someone try to murder them?" I argue.

"I guess the odds are in your favor from here on. But I wish you had a gun. Couldn't I at least bring you a pistol?"

"Do you have a shotgun? Like a 20-gauge?"

We plan for Wayne to bring me a 20-gauge pump action. Next, I call Wylie to get me a sub for tonight at Hopper's. Flo and I go back to bed. I meditate and focus on my breathing and thank God I'm alive. Then the tears come. I cry for my father, who died too young. And for my home in Tulsa. Even a little bit for the old Pete, before he started climbing the corporate ladder. I cry with anger at the thought of Randy Farley wanting to make an easy buck and stepping into the drug world's pool of evil. I cry because my feelings are hurt by Bridgette's attack, and I weep from exhaustion.

I DRIFT off and wake up two hours later, weak and disoriented. I raise my hand to see it shaking. Then I remember that after the excitement, I fell in bed, prayed, cried, and passed out. I need water, tea, and food. In the kitchen, I'm rounding up some grapes and cheese while my tea steeps. Flo growls and dashes to the front window. Well, hell. What now?

She wags her tail—she recognizes the truck. Finally, I do, too. It's Wayne. I make a dash to the bathroom to brush my teeth and check myself in the mirror. I'm feeling better, I know, because I care about how I look. I let Wayne in, and we sit in the kitchen while he gives me a short course on operating a 20-gauge.

My phone rings. It's L.B. Wayne gets up to leave and I wave him back to his chair.

"Hi, L.B."

He gets right to the point. "I know this is a big favor to ask, but Randy Farley wants to see you."

"Why?"

"He wants to see Flo, and he wants to apologize."

"Tell him I accept his apology via proxy."

"You'd be doing me a big favor if you'll play along."

"How's that?"

"Farley says he'll give us more evidence, now that Bruno's caught. But first, he wants to see you and Flo."

"Okay," I say. "I'll come by the jail tomorrow. If I'm up to it. I might discover some sore spots that I'm not feeling today. I've never been in a real fight like that."

I end the call, and Wayne asks, "Are you dating L.B.? Sorry, but I have to ask."

"Heck no," I say. "L.B.'s not my type. He's a good sheriff, but he's not my type."

"What is your type?"

"You are."

He takes my hand. "I'd say you're my type, but you're one of a kind."

Aw, shucks. All I can do is accept the compliment. I tell him about Randy's request.

"Sorry, but I need to know this, too. What about Charley?"

"We're very good friends. We cross paths because we're both in the beauty business." I should tell him the whole story, but not now. Too much effort. I should ask him about that first wife of his, but that's too much effort, too.

We sip tea and re-hash what's happened since I moved to the Gap.

"You're getting all the bad luck out of the way, and from here on, life will be smooth," Wayne says, serious as an Old Testament prophet.

"Let's make a date," I say, as much to change the subject as to move the Wayne-and-Lou project forward.

"I'm flexible if it's not early in the morning," he says. "I get my best work done between six and ten."

"Let's plan dinner for Thursday. I'll take the night off from Hopper's. Wylie's got a good stand-by for me. And on Saturday, we can go to the Railroad Centennial."

Wayne looks stricken. I laugh. "You don't like that kind of thing, huh? Well, here's the deal. It's good for my business to be a part of the community, so we'll go for a little bit. Then we can do whatever. I need to play at Hopper's that night."

Wayne nods. "When do you want to finish the fence?"

"It's not high priority right now."

As he leaves, he kisses me lightly. A little brush across the lips. He hugs me, warm and solid, but careful and gentle. And I like the way he smells. He's such a contrast to stove flues full of drugs, intruders in my house, and crazy women picking fights—so comforting—I almost cry again, but I tamp it down until he's gone. I look at the metal bulk of the shotgun lying across my kitchen table and cry some more.

Jailhouse Hangout

At the sheriff's office, a woman whose nametag reads "Gloria Marquez" greets me. She's a new deputy. "Just started last week," she says. I introduce myself and Flo. "Good luck!" I say. "I hope you like the town. I'm a newcomer, too."

"My family has reunions at the lake at my cousin's house."

I'm learning small-town ways, so I ask, "Who's your cousin?"

"He's the game warden—J.J. Rodriguez."

"Yeah, I've heard of him. Between him and L.B., Sulfur Gap's got good law enforcement."

"So true." Gloria keys in passwords to get us through a couple of doors leading into the jail area. Down a long, windowless hallway lit with flickering fluorescent lights, another locked door leads to the visitation room. Flo bristles and growls, but she stays beside me, looking around warily. Gloria touches a buzzer, and Randy Farley is escorted in by a deputy jailer. Gloria leaves, while the jailer, a body builder type, stands aside. When she sees Randy, Flo whimpers. She tugs against the leash, so I let go. He drops to his knees and hugs his dog as she licks his face. Farley looks youthful, until I notice the missing tip of his index finger and a network of fine facial lines. Life has begun to take its toll. And jail doesn't suit him.

Officer Body Builder clears his throat. "Y'all need to sit at a visitor's table."

We sit opposite one another, Flo beside Randy. She puts her front paws in his lap while he strokes her head. "Thanks for bringing her. I've worried about her."

I'm not feeling civil, since Randy has caused me all kinds of trouble with his lame plan to leave his coke in my stove flue. "Why'd you drive off and leave her?"

He looks down at Flo. "I'm sorry, girl. I was scared." He looks back at me. "I hear you've met Bruno."

"Yeah, thanks a lot."

"He'd been to the house. I was dragging my feet, didn't want to get into the heavy drug deals. Flo tried to keep him off the front porch, and he kicked her, busted a couple of her ribs. Then he barged in and slammed me up against a wall and threatened me and said he would kill my wife Rhonda and my brother Wes —he lives here. The whole time, Flo dragged herself across the porch and barked like she wanted to kill him."

"Very traumatic for her," I say, not ready to give Randy any sympathy.

"The day we lost Flo, we'd loaded in a hurry. I actually found a good job lead the day after Bruno threatened us, and I decided to take off. I got hold of Bruno and told him I was moving for another job. I told him I'd left the last of the drugs in the stove flue. I figured he'd pick them up right away. There was a key hid in the barn —still is."

I will go straight to the hardware store and buy new locks.

Randy squirms. "We stopped at Stripes to gas up, and Flo saw Bruno inside the store. She freaked and jumped out of the car and ran off, sore ribs and all. I just wanted to get as far away as possible, so we went on. I convinced Rhonda we'd hear from someone and we could get her back later. It was all for nothing." He begins to cry. "Bruno found me and told me I had to get the drugs, and that's how I got caught and landed here."

"All Bruno's fault, I say." Randy reminds me of some of the seventh-graders I used to work with.

"Rhonda left me."

Oh, the injustice.

"I just wanted to apologize for pulling you into all this. I'd have felt terrible if Bruno had killed you."

"Do tell."

He wipes his face with the backs of his hands.

"Would you like me to tell you what I'd consider a sincere apology?" I ask.

"What?" He looks scared, like this might be hard.

"Tell everything you know about Bruno and his network. Give every detail. Don't hold back."

"They'll kill me in prison."

"Get them to send you somewhere far away. Maybe they can do that. But if you want to save lives like mine, you need to tell it all. Everything you learned while you were in the business with those toads."

Randy looks hopeless for a moment, but something takes hold of him and he begins to smile.

"That would set things straight, wouldn't it? With you—and with Him?" He points toward the ceiling.

"I can't speak for God, but I'd consider it a fair deal if you give the sheriff every piece of information you can dredge out of your memory."

He looks at me like I'm giving him a pep talk. He's inspired, but I'm not enlisting as his life coach.

"Okay, Lou, I'll do it."

Flo has wandered back to my side of the table.

"Will you write to me in prison?"

Oh, hell. I want to be free of Farley, but I say, "Yes, but do not get the wrong idea. I can keep you updated on Flo —and your brother—Wes, did you say? We can email occasionally—with that understanding. Okay?"

Farley agrees. He gives Flo one last hug and begins

crying again as he's led back to his cell. He's on some path to redemption, but it'll be up to him to stay on it. Flo seems sad, too, but when we're outside in the fresh air and sunshine, she bounds into the truck with her usual lightness and waits to see where we're going next. I love the way dogs live in the moment.

I've got locks to buy, orders to take, deliveries to make. At the warehouse, Flo settles in until lunchtime, when I take a break to go see April. She wants to meet Flo.

And she's going to love this story.

New Friends and Old Enemies

The chicken parmesan simmers, salad ingredients ready to toss. Flo runs to the front window and wags her tail.

I wear a white gauzy shirt, slim-leg jeans, and white sandals, showing my pedicure. He called to confirm yesterday and to tell me Luck wasn't coming. My heart beat a little faster.

Wayne's handsome enough, but that's not the attraction. He's *true*. From what I've seen, he's direct—never tries to impress, dodge the truth, or do anything unkind or unfair. He doesn't mince words and I don't have to step around any egg shells. I'm at the door before he knocks.

He puts his hat on the hall tree. "Smells good." He sniffs. "Italian?"

"Yep. Hope you don't mind if we dispense with the

niceties and dive right into dinner. I'm starved."

"Sure. Me, too."

We sit on opposite sides of the table. I've put on a medley of fun songs—"People Are Crazy," "Who's Your Daddy," "Suds in the Bucket"—make-you-wanna-dance songs.

We click our wine glasses and dig in. Wayne says, "I had coffee with Charley this morning."

"Yeah? How's Charley today?"

"He tells me you're his aunt."

My stomach does a flip. "I'm so glad he told you!"

"How come you didn't tell me? Giving me this line about 'good friends.'" He shakes his head.

"I've been too preoccupied to get into it. I'd have told you, though. He's your adopted nephew, and now you're friends with his aunt."

"I'm happy for Charley. And his mom."

"Yeah, learning about the family gave April a pick-me-up. I hope she gets more traction and digs herself out of the rut." I refill our wine glasses. I love the idea that Wayne's already part of the family. "You've been here for Charley when he didn't have much of a family."

"I've known Charley since before Luck came along."

"Back in the Lucy days?"

Wayne's eyes narrow. "Yep, I guess so."

"I'm interested in Lucy because I'm interested in you."

He relaxes some. "Well, if you're curious why she left,

the best way I can explain it is that something was eating at her, made her want to get away—and it wasn't me. Not that I'm the perfect mate. That's not what I mean. She had layers to her, and they got more complicated, and so did she. She wasn't cut out for marriage and raising kids, for starters, but her mother was a nut job and she had a load of grief from that. Her dad's decent, kept her from going off the deep end, but there's more to it. She's not bad. Mixed up. No good with feelings or frustrations but liked to stir up trouble."

"Y'all were too young."

"Yes, we were. If we'd been even a little older and wiser, we'd never have gotten together, and then I wouldn't have Luck. Raising him has been the best part of my life, so far."

The music mix cycles in the background. We clean the kitchen, and I sing and dance along to Faith Hill, but substitute "Oklahoma Girl" for "Mississippi Girl." Wayne sings the songs he knows. He's not a singer, but he sure can dance. We spin to the living room to dance and sing while Flo watches as if we've lost our minds.

"Why don't you come dance at Hopper's more often?"

"Nobody there I want to dance with. You can't dance because you're busy playing." And he sings (if you want to call it singing), "I only wanna dance with you." Flo doesn't howl. She's tone-deaf, too.

"We'll have chances to dance," I say.

With that, he dips me and he kisses me. A deep kiss that lasts while he drops to his knees. My knees would buckle if I were standing. We hold each other's eyes as we lie on the floor.

"I didn't think things would happen this fast," he says.

"I don't believe in putting things off," I say. We get up, and I take his hand and lead him to the bedroom.

LATER, he says, "This is weird. It feels so normal."

"I know. And I don't have any reservations."

"Ordinarily, I'd worry about not getting burned again. But right now, I'm all in, no second thoughts."

"Yeah, me, too. We will, at the least, turn out to be good friends."

"With benefits?"

"With everything. This feels like home."

"Good," he says, and pulls me closer.

AT THE FIRST sign of light, Wayne is up. I lie still, enjoying the warmth he leaves beside me. He creeps around the room, trying not to wake me.

I stretch and kick off the covers as Flo jumps down.

"I'm sorry, Lou. I can't find my drawers."

"Good."

"Really. I've got to get started before it gets too hot."

"Okay. But if you're not too tired, come by Hopper's tonight, at least for the second part after the break."

Darla's practicing with the band at Wylie's today. She's going to sing and play keyboard with us on a song. She's back from taking care of some business at College Station, and she wants to surprise Charley by showing up and singing.

"Okay, I'll be there. Now where's my underwear?" Wayne looks under the bed.

I get out fresh undies for myself and help Wayne find the ones I removed from him last night. I insist he take twenty minutes for coffee and French toast.

I CLEAN house and do laundry. Flo and I make a run to the warehouse. Everything takes less effort, I'm so happy. The band gathers at Wylie's to run through Darla's song—a Miranda Lambert. Her voice is pure and clear, with a good range. Firm on the keyboard, too.

"Darla, how often do you do this kind of thing?" I ask her as we step onto Wylie's porch.

"I played a lot of dances at the community center when I was in high school. Sang in chorale at A&M, but I haven't done much night clubbing because of my age—I just turned twenty-one."

"I imagine the pre-vet track is demanding, too. No time for hangouts."

"Yes, and I want to keep my scholarships. I don't want my parents spending any more than they have to. I like to be self-sustaining."

That's the independent little Darla that Charley described. Her father's loaded, but she wants to pay her own way.

At Hopper's I wave to Charley as he heads for the pool tables. We play our opening number, but the dancers are slow to rouse. A crowd gathers around one of the tables. Charley stands up straight, rising above the knot of people, so I know he's got a game going. But the crowd disperses in no time. Charley must have run the table. He cleans up like that when he wants to put someone in his place. There are some out-of-towners here for the big railroad celebration tomorrow. Some poor dope must have riled Charley and challenged him to a duel at the pool table.

Charley and his couple friends, Jarod and Sue, stake out a table near the bandstand. At the break Darla shows up in a red sequined jacket that makes me wonder if she's on her way to Vegas. I join them and settle back as Wayne puts his arm around me. Charley gives Wayne an "I'm-onto-you" look.

After the break Darla wows the crowd. Her voice is well-trained, and she plays the keyboard with professional confidence. I love it when the dancers stop to listen. And I love seeing Charley so blown away by Darla. She's a doll, she's darling, she has it going on, and she's clearly twitter-pated over Charley. There's a song in there. And nobody but her could get away with that red sequined jacket.

WAYNE PICKS me up for the Railroad Centennial. He wants to get it over with so we can spend the day together doing something else. I know what that will include, besides meeting his folks.

We park in front of the courthouse. In the big lot behind the railroad depot, a Ferris wheel spins and kids drive bumper cars. Further on, a crowd claps along to a bluegrass band. To my surprise, Wylie is playing the guitar and singing through his nose. That old ham will do anything for an audience. Forrest the guitarist plays banjo.

We explore the booths—smoked turkey legs, waffle cones, matching sets of pot holders and tea towels, carved mesquite knick-knacks. Around the antique and vintage clothing store, a mixture of junk and treasure lines the shelves and sidewalk racks.

Wayne overcomes his glum mood when he finds the dunking booth. Sitting on the shelf above the water is none other than L.B., hatless and weaponless, wearing a track suit. "Oh, my cow." Wayne stares. He watches as several men and a few high school boys line up to pitch at the lever and knock L.B. into the water. Wayne mutters, "C'mon, get 'im," teeth clenched.

"What's up, Wayne? Can I get you some darts . . . or a gun?" I ask.

"I'm not a fan of L.B.'s. We've gotten on each other's nerves for a long time."

"Why don't you vent a little? What is it? Five bucks for three throws? I'll treat you."

"I'll take you up on that."

I have nothing against L.B., per se, and I'm grateful for all his quick responses to the Middleton place. But something about him makes me want him to take a splash. Before we pay the fee for Wayne's throws, the parade starts, so our evil plans have to wait. Marchers have stacked at the corner, backed up on Sunset Avenue, and it's time to start. We wave at the Grand Marshall, a World War II veteran wearing his uniform jacket and sitting a horse with confidence. He's followed by the beauty pageant winners—the Centennial Queen and the two runners-up, on horseback in their best western regalia.

The high school band follows and floats created by the Boy Scout troops, Lions, Rotary, and Kiwanis Clubs roll by, some with no theme other than members sitting on the trailer in folding chairs, waving to the crowd and throwing hard candy. It's a raucous bunch marching along Buckskin Road and turning onto Main.

After the last float rolls by, Wayne makes a beeline back to the dunking booth, not to be disappointed. L.B. waits there for his would-be dunkers. He leans against the framework built around the trough full of water. I pay Otis, who wears a red pocket apron and sells chances to knock his boss off his perch. Proceeds go to Toys for Tots.

L.B. gives me a confident wink and starts the trash talk when he sees Wayne. I have to credit him for being a sport. Wayne is dead serious, tossing the ball in one hand to feel its weight, judging the distance to the lever.

"Good luck, Cheadham. You can't hit a mule in the butt with a tennis racket," L.B. taunts.

Wayne winds up. The ball hits the lever, but not hard enough. L.B. sits up straighter on his perch and holds the edge. Otis tosses out a new ball. Wayne concentrates.

"Put a little muscle in it, Wayne!" someone in the crowd shouts. Everyone loves to topple authority.

"What muscle?" L.B. mocks. "C'mon, Wayne. Betcha can't throw this far. All wore out from the first try."

The sheriff gets some laughs. Wayne lines up for his second pitch, and people whistle and clap. The ball whaps against the tarp backdrop. The crowd breathes an "aww." He takes his time for the third throw. On the other side of the crowd, I see Charley's head above the throng. The people shuffle a bit, and there's Darla, peeking through—cute, tiny thing.

Wayne loosens his shoulders and moves his head

from side to side, stretching his neck. He winds up and throws a solid one. Bang! And splash.

L.B. comes up dripping and hollers, "Aw, man! He got me!" He climbs from the tank to clapping and whistling and looking skinnier than ever in his wet track suit. He salutes Wayne and smiles. They might not like each other, but L.B.'s got his next election to think of.

"Wayne! Lou!" We look around at Darla's call. Charley and Darla catch up, and we explore the exhibits. We know almost everyone there—Jarod and Sue stop to form a friendly knot with us on the street. Other fans of L.B.'s downfall congratulate Wayne. No one actively dislikes L.B., as far as I can tell. They enjoyed the show, though.

We meander, headed in the direction of the court-house. L.B. steps from the depot, where he's changed back into his sheriff's gear, his stint at the dunking booth done for now. The high school principal is the next victim, and students push to line up. L.B. settles against the railing to visit with Brenda, who lights up more than usual. Maybe Brenda is the one for L.B.

As we near the intersection with Main Street, we hear shouting—not the fun kind. Beside April's parked van, Charley stands over an old man in a seedy suit.

"Oh, no," Wayne mutters. He rushes toward Charley, so I follow. L.B. lopes past me, his gear flapping.

April's tear-stained face is framed in the window of her van. Poor, dear April. She tried to enjoy the parade, and something or someone has made her cry. I drop my shoulder bag on the pavement and start to move in. Wayne's firm grip on my arm stops me from charging in to confront the stranger who must be the source of the trouble. We stand close by as others stop, attracted to the knot of tension.

"What kind of person rejects a father?" the old man shouts.

"You're not her father," Charley returns. "You're a fraud. A phony preacher and a fake father. You kept her and her mother in fear for too many years. I'm glad I never knew you." Charley doesn't need my help.

L.B. steps between them just in time. "No fighting, guys. This is a festival, not fight night." He asks April, "Is this man bothering you?"

April says, "I'm shocked to see this jackass after so many years."

April's strong voice penetrates the crowd. The old man makes a growling sound, then addresses April as though she's a child. "Now, Missy, that's no way to talk."

"Shut up, Frank!" Now she's the one shouting. She brushes the tears from her face and works her way out of the van to face the slack-faced, stooped man. He's a dissipated, bedraggled, senior citizen, with a furtive look about him. Once, he might have been handsome.

April stands before this Frank person. He's Frank Bristow, the man she thought was her father until I showed up with Pop's letter. She hasn't seen him in at least twenty-three years. She draws strength from Charley and L.B. and points a finger at Frank. "You're a cockroach, a creep of the worst kind." She tells the gathering crowd, "He posed as a father and a preacher, but he abused me and my mother on a daily basis." She points toward me and addresses Frank. "See her? That's Lou Trainer, my sister. She found me, Frank. My father was a decent man. I have a new family, and you can go straight to hell. And furthermore," she says, turning to the sheriff, "I believe this man killed my mother. He and my mother left Briargrove in a hurry when he jumped bail on assault and battery charges, and I haven't heard from my mother since."

"That was so long ago, statute of limitations applies," Frank sputters.

"Then you admit to the assault charges?" L.B.'s got his hand on his night stick.

"No, I admit nothing, you idiot," Frank growls.

L.B. doesn't seem offended, but he can certainly twist the screws on Frank. "Miz Irwin, are you reporting your mother as missing?"

"Yes, my mother would have contacted me if she were alive."

"Then, Mr. Bristow, you'll have to account for her whereabouts, since you were the last person seen with her."

"I want a lawyer," the Bristow fellow blusters.

And before we know it, L.B. is walking the old man

down the street to the sheriff's office. Darla stood at Charley's back the whole time, along with me and Wayne. We sigh with relief as the rest of the crowd disperses. "And I just met his mother," Darla says. "And now her stepfather. Some family reunions are more fun than others."

April leans against Charley. She assures me she'll be okay.

"April, call me if I can do anything—anything at all," I say. And I blow her a kiss. Wayne puts a reassuring hand on Charley's shoulder and nods to Darla. As we walk back to the truck, I'm shaky. Too much excitement so soon after Bruno's attack. Wayne notices my pallor.

"If you're not up to having lunch with Mom and Ernie, we can beg off," he says.

"I hate to put them off, after Katy's made lunch."

"It's okay. Mom will be disappointed. She knows how smitten I am, and her curiosity is about to kill her. But she'll survive a few more days."

"You know, I think she and Ernie would enjoy hearing what happened today. And they'll be proud of April. They're like grandparents to Charley."

Down the highway, we race past the turnoff to the Middleton place and into the low hills on the horizon. As we turn onto a private road, Wayne gestures beyond an old windmill. "I live down that way." A steep copper roof with attic dormers is visible above the ridge.

"Looks pretty big for just you and Luck," I say.

"I keep part of it closed off. Cynthia had me build on a big addition, and I don't go in there unless I have to."

We cross a second cattle guard, as the road swings toward Katy and Ernie's house. Ernie's getting out of his pickup and walking stiff-legged into the house. Katy steps onto the porch. Her gray hair is pinned at her neck, and she looks at the noon sky, shading her eyes. She wears a big denim shirt and comfortable pants stuffed into work boots.

"Howdy!" She walks to greet us. "Y'all forgive my dirty boots. I've been pulling a few weeds. We've had snakes, so I don't go in the grass without my boots. Lou, Wayne's told us all about you!"

"Well, I'm flattered."

"I'm glad to meet this fascinating lady who plays drums and works in Alaska, and, most of all, is Charley's aunt!" She guides me through the heavy front door into a cozy living room. "Let's sit here until time to eat," she says. "Ernie!" she yells over her shoulder. "At least there's no football to distract him this time of year, but he'd watch paint dry if it were on a television screen. Ernie!"

"I'm here, quit yelling." Ernie scoots in wearing house slippers.

His handshake is firm, but he has a distant look in his eye, as if he's not all the way in the house. Maybe he left part of himself outside in the noonday sun.

We relate the dust-up at the centennial. They love

hearing about Charley protecting his mother and her sticking up for herself.

"It does April a lot of good to know she has you for a sister," Katy says.

Before I can say thank you, Ernie inserts himself. "That Bristow fella. They can't hold him. All they can do is question him. They'll need a body to prove he did anything to his wife."

Wayne says, "I wonder why he came back here."

"Might be out of options. No new scams going at the moment," I say. "He strikes me as delusional—so full of himself, he thinks he can pull it off, coming back here. He could have somehow found out that April came into a bit of money."

I ask the Cheadhams how long they've lived on this land and about their parents.

Ernie tells me about growing up on his father's ranch —a ranch that failed because further west, wolf packs preyed on the livestock. Lesson number one was to move east. He adds, "You know, you're the first one of Wayne's gals that seemed to care to know anything about us."

Wayne says, "Lou's one of a kind. But could we not compare her to her face, even favorably, with my exes?"

"Thanks anyway, Ernie," I say.

"Let's eat," Katy ushers us to the dining room.

Luck joins us—a nice surprise. He was reading in the back bedroom. He swallows me in his long arms. He's so sweet, with a touch of Wayne in him, and I'm sure a whole lot of his mother. I'm still curious about her.

"I'M NOT SHOWING off my house, mind you," Wayne says. "I want you to know where I live. And I need to prepare you. I've got a bridge in front."

"Are you beside the creek?"

"No. I have a bridge on dry land. I had it hauled in three years ago when they replaced it with a new one. I had my reasons."

I remember the guys at the Navaho ribbing him about buying a bridge. Now I get to see it.

"Are you keeping people out or yourself in?"

He laughs. "A little of both."

Around a curve, his bridge appears. Not as big as I'd pictured. "Well, that's a solid-looking bridge."

We park in front, between the bridge and the gate. The empty expanse of the porch and formality of the creaking, bevel-glass door give off a deserted home vibe. I feel a chill. Cynthia's ghost? But inside, the house is neat and cozy. Leather furniture, cow hide area rugs—practical and down-to-earth, but creative and quirky. He likes gadgets. A mantel clock chimes "The Eyes of Texas." It's already three o'clock. I wonder about the closed double doors to the back of the house.

Our hands come together. The afternoon could run

into evening, and I'll have to watch the time. I'm
expected at Hopper's tonight.

His cell phone chimes. "It's Eliza, my oldest step-
daughter." He answers. "Hey, girl, what's up?" He
listens a while. "That's wonderful. Come see me when
you can get away. Put Abby on." He visits with Abby a
moment, while I look out a window at a yard in need of
some TLC.

"That was both of my stepdaughters. They're at UT,
finishing the semester. You'll meet them this summer."
He's interrupted by another call. He glances at caller ID.
"It's Charley. After what happened today, I'd better take
this. Sorry, Lou."

I wave him off.

"What's up, Charley?"

Charley's voice is distressed. I hear something about
his mother, and the word "hospital."

Wayne says, "Bring Darla here and go meet the
ambulance at the ER. That'll be quickest."

He clicks off. "April called Charley to tell him she
shot Frank Bristow. She's pretty sure he's dead. Charley
and Darla were picnicking at the windmill. He's bringing
her here and heading to the hospital."

"I need to be with April!"

"I think it would be best to wait here until Charley
calls."

We stand on the bridge, waiting for Charley's car to
appear. Within five minutes, Darla hops from the

passenger side and Charley takes off, his car bucking along the dirt road and out of sight. We all watch him drive away.

"What happened?" Wayne and I both ask.

"April called Charley and said she'd killed Frank—shot him when he broke into her trailer house. Charley called 911, and then he called L.B., and L.B. said to meet them at the hospital, that April would need to be checked by a doctor and might be in custody."

"What? Why?" My mind's having trouble grasping that April did anything illegal.

"I hope he's dead. Sorry if that's cruel," Darla says.

"No, I get it," I say. "If it was a clear case of self-defense, no charges will stick, I imagine."

"Probably not," Wayne says. "Of course, L.B. will have to make it as hard as possible."

"What's this beef you've got with L.B.?" I say. Wayne shuts his lips tightly. Well, now is not the moment to discuss an old grudge. "Anyway, there has to be an investigation when someone gets *killed*."

We move to Wayne's living room and lay our cell phones on the coffee table. Finally, Wayne's phone chimes.

Charley says, "Mom's with the doctor. She's okay. She shot Frank when he broke in. I didn't even know she had a gun."

"Me either," I say. "I thought Frank was with L.B."

"He didn't have any reason to hold him. Wait, the

doctor's calling me in. I'm going to have to go. Call you later."

We wait another hour. Finally, Wayne's phone lights up again.

"L.B. interviewed Mom with me and Wallace Derby in the room."

"Oh, hell," I say. "You're not hiring him, are you?"

"No, he tried to get us to pay a retainer, and I told him he could be a good sport and stick around as an advocate, or he could get out."

"Good thinking, Charles," Wayne says.

"Anyway, Mom said Frank would have hurt her if he'd gotten to her. He broke the window in her door and reached through to release the locks. She warned him, but he didn't believe she'd shoot him."

"And he's dead for sure?" I ask.

"Yeah, he went straight to the morgue. Anyway, they're keeping her for observation. The doctor isn't too impressed with her lab results. She told me they should have seen her a couple months ago, before she stopped drinking. That blew me away. I didn't know she'd stopped."

Neither did I.

"Hang in there, Charley," Wayne says. "What can we do?"

"Meet me at Hopper's later? Mom's quit drinking, but I'm going to need a few beers."

"I'll see you there, Charley," Darla says.

Voices from the Past

I still haven't finished the fence. The posts stand in the corner of the hayfield near the live oak. Every time I imagine myself finishing the fence project, I get a superstitious feeling it'll invite trouble.

After the shooting, I visited April in the hospital. I followed the aqua stripe down the middle of the shiny hallway floor to her room. She sat in bed, wires snaking from her nightgown to the heart monitor. On her lap, she scrawled on an open spiral notebook. She snapped it shut and pushed it under the sheet. "Hi, Lou!"

"Oh, honey, are you alright?" I kissed her on the forehead. She didn't shrink away like she usually does when I try to show affection.

"You're not going to believe this, Lou, but I'm more 'alright' than I've been in a long time. Frank Bristow's never coming back." She sighed with relief.

"I was always afraid he'd come back. It was good to be rid of him, but not knowing where he went with my mother always bothered me. I wasn't going to let him hurt me again. Ever." Her eyes flashed. No more haunted look. "And another thing, L.B. says he's put out notices on cold cases from the mid-eighties. If my mother's body was found, there'll be a record."

I sat in a chair, leaning an elbow on the bed as I listened to April recount the afternoon, winding back to her childhood, and moving to the hope that she would know her mother's fate.

"And I have you to thank," she said, putting a warm hand on my arm. "You showed up three years ago. Changed everything. Before that, Charley was all that kept me alive. Without him, I'd have killed myself." She pantomimed pulling the trigger. "But when you came to town, I realized if I had a different father and a sister like you—and brothers—well, it opened all kinds of possibilities. Mainly, my father wasn't scum." Her eyes widened, shafts of afternoon sun from the window reflected in them.

"I'm grateful to be part of it," I said.

"But you had to take the risk and trouble of coming here to tell me. It took me a long time to recognize what you did. You could have kept the money and decided you didn't want to dig me up, and Charley and I would be going on the way we always did, me hiding in the trailer, Charley trying to smooth things out for me, make me happy."

As I was about to leave, Brenda's little bird-like face peered around the door. I didn't know she and April were friends, but Brenda kept up with everything and everybody. If she's seriously dating L.B., she'll be a great asset to his job. She ignored the "family only" sign, and April didn't mind.

I left the hospital feeling good, even if the idea of April having to kill a person hovered sadly in my mind.

At the night club, Charley's friends had gathered to support him. I put my head on auto-pilot and made music for the crowd. Many had shown up in hopes of seeing Charley and getting the story on how April killed Frank Bristow. Everyone knew now that April and I were sisters—news like that travels fast. At the break, Charley and I danced and sang to "True Love Ways" from the jukebox. Wayne and I planned a night together at the Middleton place, after the dancing was over.

EARLY THE NEXT MORNING, I made veggie omelets, a bit wistful about my garden, which would soon be producing had I finished the project.

"Let's go feed and check troughs and then go to church," Wayne said.

"Church?!" I was surprised.

"I'm not suggesting the rattlesnake round-up, just church."

Wayne's Episcopalian. I'm bothered by some churchy types who ask questions like "Have you been saved?" If I'm feeling smart-ass, I say, "From what?" Or they say, "Do you know Jesus?" And I say, "Yes, but he pronounces it 'Hay-SOOS.'" Episcopalians aren't as nosy.

I sat between Wayne and his mother. I felt the comfort of sitting between two of my favorite people in the somber, old chapel. After church, I met Pam and J.J. He's the game warden, a huge man who disarmed me with his crinkled smile. We all lunched at the Navaho.

J.J. asked Wayne, "When you lived in Midland, did you ever get over to the Petroleum Museum?"

"Luck was born in Midland, right?" Pam asked, and then darted a look to make sure I wasn't offended by a mention of Wayne's past life.

I said, "You guys can speak freely. I know Wayne has a son and two previous marriages. I'll be glad to know where all the skeletons are buried."

APRIL'S MADE SPEED-OF-LIGHT PROGRESS. She's eating healthy, going to AA, and staying off cigarettes—she had already committed to those goals before Frank showed up. She revealed that she'd been seeing a counselor since soon after she learned about me and my family—*her* family.

The days pass quickly while I make deliveries. Since Wylie found a replacement drummer, I'm free every night but Saturday. After driving to Big Spring and all my little towns, I call it a day.

Wayne offered to make dinner. Luck and Katy went to Dallas to shop and see a movie. "Lucy and I figured out how to make this," he says, setting a pan of lasagna on the table. "She threw a shoe over the idea of serving company one more meal of steak and baked potato." He pauses. "She threw a lot of shoes."

I don't want to hear about Lucy now. What I want to know is what lies behind the double doors. I dive right in. "You've got the house barricaded. Bridge in front, closed door to the back. How come?"

"Well, the back part used to be the family room. When Cynthia died and Eliza and Abby went to live with their dad, Luck and I didn't need the space. And I didn't want to sit in there with the echoes."

"I'm sorry, Wayne."

"It's all right. I should use it. It's got a great view of the south pasture. Come here, I'll show you." The doors swing into the room, swooshing over the hardwood floor. The large, musty area is partitioned into a study cubby and TV zone. There's no furniture, nothing. A lone TV cable dangles from the wall. Wayne opens the tightly closed plantation shutters to reveal acres of grass dotted with new cedar and mesquite. Far out, a green field of cotton drapes over a rise in the land and disappears.

"How's the cotton coming?"

"Afraid it won't make much, with no rain in sight."

The evening sun draws the shadows of the mesquites on the land. "Beautiful view," I say.

Just as I'm feeling trapped between Lucy's lasagna and Cynthia's memories, he turns to hold me. I forget former wives. I'm the one who's here.

His cell phone rings an hour later. A whole hour to ourselves before Lucy throws her latest shoe into Wayne's life. Wayne rolls away from me, glances at his caller ID, and shouts, "Good God, it's Lucy!!" He levitates off the bed, holds his cell between his ear and shoulder, and hop-scotches into his boxer briefs. He carries his jeans to the kitchen and puts his phone on speaker, so he can use both hands to finish dressing.

I hear a muffled Lucy. Her voice rises to say, "Are you tongue-tied? Don't you have anything to say, one way or the other?"

I've thrown on the kaftan I brought. I don't like listening in, and I'm intrigued that we both cover up to talk to Lucy. Wayne grabs a post-it note and pen and scratches, "Should I introduce you two?" I shrug. His call.

"Lucy, it's been a while since I've heard anything from you, so I'll have to think about the idea of Luck spending the summer in D.C. But for now, I'd like you to meet Lou, my girlfriend. We're on speaker phone."

"Oh, hello, Lou!" she says, a cultivated sparkle in her voice. She switches her tone right away, when she learns someone else is listening. "Nice to meet your voice."

"Yes! Nice to meet you." I muster my phoniest microphone voice. "Luck is such a nice young man," I add. Wayne raises his eyebrows at me. He knows I'm slathering it on, and I push his arm. He must not make me laugh.

"Well, thank you, but as you probably know, I can't take a bit of credit." Her laugh is melodic, forced.

I wish I could tell her she's never come up in our conversation. At the same time, I feel sorry for her and her priorities, so I say, "Maybe you passed along some brains to him." Wayne does his best to look hurt, and again I tamp down a laugh.

"Well, thanks, Lou. So, Wayne, why don't you and Luck put your heads together. I've talked to Luck, and he's interested."

Wayne says, "Okay, Lucy. We'll figure something out. I doubt I can spare him for the whole summer. He's got plans of his own, too."

Lucy laughs again. I have no idea why. "Okay. I know I have no right to call out of the blue after such a long time and ask to take Luck for the summer."

"Where in D.C. are you?"

"I have a condo in Dupont Circle."

"Mind if I come up with Luck and have a look before committing to his staying?"

"Not at all! Come ahead. Just say when, and I'll book you a hotel. Bring Lou!"

I shake my head with such vigor, I pinch a nerve in my neck.

"We'll get back to you," Wayne says.

"Okay, Wayne. I'll respect your decision."

They hang up, with promises to be in touch. She's completely lost all traces of a small-town Texas accent.

"Well, now you've met Luck's mother."

"Oh, I was dying to!"

"Okay, smarty pants, master of sarcasm." He grabs me and we head for the bedroom.

Dousing Fires

D amn, the cell service is out. Must be some lightning in the area. I've spent the day playing catchup—grocery shopping, working out, cleaning the warehouse. The wind gusted, rattling the metal roof of the warehouse. A strong wind could peel it off. I congratulate myself that I carry insurance.

At home in the late afternoon, I try to call Wayne. But there's no signal. The wind has strengthened. I check the weather on my laptop. The National Weather Bureau has issued a Red Flag Warning for our zone, alerting us to potential fires. A dry thunderstorm is brewing. The crack of distant thunder vibrates the windows. Flo sits up and looks at me as if to ask, "Are we running away now? I'm ready." I pat her and tell her not to worry. She doesn't believe me. I don't believe me, either. I pack a bag, just in case.

I watch television until Flo raises her head, her nostrils working. She puts her nose under my arm to make me get off the couch. It's dark, so I can't see if there's smoke, but outside, I smell it. I'm hauling my drums to the truck when Dick Raney races up the lane, pulling a stock trailer full of bleating goats. He lowers his truck window as he brakes, throwing a goat or two toward the front of the trailer, no doubt. I sense his urgency.

"What the hell, Dick?"

"Lou, there's a grass fire. Looks like you're already evacuating. I'm helping give notice to everyone in the area. Lightning started a fire north of here, at the Marshall place, and it's burning along a band across my north pasture and toward the creek."

"Won't the creek stop it?" The strong, acrid scent of the fire has increased.

"No, the creek's too dry. There's lots of weeds and dried grass to fuel it."

I've heard that the past year's growth of ground cover can serve as tinder for lightning strikes. Flames can shoot to six feet where Johnson and bunch grass grows, and although the glowing line of an oncoming fire looks nothing like a forest fire with great flames swallowing trees, a grass fire can race as fast as the wind blows. With these wind gusts, the fire could move forty miles an hour. Anything in its path becomes fuel. My brain must have been down, along with the cell towers, when I sat around watching cable TV without thinking of this.

"What about the Cheadhams?" I ask.

"They're in the path of the fire, if the volunteer fire department can't stop it. Wayne's on a water truck now, I'm sure." I draw a sharp breath. "It'll reach the Cheadhams if it drives straight ahead. If it spreads at the flanks, it'll be at your back door. So far, we think it's only a few thousand acres."

"A few thousand?" That sounds huge to me.

"That's small, but with this wind, who knows?" He gestures toward the swirling branches of the oak tree. If it were daylight, great gray billows would appear ahead of the fire line. "Ida's left to go to her sister's in town, but I've got some other people to notify and a trailer full of goats to move. Thank God I had 'em penned. Where will you go?"

"Andrea Harper's house. She offered when I was having trouble with the drug dealers. What about cattle?"

"I hope they've stayed over to the east."

Dick shouts this last bit of information over his shoulder as he drives away. I watch his taillights disappear into the haze. The smoke veils the guard light. My throat tingles as I grab my overnight bag, my old guitar, and Flo. She waits while I finish loading my drum set, craning her neck to keep an eye on me as I run in and out the front door. I'm not careful with the drums. Better to make haste now and repairs later.

The smoke thickens. I can't see the flames, but if I could, Flo and I would be toast. My most precious items are aboard—Flo, my drums and guitar, and a jewelry pouch holding my grandmother's pearls. I give the house a last look and roll away.

I RING ANDREA'S DOORBELL. After a minute or two, I hear her footsteps. The porch light switches on, blinding me. She opens the door a crack.

"Lou? What's happened?"

"I'm all right, Andrea. There's a range fire on the Raney place, and the wind's blowing just right to bring it to my house. Can Flo and I stay with you?"

"Get in here! Y'all are welcome. I wondered about the sirens, but I haven't listened to the radio."

Andrea's is a roomy ranch-style house. She fosters so many dogs and cats until they can be adopted, she's had tile laid in all the rooms, slick and clean, like her clinic. Flo greets her two current residents—a pit bull and a dachshund mix. While the dogs conduct the sniffing ritual, Andrea shows me to the guest room.

"Will you be able to sleep? Should we sit and have some chamomile tea?"

"That'd be great, but I don't want to keep you up."

"I'm up. We can listen to the emergency channels on my computer if you want."

"Wayne's on a water truck—whatever that means."

"It means he's hosing the fire from the black side, the part that's burned already. He's upwind, standing on the truck with some other guys with water hoses, and he's dousing flames. They're trained, so they'll stay safe."

"I'll take your word for it."

We sit at her breakfast bar and catch up. I tell her April is waiting to hear about the DNA results from a Jane Doe in East Texas. She was found about the time Frank disappeared with April's mother. I tell her about meeting Lucy via speaker phone while dressed in my kaftan.

Andrea laughs. "Lucy? Out of the blue? How long has it been?"

"Years. Wayne put the phone on speaker so I could hear her. She sounds so phony, like she's talking from a sound booth. Kinda sad." I shrug off this line of conversation. "Wayne was probably watching the lightning from his vantage point up on that bridge of his."

"Hope he wore rubber-soled shoes." We both snicker.

I finally feel drowsy, and Flo and I bunk in Andrea's guest room for the night. I'm grateful to lie on fresh sheets with Flo curled by my feet and my drums in the truck, parked in Andrea's garage. I pray for people's safety, for the Cheadhams, the Raneys, the Standleys, and Mattie Gilstrap, and all the people on the smaller tracts of land like the Middleton place. I pray for the animals at the mercy of the fire.

I listen to the wind as its driving gusts settle. The weather can change so quickly.

I'M DEAD ASLEEP, dreaming I'm back in Tulsa, and someone rings the doorbell. And rings again. Flo jumps down and stretches, and I'm confused. The log-jam in my head begins to clear. I remember where I am, and panic. Is it bad news? I run to the hallway and almost crash into Andrea, who's been jarred awake, too.

The hall clock says it's seven.

Wayne stands on the porch, smudged with black. His hair stands in bunches, and a few reddish bristles from his unshaven beard glow in the morning light. He smells like smoke. A line across his shirt marks the border of the protective overalls he wore last night.

He pushes past Andrea, who's more than glad to yield the right-of-way, he's such a sight. He grabs me and holds me.

"Thank God, you're all right."

He and I stand with our arms around each other. Andrea clatters in the kitchen, talking to the dogs, and the part of my mind that always tunes in to coffee hopes she's starting some.

"How'd you know where to find me?"

"I radioed Dick."

"Have you been up all night?"

"Yes. I love you."

"I love you, too."

We both smell the coffee. Andrea leans against the counter and smiles.

"So how much damage did the fire do?" she asks.

"It burned out the Marshall place, where the heirs tried to have a wildlife refuge. Lots of fuel there, all the mesquite and dry brush. It spread onto Dick's property, and the water trucks got behind the burn line, kept it from going toward my land, but the wind shifted and headed across Dick's neck of land that he got from the Middleton estate."

"I could tell it was headed my way. I hope it died out!" That house isn't mine, but it could be. It's where I found Flo, where I fought Bruno, and where Wayne and I fell in love.

"I'm sorry, Lou, but the Middleton house and barn burned down."

I groan.

"The important thing is you're okay. I'm lucky I got Dick on the radio to find out where you'd gone. I'd have done something stupid." Wayne holds my hand while I absorb the news.

"I tried to call you, but the cell service was out," I say.

"Still is. Are you upset about your house?" Andrea is puzzled by my low-key reaction.

"It's a shame. It's a historic old ranch home. But I've got Flo. And my drums are safe in your garage, Andrea. I'd hate to lose them."

"You took the time to load those drums?" Wayne can't believe it.

"Yes, and my old guitar, too. My dad gave it to me."

Wayne rubs his hands over his face and through his mess of hair. "From what Dick told me, you got out maybe fifteen minutes ahead of the fire."

"Well, I wasn't going to stay and try to spray it with the garden hose." His expression is so intense, I say, "Thank you, Wayne," and decide not to joke about the fire any more. "I know you and those firefighters saved lives last night."

"Yeah. No human casualties that we know of. Dick and Buster lost some cattle, and we might find some feral hogs."

Andrea says, "Lou, you and Flo are welcome to stay here as long as you like."

I thank her, but Wayne says, "Lou, why don't you stay with me? I've got the space. We can set it up however you want, and Flo can keep being a country dog."

"I'll think about it." I already know the answer. I'm not flippin' crazy. I just don't want to hurt Andrea's feelings.

Wreckage and Rejuvenation

The charred remains of the Middleton place rise beyond the blackened hayfield. The chimney stands among the smoldering ruins and a few salvageable items—the claw-footed tub, the hat tree. The fence posts stand undisturbed. The remains of my porch swing are jumbled into a pile of burned lumber. The fire spared the old oak in its dirt-trodden patch, leaving singed leaves on the bottom branches. Under blackened beams and barn siding, rolls of chain link for fencing remind me of what happens to best-laid plans.

"Well," I say, surveying the damage, "I guess this means I'm moving."

"The question is, where?" Wayne pulls me to him.

"Your place."

THE MOVE IS easy since I don't have any stuff. I'm not hot on the idea of occupying a Cynthia-shaped vacuum, but I'll fill it soon. On my first morning at Wayne's, I get up after he's left for early morning rounds and stand in the middle of what Cynthia called the "parlor." I ask her spirit to let me in. I move into the addition she created. Noting her attention to the fine points in the kids' nook, I re-dedicate the space to drums and music. Moving on through the house, I note the details of wall paper and paint trim throughout, and I feel all the love she poured into this home. I feel welcome.

Luck appears from his room, squinty from sleep, and, seeing me, rushes into the kitchen to make coffee, even though he doesn't drink it himself. I drink his watery brew with pleasure. I can stop by the Navaho for the real thing later.

Still, it's experimental, like when I lived with Pete, but with a lot more chance of surviving the test of time and temperaments. Deep down, I know Wayne and I will make it. Over the next days, Lucy calls a couple of times, but it's no concern of mine. Luck and Wayne will work out how to set up a visit to Lucy. They'll do what's fair and kind.

Days later, Flo and I laze on the porch chairs. She's never tried to run away, back to the ruins of the Middleton place. She knows her home is with me. I study the bridge, wondering how I'll get used to it. I decide I'll hang crisscrossing light strings and spiral them around the girders. If you're gonna have kitsch, it needs to be really kitschy. When you take tacky to the next level, it all comes together. We could have yard parties, with the band playing on the bridge.

Wayne drives up and parks under the carport. He walks to the front, eyeing me. "You making plans to get rid of my bridge?"

"No. I want to exploit your bridge." I tell him about my ideas for lights and parties.

"And maybe we'll have something big to celebrate, if you say yes," he says.

I know what he means. If he hadn't asked soon, I would have. "Yes," I say, and we lean against each other and look at the bridge.

Wayne says, "I'm tired of the old windmill being a parking spot for the teenagers. Am I becoming an old fart?"

"Yes," I say. "That's your job. What do you have in mind?"

"I'd like to get the windmill working again and have a water reserve."

"No koi pond?"

"Nope. Not enough shade. But we could fence it and do something with the spot."

"Let's go look at the place. See what ideas we get." We take my truck, since the path is muddy from recent rains. At the windmill, the ground is packed from years of traffic. Graceful old mesquites cast lacy shadows.

"We could fence this all in." Wayne waves his arms.

"We could put in some ornamental plants, maybe some sand sagebrush there and some wild petunia here."

"I'm not much of a gardener."

"I am, but this stuff grows wild. And there's this place in Sprocket where we can buy trellises and outdoor tables."

"I've seen it. Looks like a bunch of crap to me."

"We could have our wedding here."

"When?"

"July? Will that be enough time to get it done?"

"It'll be hotter than hell for an outdoor wedding."

"We'll use mist machines and canopies."

Wayne's resistance fades and excitement builds as we plan. The clinking of rocks on a car's undercarriage interrupts us.

"Charley and Darla!" We wave to the oncoming Buick.

"What're y'all up to?" Charley hollers as they walk to us.

"We're planning the wedding," Wayne says.

Charley starts to laugh but realizes Wayne is serious. "Well, you rascal! That was fast."

"You're one to talk," Wayne counters.

"I'm learning the waiting game," Charley says, looking at Darla.

At the house, Charley says, "I found my grandmother

in Briargrove today, while Darla was singing in my father's church choir, filling in the high notes."

"And Charley looks just like the Reverend Woodruff!" Darla says.

"Does the Reverend know yet?" I ask.

"No, but he will as soon as Doris—that's my grandma—gets hold of him. I didn't mean to, but I surprised her. She was mad and suspicious—thought I was casing her house. But she was excited when she found out who I was."

"I'm happy for you, Charley."

It's Aloha Night at Hopper's. The Hawaiian themed dance has morphed into a family reunion. If I'd had more notice, I would have tried to get my brothers and mother here, but I want them to come for the wedding anyway. My only nod to the theme is to wear a plastic lei. Those who play drums don't have to play dress-up. I'm checking the drums when Charley and Darla arrive.

Darla grabs my hands and looks around to make sure no one can hear. "Have y'all set a date?" she asks.

"July the twelfth," I say. "We still have to decide who's going to officiate. If we like the Reverend Woodruff, we'll ask him," I say, winking at Charley. As if we wouldn't like Gunnar, even if he did chicken out and miss Charley's upbringing. We have to forget all that and give people a chance.

Gunnar steps in the door and holds it open for two women. Gunnar is a fortyish version of Charley. One of the women who follows him is a pretty, dark-haired woman. The other looks distinguished, with a crown of white hair. No guesswork on which is Charley's grandmother. At the big table Charley has staked out for his dance guests, he makes introductions. "My grandmother, Doris Woodruff. My father, Gunnar Woodruff, and his wife, my stepmother, Celia. And these are my good friends, Wayne and Lou. Wayne's like an uncle, and Lou really is my aunt. But we don't talk about it."

April joins us, looking foxy. Her hair glistens. She has a rosy glow now that cigarettes and booze no longer sap her vitality. She's been sober for a few months, watching her diet, and sticking to AA. The bloat has dropped, along with forty pounds. Capris and a white linen shirt flatter her slimmer shape. She, Gunnar, and Doris reunited over coffee at the Navaho, but tonight she meets Celia for the first time. Both are so gracious, I'm relieved, although I hadn't really worried until the millisecond before their hands met.

Our band plays as Darla's mom and stepfather join the group and others follow. A handsome couple whom I take to be Darla's father and stepmother arrive. People in these small communities have to get along—divorced, estranged, or pissed off—unless they want to be miserable. They can't avoid one another. All the in-laws and outlaws share pieces of history and loved-ones. The salon ladies are here, and most of the crowd knows this is a celebration for Charley. I'm supposed to sing a special song he's requested for Darla. The word gets passed as we play "May I Have This Dance?" Charley waltzes Darla toward the middle of the floor, and the other dancers fade off to form a circle around them. She's crying, and I do my best Anne Murray impersonation.

Before we break, Wylie says, "How about that Lou? Lou Trainer, folks. Let's hear it!"

I grab my mike and stand for a bow. "Thanks, everyone. There's romance in the air, so it's a good time for my announcement." Beer mugs hang in mid-air, faces turn toward me, and conversations die. A few people, already sensing the subject of my news, look for Wayne. "Wayne and I are getting married," I announce, confirming their suspicions. A few gasps are mingled with applause. I know it seems fast to the gaspers, but for Wayne and me, it's about damn time. "I'll be sticking around Sulfur Gap," I add. The band guys crowd in for hugs and backslaps. Others pound Wayne on the back, and April fans herself, she's so thrilled. My girlfriends collar me and ask questions until I have to hold up my hands and beg for some time to go to the bathroom.

"Suck it up, Buttercup." That's my final advice to Wayne on the subject of whether L.B. will be invited to our wedding. "If you can give me a viable explanation for how L.B. would mess up our wedding, then I'll agree not to ask him. I'm inviting his deputies—the sheriff's department saved me. And the sheriff is dating my good friend Brenda, who is a big reason I'm here." Wayne won't discuss it any more, I can tell, by the distant, calm look on his face. I'm sure his detachment irritated Lucy.

Wayne and Luck made a quick trip to Washington, D.C., and came home with the verdict that it was a nice place to visit—for a short time. Luck learned about changing planes and getting around on the Metro. He can go on his own from now on, if Wayne is satisfied he can trust Lucy to assume responsibility for keeping an eye on a teenager in the big city. Wayne said a place like D.C. was just right for Lucy. Ever since she'd graduated from college, she disliked the ranch. "But I think it's something else," he added. "I'll never know."

Later, Wayne says, "I'm not sure I can explain how I feel about L.B. Maybe it's a bad habit I need to break. He's bothered me ever since kindergarten."

"You should have had little brothers. That would teach you about being bothered," I say.

"I know. My personal space gets cramped pretty easy."

"Are you sure you don't feel crowded now?" I hover close to his face.

Wayne looks through me, his eyes almost crossed. He's mentally piecing together a history. "In kindergarten, Larry Bob was a pest. He liked to get right behind me—in line for recess or lunch. Every time I let my guard down, he'd goose me in the ribs or holler 'boo'. If I jumped, it made his day. I got tired of it and punched him. Figured it'd be worth the trouble, except Ernie warmed my pants pretty good when I got home, and I had to sit in 'time out' for what seemed like weeks."

"I gather he provoked you a lot. That pestering verges on bullying. Back when you were in kindergarten, the teachers weren't as sensitive to the various forms of bullying as they are now. You were on your own."

"I hadn't thought of it that way—well, hell, I was traumatized! See? That's why L.B. shouldn't be at the wedding." He slaps the table, pleased with his conclusion.

"You're over it," I say.

"Yeah, but there's more. After I punched him, he quit testing my startle reflexes."

"Good. You made some progress."

"He still played tricks. The mean thing was when he threw a big wolf spider at me."

"Poor spider."

"It got stuck in my shirt collar and I tore out of my shirt and sent the spider sailing away. The other kids laughed. So, I jumped L.B. and we rolled in the dirt until the teachers broke us up. We both were in trouble, but he kept his distance after that. He really caught it from his dad, too."

"What kept the resentment going?"

"Going through school, he'd chime in when I was hanging out with friends."

"Did he have friends?"

"He always had one or two of the awkward types that he stuck with."

"He must have wanted to be part of your group."

"Yeah. And then there were girls. He flirted with my girlfriends. He asked Lucy out before we started dating. When he called you about visiting Randy Farley in jail, I thought, 'Here we go again.' Glad I was wrong. I have to admit, he's made a pretty good sheriff."

"He's been nothing but professional with me. And he was really good with April when she shot Frank. And April said he helped Charley's second wife get to the mental hospital."

"Yeah. L.B.'s suited for his job. Maybe someday we'll be friends."

I leave L.B. on the guest list beside Brenda, marveling at the Wayne versus L.B. quagmire. Wayne is a network-builder, not one to exclude others. His stepdaughters, Abby and Eliza, and Lucy's father, Baker Paxton are invited. Wayne claims Leo Hastings, Cynthia's ex-husband, as a relative because he shared Abby and Eliza with him and Katy, when he didn't really have to.

At first, we planned to invite only family—my mother and brothers and their wives, Katy, Ernie, Luck, Wayne's aunt, the cousins and their husbands, Charley, Darla, and April. And of course, Guillermo and Billy. Then we added Charley's newfound father, Gunnar, since he's officiating. And Gunnar's wife, Celia, and his mother, Doris, Charley's grandmother. And, we couldn't omit my friends and clients, the regulars from Hopper's —including Brady Hopper and wife, Jarod and Sue, and my band fellers and their significant others. And of course, there's J.J. and Pam, who have seen Wayne through it all, and his coffee group and their mates, which includes Dick and Ida Raney. And friends from Tulsa. We have a large, extended family, we decided.

I put away the guest list. "I'm glad I finally understand a little better why it's dicey between you and L.B., but I have something more important to discuss."

"And what's that?" he asks, taking my hand.

"I'm pretty sure I'm pregnant."

Ties That Bind—2008

K aty pulls to the front of her house in the Tahoe. Mom and I check our makeup in the hall mirror one last time. We step out the front door and down the porch steps.

In the Tahoe, Katy says, "Y'all are gorgeous! Helen, I'm still amazed at how much Lou looks like you." She turns the wheel to drive to the windmill. She punches a number on her cell phone and says, "We're leaving now." That's Wylie and Chad's cue to take their places at the front, under the canopy, where the guests sit in white folding chairs. We've picked some old country songs for guitar and fiddle. They'll wait one minute to begin playing "Lover's Waltz."

We take it slow on the five-minute drive. Katy suggested I keep my wedding dress at her house and get ready there, so Wayne would have no chance of seeing me. Our one nod to superstition, except for throwing a bouquet. I won't carry flowers, but I have a bouquet ready at the reception so I can throw it straight into Darla's hands. We don't want to rush Charley and Darla, but they'll be the romance of the moment in Sulfur Gap. But there's L.B. and Brenda, too. After the wedding today, Wayne and I won't be of interest, and we'll settle into the rest of our lives.

Katy's right. Mom makes the prettiest matron of honor. We have matching dresses, except mine is ivory lace, and hers is light gray. They're sleeveless, with V-necks and backs, knee length in front and tapering down with light gathers in back to brush the tops of our western boots. Mine are white with glitter inlays, and Mom's are a dark gray version.

The weather magically cooperated—low nineties with a few weak wind gusts that won't stir up dust. We couldn't ask for more in mid-July. The road was recently graded and the washed-out places filled in. It'll take quite a few rainstorms for new hollows to appear. Everything's as good as it can be for a country wedding.

I have a small baby bump, and besides Wayne, the only one who knows I'm pregnant is Mom. Earlier, I looked at my profile in the form-fitting dress and said, "This will be the baby announcement. No need to send out cards!"

"I don't think so, Lou," Mom said. "I wouldn't notice it if you hadn't told me." She stood beside me with her arm around my waist. "Thank you for asking me to be your matron of honor. It's a *big* honor."

"Wayne and I couldn't think of anyone more appropriate to stand up with us than you and Luck. You're our closest kin until we become next-of-kin." She kissed my cheek and pulled back to make sure she hadn't disturbed my blush. I didn't care.

As we approach the windmill, I roll down the passenger's window. "Sounds like Wylie and Chad timed it just right." Katy stops behind the thickest mesquite, its drooping limbs providing a perfect curtain. She looks darn good herself, in a gauzy skirt and blouse with dress boots. Katy walks ahead of Mom and me, through the gate and under the canopy, as the crescendo peaks. The song has all of us teary-eyed.

Mom and I walk arm-in-arm into view, and "Lover's Waltz" rises to the finale. Wayne, Luck, and Charley stand in front of the trellis. Katy takes her place opposite Charley. Wayne clamps his mouth shut. He'd gone slack-jawed when he saw me, and all the secrecy with the dress is rewarded. I told the guys to wear their best boots, jeans, and shirts. "If you wear a jacket, I'll make you take it off. It'll be too hot, and not one of you is allowed to faint," I said. They readily agreed, but Wayne and Luck crinkled brows at each other, amused at the idea of heat sensitivity.

Gunnar motions our guests to sit. I look behind me at our friends who've come to this mesquite haven to witness our vows. Above me, the arch of the iron trellis I hauled from Sprocket is studded with big sunflowers that have stayed bright. In the opposite corner of our new, flagstone windmill "plaza," Wayne and a mason built a cement block water tank. The windmill has been repaired to working order, and water gurgles into the small reservoir, filling the air with a pleasant, earthy aroma. In the lacy shade of the big mesquites, dragon-flies hover above the surface of the pool.

The reception will be in our front yard. The band will play on the bridge, its new lights twinkling as the sun sets. I can't believe how pain-free it's been to pull all this together. When I made this observation to Wayne, he said, "It's about time something came easy for you." I reminded him that my job at Hopper's awaited me when I came to town because of Wylie's chance discovery that I'd stayed at the Navaho Inn three years ago. I easily found an independent business to build, thanks to Brenda. And, I found my sister and nephew. Despite drug dealers, Bridgette, and a range fire—a trifecta of seeming woes—I met Wayne, we're in love, and I'm having a baby.

I had resigned myself to never having children. The time never seemed right, and Wayne and I didn't have a chance to ponder the idea. It simply happened. Such events often turn out to be the greatest of life's gifts—the things we don't plan.

Gunnar welcomes our guests. When we discussed the

wedding, I told him not to get into any of that stuff about Wayne being Jesus and me being the church. And I told him not to preach. He laughed and said, "Done. I wouldn't dare!" We decided that other than the parts about the husband being dictator, traditional vows will be fine.

Before we know it, we've said those vows and kissed and we're leading a procession to our house, to the tune of "Shove the Pig's Foot Closer to the Fire." Sounds awful for a wedding recessional, but only a few will know the title. It's a great fiddle tune, snappy and festive. Wylie and Chad play it as we walk. I wonder if I'm the only one who feels like skipping. Our kick-off dance is "Head Over Boots." We don't care that we're dancing on grass. And I like the idea of dancing on Cynthia's grass, shaded by Lucy's trees. Wayne is the person he is today because of what he learned from those two marriages. So is Luck, my new son.

We won't make our guests stay in the yard if they don't want to. The whole house is open and the kitchen set up with drinks at the counter and a taco bar. Flo is ensconced on her porch throne, accepting ear scratches. Wayne and I cut the cakes right away so everyone can have dessert.

FEBRUARY COMES ALL TOO SOON. I've told people I don't *feel* pregnant, and they laugh and look at my belly. I'm making a delivery in Briargrove when I get the first warning. The contractions are regular, maybe fifteen minutes apart when I reach the hospital in Sulfur Gap. My hope is met when I learn Pam's on duty in the ER today. I've never liked name-droppers, but asking for Pam expedites my reception at the hospital. Wayne arrives close behind me. Before long, I'm dressed in a hospital gown and hooked to more monitors than I thought possible. I was tired of the phrase that I was at the borderline age for an at-risk pregnancy, but maybe the monitors are a good idea.

Pam returns to her shift in the ER, and Wayne takes over. I'm surprised there's no pain. A nurse checks me and looks alarmed. Wayne jumps out of his chair and I raise up on my elbows.

"You're fully dilated," she announces.

I'm the only expectant mother in labor at the moment. Dr. Gupta walks the short distance from her clinic. The labor nurses get me into position, and Wayne stands out of the way. I feel his hand on my shoulder. Dr. Gupta makes it in time to catch Hannah as she dives into the world.

Later, Wayne pulls off his boots and lies beside me in the hospital bed. He spoons me and says, "That's the fastest delivery I ever saw."

"How many have you seen?"

"Oh, kid goats, calves, a few foals. I wasn't allowed in when Luck was born, but that was Lucy, not the hospital. She was hysterical before, during, and after."

"But Luck turned out all right," I say.

The door opens and a nurse rolls Hannah into the room in a bassinet. We both prop up and reach for her.

"Me first." I say, and we lie back down together to get acquainted with our new baby girl. Eventually, we have to let the others see her, so I brush my hair, put on a robe, and sit in an easy chair, holding Hannah. I don't want to let her go. Everyone who wants to hold her will just have to wait.

Mom has stayed with us the last few days. She comes in first and runs her fingertips over Hannah's wispy red hair. "My first grandbaby's a redhead," she says.

Luck gets away from school early to meet his sister. "I can't tell who she looks like," he says, bending over her bassinette.

"Neither can I," Wayne and I say at the same time.

"She's uniquely beautiful, then," he says. "I called Eliza, and she and Abby plan to be here to meet *their* new sister next week."

The extended family trickles in and out. I feel over-extended and drift off to sleep with Hannah beside me in her bassinet. Wayne gets back in bed with me, and we sleep until the baby wakes us up. Life will never be the same.

Epilogue—A Skeleton Arm—2013

I sit on the tractor beside the south gate and think about that damn skeleton. It screwed up my gravel pit deal. I look at the big gash in the land. And I realize the guy sure didn't ask to get buried there. I quit thinking of money so much when L.B. told me it was a guy from Sulfur Gap, a guy with a name. A .9-millimeter bullet in the skull. This will eat at me, but what can I do?

Earlier on the porch with L.B., I heard Hannah beating on her drum set. The noise reached from the back room to the front porch. Boy, I am in for it with two drummer-ladies in the house. But when L.B. said what he did about the .9-millimeter bullet, Hannah's ruckus faded away. My mind jumped to Lucy. She was a good shot and could do and say things most people would never consider.

I took off without telling Lou and drove the tractor to the gate in the south field, not only to follow L.B.'s advice about *blocking the entrance. I wanted to sit and try to picture Lucy burying a guy there. I could see her doing that, back when we were married—not for meanness, but if she was cornered.*

All I know to do is call Lucy's dad. Baker might remember if she knew or mentioned Tim Connelly. Only one way to find out, so I pull out my phone and hit Baker's name on the speed dial.

He picks up in a few rings. "Hello, Wayne."

"Hey, Baker. Sorry to bother you."

"No problem. What's up?"

"I guess you've heard about the skeleton found in my gravel pit."

"Yeah. A shocker, wasn't it?"

"Yeah. I just learned who the skeleton used to be. L.B. made a special trip to tell me before it hits the news and the media people come snooping. Told me to close the bar on the cattle guard and park the tractor behind it." I pocket the ignition key and hop off the tractor to walk along the horse path in the direction of the barn. From there I'll walk the road toward home.

"That was nice of the sheriff. Can you tell me who it was? Anyone I might know?"

"Does the name 'Tim Connelly' ring a bell?" I say. Baker catches his breath. There's a long silence. "Baker, you there? Did you know the guy?" I stop walking so I can hear better.

Baker says, "Yes. I remember the guy." His voice is low, a different tone from any I've heard from him. We've seen some high and low times together, and he's never used this tone. "I remember him from when Lucy was four."

"So y'all knew him?"

"Yes. Gosh, I thought he'd left town and I'd never have to hear his name again."

"What happened, Baker?"

Again, I think the connection dropped off. Finally, he says, "Can you meet me at the Navaho?"

We agree to meet in an hour for after-dinner coffee. I walk back to the house. Lou's chicken parmesan meets me before I get to the door, a delicious odor reminding me of our first . . . uh, get-together. I tell Lou some developments are unfolding regarding the investigation, and I've got to go meet Baker. I eat a fast supper with Lou and Hannah.

"Daddy," Hannah says, "I'm gonna play some drums for you."

I'm so preoccupied with this skeleton business, I almost tell Hannah to go ahead, pound away, but Lou's paying attention and says, "Not now, Hannah, I think finishing supper is a better idea, don't you?" Lou can convince Hannah to curb her enthusiasm for mayhem lots better than I can. Luck was easier for me. Maybe because he was a boy, maybe because I was young and didn't think about parenting as seriously as I do now. We finish eating in peace, and I say, "Gotta get to the Navaho. Thanks for the good supper."

On my way to town, I try to imagine what Baker knows about Tim Connelly. He waits in a booth in back, blowing on his coffee.

"Thanks for meeting me," he says. "I couldn't talk about this on the phone."

"Sure, Baker. You sounded pretty upset when I mentioned the guy's name."

Telling his story, Baker stops to clear his throat and pat his lips with a napkin several times. He's grayed lots since I was married to Lucy, but now even his ears look gray. The story's not long, but for him it is. He tells me Lucy stayed with a nice babysitter when she was four and Madge went to work as a clerk at the courthouse. The babysitter's teenage son, Tim, did some awful things, sexual things, to Lucy when his mother left her with him while she went to get groceries. It happened more than once, and finally, Lucy came home crying and told Baker and Madge what had happened. She told it as well as a four-year-old can, he said.

My pulse swishes in my ears when I consider that Lucy was the age Hannah is now. And some pervert was messing with her? For a moment, I want to rip out the table, throw it through a window. I stuff the anger and listen, trembling all over.

Baker says, "I've always regretted not calling the sheriff. I let Madge convince me there was no way to prove Lucy was telling the truth. Madge didn't believe her, but Madge was not a good mother. And I was a weak father." He blinks back tears. I know Baker is a decent man, wants to do what's right, and I know being married to a strong-willed, crazy woman eats away at your core. Lucy did us both a good deed, leaving and making her own life, far away from where all this happened. I don't contradict Baker about being weak. I hope he'll make his own peace with that.

"What do we do now?" he asks me. He's made the same leap I have. He thinks Lucy crossed paths with this Connelly fellow and shot him. He'd been missing since right about the time Lucy got her first college degree.

"I don't know," I say. "If Lucy did this, he threatened her somehow, and when he did, she could defend herself."

"She keeps up with the news in Sulfur Gap. She'll see something about it."

"She's lived with it a long time, if she did it."

We sit a while. Finally, I say, "I'm not saying anything to L.B."

Baker lets out a breath. "Thank you, Wayne. I don't see any good to come from bringing Lucy into this—if she did it. I'll call her and tell her about it. Let her know we've talked, if I can tell she's worried. Maybe she'll even tell me the truth."

"Okay. I agree there's no point getting Lucy involved. Heck, we're acting like we know she shot the guy, and we don't know squat, right?"

"I guess not." Baker gives me a weak smile.

ALL I CAN THINK of on the way home is getting there and holding Hannah. I find Lou and my little girl curled on the sofa, reading a book. Hannah's almost asleep, and I sit next to

Lou and slide Hannah onto my lap. I have to concentrate not to squeeze her too tight.

"Sorry to be so busy, but now I can catch you up," I say. "But you first. How's your day?" I want to let Lou talk about mundane stuff, our everyday life, so I can settle into the sound of her voice and the feel of my child, falling asleep in my arms.

"I stopped by the Wild Hare. Charley's added two more stylists," Lou says. She thinks a minute and adds, "Gramma Helen and Dick are coming to dinner tomorrow and will keep Hannah so we can go to the dance at Hopper's." Lou's mom, Helen, dates Dick Raney. She moved to Sulfur Gap after Hannah was born. Dick's wife died not long after Helen came.

Lou has more to tell me. "After you left to see Baker, Luck called, touching base. He's bringing his boyfriend to meet us."

"I hope the guy doesn't go into culture shock, coming here."

"I doubt it. He's from Pecos. Now, tell me what L.B. said. And why you drove off on the tractor."

"Okay, let me put this girl in her bed." I ease off the couch and carry Hannah to her room. I lay her in the bed and arrange stuffed animals so she can reach for them if she stirs in the night. I lean against the dresser, taking deep breaths to calm myself some more. The waves of shock at knowing what happened to Lucy have lost strength, here at home.

Back on the couch, I tell Lou the whole story. She balks at the idea that Lucy might be a killer. "You can't believe that!"

"But it felt like something Lucy might do. Kill someone,

bury the body, and move on with life. I thought if she did, she'd have had a good reason, and Baker confirmed it."

"You feel it in your gut, huh?" Lou thinks a while. "You know, however it happened, Lucy would have to bury him."

"How's that?"

"She would have had to dredge up the old story in her defense."

"Yep." I don't sound as matter-of-fact as I would like.

A thought sparks in Lou's eyes. "Oh, my God," she says. "She was Hannah's age. Poor Lucy. What a burden to carry. Her mother must have been a piece of work. And then, back in the seventies, there wasn't near the awareness of sexual abuse."

"I realized the age similarity when Baker and I talked. Twisted my gut. It'll take a while to wash out the feeling." Lou puts her arms around me, and we stare at the blank TV screen.

Finally, Lou brushes a tear off her cheek. "I wish I could call Lucy and congratulate her for all she survived."

"Maybe when she's older and more mellow," I chuckle now. I can't picture the conversation, and the absurdity breaks through my sadness. And my wife is so kind, wanting to reach out to Lucy. What if we all were so compassionate?

Acknowledgments

Many thanks to my friends and family for all the encouragement. And to those readers who kept asking, "When's the next 'installment' on Sulfur Gap coming out?" That inspired me to begin thinking there might be a series here!

To Chell Morrow, who designed the eye-catching cover and provided expertise to bring *Low Water Crossing* through the steps to publication.

To Bill Adams, friend and editor, who challenged the existence of some of my scenes. Thanks to Bill, I now have a "boneyard" of hilarious snippets that might later become short stories but will not distract readers of *Low Water Crossing*. Bill meticulously read two early drafts, keeping me on my toes.

To friends Leigh Harbin, Shelly Suksta, and Deanna

Lange, who provided important suggestions early on, braving their way through the ponderous first draft.

To K.J. Wetherholt, developmental editor, whose invaluable guidance encouraged me and helped me unify the plot and chisel characters.

To the San Angelo Writers' Club, for providing inspiration, education, and friendships.

To Readers P.S. Book Club (the "oldest" in San Angelo) for friendship and a shared love of good writing.

To my dear friends and my sweet husband who've encouraged me so much. Don't know what I'd do without you.

Group Discussion Guide for Low Water Crossing

The events of *Low Water Crossing* span the years from 1988 to 2013, with major events taking place in the fictional town of Sulfur Gap, Texas, and also in real places such as Columbus, Mississippi, and San Angelo, Texas.

1. Sulfur Gap is a small West Texas town. It has small-town geography and small-town culture. In what ways is it similar to other small communities, regardless of location? Does its West Texas location add differences from other small towns? If so, what are the differences?

2. Within Sulfur Gap, certain landmarks figure into the story. Which landmarks stand out to you?

3. The low water crossing on Wayne's ranch provides the title. What makes it significant enough that it forms the title? What theme does it express?

4. The novel begins with the discovery of a human skeleton in Wayne's gravel pit operation. What does this 2013 event add to the rest of the book? Who narrates this episode?

5. The next narrator is Lucy Paxton. What are her strengths and weaknesses? What is her main motivation at first? How does it change? How did Lucy's childhood affect her?

6. How does your opinion of Lucy change by the end of the novel?

7. What humor did you find in Lucy's telling of her story? How would you describe Lucy's humor? Was the humor always intentional on Lucy's part?

8. Many of us would agree that when tragedy occurs, the details can be ludicrous. Sometimes we don't see this until time passes. An example might be Lucy's trip with her parents to the ranch for Thanksgiving. While her home life is not a laughing matter, the details of this drive could be. What are the details that provide humor in this situation? What aspects

of Lucy's life are tragic with *no* silver lining of humor?

9. During the "Lucy phase," what insight do we get into Wayne's character? What characteristic of his creates the most trouble for him?

10. Cynthia Hastings is the next narrator. What is she like—strengths and weaknesses? How does she differ from Lucy? In what ways does Cynthia grow as a person during the time we know her? Her religion is important to her, but what is her primary focus?

11. How does Cynthia's religiosity affect her relationships? What insight do we get into Wayne's character during the "Cynthia phase"? How has he matured since his marriage with Lucy?

12. What challenges does Luck present for Cynthia?

13. We meet Lucy and Wayne's son, Luck, through Cynthia's eyes. What makes Cynthia a good narrator to present Luck as a character in the book? How has being a father shaped Wayne?

14. What humorous situations occur during Cynthia's story? Does she always see humor in these situations?

15. Cynthia is tormented by a secret. What is it? How does her secret compare with Lucy's?

16. Lou Trainer is the next narrator. How does she

differ from the first two? What are Lou's
strengths and weaknesses? What is her
motivation, her great desire?

17. Given the overall arc of the plot, the reader is
    prepared for Lou to be "the one" for Wayne.
    What heightens the suspense that she might
    not be?

18. Lou is intentionally funny. Cite some
    examples. Is Lou able to laugh at herself?

19. Flo the dog is an important character. What
    does Flo add?

20. Wayne's narratives form the prologue, the
    bridges between main parts, and the epilogue.
    What purposes do these segments serve?

21. Several themes run through the novel: secrets,
    compassion, recovering from life's pitfalls,
    varieties of love, family ties, and romantic
    love. What statements does the novel make
    regarding these themes?

22. Søren Kierkegaard, existential philosopher,
    said, "The more one suffers, the more, I
    believe, one has a sense for the comic."
    Suffering can strip away pretense and false
    values. What is the suffering of each main
    character, and how do they become
    "lightened" or "enlightened," if at all?

23. A large cast of supporting characters appears:
    Charley Bristow, Wayne's protégé and main

character of *The Lark*; Sheriff L.B. Sparks;
Lucy's parents, Baker and Madge Paxton;
Cynthia's ex-husband, Leo Hastings, and her
daughters, Abby and Eliza; Wayne's son, Luck,
and Wayne's parents, Katy and Ernie
Cheadham; Wayne's long-time friends, J.J. and
Pam Rodriguez; and groups such as Lou's
band members, customers, fans, and friends;
also, Dick Rainey, Lou's landlord and member
of Wayne's group of coffee buddies; Lou's
sister, April. Some of these supporting
characters evolve, becoming dynamic
characters. What are some of the most
dynamic ones? How do they evolve?

Made in the USA
Columbia, SC
28 January 2022